Strike Back

Also by Chris Ryan

The One That Got Away

Fiction
Stand By, Stand By
Zero Option
The Kremlin Device
Tenth Man Down
The Hit List
The Watchman
Land of Fire
Greed
The Increment
Blackout

In the Alpha Force Series
Survival
Rat-Catcher
Desert Pursuit
Hostage
Red Centre
Hunted
Black Gold
Blood Money
Fault Line
Untouchable

In the Code Red Series
Flash Flood
Wildfire

Non-fiction
Chris Ryan's SAS Fitness Book
Chris Ryan's Ultimate Survival Guide

CHRIS RYAN
Strike Back

C̄

Century · London

Published by Century 2007

2 4 6 8 10 9 7 5 3 1

First published in Great Britain in 2007 by
Century
Random House, 20 Vauxhall Bridge Road,
London SW1V 2SA

www.randomhouse.co.uk

Addresses for companies within The Random House Group Limited can be
found at: www.randomhouse.co.uk/offices.htm

The Random House Group Limited Reg. No. 954009

A CIP catalogue record for this book
is available from the British Library

HB ISBN 9781844135356
TPB ISBN 9781844135479

The Random House Group Limited makes every effort to ensure that the papers
used in its books are made from trees that have been legally sourced from well-
managed and credibly certified forests. Our paper procurement policy can be found
at: www.randomhouse.co.uk/paper.htm

Mixed Sources
Product group from well-managed
forests and other controlled sources
www.fsc.org Cert no. TT-COC-2139
© 1996 Forest Stewardship Council
FSC

Printed and bound in Great Britain by
Clays Ltd, St Ives plc

ACKNOWLEDGEMENTS

To my agent Barbar Levy, editor Mark Booth, Charlotte Haycock, Charlotte Bush and all the rest of the team at Century.

PROLOGUE

The Mediterranean: Tuesday, 12 September 1989
John Porter folded the telegram into the inside breast pocket of his olive-green combat uniform. He permitted himself a brief smile, then walked swiftly up the grey gunmetal stairs that led up to the deck of HMS *Dorset*. A stiff breeze was blowing up from the Lebanese coastline, and he could feel it catching his jet-black hair, thrusting it down into the bones of his face.

'*Baby Girl. Born 23.11, 11.9.89. 7lb. Sandy. Love Diana,*' the telegram had read. The words were already stencilled into his mind. My first kid, he thought to himself. Sandy. I can hardly wait to see the smile on her face when she lays eyes on her dad.

All I need to do is try not to bugger things up by getting myself shot in the next few hours.

He walked purposefully towards the rest of the unit. The *Dorset* had been anchored off the Lebanese coast for three days now, waiting for the spooks to assemble enough info for the mission to kick-off. A British businessman, from one of the arms manufacturers that racked up billions in vital exports every year, had been held in one of the brutal basements of Beirut for the last four months. There was no way the government was willing to negotiate with his captors: they were already armed to the teeth without handing over the sophisticated missile systems they were demanding for Kenneth Bratton's release. So the government had done

1

what it always did when the going got tough: called on the Regiment to sort out the mess. Their mission was to go in, and bring Bratton out. Preferably, though not necessarily, alive.

'Congratulations.'

Porter's eyes swivelled round. Major Chris Pemberton was standing only a couple of feet away. A tall man, with more lines chiselled into his face than was normal for a man in his late forties, he was smiling, but there were still traces of ice in his steely, grey eyes. He had a rich Yorkshire accent, and a scar sliced down the side of his right cheek.

Porter nodded. 'Thanks, sir,' he replied.

'A girl?'

'Called Sandy.'

'Just as well,' said Pemberton. 'Girls love their dads. Always. Doesn't matter what a useless old bugger you are.'

'Is that . . .'

Porter could have finished the sentence, but he could tell the Major had already lost interest. He wasn't here to swap tips on brands of nappies. A harsh wind was blowing in from the coastline, and a few miles across the horizon some black-looking clouds were starting to swirl out across the sea. If they were going to fly in tonight, there wasn't much time left. It looked as if a storm was brewing.

'We can stand you down if you want to,' said Pemberton. 'We have backup.'

Porter paused. Stand down? Why the hell would he want to stand down? He had spent eight years in the Irish Guards, and seen plenty of contacts across the water, then, a year ago, he'd made his third request for a transfer to the SAS. When he'd been accepted into the Regiment, it was the best moment of his career. Now he was about to go on the first mission where real blood was at stake. He'd sooner toss himself over the side of this ship than stand down. This is what it had all been about.

'Appreciate it, sir,' he said tersely. 'But I'll be fine.'

Pemberton examined him closely, the grey eyes flickering across his face, scrutinising him for any sign of weakness. 'We don't like to send men out when they've got other things on their mind, and this is an important mission. We can't afford any fuck-ups. You're entitled to forty-eight hours leave when you have a kid, and if you want to take it, no one will think any the less of you.'

'I'll be fine.'

'You've already proved yourself, Porter. You don't need to prove yourself again.'

'I said, I'll be fine . . .'

Pemberton patted him on the shoulder. 'Good man,' he muttered.

Together they joined the rest of the unit. Steve, Mike, Dan and Keith were all far more experienced than Porter. Mike had only been in the Regiment two years, but the other three had clocked up fifteen years between them. They should know what they are doing, Porter reflected. *And if they don't, then God help us.*

'The mission is set for 2000 hours,' snapped Pemberton. 'There will be a full briefing in fifteen minutes.'

Porter could feel the adrenalin surging within him. It was only forty-eight hours since they'd been assembled in Hereford, and put on a plane to Cyprus. From there they were flown out here on the same Puma chopper that was going to take them straight into enemy territory in the next couple of hours.

'Well done on the kid, mate,' said Steve.

He grinned. A Welshman with a neat line in patter, Steve was the only other man on the unit with a wife and kids at home. He joked all the time about how he'd rather be back in the Falklands than pushing prams around Newport.

'We can organise a nice little flesh wound, if you like,' said Keith. 'Get you a few months in hospital chatting up the

3

nurses, and by the time you get back, you'll have missed all the nappies.'

A Londoner with an easy charm, Keith was the joker of the pack, and always the first of them to organise a night out. Porter laughed. But there was no time left to mess around. The five-man unit trooped below deck to the *Dorset*'s ops room. Pemberton was standing in front of a white screen, tapping the palm of his right hand with a well-chewed pencil. At his side, Porter noticed a guy of maybe twenty-seven, twenty-eight, with dark blond hair, the colour of biscuits, and a nonchalant cocksure manner that Porter didn't much care for. 'This is Peregrine Collinson,' said Pemberton. 'Irish Guards. He's going to be observing us today.'

'Call me Perry,' Collinson interrupted. His voice rang out around the tiny room, at least a couple of decibels too loud. We're just having a chat, mate, Porter thought. You're not addressing a battle-ready battalion.

'I'll call you Gloria,' muttered Steve.

Porter was already laughing when he heard Pemberton snap: 'What was that?'

'Glorious, sir, glorious,' said Steve.

Pemberton ignored him. 'I know we don't usually include men from any other regiments on our briefings, but Perry is a fine soldier, and I'm sure he'll be able to help out.'

There was no time for any of the men to worry about him: they had just a few minutes to memorise their instructions. After weeks of patient detective work, the Firm had identified the address where Bratton was being held. Hostages were moved every eighteen to twenty-four hours to reduce the chances of their location being revealed, usually using Hezbollah operatives posing as taxi drivers. Agents inside Beirut had managed to turn one of them: the man was desperate for money, and grateful for the fifty thousand dollars handed over in crisp, clean notes. In return,

4

he'd been given a Coke tin with a satellite tracking device hidden inside it. When he had a fix on the hostage's location, he crushed the tin to activate the tracker and dropped it in the gutter outside the house. He'd left it there two hours ago, and ever since then the Firm had known precisely where Bratton was. But they had to go in tonight. By morning, he could have been switched to another location.

Intelligence reckoned there were twelve Hezbollah guards, on two rotating shifts of six men. There was backup not far away, so they would have to move fast. Thirty minutes was the maximum window from touchdown to evacuation. Any longer than that and they would be overrun by the enemy. The plan was what they'd trained for over the years. Standard hostage-evacuation procedure. A Puma chopper would take them in, and drop them onto the roof of the building. They would go in hard, kill everything that wasn't nailed down to the floor, then get the hell out. If anything went wrong there was a backup unit waiting on the ship. They had all done it at the killing house back in Hereford a dozen times. There was no need to change the formula now. *Just make it work.*

'One word of warning,' said Pemberton, his voice turning grave. 'The Firm reckons its man inside Hezbollah has put this marker outside the right building but you never know if you can trust any of those bastards. Beirut is the most dishonest, double-crossing few square miles of real estate in the world. They could have turned our informant, or he might have been double-crossing us all along. Just be prepared to have a welcoming party waiting for you.'

His eyes rested for a brief moment directly on Porter. 'So you could be walking straight into a trap. The moment you smell anything fishy, don't stop to investigate. Shoot your way clear of danger then get the hell back to base. The last thing we need is five British soldiers taken prisoner in that hellhole, and we won't be able to do a damn thing to help you if that happens. Remember, just living to fight another day is a victory in itself. So good luck, and give them hell.'

Porter was next to Steve as they climbed up towards the deck. The Puma chopper was revved up and ready to go. Before lift-off, each man was responsible for his own kit. Porter ran a quick inventory of his pack. Two stun grenades, two regular grenades, a pistol, a knife, a first-aid kit, a water bottle and, most important of all, an M16 assault rifle, with two hundred rounds of ammunition.

They moved out swiftly along the metal staircase, twisting through the narrow spaces that led up to the metal deck. It was already two minutes to eight: the mission was scheduled to kick of 2000 hours. Porter heard a snapping sound behind him, then a muffled cry. As he turned round, he could see Dan keeling over, his face contorted with pain. Porter had seen that face a dozen times playing football. He's ripped open a tendon, he thought. 'You OK?' he said.

Dan was trying to stand up, pushing himself towards the staircase, but tears of pain were streaming down his face every time his foot touched the ground. 'It's no bloody good,' hissed Steve. 'You're useless like that.'

'I'll be all right.'

'Sod the heroics, mate,' growled Porter. 'You're sitting this one out.'

'I'll take his place,' said Perry, standing at Porter's side.

Porter turned to look at him. 'This is a Regiment job, mate,' he said. 'Get yourself down to Hereford and pass the selection test, and then we'll consider you.'

Pemberton had already joined them. He was looking from Porter, to Steve, then across to Perry. There was a frown creasing up his forehead. Not surprising, thought Porter. One minute to take-off, and we've screwed it up already. 'You're a man short,' he said.

'We'll be fine as we are,' said Mike.

'You need the men,' said Pemberton.

'Get one of the backup guys,' said Steve.

Pemberton shook his head. 'They're too far away.'

He glanced at Perry, as if he was assessing the man's character. 'You're in,' he snapped. 'Now the lot of you should be on that chopper in thirty seconds.'

Porter started running. Within seconds he was out on the open deck. 'I can't believe we've some fucking Rupert coming with us,' snapped Steve. 'I reckon we just tip the snotty-nosed little git out into the Med.'

'Who the hell is he?' asked Porter.

'His old man was a general, Daniel Collinson,' said Steve. 'Then he made a second career for himself in the City. His godfather's Sir Arnold Langham, used to be at the Ministry of Defence. Collinson knows where all the strings are and how to pull them. The bloke has got more connections than bloody British Airways. Doesn't mind using them either.'

The chopper was revved up, and ready to fly. Porter climbed inside, pushing his back to the machine's steel frame. Steve, Mike and Keith were squeezed in next to him. Perry was sitting a few feet away. As the chopper soared upwards, Porter could feel a giddy moment of weightlessness. He looked into Perry's eyes, wondering what he could see there. Fear, maybe? No. It was contempt. For the lads or for the enemy, it was impossible to tell.

The roar of the Puma's blades was deafening. Each man had a two-way radio tucked inside his helmet, allowing him to receive instructions from the pilot. Nobody was speaking. In the moments before a mission kicked off, nobody ever spoke. Each man needed a few minutes of silence to settle himself, and to make his own peace with the certain knowledge that although there was a decent chance of coming back alive, the odds weren't what any sane man would accept.

'As Sir Winston Churchill said on the BBC, in July 1940,'

starred Collinson, speaking over the radio so that his words were delivered crisply to each man on the chopper, '"This is a war of the unknown warriors; but let all strive without failing in faith or in duty, and the dark curse of tyranny will be lifted from our age."' He paused. 'I just thought we should remember that in the next couple of hours, and maybe draw strength from it.'

Steve rolled his eyes. He took off his helmet, and pulled out the headphones embedded inside. 'Funny, can't hear a sodding thing,' he said, shouting to make himself heard over the din of the engine. 'Bloody kit must be on the blink already.'

The Puma had rolled high into the air as it approached the coast, but now it was dipping low, hugging the ground, as it flew over the docks, and took them straight into the heart of the city. By staying as close to the ground as possible, the chopper would be impossible to detect on radar, and a lot harder to hit with a missile launcher: the enemy had no time to get it in their sights before it had disappeared from view. But it made for a stomach-churning ride. Porter had done it a couple of times in Ulster, flying low over dangerous border country when it was controlled by the Provos, and he'd learnt not to bother eating anything in the few hours before a mission. It just ended up on your shoes. Glancing around, he could see Steve and Keith hanging on to the side of the machine, their expressions grim. And glancing across at Perry, he noted with just a touch of satisfaction that the man was holding on to his stomach. You're going to be a bloody liability on this gig, mate, he thought to himself.

'Twenty seconds, twenty seconds,' shouted the pilot over their headphones.

The chopper shook violently as it dropped the last few feet out of the sky. The pilot knew exactly where the house was: the Coke tin in the gutter was sending out a signal powerful enough to guide him right home. But he was flying low now, skimming right through the streets, at roof level. Any higher, and it would give an opponent a chance to lock onto the Puma with a rocker launcher. Suddenly the chopper lurched violently upwards, and Porter could feel his stomach heaving. It shuddered then hovered in the air.

Porter gripped his M16 tight to his chest. Lights were flashing on the Puma, and the roar of the engine as the hatch opened was deafening. 'Go,' shouted Steve. 'Bloody go.'

Four sets of ropes were tossed out of the side of the Puma. With his legs kicking across the metal, Porter pushed himself out. Steve went first, then Porter, then Mike and Keith. Collinson was hanging back, Porter noted. A cloud of dust was shooting straight up into the sky as the chopper hovered a foot above the building, creating a brilliant, illuminated light that made it impossible to see anything. Porter gripped hold of the rope, and slipped down it, then threw himself down hard onto the roof of the building.

'Move up,' shouted Steve, his voice raw and hoarse.

They had practised this manoeuvre a hundred times back at the killing house. Go in hard and fast. Maximum speed and maximum aggression. The tactics were settled. But it was always different in real life. Back at base, the opposition was just pretending to kill you.

They had landed on a flat roof, with a single doorway leading down inside the two-storey building. Steve and Mike had already shot the door open, and the two men were fearlessly leading the way. Porter ran after them, his ears cocked for the first round of gunfire that would inevitably greet them, and weapon cocked tight to his chest, his finger poised on the trigger, ready to fire. Collinson was lagging a couple of yards behind the pace.

'Take out, take out,' Steve shouted.

Porter dropped to his knees as soon as he hit the first-floor landing. He could see the man clearly enough: a solitary figure, swathed in black robes, with an AK-47 tucked into his chest and dark glasses covering his eyes. Pressing the trigger on his M16, Porter loosed off a barrage of fire. At his side, Mike and Keith had done the same. A lethal hailstorm of bullets was biting chunks out of the bricks and mortar. Enough of it lodged into the chest of their sole opponent to send him crashing back against the wall, blood spurting from a dozen different wounds, and a pitiful moan erupted from his lips as he clung miserably on to the last few seconds of his life.

Steve kicked the body out of the way, affording it the merest glance to make sure there was no more breath left in it. The house was a simple, flat-fronted concrete structure, and it was only the intelligence reports that told them it was the front for an underground complex of bunkers. Another man was already running into view. A burst from their assault rifles quickly finished him off. Another bullet-ripped corpse lay in front of them. Porter could feel the excitement rising within him, making him stronger as each second passed.

With a rapid burst of fire, Keith and Mike had kicked their way through to the ground floor of the building. There was a simple square room, measuring twenty feet by twenty-five, with a couple of motorbikes stored in one corner. It smelt of soldering irons and diesel oil. To the back, there was a staircase, leading downwards. A pale light was snaking its way up to the surface. Porter paused for a moment. There was a brief, eerie silence as the guns stopped their murderous fire. He looked left, then right. Suddenly there was cry, followed by a burst of fire. Porter could feel a chunk of the wall right next to him being cut open by bullets. He dropped to his knees and squeezed the trigger on the M16. He didn't even know what he was firing at until he saw his assailant keel over.

'How many have we killed?' he barked.

'Three, maybe four,' said Steve. 'But there must be more of the bastards.'

Porter walked towards the staircase. They could be certain there would be more Hezbollah fighters downstairs.

'Stun grenades,' muttered Steve.

Both men unhooked the oval devices from their ammo belts, pulled the cords, then tossed them down into the stairwell. There was a delay of three seconds, then the muffled sound of an explosion. The blast of the grenade unleashed a wave of heat, followed by a rolling cloud of gas that would temporarily disable anyone who encountered it. In the two minutes it bought them, the unit had to get their man.

'Let's go,' shouted Steve.

Behind him, Porter could hear the sound of puking. At the side of the room, Collinson had just thrown up. He was leaning against the wall, looking down at his vomit in shame, clutching his chest as he tried to recover his breath. 'You OK, mate?' said Porter.

'Bloody fine,' snapped Collinson.

'You don't look it.'

'I told you, I'm fucking OK,' said Collinson.

'You can stay here if you —'

'Leave the fucking bed-wetter,' shouted Steve. 'We're going down.'

Mike, Keith and Steve had already started to descend the staircase. Their boots were rattling across the bare concrete, sending a ripple of echoes resounding through the enclosed space. Porter followed swiftly in their wake. At the bottom of the stairs, there was a narrow corridor that stretched for twenty feet both left and right, with two doors in both directions. One man was lying unconscious on the floor, blood streaming from his nose: he had been knocked out by the smoke from the stun grenade. It was still filling the room with a noxious, brutal odour. A couple of pale light bulbs were filling the room with an eerie glow that struggled to break through though the fumes. With one swift movement, Steve emptied three rounds of ammunition into the skull of the man lying at his feet, shooting his brains out. The corpse twitched on the impact, and a chunk of broken skull bone skidded out across the concrete, but in less than a second the corpse had stopped moving.

'Two men left, two right,' shouted Steve.

His voice reverberated around the corridor, and was still ringing in Porter's ears as he peeled right and started striding through the sealed concrete passageway. His M16 was cocked, as both he and Steve edged their way closer to the first doorway. They had already worked out the standard operating procedure back on the boat. Porter would kick the doors down, and Steve would stand behind him ready to shoot anything that moved. There was no need for either man to say anything.

From the corridor behind him, Porter could hear the rattle of gunfire, and then the sound of a man screaming. Without pausing to think, he held his rifle in his left hand, balanced himself, then threw his entire weight into the wooden doorway. As it flung open, Steve was already kneeling down at the entrance, his gun held in his arms. It took just a fraction of a second to establish there was no hostage inside, and the decision made, Steve loosed off a volley of fire. The bullets splattered around the ten-by-ten room, taking down the two guards who were still trying to recover from the fumes of the stun grenade. Neither man knew what had hit them: before they had time to reach for their own weapons, their lungs had been perforated with bullet wounds, sending both of them collapsing to the ground.

They were solid, trained opponents, noted Porter: they were keeping their discipline, and trying to regroup, but they had been overwhelmed by the speed and scale of the attack.

Porter heard a movement. Up ahead in the corridor, another door was opening. He could see just a sliver of metal emerging through it. Porter recognised it at once. The muzzle of an AK-47. He waited, counting the beats of his heart as he allowed the sniper to expose just enough of himself to waste his own life. An inch, then another inch. It would take just an instant for the man to turn and fire. Porter waited, ticking off one second, then another. The hand was in view. Steadying the M16 cupped into his shoulder, Porter aligned the sights. The man was about thirty, with a slim build, and a scraggy, dirty beard. With a squeeze on the trigger, the bullets exploded from the barrel of the gun. The AK-47 dropped to the ground, as the shards of hot metal turned the hand gripping it into shredded ribbons of torn, bleeding flesh.

With a roar of controlled anger erupting from his lungs, Porter leapt forward, turning the M16 on the wounded man and finishing him off with a rapid burst of fire. Looking up, he could see Kenneth Bratton tied up to a chair that had been nailed to the floor. His arms were bound by rope that was cutting into his bare skin, and a gag had been stuffed into his mouth, and held in place with thick layers of plastic tape. He was wearing a black boiler suit, with staining down the front. In his eyes you could see the look of pure terror: the cringing, pleading fear of a man who knows he is clinging to life by the most slender of threads.

Behind him, there was one more guard. He was a boy, maybe no more than fifteen, with a shaved head and a week of untrimmed beard growing on his face. In his hand, there was a Browning BDA 380 snub-nosed pistol. And it was pointing straight at Porter. For a second, Porter could feel a cold sweat pass across his skin: he thought briefly about Sandy and reflected sadly that maybe he never would get to meet his new baby daughter. He'd had guns pointed at him before. But not with the same lethal certainty that they were intent upon killing him.

'Easy, mate,' said Porter.

The boy barked something in Arabic.

There was a hit of nervousness in his voice, Porter noted.

He's just a kid. *He's bottling it.*

Porter stood his ground, pointing his M16 straight at the man, his finger poised on the trigger. He could kill him in an instant. And yet he knew that in the same moment, the Arab could kill him. Or the hostage.

'Drop the gun,' snapped Porter.

'Back, back,' shouted the Arab.

He was gesturing wildly with the Browning. Porter kept his gun level with the boy's head. Let him lose his rag, he told himself. Maybe then I can get a clean shot at the bastard.

'Back, back,' the boy shouted again.

His voice was ragged and there was sweat pouring off his face.

Porter could see his hand waving with the Browning first at him, then at the hostage. He was moving too fast to get a decent shot, he reckoned. His finger started to close on the trigger of the M16. Right then, a sudden burst of gunfire rattled through the room. The first bullet caught the Arab on the chin, smashing the bone, and snapping his head straight back. A flicker of flame lashed out of the muzzle of the Browning as the shot was fired, but it struck the wall harmlessly, loosening off a chunk of dusty concrete. The boy staggered backwards with blood already pouring from the lower half of his face. He was trying to cry out in pain but his mouth was smashed to pieces. Porter twitched the M16 towards him, and put one bullet straight into his skull. By the time the third bullet pierced his heart, he was already dead.

Ugly work, decided Porter. *But you started it . . .*

Steve was standing in the doorway, the smoke still smouldering out of the barrel of his M16.

'Nice work,' muttered Porter.

'You've done all the heavy lifting, mate,' said Steve. 'Now let's get the fuck out of here.'

With their Regiment-issued Spider knives, it took just a few seconds for the ropes that bound Bratton to his chair to be severed. His hands snapped free of their captivity, but with the tape still covering his mouth he was unable to speak. Porter grabbed his shoulder, helping him to his feet, but, like a man who has had his leg in plaster for a month, his nerves had grown rusty and he couldn't find his balance. He was holding on to Porter's shoulder as they navigated their way back towards the staircase. Porter could feel his pulse slowing down. The buzz of the adrenalin was starting to drain out of him as the immediate danger passed, and he felt empty and exhausted.

As they reached the end of the corridor, Mike and Keith were standing next to them. Collinson was at their side, some grime on his face. 'Bloody good show, men,' he said.

'I didn't see you lining up to take a bullet,' snapped Steve. 'Where the fuck have you been?'

Collinson was about to say something, but then stifled his words. As he glanced into his eyes, Porter could tell he had been humiliated, and the pain was stinging through him. 'Let's just get out of here,' he said stiffly.

'Leave it to some proper bloody soldiers,' said Steve. 'The fighting kind.'

He pointed to Keith to keep hold of Bratton, then started climbing the stairs. Mike and Porter followed him with Collinson bringing up the rear. As Porter pushed his head up into the main room, the way seemed clear enough. They just had to get back up to the roof, then the chopper could pick them up and they could fly home.

'Clear,' said Steve, as he looked out around the empty room.

Porter motioned down the staircase. Keith and Mike started helping Bratton up the staircase.

In the next instant, an explosion splintered the night air.

Porter looked round, startled. His pulse was beginning to race again.

The grenade had exploded just inches from the front door. Steve had already fallen back, crouching down low next to the staircase. 'Covering fire,' he snapped at Porter.

Without thinking, Porter laid down a burst of fire in the direction of the doorway. One fighter appeared, and was killed instantly, then another walked into the same hailstorm of bullets. Both corpses were lying bleeding across the doorway. Then a grenade was tossed into the doorway, ten yards in front of him, and for a split second Porter could see it hissing. His blood was pumping. He could tell it was about to blow, possibly bringing the whole house down and killing all of them. He ran forward, grabbing hold of it, tossing it through the doorway and watching as it rolled back down the alleyway: two seconds later, it exploded, bringing down half a wall in a heap of rubble.

'Take the doorway,' shouted Collinson behind him.

Porter glanced back. With his right hand, Collinson was directing him towards the doorway. Straight into the line of fire.

'Go, man,' screamed Collinson, his face red with anger. 'I'll cover you.'

'Since when were you in charge, you tosser?' snarled Steve.

Moving forward, Porter crouched in the doorway. Amid the deafening roar of the explosion from the grenade, he took a second to catch his breath. His pulse was racing and his nerves were shredded. As his lungs filled with smoky, dusty air, the sniper eluded his gaze. It was only later that he realised the bastard must have been perched right in front of him. The shot came as if from nowhere, and the first Porter knew of it was when he felt the index finger of his left hand dropping clean away from his body. He looked down, at first unaware of the pain, then felt a strange tingling sensation running through his arm, like a mild electric shock. He was using his right hand to position the M16, looking through the murky night to see if could get a fix on his assailant. Then the second shot struck, hitting him just below the existing wound, and smashing the bone that connected another finger to his left hand. This time he felt it. The numbness and the shock had started to subside, and the pain was like a blistering explosion. His nerve endings were screaming from pain, and the gun dropped from his right hand. He could feel the blood pouring from the wound, but the tears already welling up in his eyes meant he could hardly see anything. Another shot blasted the concrete in front of him, and instinctively Porter fell back from the doorway, edging back inside the room.

That's just a hand, he thought to himself. He could feel the desperation rising within him. There was no way of telling how many of them were out there, or how long the firefight would last. The next shot was going to be far worse.

'Get up here,' shouted Steve down the staircase.

Keith and Mike ran up the passageway, their guns blazing, but Collinson had already fallen back, dropping down the stairs where he was out of the line of fire. The assault was starting in earnest now. Three, four, then five heavily armed men started to charge the doorway, their guns cocked, their expressions grim with the determination of soldiers who had already prepared themselves to die. Steve was holding their position, managing to shoot a couple of guys as they approached the entrance. Keith took out another one, then the fourth and fifth, slicing into them with deadly fire, but there was still no sign of the attack abating.

It's us against . . . how many? Porter wondered. A whole bloody city.

Suddenly, Porter could see something rushing towards him. Twenty feet away, it was coming at him from the left: it must have slipped in through a hidden window, or

17

crawled up through the sewers. A small dark figure, no more than three and half feet tall, and weighing seventy or eighty pounds. A child. The bastards were using kids to break through the lines. There was what looked like an explosive charge strapped to his chest, and he was heading straight for Porter. Desperately, he reached for the gun that had dropped to the floor. Then he realised, he couldn't shoot the kid without detonating the explosives. That's what the bastards wanted. To blow the whole place up. The kid was reaching for his belt, just feet away from him now, searching for the cord that would take them all to meet their God. Porter lunged forwards, grabbing hold of the kid by neck, pushing him to the ground. He fell on top of him, smothering the child with his body, determined that even if the explosives did blow he would absorb enough of the force himself to save the others.

The black robe that covered his face fell away. Porter looked down. He was a kid, no more than twelve, with a slight, delicate build. Porter could feel his anger rising at the way the terrorists were using children to fight their battles for them. Why can't they send in men to take us on? he asked himself. The boy's eyes were a soft brown, and the expression of terror on his face suggested that whoever had persuaded him to die for his cause hadn't finished the job. His mouth was twisted out of shape, with the lower lip looking as if it had been severed in half, and at first Porter thought it was just the fear, but then he saw the poor kid must have been deformed at birth.

Porter took the knife from his belt, and raised it a couple of feet into the air. He was about to plunge it straight into the boy's neck, when his eyes caught him. He was looking straight at Porter. 'Please,' he said, in broken English, his voice croaking with abject fear.

Blood was dripping from Porter's wounded hand, and the bolts of pain from the wound were jabbing up from his left arm and thumping straight into his chest. It was like having a hundred hammer drills boring into your body at the same time.

'My, my . . .'

The boy was struggling for the words in English but they wouldn't come. A burst of Arabic, frantic and desperate, erupted from his lips, then he subsided into the stunned silence that sometimes overwhelms even children when they are certain they are about to die.

Ten yards behind him, Steve and Keith were holding the line, using assault rifles to fight back another wave of Hezbollah attacks. Amid the din and roar of the gunfire, the hostage had bottled it, screaming his lungs out with raw fear.

Porter held the knife in his hand, his eyes flicking across the smooth skin of the boy's neck as he searched for the windpipe he would need to sever to make the death as quick and painless as possible.

He lowered the knife into position, nicking the skin, and drawing a speck of red blood. He thought briefly of Sandy. How old was she now? Into her second day, allowing for the time the telegram had taken to reach the ship.

'Fuck it,' muttered Porter, the words wheezing through his exhausted lips.

He's just a kid.

With his left hand, he ripped the explosives off the boy's chest, flinging them to one side. He folded the knife into the palm of his hand, using it as a weight rather than a weapon. Tensing his shoulder muscles, he smashed his right fist into the side of the boy's face. His deformed lips quivered, then he spat some blood and a broken tooth up into Porter's chest. '*Amiat al-Ikhwan al-Muslimun*,' he whispered. His eyes closed, and Porter could tell there was no fight left in him, but he punched again, and then again, draining the last few ounces of consciousness from him. Slowly, he lifted himself from the boy's body. You'll take at least three hours to wake up from that, mate, he thought. But you'll live, at least. Maybe even find something better to do with your life.

In front of him, Steve and Keith had dealt with the latest wave of attacks. The firing had subsided long enough for them to rush up towards the roof and the Puma. 'Get out to the chopper,' shouted Steve. 'We'll lay down the covering fire.'

'I'll stay and fight my way out of here with the rest of you,' said Porter gruffly.

Steve took two paces forward, standing so close Porter could smell the sweat and grime dripping off his face. 'You're fucking wounded, you tosser.'

Porter was clenching his left hand. The pain was aching, and the blood was still dripping from the two stumps where his fingers had once been. He could feel the strength bleeding out of him. 'I can hold on until we get the hostage back to the chopper.'

With a flicked shake of his head, the anger was evident in Steve's eyes. 'You're wounded, and we have to get the hostage out. We'll put down some covering fire, and keep the Hezbollah bastards back. No one gives a fuck whether we get shot, but if we lose Bratton then we're all in the shit. Now run like fuck, get on that chopper and get back to the ship, and there's a chance the medics can still save that hand. Tell the pilot to call in the backup, and we'll get out of here as soon as it's safe.'

'My hand –'

'Bloody move, man,' snapped Steve. 'This is the Regiment. We get paid to fight and win. Not to lose a hand, and spend the rest of our careers behind a desk because we're too sodding stupid to know when to clear out.'

Porter paused. He was about to speak, but he could see that Steve was already telling Keith how they could make certain the building was safe enough for the chopper to drop down onto the roof.

He held tight to his gun, then glanced up at the staircase. Bratton was standing right next to him: the man was shaking with fear, and his nerves were so shot he could no longer speak. Porter's feet were pounding against the concrete as he started running. Behind him, he could hear one shot ring out, then another. He dragged Bratton with him, up one flight, then up the second, before bursting onto the open roof. Down below he could see the rest of the unit laying down more fire to keep their attackers at bay. Up ahead, he could see the chopper hovering a few feet above the roof. Within seconds, he had covered the last few remaining yards, and grabbed hold of the Puma's doorway. He pushed the screaming Bratton through the open door, and flinging himself onto the floor, he shouted to the pilot to take him back, then unhooked a first-aid kit from the floor of machine. As the Puma lifted up into the sky, and started to soar over the city and out towards the sea, Porter found the disinfectant. He winced in pain as he splashed it over the raw, stubby mess where his fingers had once been. If he didn't clean the wound soon, he knew there was a chance the thing might have to be chopped off at the wrist.

And the Regiment has no use for a bloke with only one hand.

Porter walked slowly from the operating theatre. The anti-biotics they had pumped into him had made him woozy, and the local anaesthetic injected into his arm and chest left him numb and dopey. It had been a terrible hour, but at least the worst was over now, he told himself. After being dropped down onto the *Dorset*'s deck, Bratton had been led away, still shaking and sobbing with fear, and he'd been rushed down to the medics, who quickly concluded they could save the hand, but only if they cut through the remaining flesh and bone and reduced both missing fingers to nothing more than stumps. There was an operating theatre on board, but he'd probably be sent on to Cyprus at daybreak to get some more treatment. 'If you'd kept the fingers we could have had a go at sticking them back on,' said the doctor with disturbing cheerfulness as he sawed through what remained.

'Yeah, well, some Arab buggers were lobbing grenades at us,' growled Porter. 'So there wasn't really much time for looking around for any bits of your body that might have been shot off.'

In total, the operation had taken no more then twenty minutes, and the doctors assured him he should be fine so long as he kept it clean, and took some heavy duty antibiotics for a couple of weeks. He'd been lucky, they told him. The wound had staunched quickly enough for him not to lose too much blood: any more and he'd have passed out.

No point in signing up for the Regiment if you are going to complain about getting hurt, Porter told himself as he climbed the stairs back towards the deck. It had been that tosser Collinson's fault for sending him up to the doorway, but those were the breaks. In combat, stuff happened. You just had to live with it.

He looked out at the sea. Taking out a packet of Rothmans, he cupped his hands against the wind, and lit a cigarette. He'd promised Diana he'd give up when she got pregnant, and had managed not to smoke at all on his last leave, but he knew the nicotine would help to dull the pain that would inevitably come raging back once the anaesthetic wore off.

Lucky I don't hold the fag with my left hand, he grinned to himself as he chucked the ash into the sea swelling up around the side of the ship. With luck, it shouldn't hurt his career too much. There were plenty of guys in the Regiment who'd lost fingers, but if they could still hold a gun straight, it didn't count against them. So long as it didn't disable you, a wound could even help you get ahead: it showed you could take the punishment.

He heard the chopper first, its engine growling out over the sea, then saw its lights. It was flying low, skimming over the waves, before gaining altitude as it came in for a landing on the *Dorset*'s deck. Porter glanced at his watch. It was now just after ten at night. They'd set off two hours ago for the ten-minute flight. They had a maximum half-hour window to complete the mission. Porter had been on Lebanese soil for only twenty minutes. They should have been back an hour ago at least. What the hell kept them?

Turning round, he watched the Puma hover for a fraction of a second above the deck before the pilot brought it in to land and killed the engine. As the blades stopped turning, you could hear just the lapping of the ocean against the *Dorset*'s hull, and the humming of her propellers beneath the waves. Six sailors were already running towards the Puma, securing the machine to the deck, and flinging open the hatch.

Porter took a deep drag on the cigarette, letting the nicotine mix with the anaesthetic to soothe his nerves. He watched as the first man stepped out of the chopper. Collinson. The little prat, thought Porter. Didn't fire a shot throughout the whole mission.

Collinson was reaching inside the chopper. 'Stretchers,' he shouted to the waiting sailors.

'Shit,' said Porter, his voice no more than a whisper quickly stifled by the sea breeze. *I hope to hell we didn't take any more casualties.*

Two sailors had already disappeared inside the chopper carrying a stretcher, then two more, then two more. There was a wait of a few seconds. Porter took a step forward, taking a final hit on his cigarette. A stretcher was emerging, carried flat out of the helicopter.

With a white sheet covering it.

'Fuck, no,' Porter muttered.

He could feel the pain stabbing up his left arm.

Another stretcher.

And another white sheet.

Porter could feel his heart thumping. He took another step forward, then stopped. He couldn't bear to go any closer.

One final stretcher emerged from the Puma.

And it too had a white sheet covering it.

Porter wiped away the bead of cold sweat that had formed on his brow.

All three of them, he thought to himself. Steve, Mike and Keith. Dead.

How the fuck did that happen?

'Porter.'

The voice was sharp, insistent.

Porter turned round. A young sailor was looking straight at him.

'You're needed in the debrief room,' he snapped. 'Now.'

With his pulse still racing, Porter began to walk. He knew exactly where to go: the same room where they had been briefed on the mission just a few hours ago. He was walking slowly, gripping on to the rails of the metal staircase. When he left them, Steve said he had the situation under control. He told him they just needed to secure the building, then evacuate. Now the three of them were dead. And I wasn't there to help them.

He pushed open the door to the debrief room. Pemberton was already there and so was Collinson, flanked by a pair of officers. Nobody was smiling. Pemberton looked at him coldly. 'Come in, Porter,' he said slowly. 'Glad to see somebody survived the bloody mission.'

One chair had been positioned directly opposite the main desk. 'Take a seat, Porter,' said Pemberton.

'I prefer to stand.'

'I said, take a seat,' he repeated icily. 'You're injured, you need to rest.'

Porter pulled out the chair. He didn't recognise the two other officers, but he could see that one of them was taking notes. 'What happened, sir?' he said. 'To the other blokes, I mean.'

Pemberton rested against the edge of the desk but didn't sit down. 'I'll let Collinson tell you,' he said.

Glancing up, he could see Perry taking a step forward. He was standing just three feet from where Porter was sitting and you could still smell the gunpowder on his uniform. There was a tear on his jacket, and a plaster covering a cut on his face. 'It was like this,' he began. 'We evacuated you as well as the hostage. Steve wanted to secure the building. It was a sound enough plan. Steve's a good man. We laid down some fire, enough to keep the Hezbollah guys at bay. It shouldn't have taken more than a few minutes. We were getting ready to clear out when the little Arab fucker you left unconsciousness suddenly came round. He'd crawled across the floor, and picked up one of the AK-47s his mates had left on the floor.' He paused, glancing towards Pemberton before continuing. 'Then he sprayed the place with bullets. Took Steve and Keith down instantly. Poor blokes didn't have a chance. Mike managed to start returning fire, and might have winged the kid, but by then he was running backwards out into the alley. He managed to hit Mike just as he was disappearing from view. He was still alive for the next twenty minutes or so but he was losing a lot of blood, and there wasn't anything I could do to help him. I knew the chopper would be waiting for us, so I laid down as much fire as I could, and started to make my way upstairs. I was lucky. I reckon the kid had already legged it. I told the pilot to stay put, then I went back to get our boys.'

'I left him out cold,' snapped Porter.

'Then I suppose your punch isn't hard enough,' said Collinson. He paused, wiping away some greasy sweat from his forehead. 'There were two firefights as I went back to collect the bodies. A couple of snipers were trying to get me. I think I may have killed one of them, I'm not sure. Took three runs to get our men, and I don't mind telling you it was a bit hairy. Still, at least we got out. And, after all, the hostage was rescued.'

Porter's eyes remained rooted to the floor. If he could have drilled a hole in the bottom of the boat, he would have gladly sunk himself to the bottom of the ocean. Steve, Mike and Keith. *Three of the best mates I ever worked with. All dead. And all because I didn't finish off that little Arab bastard when I had the chance.*

'So, as Perry says, mission accomplished,' said Pemberton. 'The hostage is back, and unharmed. But three of our men died, and the Regiment doesn't take casualties lightly. This is our worst day since the Falklands. So, the question is this, Porter. Why didn't you kill the boy?'

Porter's eyes were still rooted to the floor. He couldn't move them. He wasn't sure they would ever move again. 'I . . . I . . .'

He could start the sentence. *But how the hell could he finish it?*

'Well, man?' snapped Pemberton. 'What's the bloody answer?'

He was just a kid, thought Porter. He was begging me. A child . . .

'Sod it, can't you even speak?'

'We're not butchers,' said Porter suddenly. 'I left him unconsciousness. There was no way he should have come round.'

'But he did, didn't he?' said Pemberton. 'And three good men lost their lives. I can't discipline you, Porter. In this Regiment, every man makes his own decisions in the moment of combat. We don't have a lot of officers analysing them afterwards.'

Pemberton leant closer into Porter's face, and he could

smell a trace of whisky on his breath. Burying his face in his hands, Porter was desperate for a drink. Any kind of drink. 'Under the Geneva Convention, you're not supposed to kill a child, so I don't think I can court-martial you, as much as I might want to.' He paused. 'But I will say this. Perry here deserves a bloody medal, and I'll make sure he gets one. And you . . . well, I wouldn't want to be looking at your face in the mirror every morning knowing that I had the blood of three of my mates on my hands.'

Porter turned round, and started to walk back towards his cabin. He felt empty and bitter inside. Nobody was looking at him, but he heard one man whisper: 'There's going to be a lot of dead eyes looking at that bloke.'

ONE

Vauxhall, London: Monday, 23 October 2006
Porter could feel the dampness in the sheet of cardboard that was covering him. There had been some light drizzle during the night, and although he had taken shelter inside a railway arch, that didn't stop the rain from seeping in. On Goding Street, between the Albert Embankment and Kennington Lane, it was one of a strip of arches that the developers hadn't yet got their hands on. He could feel a dirty light from the river flicking down the alley, and painfully opened first one eye then the next. Some rubbish from one of the local kebab shops was overflowing in the bin next to him – the guys running the shop tipped it out there when they shut up at three or four in the morning – but from the smell he could tell there was nothing that he'd want to eat. One dog had already walked past without stopping.

He pushed the cardboard aside, and stood unsteadily. A thumping pain was ringing through his head, like having your skull drilled open. There was a pain in his left leg. The nerves were shot to pieces, he could tell, and there was some nasty bruising. He knelt down to take a look and noticed the state of his feet. It was more than a week since he'd taken off his shoes and socks, and although he didn't much feel like taking a look, he sensed there was some blood starting to coagulate somewhere around his toes. Just ignore it, he told himself. What difference does it make anyway?

He started walking, trying to put as little weight on his left

28

leg as possible. For a brief second, he thought about his daughter Sandy, and wondered what she might be doing. What day was it today? he wondered. The weekend? He glanced towards the tube station. No. Too many men in suits. Must be the week then. Maybe the start of a new one. Not that it makes any difference. One week is much like another down here.

The Travel Inn was a half-hour walk away, along the side of the river. Pleasant enough if you were in the mood for walking, but Porter found the pain in his left leg was increasing the more he used it. Something was definitely wrong there. He'd take himself to a hospital, but if there was anything seriously wrong with him, they'd make him stay in. And then how was he going to get a drink? No, he told himself. You'll be OK in a day or two. And if not . . . well, who cares anyway.

Washing-up wasn't a great job, but when you lived on the streets it was usually all that was available. The Travel Inn wasn't a classy place, but they often needed someone to clean up the breakfast dishes. They didn't pay even the minimum wage – not many hotels in London did any more – but the work wasn't too hard, even though the two missing fingers on his left hand made it hard to keep a grip on the plates. And they didn't mind too much if you finished off some of the grub left on the plates before you put it in the bin. All in all, there were worse ways to start the week.

Porter knocked on the back door. The kitchens were run by a guy called Dan, a rough Ulsterman who claimed to have spent a few years in the Territorials, although he could never tell you which regiment. In truth, Porter didn't much care for the man. He had a sarcastic manner to him, and he ran his pitiful little empire like he was commanding the household cavalry. There were three chefs, and six waitresses, and he bullied the blokes and hit on the girls, but he still skimped on their wages, and everyone said he kept half the tips for himself. Often he'd ask for a kickback of twenty or thirty quid before he'd give anyone a job.

'What the fuck do you want?' said Dan, as he opened the door.

For a few seconds, Porter just stood there. What do I want? he wondered to himself. He tried to hold on to the thought for a moment, but the splitting headache soon drove it away. 'Some work,' he said plaintively.

'Nothing doing,' snapped Dan. 'Now piss off.'

Porter stepped inside. It was warm in the kitchen and the grilling of sausages and the frying of eggs filled the room with cosy warmth. Over by the sink, he could see a pile of dishes, at least fifty of them. 'There's work,' he said. 'I can see it.'

'Which of the two words "piss" and "off" are you having trouble understanding?' snarled Dan.

Porter stood his ground. Anelka, a Bulgarian or Romanian or maybe Ukrainian girl with dishwater-blonde hair and a sullen face, stared at him. There was a shudder on her face as a gust of hot air from one of the ovens caught Porter and carried his smell straight to her. 'Maybe tomorrow?' he said.

'Forget it,' said Dan sourly. 'There's plenty of Bulgarian blokes looking for work right now. They put in a full shift for a pound an hour, they don't nick the grub, and they don't stink of Special Brew. Now piss off.'

But Porter kept walking forward. Dan had already been distracted by a waitress shouting at one of the chefs that some eggs were overcooked, and was no longer paying attention. The words bounced off him, the way rain bounced off the windscreen of a car. It just gets wiped away, he thought. So many humiliations have been endured already, one more doesn't make any difference. Maybe try Bulgaria, he decided with a wry smile, at the same time as he took half a sausage from a dirty plate. So many of their blokes are over here, there must be some work going spare there.

'Hey, leave that food alone, you old tosser,' snapped one of the chefs.

Without thinking, Porter kept on walking through the kitchen, and out into the lobby of the hotel: there were so few staff on duty nobody tried to stop him. A clock on the wall said it was just after eight. Nobody was checking in yet. Too early. One of the cleaning girls was arranging some freshly cut flowers in reception. She glanced at Porter suspiciously, then looked quickly away: she could tell he didn't belong here, he realised, but it wasn't her job to deal with him. Too scary.

In the corner of the lobby, a flat-screen TV pinned to the wall was tuned to Sky News. The half-sausage he'd just eaten had made Porter realise how desperately hungry he was. It was more than a day since he had eaten: yesterday's calorie intake had consisted of half a pint of vodka. There was no money in his pocket, however. And little prospect of getting any, not now Dan had refused to give him work.

'Now for the latest on this morning's breaking news,' said a smooth-faced young presenter. 'The capture of Sky News reporter Katie Dartmouth in Lebanon. At one in the morning, local time, masked men stopped the Sky News van that was heading towards the border at gunpoint. The cameraman and producer were forced out, then Sky's Katie was bound and led way. We now believe she is being held hostage somewhere in the Lebanon. More after the break . . .'

Porter paused, enjoying the warmth of the hotel lobby. The Lebanon, he thought. More hostages. *It never bloody stops, does it?*

A couple of ads flashed by, but Porter didn't feel like moving. Where would he go, anyway?

The presenter came back on air, with an interview with Doug Freeman, the producer who'd been in the van when it was held up. It had been a short and terrifying experience, he said. They had been driving along a main road, when suddenly their way was blocked. There were six men in total. At first they thought it was a robbery – bandits were everywhere in the Lebanon once you got away from Beirut. But they didn't want the cameras, or the van, or any of their credit cards. 'They wanted Katie,' said Freeman, looking straight at the camera. 'They knew who she was, and they'd come to get her.'

'Do you think they meant to harm her, Doug?'

'I hope not,' he replied. 'Katie is one of the finest reporters I have ever worked with.' He paused, wiping the sweat of his face. 'Our prayers are with her this morning.'

Porter could feel a tap on his shoulder. As he turned round, a young girl was standing right next to him. She was wearing a Travel Inn uniform, and name tag pinned to her chest said Sarah. From the way her nose was wrinkling up, Porter could tell she was freaked out just to be standing next to him. 'I'm going to have to ask you to leave, sir,' she said.

'One minute,' snapped Porter.

'I –'

'One minute, I said.'

He looked back towards the screen. The words 'breaking news' were flashing on the screen once again.

'And now we can go over live to Downing Street, where Sir Peregrine Collinson, the Prime Minister's special envoy to the Middle East, will be speaking live to Sky's Adam Boulton. Adam, what can you tell us?'

Porter kept watching. Collinson, he thought. The last time I saw you, you were puking up in the corner because you were too afraid to carry on with the mission. You should have taken the rap for what went wrong on that mission. *Not me.*

'As most viewers will know,' began Boulton, looking into the camera. 'Sir Peregrine Collinson is one of Britain's most decorated fighting men, with a book of military memoirs still on the best-seller lists. Now we learn that Sir Perry has been put in charge of securing the release of Katie Dartmouth.'

Porter watched as the camera panned out to show a tall man, elegantly suited, and with his dusty blond hair just a touch longer than would ever have been permitted when he was still in the army. It's been seventeen years, reflected Porter.

'What can you tell us, Sir Perry?' asked Boulton.

Collinson pursed his lips and furrowed his brow thoughtfully. He conjured up an air of seriousness. 'There's only so much we can say at this stage, Adam,' he began. 'We don't know who has taken Katie Dartmouth, where they've taken her, or what they want. But the PM has asked me to take full charge of the investigation, and I can assure you that every muscle we possess will be strained to bring Katie back safely.'

'And you really don't have any clue where she is?'

Collinson shook his head. 'At this stage, I'm afraid there is nothing firm to go on. All of our efforts, however, will be devoted to getting her back. There may be testing hours and days ahead, but together we will pull through them.'

As Porter watched the screen, he pondered how much better the years had been to Collinson than they had been to him. After coming back from the raid in Lebanon, he knew he'd never been able to get himself back on the level again. The physical damage to his hand healed in time, but the mental damage remained as fresh and raw as if he'd been wounded only yesterday. He'd done his best to reintegrate himself back into the Regiment, but all the men seemed to know that Porter was the guy who'd spared the life of an Arab kid who had then killed three of their men. They didn't say anything to his face, but then they didn't need to. He could see it in their eyes. He could feel it in the way he was shunned in the bar. He could sense it in the way no one was ever going to trust him again. When the chips were down, no one could count on John Porter. And the Regiment didn't have much space for those who couldn't be relied on.

Within three years, he'd left active service, and been put on firing-range duty: there was no more humiliating posting for a Regiment man. After another couple of years, he'd left the army completely. The only career he'd ever planned for himself was over. How do you put your life back together after something like that? Porter wondered. If there was an answer, he'd never found it.

Porter could suddenly feel a hand on his shoulder. As he spun round, Dan was looking straight at him. 'I thought I told you to piss off.'

'I'm just —' started Porter.

'You're just stinking the place up,' snapped Dan. 'Now scarper before I call the police and get you banged up for the night.'

Porter was about to say something, but the words stalled on his lips. The aching in his head was terrible, and the pain in his left leg was growing worse: a tingling sensation, that seemed to numb him all the way up to the knee. With his head bowed, he started walking.

'The bloody back door,' shouted Dan.

Porter ignored him, and kept on walking. He stepped out of the foyer of the Travel Inn into a murky, overcast street. There was a McDonald's round the corner, and he glanced towards the bins, but so far as he could see they'd been emptied recently. No chance of getting a bite to eat there then, he reflected.

He walked slowly across the river. There was a hole in one of the old canvas shoes he was wearing, and it was letting in the dirt, but his left leg was already in such terrible condition, it probably didn't make any difference. There were plenty of people around him as he walked across the bridge, and up the busy road that led towards the prosperous houses, shops and bars of Chelsea and Fulham.

'Could you spare me some money?' he mumbled to a man who was walking past him towards the tube station.

The man looked away, not saying anything.

'Just a couple of quid to help me out,' Porter muttered to another guy who standing right next to him.

He snapped something in what sounded like Polish, then headed past him.

'A quid for a cup of tea, love,' he said, trying to meet the brown eyes of a girl who was rummaging around in her handbag for a ringing mobile phone.

She said nothing, glanced at him once, then started smiling as she answered the phone.

'Jesus,' Porter muttered. 'Doesn't anyone . . .'

A woman brushed passed him, ignoring him as he wobbled on his feet. His head was spinning and he was having trouble concentrating. 'Watch where you're fucking going,' he shouted.

She turned round and looked at him. She was forty or so, with dark brown hair, a well-cut black trouser suit, and a briefcase under her arm. 'Piss off,' she snapped sharply. 'Some of us have got jobs to get to.'

Porter walked towards her menacingly. He wasn't sure what he was going to do. He couldn't even think straight. The splitting, beating noise in his head was getting worse. There were stars flashing in front of his eyes, and he was finding it hard to balance. He was swaying as he walked, unsure how much longer his feet would support him. 'Watch your fucking mouth,' he shouted, surprising himself with the strength and anger he put into the words. 'You know nothing about me. Fucking nothing.'

He knelt down. She had already turned and fled, but as she'd moved swiftly away she'd dropped her purse from her handbag. Quickly, making sure nobody could see him,

Porter slipped the wallet into his ragged, filthy jumper and started to walk away. He'd moved on a hundred yards towards the New King's Road before he paused to check what was inside. Fifty pounds, he noted with pleasure. In crisp ten-pound notes. That and a couple of credit cards.

Enough money for a man to get plenty drunk.

Enough money to get through another miserable day.

TWO

Porter held the bottle of Asda own-label vodka in his right fist, twisted the screw cap with his teeth, then poured it slowly into his mouth. His throat felt like sandpaper, and the alcohol tasted rough and raw, but he could feel it taking him closer and closer to oblivion.

A bottle a day keeps the memories away, he reflected to himself. Hum it, and you could even turn it into a pleasant enough tune.

Some light rain was starting to fall. Porter wasn't quite sure what time it was. He'd been sitting here for a few hours already, he felt sure of that. After taking the money from the purse, he walked slowly back in the direction of his familiar arch, stopping at the supermarket to pick up a couple of bottles of his favourite liquid. Even with fifty quid in his pocket, he stuck to the own-label stuff. No point in wasting the money. There was no way of knowing when he might see some more.

A half-eaten kebab was lying at his side. It was getting slight damp from the drizzle, but that made little difference to the quality of the grub. He'd collected it from the shop round the corner, the same one where the guys tipped the day's refuse into the bins in the middle of the night. He couldn't say there was much difference between the stuff they sold over the counter and the stuff they put in the garbage. But maybe my taste buds have just been shot to pieces, he thought. It was so long since he'd had a decent meal he wasn't sure he'd know what one tasted like any more.

He took a slice of the stringy meat, unsure whether it was lamb or chicken, and chewed on it slowly before taking another hit on the vodka. There was still about thirty quid in his pocket, he realised. Enough to stay drunk for a week.

'Hey, Jimmy,' shouted a voice.

Porter glanced up. He could see two figures swaying towards him, but whether they were swaying because they couldn't walk straight, or because his vision was gone, Porter couldn't tell. Maybe a bit of both. I'm drunk, they're drunk, everyone who kips down in this alley is drunk. *Why the hell else would you be here?*

'What you got, Jimmy?'

They were getting closer now. Porter was sure he'd seen them before. A pair of Scottish blokes, he couldn't remember their names. They used to kip down up by Waterloo station, but their old spot was being dug up while some new cabling was put down in the street, and they'd moved down to Vauxhall. They'd been builders by trade, or so they said, but from the look of them it was years since either of them had done a decent day's work. What were the names again? Porter wondered. Bill or Bob or Bert. Something like that. Down here nobody really needed a name, he reflected. It wasn't as if you were fending off calls all day.

'Have you nae got a wee dram for yer mates?' said the first man.

He was leaning into Porter's face, and there was a nasty snarl on his face.

'Just a wee dram,' he repeated, revealing a set of rotting teeth, and a tongue the colour and texture of tarmac.

'Piss off,' muttered Porter, gripping on to the neck of his bottle of vodka.

The second, shorter man knelt down. He smelt of stewed meat and his eyes were like tiny black pebbles swimming around in pools of scabby flesh. 'Piss off, yer say, Jimmy?' he croaked, his voice harsh. 'That's not very friendly, is it, Jimmy?'

'It looks like you've been doing all right for yerself, Jimmy,' said the taller of the two men. 'A nice drinky, and some food as well. All very lush, Jimmy. You've probably got a pair of lasses tucked underneath that pile of cardboard boxes as well.'

'And you'll be wanting to share with your mates, won't you, Jimmy?' chipped in the shorter man.

The rain was starting to come down heavier now. It was dripping into Porter's hair, and he could see a small puddle starting to form inside his half-eaten kebab. He edged backwards into the archway, but the two men moved forwards, so they were both kneeling just a few inches from his face.

'Because that's how it works here on the streets, doesn't it, Jimmy?' persisted the shorter man. 'One bloke has a bit of lucky, and he shares with his mates.'

'And we're yer mates, Jimmy,' said the taller man.

'Then get your fucking hands off my booze,' Porter snapped.

'But nobody's taking your stuff, Jimmy,' said the shorter man. His hand was reaching out for the vodka bottle. 'Sharing, that's all —'

Porter snatched the bottle away. He put its neck to his lips, and took a hit of the alcohol, relaxing as the vodka mixed with his bloodstream, dulling his senses, and easing the terrible aching in his left leg.

'If we all shared, maybe the world would be a better place, Jimmy,' said the taller man. 'Maybe men like us wouldn't have to live out on the streets.'

Porter suddenly snapped to attention. The rain was coming down harder now, lashing into his face. 'The world is full of thieving, useless scum like you two. That's why there's blokes like me on the street. That's why —'

The sentence wasn't finished, but Porter knew he would never get to complete it. The first blow had landed straight in his stomach, knocking the little wind he had left out of him. The second collided roughly with his jaw, snapping his head backwards. The vodka bottle had loosened from his hand, and as his balance wobbled, the taller man had jumped up and taken it. He put it straight to his lips, drinking three or four shots in one go. The effect on him was as instant as it was ugly: his face folded up into a snarl, and his boot crashed hard into Porter's side, breaking into his ribcage. 'Fuck off, you Scottish bastards,' yelled Porter.

The scream rose up through the alleyway, but he could tell no one was listening. You could run through the streets with an axe through your head in this part of town and no one would pay a blind bit of attention. Even the police didn't bother to venture down these alleyways: they couldn't stand the smell. I can scream all I want to. Nobody's going to come and help me. Not now. Not ever.

The blows were lashing into him now, as hard, as relentless and as unthinking as the raindrops. Both men were standing up, handing the vodka bottle to one another, taking long, deep swigs on the pure alcohol. It was cranking up their aggression, turning a robbery into a beating. Their sturdy, leather boots, the one bit of clothing on them that wasn't falling to pieces, smashed into his chest, into his face, and into his legs. He was absorbing the blows, rolling with each one, unable to offer any resistance. The vodka he'd already drunk dulled the pain, and he hardly felt the blows as they crashed into him, but he could tell how much damage they were doing to his already weakened body. There was blood everywhere, on his face, his hand, inside his sodden trousers, but still the blows kept coming. All I can do is wait for them to get bored of kicking me. And then see if I'm still alive at the end of it.

As he lay on his side, Porter could hear the Scotsmen

staggering down the alley, laughing drunkenly. He watched as a trickle of his own blood spat away from the cuts in his face, and, caught up in the lashing rain, swirled away towards the gutter.

Where it belongs, he thought bitterly, as he closed his torn and cut eyes and let consciousness slip away from him.

Groggily, Porter opened one eye then another. He was lying flat, his face down in a puddle of water that was crimson from his own blood. His whole body ached, and another of his remaining teeth appeared to have come loose.

Slowly, he tried to lift himself up. He had no idea what time it was, but it was already dark, and the lashing rain had been replaced by a slow drizzle. Porter looked around for the vodka bottle, but it was gone. So was the kebab he'd been eating. Reaching down into his pocket, he looked for the thirty quid he had left. Gone. 'Bastards,' he muttered.

Standing up, he wobbled a bit, then managed to find his balance. The pain in his left leg was hardly noticeable any more: every nerve ending in his body was screaming out in agony, overriding whatever was wrong with his leg. Got to get myself cleaned up, he told himself. I'm going to die if I stay out here tonight.

He walked slowly towards Vauxhall Bridge. The traffic was snarling past him, an angry, swelling chorus of horns and engines. A cyclist sped past on the pavement, shouting at Porter to get out of the way. He staggered forwards. Only half a mile, he told himself. Maybe the hostel will help me.

The Orchid Centre was the only place he could think of right now. Run by a charity, it provided beds for the night for the homeless, gave you a shower and some medicine, and a hot meal if they had any volunteers coming in to man the kitchens. It was financed by one of the big American banks in the City as part of their 'corporate responsibility' programme, and sometimes you'd get American bankers spending part of the evening there, helping out with the dossers, before getting their chauffeurs to take them back to their mansions in Notting Hill. Still, it wasn't too bad, Porter had decided over the couple of years he'd been a regular visitor. At least they didn't try and stuff any religion down your throat like some of the shelters. The only religion these bloody bankers knew was money, and there was no chance of any of the guys kipping down in the hostel catching that.

'Have you got a place?' he said, leaning up against the door.

It was opened by a young guy in black jeans and a sweatshirt. Matt, maybe that was his name, Porter thought, struggling to remember what he was called. He was OK, the way he recalled it from the last time he'd been here. Didn't lecture you, and didn't suggest you got a job. Just gave you a hot shower, and some antibiotics, and let you get some kip.

'What the hell happened to you?' said Matt.

Porter hadn't looked in a mirror − it wasn't a piece of kit you carried around with you when you lived on the streets − but he imagined he looked terrible. There was still some bleeding on his face, and some minor flesh wounds from the beating he'd taken. His clothes were cut and torn, and he was soaked through. Everything is relative, but even in a Vauxhall hostel for the homeless, he looked like crap.

'I need a drink, mate,' growled Porter. 'A drink and somewhere to kip . . .'

Matt took a step back, and Porter followed him. The entrance hallway to the Orchid Centre was painted lime green, and smelt of disinfectant and boiled cabbage. Matt's office had an electric fire, and a small TV. The clock on the wall said it was just after nine. 'There's no booze here, Porter,' said Matt sharply. 'You know that.'

Porter was wobbling, trying to hold on to his balance.

There was still enough vodka swilling around inside him to make it hard to stand up straight. On the TV, he caught a glimpse of Perry Collinson. He was talking about Katie Dartmouth: it was a replay of the same interview he'd seen earlier in the day. As he finished his Churchill quote, the report cut to a blonde, smartly turned-out woman in her late fifties. It was an interview with Katie's mum, from her home village in Hampshire. There were tears in her eyes as she said how worried they were about Katie, and how desperately they wanted to see her again. 'We'll be back right after the break with the all the latest on the Katie Dartmouth kidnap drama,' concluded the newscaster. And the screen faded to an elegant picture of Katie Dartmouth, looking blonde and radiant, while the wistful opening chords of Elton John's 'Someone Saved My Life Tonight' played on the sound-track.

'I need a fucking drink,' Porter snapped, looking away from the TV screen.

'Like I said, there's no drinking,' said Matt, turning angry. 'We can sort you out with a bed. From the looks of you, we should probably try and get you to a doctor in the morning as well.'

'It's a drink I need, not a bloody doctor.'

Matt took a step closer. He was slightly built but he'd worked in the hostel long enough not to be intimidated by any of the guys who kipped down there. 'You need to learn to play by the rules, mate,' he said.

'I'll bloody pay you,' Porter snapped.

He fished around in his pocket, and took out the two credit cards he'd taken from the woman's purse that morning. The Scots guys had emptied the cash out of his pockets, but hadn't bothered with the plastic. They knew that even the dodgiest off-licence in Vauxhall wasn't going to let them pay by card. Porter shoved them at Matt. 'I'll pay for some booze.'

Matt glanced down at the cards. 'You're called Helen now, are you?' he said, reading the name that was written across the thin strip of plastic. 'Very fetching. It suits you.' He looked straight into Porter's swollen, bloodshot eyes. 'We're here to help guys like you, and we do a pretty good job, but we aren't interested in bloody thieves.'

'I need a drink, man,' cried Porter. 'Just one bloody drink. Look at the state of me –'

'Get out of here,' said Matt.

'I'm bloody desperate, man. What's one fucking drink?'

Matt pushed him back. Porter wobbled, but managed to hold on to his balance. 'Get lost,' he said. 'We might be a charity, but there's a fucking limit, and you just crossed it. Sober up, and we'll help you. Stay like this, and you're on your own.'

'Fuck, there's just no sodding point,' Porter snarled.

His face was suddenly creased up with sadness as he turned round and started walking back into the rain. Behind him, Matt was turning the sound up on the TV. Porter could hear the strains of 'Someone Saved My Life Tonight' whistling through the cold air.

Turning left, he walked through the slowly falling rain. He was heading towards the river. No point going back to his old archway. The Scots bastards would just give him another kicking. There was a spot close to the bridge, next to a new apartment block, where some blokes sometimes kipped down for the night. Maybe I'll go there, Porter thought. See if I can find some way of keeping warm. And see what tomorrow brings.

THREE

Porter looked down at the river. A dirty puddle of water was lapping up by the muddy shores of the Thames. He dipped his hands down into it. The water felt cold and refreshing, and he sloshed some across his face, trying to clean away the blood that was clinging to his skin. He'd already walked a mile or so along the riverfront, looking for somewhere to kip down for the night. One spot underneath the first arch of Vauxhall had already been colonised by some Macedonians who'd built a campfire and seemed to be heating up some tins of grub. Porter had gestured that he might join them, but if he didn't already know the Macedonian for piss off, then he did now. An abandoned petrol station where guys sometimes kipped down had been taken over by a couple of brawlers, and Porter was in no mood for another fight. Just somewhere to rest his head until he could pick himself up and start again.

But there didn't seem to be anywhere. In London, he couldn't even find anywhere to sleep rough and not be disturbed by anyone any more.

Somewhere up above, a few beams of moonlight were trying to break through, but mostly the sky remained dark and angry. He sat down on a concrete ledge, looking out at the river, and felt a stiff night breeze blow through him. Just got to try to stay warm, he told himself. Until tomorrow.

'John,' shouted a voice.

It ran out across the empty stretch of concrete that led down to the water.

Porter hunched his shoulders, and looked out again over the river. When you were called John you got used to hearing your name, and no longer assumed they were looking for you. Who the hell would want to talk to me anyway? he thought bitterly. This or any other night.

'John,' the voice shouted again, drawing closer this time.

Porter glanced round. He recognised Matt's voice now, and, looking closely into the murky, hazy light, he could see him. About a hundred yards away down the river, with someone at his side. A doctor maybe. I'm in no mood to see a medic, Porter decided. Not unless they've started handing out bottles of vodka on prescription.

'Piss off,' he said.

His voice was carried on the breeze, and moved swiftly down the river. He looked back at the shoreline, watching the slow progress of a barge moving towards the sea. The day had been bad enough already. All he wanted to do was to get it over with. Move on to the next one.

'I've someone to see you,' Matt shouted.

Porter glanced to his left. Matt was maybe fifty yards away from him now. The shape at his side was hard to make out. An overcoat was all he could see. Bollocks, he thought. It's a trick. They've brought a doctor, or the social, or the police. They're going to section me. Or arrest me. Or something worse.

'Piss off,' he said again, louder this time.

'Just wait there,' Matt said.

Porter stood up, and began walking upstream. His legs were exhausted and he could feel the bruising all over his body, but he still had the strength to get away if he had to.

'This woman needs to speak to you,' Matt shouted.

Porter turned round, looking straight at him. The shape at his side was moving closer now. Maybe thirty yards from

46

him. She was wearing a long, blue overcoat, smartly tailored, and she had thick black hair that tumbled about five inches past her shoulders. Just a kid, really, thought Porter briefly. No more than seventeen or eighteen. A looker, though. She had sharply elegant features, high cheekbones and a strong mouth.

Not just any kid, he realised. *My kid.*

Sandy.

It shouldn't be hard for a father to recognise his own daughter, should it? Porter asked himself. Diana had thrown him out of the house eleven years ago, when Sandy was just a child of six, and he hadn't seen her since. She'd changed a lot, and so had he, but her face was printed onto his soul, and he'd no more forget it than he'd forget his own name.

'Dad,' she said, her voice hesitant and gentle. 'Dad? Is that you?'

The words pierced Porter's skin more painfully than any of the blows that had rained down on him in the alleyway earlier that day. Her voice settled in his ears and, for a moment, he wanted to run to her, and take her in his arms. Then he paused. It's not me, is it? I'm not her dad. I abandoned that job eleven years ago. I couldn't hack it, and her mum couldn't put up with my drinking any more, and I can't say I blame her. I can't change that now. There's no point in even trying.

'I'm nobody,' he growled.

'It's me, Dad,' she said. 'Sandy . . .'

He could hear the determination in her voice, and it reminded him of her mother. She was always the strong one: I might have been the soldier, but she was the one who knew how to fight.

'Piss off,' shouted Porter. 'I never heard of a girl called Sandy.'

He turned round and started walking along the river. It wasn't true of course. There wasn't a day that had passed in the last eleven years when he hadn't thought about her. Probably not even so much as an hour. But he couldn't look at her now. Not like this. Nobody wants a dad who lives out on the streets, who doesn't have a house to live in or a car to drive, who smells likes a sewer. What's the point of a parent like that? Better just to keep on moving. She'll get by without me. She has done so far, and it'll only get easier as the years go by.

Suddenly he heard footsteps running down the pathway. The wind was blowing up stronger now, and the clouds briefly cleared, sending bright shafts of moonlight flooding out across the river. Porter felt a hand on his shoulders. He spun round. Matt was standing right next to him, his face sweaty. 'For fuck's sake, you old bugger,' he snapped. 'It's your daughter.'

Porter paused. He could see Sandy standing twenty yards away, not moving.

'She came to the hostel tonight looking for you,' pressed Matt, fighting to recover his breath. 'She's been looking for you for weeks. She contacted SAFA, tried everything, and eventually she found someone who knew you kipped down with us sometimes. I guessed you'd be down by the river.' He looked straight into Porter's eyes, his expression piercing and harsh: there was a world of judgement in those eyes, and none of it was in Porter's favour. 'She wants to meet you. Just do that for her. It's bugger all to ask . . .'

Porter nodded. It was a simple movement of the head, but it was harder than throwing the strongest punch. Glancing up at Sandy, he attempted a rough smile. 'C'mon then, love,' he said. 'We'll hit the bloody town.'

She smiled back and walked towards him. Porter felt embarrassed about the way he looked. Usually he didn't care: when you lived out on the streets it made no difference to the people around you. Now he wished he'd found somewhere to wash, maybe even had a change of clothes. It would have been good to scrape some of the blood off his face. She probably wasn't expecting much when she came looking for me, but this . . . Christ, nobody could be prepared for this.

'I'm sorry,' he said, glancing down at his wet, filthy clothes.

'It's OK,' said Sandy. 'Let's find somewhere to talk.'

Porter nodded. He walked alongside her, away from Vauxhall, up towards Waterloo station. He wasn't sure what time it was. Eleven, maybe, or twelve. Most of the pubs would be shutting but there was café he knew where the cabbies went to get a coffee and a bacon sandwich before heading out on to the nightclub shift. They didn't mind what you looked like in there, and they never shut.

Porter paused outside the entrance. He could hear the sound of bacon frying, and smell the comforting fug of grease and cigarette smoke. They had walked in silence, neither of them sure of what to say. 'I'll pay,' said Sandy as he hesitated by the door. 'Don't worry about it.'

Sitting down, Porter watched as she sauntered up to the counter, ordering them two coffees, and two bacon sandwiches. A few of the guys in the place were following her with their eyes, and one of them looked like he was about to say something to her but then he noticed Porter glaring at him and quickly went back to reading his newspaper. There was a TV in the corner, tuned to the latest in the Katie Dartmouth kidnap saga, with a few people glancing occasionally towards it. An ultimatum had been issued, according to the newsreader. She'd been captured by Hezbollah terrorists who were demanding that British troops be withdrawn from Iraq and Afghanistan by eight o'clock on Saturday night, or else Katie was going to be beheaded live on television. Porter looked away. Why's everyone so interested? he wondered. It's not like there is anything they can do to help her.

Sandy put the coffees and the bacon sandwiches down on the table. He could see her better now, with her coat off, and in the proper light. She was a strong, powerfully built young woman, with none of the playful puppy fat that he remembered from the little girl he'd left behind. She had pale green eyes, and a seriousness about her that Porter wouldn't have expected. Still, as he watched her move through the café, he couldn't help feel a pride in her simple existence. I may not have got much right – probably nothing at all when you try and calculate it – but at least she is something to be proud of.

'What the hell are you doing here?' he said.

Sandy looked straight at him, and Porter was taken aback by the affection in her eyes. It was so long since anyone looked at me with anything other than contempt I'd forgotten what it feels like, he reflected.

'Mum won't ever tell me about you,' she said, stirring a sugar into her coffee. 'It's like you never existed. But of course I remember you from when I was a kid.'

Sandy pushed a lock of black hair away from her face. 'Mum wouldn't give me any clues about where you were but her brother – Uncle Ken – said he reckoned you were down in London. He'd heard you were on the streets, that you'd been having a bad time, and there was a hostel where you went sometimes. He put me in touch with the Soldiers and Airmen Forces Association, and after I spoke to them on the phone a few times, they pointed me in the right direction. Ken made me promise not to tell Mum. Or Auntie Sally.' Sandy wrinkled up her nose in a way that made Porter fall in love with her all over again. 'I don't think Aunt Sally likes you very much either.'

Porter laughed. 'Women don't like me,' he said gruffly. 'You'll find that out soon enough.'

'Anyway, I've got an interview at University College London tomorrow afternoon, so Mum gave me the money to get the train down from Nottingham,' she continued. 'I'm getting the eight o'clock train back tomorrow evening. It's

50

the first time I've ever been to London by myself. The first time I've had a chance to look for you. Mum would kill me if she knew but I don't care about that. I went to the hostel, and talked to Matt. Nice bloke. He said you'd been in, and he reckoned you'd be down by the river somewhere.'

'I can't even look after myself, never mind a kid,' said Porter bitterly. 'You'd be better off without me.'

'Bollocks,' snapped Sandy. That anger again, noticed Porter. It was like sitting opposite her mother a lifetime ago. 'No one's better off without a parent. It doesn't matter how useless they are.'

'I'm the exception,' snarled Porter.

'No you're bloody not,' said Sandy. 'Nobody's an exception, not you, not anyone. You're the only dad I've got. That's probably bad luck on both of us, but we're just going to have to live with it.'

Porter paused. She was looking straight at him, and he could feel the pride swelling up inside him again. But what was the point? he reflected bitterly. How could he have a relationship with her now? What was she going to do, come down for the weekend and kip down underneath whatever archway he found himself sleeping under? Trudge around town while he looked for some work washing dishes? Maybe meet some of his mates, like the Scottish blokes. Other divorced dads could take the girls skiing, whizz them around in their Jaguars and Land Rovers. Not me. I would offer her everything I have. Except I've got nothing, and how can you offer someone that?

'It's not going to work,' he said flatly. 'Life hasn't gone straight for me, not for a long time. It's not going to change now.'

'It can change for anyone.'

Porter smiled. 'You're young,' he said. 'It's easy to believe that. I'm forty-five years old. This is what I am. There's nothing to be done about it now.'

Sandy was already fishing around in her handbag. She took out a crisp wad of notes and pushed it across the table. 'Here's a hundred pounds,' she said. 'There's nothing wrong with you that a good shower and something to live for won't fix. Get yourself bloody cleaned up, and start being a proper father.'

Porter pushed the money away. 'Where did you get that?' he said.

'I saved,' Sandy said. 'Holiday jobs. Now take it, it's yours.'

'I can't.'

Sandy stood up, and put her coat on. 'You can and you will,' she said. 'You've let me down once. Now don't do it again. When you've sorted yourself out, you can contact me at our old address. We haven't moved.'

She lashed the belt on her coat angrily into place, and started walking towards the door. A couple of guys looked over from the TV with leers on their faces, but then went back to watching the TV. Porter took the bacon sandwich, and ate it in a couple of mouthfuls. Sandy had only nibbled on hers, so he ate that as well. It was the first proper food he'd had all day, and it started to make him feel better. All I need now is a drink, he told himself.

He started walking. The café was round the corner from the station, and there were people pouring back into Waterloo even at this time of night. If you walked due south, there was a pub Porter sometimes went to, on the rare occasions he had money. The Three Kings stayed open to the small hours, and didn't mind what you looked or smelt like. The place didn't look or smell of much itself, so it could hardly start getting fussy about other people's appearance. There was plenty of vodka behind the bar, and so long as you had money in your pocket they'd keep serving it to you until you fell over.

A blast of cigarette smoke hit him as he stepped through the door. When they got around to banning smoking in public places, the Three Kings wasn't going to pay any attention. Nobody worried much about the law in here, and if the police ever raided the place, there would be a lot more than smoking bans to worry about. There were maybe two dozen blokes standing around the bar, a couple of whom Porter recognised: they were both ex-forces guys who, like himself, had fallen on hard times and spent their lives drifting in and out of hostels. Porter nodded in their direction, but didn't say anything. Like most people at the Three Kings, he was here to get drunk. As quickly as possible.

'A vodka,' said Porter, looking across at the barmaid. 'In fact, make that a double.'

He looked at the glass of pale liquid. I've seen the bottom of a lot of glasses, he thought to himself, but I've rarely seen anything as clear as I see this. There's no way back for me. I just have to forget about Sandy, the same way I did all those years ago. And pretty soon, she'll forget about me as well.

Taking a hit of the vodka, he threw it down the back of his throat. He felt the warm, smug embrace of the alcohol starting to take hold of him as the vodka swirled through his bloodstream. He could feel his muscles start to relax. And the questions in his mind started to beat less ferociously, like a storm blowing itself out. After all, he repeated to himself, how the hell could a guy like me get his life back on track? It's all very well Sandy saying I can change now. But what does she know about life? She's just a kid.

He looked towards the TV in a corner of the pub. At least a dozen guys were sitting around it, their beers in their hands. More Katie Dartmouth nonsense, Porter reflected. The whole country's going crazy.

He took a step forward, his vodka glass still in his hand. The newsreader had already talked about how frantically the security services were searching for any clues to her location. There was an Arab guy on the TV. According to the strapline, his name was Hassad Naimi, and he was one of the senior commanders of Hezbollah who had taken Katie hostage. He'd been filmed on a webcam, and the footage had been broadcast by al-Jazeera. He was explaining how Katie was going to be beheaded on Saturday night. The execution would be broadcast live on the Internet. 'Unless the British war criminals take the infidel invaders out of Iraq and Afghanistan by this hour, then she will die,' he was saying, looking straight at the camera. 'I say to the people of Britain, her fate is yours to decide. Tell your leaders it is time for your soldiers to come home. Or the blood of Katie Dartmouth will be on your hands.'

Porter watched him speaking. He was not even really listening. He was just looking at the man's face. He watched his soft brown eyes as he spoke. And he watched the lower lip tremble and shake as he stuttered out each sentence.

The lip was deformed. Badly deformed.

Jesus, thought Porter. *I know that bastard.*

Heading back to the bar, Porter ordered another vodka. He threw it down his throat in one gulp then signalled to the barmaid to pour him another.

I know that bastard, he repeated to himself.

It's the same kid I spared in that basement back in Beirut seventeen years ago. The kid who went on to kill Steve, Keith and Mike.

Porter gripped the third vodka but didn't drink it.

Maybe Sandy's right. The thought hit him with the force of a hammer. Maybe, just maybe, there is a way back for me.

He put the vodka back on the bar. Turning on his heels, he started to walk through the doors, and out into the cold, dark streets. The chords of 'Someone Saved My Life Tonight' were crashing through the pub as Sky News flashed up a picture of Katie Dartmouth and faded into the ads.

Just for once, Elton, thought Porter with a wry smile, you might be right.

54

FOUR

The river looked better in the morning, Porter thought. The tide was high, and the water was lapping right up close to the barricades. A couple of tourist boats were heading down towards Greenwich for their first run of the day. Sunshine was breaking out across Battersea Park, sending shafts of brilliant light skimming out across the water. Hell, we all look better at dawn, Porter told himself. The day is still fresh, and we can still hope.

He glanced up at the headquarters of the Firm, right next to Vauxhall Bridge. He'd walked past it a thousand times during the few years he'd dossed down in the area. Until he saw Sandy again, and realised how much she'd missed him, it had never occurred to him to go inside.

I thought my soldiering days were buried. Until now.

Porter checked himself in the reflection from a phone box. Not so bad, he decided. After leaving the pub, he'd found a quiet spot close to the bus depot, and bedded himself down among some tossed-out cardboard boxes. He hadn't slept well, but then he never did. At five in the morning, he'd walked a mile down to the Asda superstore on the road that snaked towards Brixton. The place was open all night, it was as cheap as dirt, and they didn't mind what the customers looked like. Porter picked himself out a new pair of jeans, a white shirt, some socks and trainers, and a sweater. The whole outfit came to thirty quid. He slipped into the toilets, washed himself as best he could in the sink, then put on the new clothes. He tossed the old ones into the bins outside, then went to the café and blew another fiver on a full English breakfast, and a jug of coffee. The water, at least, was free. By the time he'd finished that, he felt almost like a human being again.

He glanced one more time at the Firm. The office was deliberately forbidding: a mass of turrets and spikes, with a huge inner courtyard. There were a dozen armed and uniformed police officers at the entrance, and no doubt twice as many plain-clothes men keeping an eye on it as well. There was no building in London more heavily guarded. Don't worry about it, Porter told himself. You can do this. It's just a matter of holding your nerve.

He walked steadily towards the building, at an even, unvarying pace. Run into this place and they were likely to gun you down. Looking across the river to the clock on Big Ben, he noted that it was just after seven in the morning. Early. But the spooks never slept. And certainly not when they were in the middle of a crisis.

The policemen looked at him suspiciously as he walked across the driveway, and into the entrance lobby, but they made no attempt to stop him. It's a public building, Porter reflected. They have to at least let people walk into the place. It was only once you checked in at the desks that they ran you over for guns and knives.

The foyer was decorated in grey, with slate floors, and a bank of glass at the front. Marble-clad walls led up to a bank of elevators. Along one side there was a reception desk with three uniformed guards sitting at it. At the other, there was a pair of black leather sofas, and a collection of the day's papers spread out on a coffee table. All of them, Porter noticed, had pictures of Katie Dartmouth on them. 'BRING OUR BOYS HOME TODAY' said huge letters across the front page of the *Independent*. 'SAVE HER' said the *Mirror*.

Porter walked steadily up to the desk. A thickset man in

his forties looked straight at him, his expression as welcoming as a chunk of granite.

'I know how to get Katie Dartmouth out,' said Porter.

Even as he delivered the sentence, Porter knew how ridiculous he sounded. If it wasn't for the fact he knew it was true, he'd be laughing at himself.

The receptionist looked at him, taking half a second to make a judgement, and then reached underneath his desk to press a button. Even though he was trained to remain impassive, Porter could tell he had already reached his own verdict. He thinks I'm a nutter. Who know, maybe he's right?

Five armed officers appeared from the door that led away from the elevators. They walked quickly across the slate floor. Not running, but moving with purpose. A few people were coming through the entrance doors, heading towards the lifts to get to their desks, but they simply made way for the armed men, paying them no attention. 'We'll have to ask you to leave, sir,' said the first officer, standing in front of Porter.

He glanced at the man's face. It was expressionless, like rock. He was wearing no uniform but he didn't need to. There was an MP-5 assault rifle strapped to his chest, and that gave him all the authority he needed.

Porter looked straight into his steely blue eyes. 'I know how to get Katie Dartmouth out.'

He could see the man's reaction in his face. Nutter, he was thinking. Just like the other guy. But he remained silent.

'I can get her out.'

'This way, please, sir,' said the officer.

Porter could feel his chest thumping. This was his one chance to show Sandy he could amount to something. To look her in the eye without feeling ashamed of himself. He'd no more throw it away than he'd throw away his own life.

'I'm the only man who can get through to her kid-nappers,' Porter shouted.

He could see a few of the office workers looking at him distastefully before hurrying on. None of them wanted to hear what he was saying, and none of them were looking in his direction. The five guards were slowly closing in on him, forming a tight semicircle from which there was no chance of escape.

'This is your one chance to save her,' said Porter. 'I was SAS, I know something about the man who's holding her, something we can use.'

He could feel a hand grabbing hold of his arm. The MP-5 wasn't jabbing into his chest, but it was definitely pointed in his direction, and the expression of the man with his finger on the trigger suggested he wouldn't hesitate to use it if he had to. They were starting to move him towards the door. Porter shrugged himself free. These goons weren't going to listen to anyone, he reflected bitterly. Osama bin Laden could walk through the door offering to turn himself in, and they'd tell him to come back when he'd made an appointment. 'I can walk,' he growled.

A fresh blast of cold air struck Porter in the face, as he stepped out into the morning air. A gust of wind was blowing through him. It can take my hopes and blow them away, Porter told himself. I must have been mad to think they would listen to me.

'Don't come back,' said the officer firmly.

A Jaguar was pulling up outside, and a man in a charcoal-grey suit was climbing out of the back seat. Porter recognised him at once. Sir Angus Clayton, the director general of the Firm. Porter had seen his picture in the papers he sometimes fished out of the bins he slept next to. He might even have used his mugshot as a blanket once or twice. A tall man, with a fast-disappearing head of black hair, and a face that was shallow and drawn, he looked tired even though he hadn't started work yet. Porter was standing only a few yards away from him. If I don't take this chance, he told himself, then I'll never get another.

'I can get Katie Dartmouth out for you, Sir Angus,' he shouted.

The man looked at him. His eyes were focused, intent, as the words struck home. He was assessing Porter in an instant, scanning his face, using a lifetime of experience in the intelligence trade to make a snap judgement on whether the man might be worth listening to. He slammed the door shut on the Jaguar, and started walking towards the entrance doorway.

The guard was tightening his grip on Porter's arm. 'We've already asked you to leave, sir,' he snapped.

Porter took a step forward. 'One minute of your time,' he said. 'That's all I'm asking for.'

Sir Angus kept walking towards the revolving glass door that led into the Firm's headquarters. From the expression on his face, you couldn't even tell if he had heard Porter.

'If you make any more trouble, sir –' started the guard.

Porter shrugged him aside.

'That woman is going to die in five days' time, Sir Angus,' said Porter. 'And I'm the only man who can do anything about it.'

The guard was tugging him back.

'One bloody minute. I'm SAS, I'm –'

'Sir, you are risking arrest,' the guard said.

Sir Angus paused. His hand was already pushing the revolving door open, but his feet had stopped moving. Slowly, he turned round. His eyes were looking straight at Porter, questioning and probing at the same time. 'You're Regiment?'

Porter nodded.

'What was the code name of the Firm's liaison officer in Hereford in 1990?'

'Zebra, sir,' replied Porter, without a flicker of hesitation.

'And do you keep in touch with Jim West?'

'Not likely, sir,' replied Porter. 'The bloke died on a black op in Somalia.'

I've passed the test, thought Porter. Only a Regiment man could answer those questions.

'A minute is too long,' said Sir Angus quietly. 'I'll give you thirty seconds.'

The guard let go of Porter, but he was still standing just a couple of feet behind him, and his gun was still cocked, ready to drop him if he created any trouble. Porter paused. Thirty seconds, he told himself. Better make this good.

'In 1989, I was in the SAS,' he said, his tone confident and strong. 'There was a hostage-rescue mission in Beirut. A guy called Kenneth Bratton. There was a young kid, one of the Hezbollah boys. I spared his life. It's that Hassad bloke, the one who is holding Katie Dartmouth hostage. I recognised him because of the deformed mouth.' Porter paused, looking straight into Sir Angus's eyes. He could tell he'd caught his interest: whether he'd convinced him or not it was impossible to say. 'He'll talk to me, because he owes me,' he continued. 'I know it might not work, but it's worth a try, and what else have you got? If you've got a secure line to him, tell him there's an SAS guy with two fingers missing on his left hand. Tell him I want to come and talk to him.'

Sir Angus glanced down at Porter's left hand. He could see at once the two stumps where his fingers used to be. He rubbed his brow as his face creased up into a frown.

Porter could feel his heart thumping against the walls of his chest. 'I'm on the level,' he said. 'I was Regiment. You can check my records.'

Sir Angus hesitated. 'Here's what I'm going to do,' he said. He nodded towards the guards. 'These gentlemen are going to take you to a secure room. A case officer is going to come down and check out your story.'

'Thank you, sir,' said Porter.

'But let me tell you my terms,' Sir Angus continued. He was already starting to turn back to the revolving door. 'If you're wasting our time, I'm going to get them to beat the bloody hell out of you, then take you to the back of this building, and feed you to the sodding fish. Got that? You can leave now if you want –'

'I'll take those terms,' said Porter with quiet determination.

FIVE

On the table in front of him, there was jug of coffee and a plate of biscuits. Porter took the jug, and poured himself a third cup of coffee, drinking it down in a couple of gulps, then eating another of the biscuits. He'd have polished off the whole plate in the next few minutes, he realised. When you lived on the streets, you ate your food quick, before someone stole it, the same way a wild dog does.

He'd been sitting here for ten or fifteen minutes already. The guards had taken him down three flights in the elevator, into the network of cells and interrogation rooms that lay deep underneath the Firm's headquarters. They'd remained silent during the time it took to bring him here: Porter could tell the guy in charge was looking forward to roughing him up if his story didn't check out. 'Someone will be along to see you in a minute,' he had said briskly, as he ushered Porter into the room.

It didn't look like a prison cell, Porter thought, but that's what it was. The door was locked behind him, and he reckoned you'd need at least a couple of pounds of Semtex to break through it. There was grey carpet on the floor, and the walls were painted a grey-white. A simple table was in the centre of the room, with the coffee jug on it, and next to it there was a chair. A flat-screen TV nestled in one corner. Otherwise, the room was completely empty.

Porter took another biscuit, and flicked on the TV. Sky News was covering the Katie Dartmouth hostage story twenty-four hours a day now. The presenter was going over live to Downing Street, where the Prime Minister was about to make a statement. Porter watched with interest, as the familiar figure appeared on the screen. He paused, and there was catch in his throat as he concentrated on what he was about to say. 'Let me just start by saying that all our thoughts are with Katie Dartmouth and her family at this time,' he began, looking straight at the camera. 'I just say this to the people who have taken her. Whatever your quarrel is with the British government, then we can talk about that, but there is nothing to be gained from taking the life of an innocent young woman. Now, to the British people I say this. They are asking for British troops to be withdrawn from Iraq, but nothing is more important than that we stay the course, and don't turn our back on the war on terror. Sir Perry Collinson has been put in charge of our diplomatic efforts to bring Katie Dartmouth out of the Lebanon. Whatever he needs to bring that about, you may be assured it will be put at his disposal.' The PM paused, coughing slightly. 'This certainly isn't the moment for sound bites,' he continued. 'But in our darkest hours, our finest men come forward. Perry Collinson one of those men.'

Porter turned the sound down. 'Bollocks,' he muttered out loud. That tosser couldn't get a Cheesy Wotsit out of its packet. He certainly doesn't know how to get Katie Dartmouth out of a cellar in Beirut.

Porter snapped rigidly to attention as he heard the lock turn in the door. A woman was coming into the room. He guessed she was about thirty-five, with dark hair that stretched down no further than the bottom of her neck, and with clear blue eyes that were set in a solid, serious face. She was wearing a black jacket and black skirt, with a white blouse and an amber necklace hooked around her delicate white skin. Just keep yourself focused, Porter told himself. Finally show Sandy that you can do something.

'My name is Layla Thompson,' she said, looking straight at Porter. 'And you are . . . ?'

'Porter,' he replied crisply. 'John Porter.'

She pulled out a chair and sat down opposite him. There was a notepad and a pen in front of her, and she instinctively reached for them, but Porter noticed she wasn't writing anything down. Just drawing a series of rectangles. 'Sir Angus says you know how to get to Hassad Naimi,' she said.

'I've been through it once with the boss,' said Porter. 'I was in the SAS back in '89. We went into the Lebanon to get out a hostage. Hassad was there. He was just a kid then, so I spared his life. I recognised him from the shape of his mouth. It's deformed, you can't miss it.'

'And you think he'll talk to you?' said Layla.

She was about to pour herself a coffee and take a biscuit, but then she noticed they were all gone.

'Like I said, I let him live,' said Porter. 'Three good men died on that mission, and I lost two fingers on my left hand. I've regretted it every bloody day since, but that doesn't change the facts. He owes me. Arabs may not be good at much, and I wouldn't trust the bastard any further than I could throw a camel. But they never forget an obligation. Not when their honour is at stake.'

'Why did you let him live?'

'Christ, he was just a kid . . .'

'A dangerous one, however.'

'We've been through all that,' snapped Porter. 'It's not important now.'

'Which years were you in the Regiment?' said Layla.

'From '88 to '92,' answered Porter.

Layla nodded. She had the same patient manner of a doctor, listening carefully to what you said, while neither approving or disapproving. 'Here's what I'm going to do,' she said. 'I'll take some fingerprints, and a snip of your hair, so we can run ID checks, and a DNA test. We need to make sure you are who you say you are. If that works out, then we can have a conversation. OK?'

Porter nodded. It was going to take time, he told himself. You couldn't walk back in from the cold after fourteen years and expect the security services to start trusting you.

It took only a few moments to snip a lock of hair and take an impression of his fingertips, and then Porter was alone again. Layla had left, locking the door behind her: they didn't believe him yet, he noted, but they weren't going to risk losing him either.

Porter flicked on the TV, but there were just replays of the PM's statement on Katie Dartmouth. One of the political commentators was talking about the by-election coming up in nine days' time, and how the government faced a potential humiliation if Katie was executed at the weekend. There were more calls from the Opposition for troops to be taken out of Iraq, and a vigil had already been started by the 'Stop the War' coalition in Trafalgar Square. Porter turned it off again. He'd watched enough by now to know how badly they wanted Katie out of there.

Alone with my own thoughts, he reflected. Always a dangerous place. An hour slipped by and then another. Porter could feel himself growing desperate for a drink. The coffee pot was empty, and the biscuits were all gone. As he stared at the walls, the doubts start to creep up on him, like maggots crawling across rotten meat. What the hell am I doing here? Who in the name of Christ do I think I am kidding?

I must be mad to want to get back into this, he decided, as he stood up to pace around the small room. Whatever it is a man needs to be made of to turn him into a warrior, I haven't got it. *And there is no point in thinking I'm suddenly going to acquire it at my age.*

He looked at the door again. If only it wasn't locked, he'd just walk straight out of here. Get back to his archway, use his spare cash to buy a couple of bottles of vodka, and get some rest. If they don't come back soon, I'm going to start banging on the door. I can't deal with this much longer. Not without something to drink.

Just then the door started to open. Layla walked in. 'OK, so you are who you say you are,' she said, sitting down behind the table.

She motioned to Porter to sit down opposite her, but he preferred to stand.

'The problem is, John Porter is a fuck-up,' she continued.

Layla glanced down at a sheaf of computer printouts she'd been carrying under her arm. 'We've retrieved your records. And indeed, you were in the SAS from 1988 to 1992. But, how shall I put this delicately, you weren't exactly gunning for any medals, were you?'

'I was good enough to get in,' growled Porter.

'But not good enough to stay in,' said Layla, her tone laced with sarcasm. 'You fucked up in the Regiment. You were sent off to be a range warden but you couldn't handle that either. After you left the army, you tried a few jobs, but you couldn't hold them down. Your wife kicked you out more than ten years ago. She divorced you five years ago – but you probably didn't even know because her lawyers didn't have anywhere to send the papers.'

She shrugged, flicking a piece of dust off the shoulder pad of her black jacket. Porter watched it fall to the floor: he knew how it felt.

'If I may put it this way, John Porter isn't exactly the first person the nation would turn to in its hour of need.'

Porter stared at the floor. I shouldn't have bothered, he was telling himself. I should have just gone somewhere I could get a drink.

'I shouldn't have come . . .'

He started to walk towards the door.

'Hold it,' said Layla.

He looked at her. She was flashing a smile at him, and for the first time he noticed how pretty she was. There's a woman underneath that black suit somewhere, he thought. But you need some sturdy pickaxes and shovels to find her, because she's buried a long way underground.

'What's passed is passed,' she said, her tone softening. 'What we do know is that you were in the SAS, and you went into the Lebanon. Do you really know this Hassad bastard?'

Porter nodded. 'I spared his life . . .'

'And you reckon he'll speak to you?'

Porter nodded. 'I already told you that.'

Layla stood up. 'If we had any other options, believe me, we'd take them,' she said. 'Wait here. I'm going to talk to the boss. He doesn't always listen to me, but if he does, well, you might have just talked yourself into a job.'

SIX

Porter glanced at Layla in the elevator. They were moving swiftly up towards the tenth floor, where all the top brass had their offices. One shot, thought Porter. That's all I'm going to get at this. Within an hour, I could be back on the streets.

A brief flicker of doubt crossed his mind. This might end up costing me my life. Then again, what sort of life is it anyway?

The elevator cruised to a halt, and as the door opened, Porter stepped out onto the thickly carpeted corridor. He'd been waiting back down in the interrogation room for three hours before they'd said they were ready to talk to him. Plenty of time to practise my lines, he told himself.

He trod swiftly down the corridor, following as Layla led the way. There were no windows on this floor of the Firm: the building has already suffered one rocket attack by a dissident IRA group back in 2000, and the walls were now built of thick, armoured steel, but there was no way a window could be made completely secure, so they had got rid of them. There was a soft artificial light along the corridor, and the walls were decorated with striking pieces of modern art. The main conference room was fifteen yards down from the elevator, sealed off behind a frosted-glass door. Its entrance was guarded by two men, neither of them in uniform, but both with MP-5 assault rifles strapped to their chests.

'Porter,' said Layla, pausing before the door to the conference room, 'if you want to make yourself look like a bloody idiot, that's up to you. If you make me look like one as well, then I'm going to have your balls chopped off. Is that clear?'

Porter ignored her, walking inside. The room was at least thirty feet long, and ten wide. It was dominated by a thin glass table, with black leather chairs all around it. There were pots of coffee and bottles of mineral water distributed along it. On the left-hand wall, there was a row of flat, black, plasma screens: they were tuned to Sky News, CNN, BBC News 24, Fox News and al-Jazeera, all with the sound turned down. On the opposite wall, there was a bank of computer screens and a table of telecoms kit. Lots of kit, Porter noticed, but you wouldn't learn anything here you wouldn't find out from watching TV at home. *They don't trust me enough to let me see any sensitive intelligence.*

The lion's den, thought Porter as he took another step forward. This is what the Christians must have felt like when they got tossed into the Colosseum. *Except at least they had some faith in themselves.*

Sir Angus was sitting at the head of the table. And directly to his right was Perry Collinson.

Porter's eyes flashed towards him, the contempt unconcealed.

Collinson returned the look, and as he did so a thin, detached smile crossed over his lips. It was more than fifteen years since Porter had last seen him, but he still looked in remarkably good shape for a man in his mid-forties. His hair had grown darker, but there was still plenty of it. There was a little more flesh on him, but he was still lean and trim.

'John, sit down,' said Layla quietly.

She pulled out a chair at the head of the table. He could see how her manner changed as soon as she saw Sir Angus: in control when she was interrogating him, she suddenly became quiet in the presence of the boss. No doubt about who's in charge of this place, Porter noted. No doubt either that he scares the crap out of the lot of them.

'You've turned up rather unexpectedly, Mr Porter,' said Sir Angus. 'And I suppose we'll find out in the next few minutes whether you are unwelcome or not.'

Porter nodded, but remained silent. Don't open your mouth more than you need to, he told himself. It's never done you any good before, and it probably won't now either.

Sir Angus waved a hand around the table. 'Let me make the introductions,' he said, nodding to each man in turn. 'Peter Thornton, the man in charge of your old Regiment, the SAS. Sir Gerald Daniels, the Chief of the Defence Staff. James Middleton, who runs the Foreign Office's Middle East desk. You'll probably recognise Geoff Bramley, the Secretary of State for Defence. Jim Muir, from Downing Street, who runs the press operations. And, of course Sir Peregrine Collinson, the Prime Minister's special envoy to the Middle East.'

'We've met before,' said Collinson.

Porter didn't flinch. 'I believe so,' he said quietly.

There was something about Sir Angus's tone when he mentioned Collinson's name that suggested he didn't like him very much. *Join the club, mate.*

'Let's forget the poxy reunions, shall we, boys?' snapped Muir. 'There's a poll out in the *Evening Standard* this morning showing that 75 per cent of the British public think British troops should be taken out of Iraq rather than have fucking Katie Dartmouth executed. So shall we just get down to sodding business?'

Porter noticed that Muir was doodling a picture of a woman with huge breasts and a very short skirt on the notepad lying in front of him on the desk. He looked back at Sir Angus.

'So you think this Hassad man will speak to you?' said Sir Angus.

'That's right, sir,' said Porter. 'Tell him there is an SAS man who spared his life in '89, who lost two fingers on his left hand.'

Sir Angus nodded. 'And if he'll talk . . .?'

'Then send me out to negotiate,' said Porter.

'Who is this guy, anyway?' snapped Muir. 'Where the fuck did you find him?'

'Actually, he found us,' said Sir Angus. 'He came in this morning –'

'Jesus, I can't fucking believe it,' said Muir, his tone exasperated. 'We spend a couple of fucking billion a year on our security services, and we have to rely on some bloke who wanders in off the street. Christ Almighty. Your budget's getting chopped in the next spending review, along with your balls.'

Muir was scribbling even more frantically on his pad – the breasts on the woman were growing larger and her skirt shorter.

'He was one of our men,' said Peter Thornton. 'Porter was in the Regiment from '88 to '92.'

'And he says Hassad will talk to him,' said Sir Angus.

'I don't think we need him,' said Collinson, leaning forward on the table.

Porter looked towards him, but made sure not a single muscle on his face even twitched.

'No offence, Porter,' said Collinson. 'Good to see you again, and all that. But we've got men scouring the Middle East, looking in all the usual rat cellars, and we're bound to turn up something. You've been out of this game for a long time.' Another thin smile started to spread across his lips. 'And all in all, it's a shame you didn't kill the man seventeen years ago.'

'You . . .' Porter was about to continue, but he stopped

71

himself at the last moment. Looking up the table, he could see Sir Angus flinch as soon as Collinson spoke. So long as he's against me, I'm in with a shout, he realised. Within the Firm, your enemy's enemy had always been your friend. I can use that, he realised. *So long as I play it right.*

'If you don't need me, I'll understand, sir,' said Porter quietly, looking straight at Sir Angus, then glancing towards Muir.

'And how many other leads do you have?' said Muir to Sir Angus.

'At this moment, precisely none,' said Sir Angus. 'And however confident Perry might be, the truth is we don't have much of a clue where she is. Could be the Lebanon. Could be Syria or Jordan. They might even have taken her to Iraq.'

'We've talked to Mossad,' said Sir Gerald Daniels. 'They've got the best network of spies throughout the Middle East, and even they don't have a clue where Hassad might be hiding the woman. They can't even give us any pointers as to why Hezbollah are pulling this stunt now.'

'Looks like this guy is the best chance we have,' said Muir.

Sir Angus looked down the table. 'Please try not to screw it up.'

Porter felt a surge of adrenalin shooting through his veins: maybe, just maybe, I've pulled this off. He glanced at Collinson. He could see a flash of irritation pass across his face, but within the next few seconds it was replaced by a relaxed smile. At his side, Layla stood up, saying she would get the technicians to put through the call. Hassad hadn't given them a phone number. It was too dangerous: even a mobile phone could be tracked by the American satellite systems, and the Firm could always borrow the CIA kit for a day. Instead he'd given them a Skype number, which allowed him to make a call over the Internet. The call would be routed through the Web, and would contact Hassad at the other end. The technicians had been trying to use the number to get a location, but it was impossible. The call was routed though a hundred different Web servers and computers, some of them just Internet cafés in the back streets of Damascus or Cairo, and some of them home computers that had been hijacked by viruses. There was no way of telling where the call had come from. Hezbollah, along with al-Qaeda, were experts in using the Internet to communicate safely, with no chance of their location being cracked.

'The guy's a fuck-up, we can't trust him,' said Collinson suddenly.

The technicians were still fiddling around with the Internet connections. The Skype call was going through so many different routers, it was taking several minutes just to reach Hassad. He'd answer, there was no question of that. He'd already been in touch to confirm he'd taken Katie hostage, and to show them the webcam that was going to broadcast her execution live to the world next Saturday night. Wherever he was holed up, he had an Internet connection, and it was kept live twenty-four hours a day. It was just a question of patching the call through.

Porter could feel his heart thumping. He knew it was still possible to blow this.

'We've read the files,' said Peter Thornton. 'On Porter's one and only combat mission for the Regiment, three men died. It was the worst round of casualties since the Falklands, and there was nothing as bad until Iraq One. So, no, he didn't exactly cover himself in glory. But no blame was officially attached to Porter, and . . .' He paused, deciding not to continue along that path. 'We haven't seen him or heard from him for at least a decade. So his record isn't great, but it doesn't disqualify him either.'

'Why are you doing this?' asked Bramley, looking straight at Porter.

'To help my country, sir,' he replied, his tone even and

controlled. 'And that young girl, well, I've seen people held hostage in the Lebanon and it's pretty bloody rough.'

'That's good enough for me,' insisted Sir Angus. 'I say we let him make the call.'

Just then Layla switched on a speakerphone placed at the centre of the conference table. 'We have Hassad Naimi on the line,' she said softly.

The room went quiet. Each man sitting around the table was suddenly rigid with anticipation.

Sir Angus leant forward on the table, speaking clearly so that his voice could be picked up by the phone. 'There's a man here who says he saved your life,' he said. 'An SAS guy with two fingers missing on his left hand.'

There was a pause, almost audible on the line. But Hassad said nothing.

The entire room remained silent. At his side, Porter could hear Layla taking a sharp intake of breath.

'Know him?' snapped Sir Angus impatiently.

There was another long pause. Nobody was looking at Porter. They were staring at the table.

'No tricks,' Hassad replied. 'The woman dies at eight on Saturday.'

The voice was pinched and dark, with a slight American accent to it.

'Do you know this man?' repeated Sir Angus.

Another pause. 'It makes no difference . . .'

Porter stood up, and walked five paces along the table. Leaning over, he wiped a thin film of perspiration from the back of his neck. Looking at the speakerphone, as if he were looking straight into the eyes of the man on the other end of the line, he started to speak. 'You said you were so grateful I was an "*amiat al-Ikhwan al-Muslimun*",' he growled. 'A debt is a debt. All I ask is that you meet with me.'

The pause was even longer this time. One, two, then three seconds during which the only sound in the room was the muffled hiss of the speakerphone. 'When can you be here?' said Hassad.

'Where is here?' said Porter.

Everyone in the room exchanged glances.

'I can't tell you,' said Hassad swiftly. 'But if you fly to Beirut . . . then we can collect you.'

Porter glanced up at Sir Angus. He'd already scribbled one word down on a piece of paper, and was pushing it down the table.

'Thursday,' said Porter. It was Tuesday today, so that gave him less than forty-eight hours to get ready. 'I can arrive in Beirut on the Thursday-morning flight.'

'Then I'll make arrangements for you to be picked up,' says Hassad. 'I owe you a conversation, I acknowledge that. But any tricks, and I'll slice off your head right after I kill the girl.'

Silence.

The phone connection had already been severed.

Up at the head of the table, Porter could see Sir Angus glance at Collinson, and he could see the anger written into the creases around the man's mouth. 'Looks like you've got a job as a negotiator, Mr Porter,' said Sir Angus. 'Welcome to the team.'

Porter stood up straight, and started walking back to his own chair. The perspiration was still running down his back, but hopefully no one would notice it. 'I'll need payment,' he said.

Sir Angus stiffened. The fingers of his right hand were tapping on the tabletop. 'I thought you were volunteering to help your country,' he said coldly.

'I did that when I was younger, thanks,' growled Porter. 'And I ended up in the gutter.'

'Then how much?' said Sir Angus.

'Two hundred and fifty thousand pounds, paid into my bank account tomorrow morning.'

Sir Angus glanced down at the papers on his desk. 'You haven't even got a bloody bank account,' he snapped. 'You haven't even had a proper job for seven years.'

'Then run down to sodding Barclays and open one,' said Porter. He could feel his confidence growing now he'd spoken to Hassad: they needed him now. If he could just put enough money in the bank to take care of Sandy, well, then at least she'd have some respect for his memory. That would make it worthwhile, even if he didn't return from the mission.

'I'm risking my life for you,' he said.

'A quarter of a million pounds is a lot of money,' said Sir Angus.

Porter was resting his hands on the edge of the table. He could feel the blood pumping through his veins as the argument took hold of him. 'You don't learn much on the streets, except that most people don't give a fuck about their fellow man, but you do learn this,' he said. 'When people are desperate they'll do just about anything. I reckon I'm the last bloke in England you want back on the payroll, and that means you're desperate. So you'll pay all right.'

Sir Angus was about to say something, but along the side of the table Geoff Bramley had already raised his hand. 'Just pay it,' he said. 'We'll send the bill to the Chancellor. Always good to ruin that miserable Scottish bastard's morning.'

Porter nodded towards the defence minister. He'd lost two fingers in the Regiment, and they'd never even paid him a proper pension, so this was the least they could do for him. 'Thanks,' he said. 'Let's get the details sorted. If I die on this mission, and let's face it, we all know there is a pretty good chance that I will, then I want the money to go to my daughter Sandy. Set the account up in our joint name, and make sure the money is paid in before the plane takes off.'

'Agreed,' said Sir Angus wearily. 'If you need a certain

colour of socks, be sure to let us know, and we'll see if it can be arranged.' He smiled at his own joke, but his expression quickly turned serious again. 'Layla's going to get you cleaned up, and back into training,' he says. 'We've got twenty-four hours to get briefed and to decide our tactics.'

Layla had already stood up, her expression purposeful and businesslike. Porter started to follow her towards the door. 'One other thing, Mr Porter,' said Sir Angus. 'What the hell is the "amiat al-Ikhwan al-Muslimun"?'

From the right side of the desk, the Foreign Office's James Middleton looked up. A thin man, with a balding head, and a shirt that seemed at least one collar size too small for him, he had remained silent throughout the entire meeting so far. 'It's a reference to the Society of Muslim Brothers, Sir Angus,' he said. 'They are the most extreme and secretive of fundamentalist Muslim sects. They were set up in Egypt in 1928, and its offshoots include Hamas, Hezbollah, al-Qaeda, the whole bloody lot of them. But the Society is where it all started – and many people think it still controls the entire Muslim fundamentalist movement. Evidently Hassad is a member, and when he referred to it to Porter all those years ago he was acknowledging the extent of his debt to him. Just to mention the name of the Society to a Westerner is a mark of extraordinary respect, and places the speaker under an obligation that he can never break.'

Porter smiled, reserving his widest grin for Collinson, still fuming at Sir Angus's side. 'Looks like I've got honorary membership,' he says. 'Praise be to sodding Allah.'

SEVEN

The doctor was young, no more than thirty, dressed in a white coat, with closely cropped black hair, and eyes that suggested he didn't like being disagreed with. His name was Simon, according to the tag on his jacket. 'Basically, you're in terrible shape,' he said. 'But I guess you already knew that.'

Porter nodded. The last time he'd seen a doctor had been more than ten years ago, before Diana had thrown him out. He'd gone to see him because Diana was driving him crazy, nagging him about his drinking. He'd dragged himself off to see the local GP in Nottingham, a kindly woman in her mid-thirties who offered to refer him for some counselling. Porter thanked her, and took the number of the therapist, but never made the call. What was the point? he thought at the time. He drank because it was the only way he could live with himself, knowing that he'd screwed up the only job he ever wanted, and carelessly thrown away the lives of three good men. No therapist could go back in time and change that. So what was the point in even talking about it?

'You want the good news or the bad news?' said Simon.

After leaving the conference room, Layla had taken Porter straight back to the elevator, and down to the operations room on the second floor of the building. A flight was already being arranged to get him to Beirut for Thursday morning. It was Tuesday afternoon now, which left them thirty-six hours to prepare him for the mission, and to

78

resolve what kind of tactics he should deploy once he was confronted by Hassad. We'll take you to the medical centre first, Layla had told him. They had to find out what kind of shape he was in before they could do anything else.

For twenty minutes, he'd been sitting back in a comfy chair while they took blood samples, and X-rayed his whole body. 'I'll take the bad news,' said Porter grimly. 'It's what I'm used to.'

'Your lungs are in the worst shape,' said Simon. 'Smoker, right?'

'Only when I can afford them,' said Porter. 'Which isn't very often right now.'

'Just as well,' said Simon. 'Anyway, you've got several different infections. I'm going to put you on some high-strength antibiotics.' He looked down at the papers on his desk. 'There are a series of problems with your left leg. You have a nasty arterial ulcer infection just below the knee. You're going to need a small operation to fix that. We'll try and get that done right away. I'll put you under for that, otherwise it will hurt a bit. You've got a series of skin fractures around your back, and your feet have a nasty case of gout, so we're going to have to try and clean all of that up. We're still waiting for a full analysis of your blood, but I think we can safely say your liver isn't a prime specimen, but there's basically nothing we can do about that in the time we have available.' Simon glanced up at Porter and tried to smile. 'As for your teeth, well, we've put in a call to one of the best dentists in London, and he'll be here later today. It's going to take a while, I'm afraid.'

He put his pen down on his sheaf of papers. 'Any questions?'

'You said there was some good news.'

Simon shrugged. 'I lied about that. There isn't any.' He grinned. 'Let's put it this way, you're still alive, which is a miracle given the way you've been living for the past few

79

years. You're basically pretty strong. Clean you up, and you'll live a few more years yet.'

'A few days is all I need,' said Porter. 'Fix me up so that I can hold out until Saturday night, and I'll be fine.'

Simon nodded. 'Then we'll start right away.'

Porter walked through to the room he'd been allocated within the Firm's headquarters. It wasn't the Ritz, but by the standards he'd become accustomed to, it was luxury. He had his own TV, a small but comfortable bed, and next to it an array of medical tracking kit. It was a cross between a chain hotel, and an upmarket, private hospital. Good to see the Firm isn't bothering with the NHS, Porter thought. They don't mind mixing it up with al-Qaeda, but they don't want their best men catching MRSA down at the local surgery.

Along one wall, there was a wardrobe and when he checked inside, there was a new charcoal-grey M&S suit, a white shirt and dark blue tie, and some black half-brogue shoes. Next to it, there were some cream chinos, a blue linen shirt, some loafers and a black sweater. Smart or casual, Porter thought, but either way, it was all a lot better than anything he'd worn for at least a decade. I guess they don't want anyone on the payroll who dresses at Asda.

On the table there was a bank statement. Porter checked it briefly. An account had been set up at the Westminster branch of Barclays. It was in the names of John and Sandy Porter, registered to her address in Nottingham. According to the opening balance there was £250,000 in the account, and it was giving 4 per cent interest, paid monthly. There were two debit cards, one in his name, and one in Sandy's. No nonsense about your card being in the post, and taking three working days to process a payment, thought Porter with a smile. Amazing how quickly you can get things done when you lean on the right people.

In the corner there was a fridge. Porter knelt down and

took a look. Some bottles of mineral water, some Coke and lemonade, a couple of sports energy drinks, and some peanuts, he noted. No sign of a bottle of vodka.

'No boozing,' said a voice.

Porter turned round. The nurse was blonde, with hair that tumbled a couple of inches past her shoulders, and a shapely figure that had a couple of centimetres more flesh on display than was strictly necessary. She was standing in the doorway, dressed in a starched white uniform with a nasty-looking needle in her right hand. According to the name tag pinned just to the side of her ample left breast, she was called Danni.

'Where do they stash the alcohol in this place, then?' said Porter.

'They don't,' said Danni, stepping forward.

'It's dry?' said Porter.

'Like the Gobi Desert, sir,' said Danni. 'You've got more chance of getting a bevvy down at your local mosque than you have in this place.'

She had big blue eyes, and a face that was friendly rather than classically beautiful. 'What's that for?' he said, nodding towards the syringe.

'It's a syringe, so you take a wild guess,' she replied. 'Now lie back on that bed like a good boy. I can do this so it hurts or doesn't hurt. It doesn't make any difference to me either way.'

Porter lay back on the bed. The sheets were crisp and white and soft, and he realised as he put his head down on the pillow that it was years now since he'd gone to sleep between white linen.

'Just hold still,' said Danni.

He could feel the needle piercing his skin, but she was right. It hardly hurt at all. He let his head rest on the pillow, and closed his eyes. In only just over a day, I'll be face to face with Hassad. I can kill him, the way I should have killed him

81

seventeen years ago. And then . . .

But before he could finish the thought, he lost consciousness.

Porter struggled to open his eyes. A fierce, white light was shining down on him. He suddenly jerked back, and sat bolt upright. He was sitting on a metal chair padded with leather, and a man in a white coat was standing next to him. There were lights and equipment everywhere. 'What the . . .' he started.

'Steady, old chap,' said the man in the white coat, pushing him back down into the chair with a firm hand.

He was about fifty, with brown hair, and a chubby, friendly face. Porter had not seen him before. His head was spinning, and his legs felt sore and weak.

'You've been under anaesthetic, and you're only just coming round,' said the man. 'We haven't got much time, so we decided to whisk you in here while you're still under. My name is Peter Shaperio. I do some dental work for these guys. I hope you don't mind me doing some work while you were still under, but since you were already out cold it seemed to make sense.'

Porter started to speak, but he could feel the numbness in his mouth. 'OK,' he said.

Not like I have much choice, he thought to himself.

'You've got a lot of problems, I don't mind telling you. I won't ask how long it is since you last had a check-up, since I suspect I won't like the answer. While you've been asleep, I've taken two teeth straight out. They are molars so you won't miss them that much. We could do implants to replace them if you like, but there's no time to do that before you head out of here. I've put another two crowns on teeth that needed to be reshaped. And I've got three fillings left to do before I've finished. So just lie back. We'll only be another half-hour or so.'

Porter put his head back on the chair, and closed his eyes. He could sense the lights coming in down close to his face, and feel their heat on his skin, but he was feeling so tired, and so drugged up by all the anaesthetics, it was hard to concentrate on anything. He could hear the drill grinding into action, scratching away inside his mouth, but he felt nothing apart from a slight headache. The dentist had put some jazz on in the background – nice, light, relaxing music – to try and soothe him, but it wasn't going to work. He was too hyped up. Too excited. It was impossible to relax, he reflected, when you'd just made £250,000 and you knew you might well die in the next forty-eight hours.

'All done,' said Shaperio, putting down his drill.

He offered Porter a glass of green liquid, which he swilled around his mouth, then spat out.

'Normally I'd give you a lecture on flossing regularly,' continued Shaperio. 'But somehow I don't think there would be much point.'

'I'll be fine,' said Porter. 'Thanks, anyway . . .'

He started to lift himself out of the chair, but his legs were weak. He was starting to wobble, and it was only with Shaperio's help that he managed to steady himself. What they'd done to his legs in the operating theatre, he couldn't be quite certain, but there was a bandage around both his left knee and his right foot. His head was dizzy, and his body felt as if he just come off the worst in a pub brawl. 'You'll be OK,' said Shaperio, helping Porter to steady himself. 'You just need some rest, that's all.'

Through the door, Layla was already waiting for him. 'This way,' she said sharply.

He followed her down the brightly lit corridor. At the end of it, both Danni and the doctor, Simon, were waiting for him. Danni took hold of his arm, and he could smell the perfume of her neck, and see at least an inch of cleavage through the one opened button on her starched white tunic.

Her skin felt good next to his. She was steering him towards a table.

Simon was already looking at him closely. 'Get some rest,' he said firmly. 'The operation went fine, and so did the dental work. I can give you something to help you sleep if you like. A good long rest, and you should be ready for action by the morning.'

'We've got you some food,' said Layla. 'You need building up badly.'

Danni put the food down on a tray in front of him: a pasta with some kind of meat and tomato sauce on it, some chips, a green salad, and bowl of steamed spinach. Porter couldn't even remember the last time he had had such a good meal: probably the last Christmas before Diana had kicked him out, although he'd been so drunk already by the time she'd got the turkey cooked he wasn't sure he'd been able to taste anything when he started eating.

'Where's the wine list?' asked Porter, smiling.

'Forget it,' said Layla.

Porter started to tuck in. His mouth felt sore and numb from all the dental work, but so long as he didn't chew too much, he was able to eat without too much pain. Simon put a row of sixteen different vitamin tablets down in front of him. 'Pudding,' he said. 'We ran a sample of your hair, and you are deficient in just about every major vitamin group.'

'Except vitamin B, funnily enough,' said Layla sharply. 'Maybe it's because you find that one in vodka.'

Porter ignored the remark, carrying on eating. No one else was having anything but that didn't bother him. He finished the pasta, and started swallowing the vitamins one by one, washing them down with the pint of orange juice that was on the table. 'I need to go out,' he said. 'Can you get me a car?'

Layla stared at him. 'You're kidding, right?'

Porter shook his head. He waited until Simon and Danni had left the room, then said, 'My daughter Sandy has been interviewed for a place at university today. I think she'll be on the eight o'clock train from St Pancras back to Nottingham. I'd like to say goodbye to her.'

Layla shook her head. From her expression, she wasn't even going to think about it.

'You can see her when you get back.'

I'm not coming back, thought Porter. I'm going to try to break Katie out. *But the ragheads will probably cut my limbs off one by one and feed me to the dogs.*

'You know how risky this is.'

'And we're not going to take a chance on losing you.'

The words were still hanging between them, when the door was pushed open. Perry Collinson had already let himself in. He glanced over at Porter, an attempted smile creasing up his lips. 'Let him go,' he said quietly.

Layla glared at him angrily. 'We'll need to check with Sir Angus.'

Collinson shook his head. 'He can take my car, it's got a permanent police escort.'

'Who running this operation?' said Layla.

'Actually, my dear, I think you'll find I am,' said Collinson. 'The personal appointment of the PM, if I need to remind you.' He looked towards Porter. 'I've spoken to the PM about you, and he's bloody pleased you've come on board. Only bit of good news he's had so far on this whole bloody Katie Dartmouth saga.'

'If it was up to you, I'd be sleeping out on the streets tonight,' growled Porter.

'The last time I saw you, you were getting your fingers blown off,' snapped Collinson. 'And letting the enemy live because you felt sorry for the little buggers.'

Porter stood up. He could feel his head spinning, and had to put his hand down on the table to steady himself. 'And the last time I saw you, you were puking up because the sound of gunfire had you rattled.'

For a moment, Collinson stiffened. His face went white, and his lips were pursed together. Then he suddenly relaxed. Another grin creased up his face. 'Let's just bury the hatchet, shall we?' he said. 'We're all working together on this one. You wouldn't have been my first choice, but now you are on the team, I'm bloody glad we're working together.'

He patted him on the shoulder, but Porter instinctively recoiled from his touch.

'My car's outside, so take it and go and say goodbye to your girl,' he said.

'Sir Angus will —' Layla started to say.

'Will listen to me,' said Collinson. 'And if he doesn't I'll just have to get the PM on the phone.'

'Thanks,' said Porter tersely.

He headed for the door and left the room. As he reached the lift, he could see Layla walking along the corridor behind him. She followed him down to the foyer, then walked out of the building and started talking to the driver in the waiting Jaguar. 'Don't be more than an hour,' she said, looking up sharply at Porter. 'If you're not back here by eight thirty, then the police will bring you back. You need your rest. That understood?'

Porter nodded, climbing into the back of the car, and telling the driver to take him straight to St Pancras. 'Understood,' he said. 'I came in and volunteered, remember. I'm not about to bugger off now.'

EIGHT

The cream leather upholstery of the Jaguar felt luxuriously comfortable as Porter sat back into it. He was wearing the charcoal-grey suit they'd left for him in his room, and he was surprised by how well it fitted. The shoes were comfortable, and even the tie wasn't pinching his neck too badly. Last time I wore one of these, I was being turned down for a nightguard job at a Tesco depot, Porter reflected. Maybe I just didn't know the right people.

The driver pulled the car away from the kerb, and started driving across Vauxhall Bridge for the short journey up to St Pancras station. I could get used to this, thought Porter. The food, the cars, the money. *Shame I'm almost certainly going to die in the next few days.*

He glanced over at Big Ben. It was already twenty to eight. Only a little more than twelve hours since he had stepped into the headquarters of the Firm, and less than twenty-four hours since Sandy had found him by the edge of the river. It seemed a lifetime ago already. His world had spun on a coin, and he couldn't be certain how long it was going to take him to get used to it.

'Step on it,' he told the driver. 'I have to be there by eight.'

There was some traffic up past Trafalgar Square: the Katie Dartmouth vigil was gathering strength, and from the windows of the car Porter could see several hundred people carrying banners, and singing Bruce Springsteen's retooled version of the Pete Seeger Vietnam classic 'Bring 'Em Home'.

The driver put the blue siren on top of the Jag, and managed to push his way through the stationary cars, and cut through Russell Square to take them through to the Euston Road. He pulled up sharply outside the station, with just a few minutes to spare. Porter climbed out, walking quickly through the evening crowds. He was sure Layla had some policemen following him, but decided to ignore them. He just needed to see Sandy once more.

His eyes scanned the departure board. The Nottingham train was leaving from Platform 5.

In three minutes.

Porter ran towards the platform and the waiting train. Walking swiftly along the platform, he scanned the passengers as he went. His eyes flickered across them as they took their seats, hooking their iPods into their ears, and opening up their books and newspapers. But he couldn't see her anywhere.

Where the hell was she?

He looked along the platform. There were people streaming towards the train, trying to decide which carriage to climb aboard. Porter pushed his way back through the throng, muscling his way past the suitcases.

'Sandy,' he shouted.

Porter could see her running towards the platform. Her hair was tied back in a ponytail, and her coat was wrapped tightly around her. She was carrying a small leather holdall, and there was a magazine tucked under her arm.

'Dad,' she shouted back.

He swept her up in her arms, lifting her clean off the ground. She gasped as the strength of his embrace squeezed the air out of her chest, then kissed him on the cheek. I might not look like a million dollars, but I at least look like a couple of hundred, he thought. A lot better than I did last night anyway.

'How'd it go?' he asked, putting her back down.

Sandy shrugged and pulled a face. 'I hate interviews,' she says. 'I never know what to say.'

Porter wished there was some kind of advice he could give her, but nothing came to mind. 'We all do,' he said reassuringly. 'I'm sure it will be fine.'

Sandy pulled away.

'You look . . .' She paused.

Cleaner. That's the word you're looking for, Porter thought with a twitch of shame.

'Better,' Sandy continued.

Porter took her holdall, and started walking with her along the platform, looking for a carriage where she could get a comfortable seat for the journey home. 'You helped me out,' he said. 'And now I've got myself a job.'

Sandy looked at him, the surprise evident in her eyes. And maybe a touch of pride as well? wondered Porter. Or maybe I'm just fooling myself about that.

'A job? As what?'

Porter knew he had to brush the question aside.

'Just advising some guys,' he said. 'A consulting type thing.' He grinned. 'Pays pretty good though.'

He could tell Sandy wasn't going to press him. She was just pleased to have made a difference.

Up ahead, passengers were slamming doors shut on the train. The station announcer was telling people the train was ready to leave. Sandy was standing by a door, ready to climb aboard.

'I just wanted to say thanks,' said Porter, putting the holdall back in her hand. ' I may be just about the worst dad in the world, but you are probably the best kid.'

He pressed an envelope into her hand. Inside were the details of the account the Firm had set up in their names. There was already £250,000 in there, and Sandy could take it out as easily as he could. 'If you don't hear from me in a week, then open the envelope,' he said. 'There's something in there you should know about.'

'But Dad —'

'Don't worry, I'm going to be just fine,' said Porter. 'I'll call you next week, OK?'

She smiled weakly. The guard was walking briskly along the platform, slamming any remaining doors shut. Suddenly there was a few inches of steel and glass separating them, and Porter was painfully aware that he might never see her again.

'I love you, Sandy,' he said, as the engine started to pull out of the station.

It took all his willpower to disguise the choke in his voice.

Even if I die on this mission, at least I'll have done something for her, he told himself. That's enough.

He waited for a minute, watching as the train disappeared along the dark track. Another train was soon pulling into the platform. Doors were swinging open, and people were starting to pour out of the carriages. Porter turned round, and started walking back towards the main part of the station. Ahead, he could see a couple of policemen watching him. Sent by Layla, no doubt, he decided. To keep a watch on me, and make sure I don't do a runner with their two hundred and fifty grand and the new suit. Maybe that wouldn't be such a bad idea, he thought with a wry smile. But then I wouldn't be able to look at Sandy without feeling ashamed of myself. That's what this is all about.

Someone was thrusting a free newspaper into his arm. 'KATIE RALLY TO BRING LONDON TO A STANDSTILL' blared the headline. Porter pushed it aside, and the paper dropped to the ground. At his side, a man was shoving him. Porter shoved him back. You expected more respect than that when you were wearing a suit as smart as this one, he told himself.

He walked swiftly across the concourse. Even after eight it was still thronging with people. He glanced a couple of times at the station pub, and the guys with beers in their hands milling around outside. No, he told himself. They'll smell it on your breath. Don't blow it.

Out on the street, a blast of cold air hit him in the face. The Jaguar was waiting for him across the road, the driver sitting reading the sports pages. Porter stepped onto the road, glancing left. He could see a black Vauxhall Astra pulling out of a parking space. Suddenly he heard a roar as the driver gunned the engine. For a second, Porter caught a glimpse of the man's eyes. An Arab, late twenties, with a stubby beard.

The car was picking up speed.

And driving hard. Straight into him.

Instinctively, he pulled back, crashing into the man behind him.

The car kept coming. The driver veered left, pushing the wheels up onto the pavement, still heading straight for him. In the same instant, Porter dragged his foot away.

The car missed him by only a couple of centimetres. Porter watched as the Astra sped away. Someone just tried to kill me, he thought.

Porter tried to concentrate, struggling to make sense of the attempt on his life. But his brain was too groggy to focus. The drugs were still playing havoc with his system, leaving him dizzy and confused. Just get back to base, he told himself.

He straightened himself up, and climbed into the back of the waiting Jag: the driver had been too engrossed in his paper to even notice anything had happened. The drive back to Vauxhall didn't take long. Layla was waiting for him in the entrance foyer. She asked how his daughter was, but Porter just brushed aside the questions, telling her that he needed some rest.

Back in the room, he splashed some water onto his face. He rummaged around in the bathroom cabinet, but there were no bandages or plasters, not even any disinfectant. They hadn't even left him a razor blade, just an electric shaver: they obviously didn't want him getting his hands on anything that could be used as a weapon.

'You need a jab,' said Danni.

He spun round. She was standing in the doorway, still dressed in the nurse's uniform, a syringe in her hand.

'I need a drink,' said Porter.

'We all need a drink after a day in this place,' said Danni, striding towards him.

'What's in that?' he asked, nodding towards the syringe.

'More antibiotics,' said Danni. 'The doctor says you need them for another twenty-four hours. There's still a lot of rubbish to clear out of your system.'

He lay down on the bed. 'You're going out to rescue Katie Dartmouth, aren't you?' said Danni, as she prepared the syringe.

Porter nodded.

'Poor girl,' Danni continued. 'It's terrible what those bastards are doing to her.'

For a moment it struck Porter that he hadn't really thought about it. He'd been so focused on doing something for Sandy that he'd hardly thought about Katie Dartmouth's plight. And better not to, he told himself. Because there is probably sod all I can do for her even once I'm out there.

'There was a picture of her strung up against a post,' Danni carried on. 'She looked terrible. And I saw her mum being interviewed on TV. I felt *so* sorry for her.'

Her touch felt soft and gentle to Porter, and he couldn't help noticing that a button was still undone on her crisp white tunic, revealing a few centimetres of her pink bra. The needle jabbed into his arm. Porter winced briefly, then let the medicine hit his bloodstream. He could feel his eyes closing drowsily. 'You're a brave man, John Porter,' Danni was saying softly. 'If it's any help, I'll be rooting for you.'

NINE

Layla put a row of pills down on the table. Green, yellow, black and beige. Next to it, there was a glass of fresh orange juice, a jug of freshly brewed coffee, a bowl of cornflakes, and some toast, butter and jam. 'More vitamins,' she said sharply. 'Make sure you take them. You're probably in the worst shape of any agent we've ever sent into the field, but we're doing our best.'

Glancing at the clock on the wall, Porter could see that it was just after ten in the morning. They must have let him sleep in on purpose. Maybe they even put something into the cocktail of drugs they jabbed into his arm last night. When he'd woken up, he had a quick shower, put on clean clothes from the cupboard, and as soon as he stepped out, Layla had already been waiting for him, leading him to breakfast. They must have a camera in the room, Porter thought. How else could they know exactly when I woke up? His eyes scanned the bed, the washroom and the walls, but he couldn't see anything. That makes no difference. The cameras they make these days are so small I'll never find them. I'll just have to get used to being watched.

'Here's your schedule for the day,' said Layla. 'This morning we're going to put you back in training. Basic firearms, self-defence and –'

'I was in the Regiment, you know,' interrupted Porter.

'And it's more than a decade since you left,' said Layla.

'Warfare has changed a lot since then. There's a lot more kit, and a lot more brainwork.'

'Lucky I'm out of it then,' said Porter, taking a hit on the orange juice.

Layla nodded, then a brief smile flashed across her face. 'Probably so.'

She poured herself a cup of coffee, then carried on. 'The training should take all morning. Then this afternoon, we're scheduling a series of planning meetings to talk through what you do when you get out there.'

'Any breakthroughs?'

Layla shook her head. 'Nothing,' she said. As she spoke, he caught the exhaustion in her voice. Her eyes looked as if she hadn't slept in several days. 'We've got every intelligence agent in the region offering a fortune to their informants, but so far we've come up with nothing. The freelancers and mercenaries know we will pay handsomely for any lead, but nobody's talking. The satellite systems are scanning the region, and our computer wizards are monitoring all the Internet chatter. And so far we've come up with absolutely sod all. She could be anywhere.'

'I thought Perry Collinson was confident he'd find something,' said Porter. 'So they wouldn't need me.'

'He was talking rubbish as usual,' said Layla. 'Everyone in here hates the guy, starting with Sir Angus. He's a complete waste of space. Unfortunately the PM likes him. He sounds plausible on TV, and he gives a good sound bite. It's only when he tries to actually do something that it all goes tits up.'

'So you're left with me.'

'Afraid so,' said Layla. 'Any questions?'

Porter paused. He finished his slice of toast, and took a gulp of hot coffee, waiting for the caffeine to hit his bloodstream. He was feeling better this morning. The headache was mostly gone, and although there was some soreness where they'd operated on his leg, he could tell it would be back to normal in a couple of days. Even his teeth were feeling better, although there was still some numbness where a couple of them had been extracted. Not exactly 100 per cent fit, he told himself. But fit enough to kill one man. And that would be all the strength he needed.

'Who tried to kill me?'

The cup of coffee almost fell out of Layla's hand. 'Someone tried to kill you?' she said cautiously.

'At the station.'

'What happened?'

'Right after I'd seen Sandy, a car pulled out and drove straight towards me,' said Porter. 'The guy was planning to kill me, but I was lucky, I saw him coming and managed to jump back just in time. I might have been out of the game for a while, but you never lose the instinct.'

'He could have been a dangerous driver,' said Layla. 'London's full of them.'

Porter shook his head. 'He was coming straight for me. I could see it in his eyes. He had orders to kill.'

'So what are you saying?'

'That somebody doesn't want me to go out to Beirut.'

'That's impossible,' snapped Layla.

The anger was evident in her voice.

Porter shrugged, knocking back the remaining coffee in his cup. Maybe I've made a mistake even talking to Layla about this, he thought. Maybe she's the one who wants me killed.

'Impossible or not, it's what happened,' he said, his voice even and calm. 'Only a few people within this organisation know I'm here. I reckon somebody wants me stopped.'

'I'll investigate,' said Layla. 'In the meantime, you're staying right here. I don't want you leaving the building until we move out to the airport. We should be able to keep you alive until then.'

Porter finished his breakfast, then Layla took him downstairs. Somewhere there was a mole, he felt certain of it. And someone was trying to stop him making it to Beirut. The gym was down in the basement: not quite as far down as the interrogation rooms he'd been taken to yesterday, but still below ground level. There was a row of fitness and weight machines, a small sauna, and an exercise room. A couple of the desk cowboys were on the cycling machines, but otherwise it was empty at this time of the morning. Sam Roberts shook Porter's hand. He was a chunky man, with a shaved head that was as round as a football. 'What kind of shape are you in?' he asked.

'Who's asking?' said Porter looking at the man suspiciously.

'Para, sergeant and fitness instructor, 2001 to 2005,' barked Roberts. 'That good enough for you?'

Porter nodded.

'Now, again, what kind of shape are you in?'

'Terrible,' replied Porter.

'We'll do what we can, but there's not much that can be achieved in a couple of hours.'

'Just do your best,' said Layla. She looked at Porter. 'I'll investigate what happened last night and get back to you.'

Sam handed Porter a skipping rope. 'Let's start with this,' he said.

Porter held the thing in his hand. 'I'm not joining the bloody Brownies,' he snapped.

Sam laughed. 'I guess techniques have changed a bit since you were last in the Regiment. Everyone skips these days. It's the best way of practising hand-to-eye coordination, which is what firing a gun is all about. If you can't skip, you can't shoot either.'

OK, thought Porter. It's just a couple of hours. Humour the bastard. He took the ropes, and tried to jump over it, but he had never skipped, not even as a kid, and the technique wasn't there. He threw it over his head, and tried to jump.

Instantly, his feet tangled up in the rope. He tried again. Same result. 'Jump, man, bloody well jump,' Sam snapped.

For a moment, Porter was transported back to a windy, cold barracks, a quarter of a century ago, back in the days when you could still smoke on the tube, and your career choices amounted to signing up to shoot people or going down the pits. He could recall himself as a young recruit, being bashed through his first paces on the parade ground. It was cold and windy, his head was shaven, and the food was terrible, but at least I had plans back in those days, he reflected. He wanted to be a career soldier: regimental sergeant major was the rank he had his eye on. That was a long time ago, he realised bitterly. He tossed the rope swiftly over his head, watched it move through the air, then jumped. One foot cleared the rope. The other caught on the back of his ankle, tangling up with his trainers.

'Fuck it, maybe I'll go out to the playground, and see if I can find a six-year-old girl to show us how to do this,' said Sam. 'Maybe send her out to Beirut. She's got more chance of getting out alive than you have.'

'I'll do it,' snapped Porter, through gritted teeth.

He closed his eyes, took a deep breath, and ignored the pain still aching through him from where he'd been operated on the day before. Tossing the rope back, he swung it over his head, and concentrated. One jump, and he was over. He swung the rope again, following its arc as it cut through the air. Over. Just get the rhythm, he reminded himself. Then it's easy.

'Ten minutes,' said Sam. 'Then we'll play with some real toys.'

By the time the skipping was completed, Porter could feel the sweat pouring off him. His shirt was wet through, and his skin felt sticky and clammy. He took the bottle of mineral water Sam offered him, and swigged it back in a couple of gulps. 'Let's start the fun stuff,' said Sam.

The swing of his fist caught Porter by surprise. Sam's arm flung back, then smashed into the side of Porter's face. The palm of his hand hit his cheek, stinging the skin. Instinctively, Porter lashed out, thrusting a clenched fist forward, but Sam had already danced out of the way, and Porter was left flailing in thin air. His lungs were gasping for air, and he was still trying to recover his breath when Sam grabbed his right arm, and swung it viciously upwards. Porter gasped with pain as Sam slowly increased the pressure on the arm. He could feel the tendons starting to stretch, and his eyes started to water. 'You've got to be faster than that, mate,' said Sam.

Porter roared, filled his lungs with air, then snapped his right arm down. The pain was screeching through him, as he thrust backwards with his legs, smashing his back straight into Sam. He could feel Sam start to wobble as his groin took the impact of the blow. For a fraction of a second, the grip on his arm weakened. Porter tugged it free. He swung round, struggling to hold on to his balance. Ducking, he put his head down, then threw himself forward, smashing into Sam's chest with his head. That was a technique he'd learnt on the street, he reflected, as he saw Sam shake under the impact of the strike, then fall back on the ground. When in doubt, headbutt the bastards. You might give yourself brain damage, but, let's face it, when you were living rough and drinking two bottles of vodka a day, there wasn't much point in worrying about that.

'That fast enough for you?'

'No marks for technique,' said Sam. 'But you're still strong.'

'Just remember, I was in the Regiment and you weren't,' Porter growled.

Sam picked himself up off the ground, and this time it was him drinking half a bottle of water, and struggling to recapture his breath. 'You need to calm down though.

You're getting riled up too easily. Take your time, figure out your opponent's weaknesses, then strike.'

Sam led him towards the shooting range. There wasn't enough room underground for a full-scale range, but there was single block of enclosed concrete with a target at the end of a forty-foot strip. The firing point was just a white line printed on the ground, and next to it, there was black wooden table with a row of about thirty guns laid out on it. From a quick glance, Porter could see they covered the complete range of global arms manufacturers. There were Berettas, Brownings, Mausers, Walthers, Enfields, Webleys, Colts and, of course, Kalashnikovs, as well as a dozen different varieties of Asian and Eastern European knock-offs. 'What do you want to have a go with?' said Sam.

'What type of kit are Hezbollah using these days?' said Porter.

'All kinds of stuff,' said Sam. 'They are pretty well financed, and of course you can buy just about any weapon you want in Beirut. It's the B&Q of global terrorism out there. For assault rifles, it's mainly going to be AK-47s and M16s you're up against. For handguns, it could be just about anything. Berettas, Walthers, Brownings, take your pick. They use the good stuff mostly. None of that Bulgarian knock-off crap that blows up in your own face.'

Porter studied the desk. He hadn't picked up a gun since he'd left the army more than a decade ago. Hadn't even thought about it. Scanning the weaponry, he picked out a Beretta 92 pistol, a firearm he could recall training with back in the Regiment. The 92 was a short-recoil-operated, locked-breech weapon. It carried fifteen rounds, and its lightweight, aluminium frame weighed just slightly under 100 grams making it easy to hold, and even easier to slip inside a jacket or a pocket. It took a moment to reacquaint himself with the feel of the weapon, but once he curled his fingers around its cold, metal barrel, it was like welcoming back an old friend.

He took two strides forward. A white line was smeared across the floor, and the target was twenty metres away. Raising the gun with his right hand, Porter steadied himself, then lined up the target in the Beretta's sights. He squeezed the trigger once, then twice, enjoying the powerful recoil as the gun kicked backed into him. A gun in your hand was like a suit and a tie: it made you feel like a man. It gave you power, and control, and certainty: and those were all the things you missed when you lived out on the streets.

'An eye,' said Sam approvingly. 'It never leaves you.'

He was walking back from the target, noting where the bullets had struck. Neither was a bullseye, but both were close enough to it to at least disable an opponent, if not kill him outright. When you were in a firefight, that was all that counted, Porter told himself. If you wanted to kill the bastard, you could always do that with a double tap to the head afterwards.

'Try it again,' said Sam. 'Legs a bit further apart, and keep your shoulders slightly squarer.'

Porter adjusted his position. He moved his left leg slightly, giving himself better balance, and relaxed his shoulder muscles. The pistol felt comfortable in his right hand, almost as if it was an extension of his own body. One squeeze on the trigger, then another. The noise of the explosion echoed around the room. Squinting, Porter could see where the bullets had struck: one just a fraction of an inch to the left of the target, and the second a bullseye.

Pretty good, he told himself. At least on a firing range. Combat will be very different.

'Here, try this,' said Sam.

He tossed an AK-47 to Porter. Grabbing a hold, Porter slipped it into his arms, the polished wooden stock of the gun and its elegantly shaped cartridge both instantly familiar.

The missing fingers on his left hand were no problem. He could grip the gun between his two remaining fingers and his thumb, while his right hand was on the trigger. Slamming down hard, he loosened off a round of fire. The AK-47 was never a high-accuracy weapon: Mikhail Kalashnikov had designed it after being wounded in the Battle of Bryansk to support close-range infantry engagements. The bullets tore out of the muzzle of the machine, chewing up the paper target and leaving a pile of smoking ordnance on the floor.

'I can still shoot,' said Porter, turning to look at Sam.

'So long as you can keep your head.'

The remark struck Porter with all the deadly force of the bullets he had just fired from his assault rifle. 'What the fuck do you mean by that?' he growled.

Sam glanced at him, his eyes clouded with suspicion. 'Nothing . . .'

'You think I bottled it, don't you?'

He was still holding the AK-47 in his fists. Now that he had turned round, it was pointing straight at the instructor's chest. Sam was staring at it, and from the look on his face, he was unsure whether or not Porter might fire it.

'Last time you heard live firing, it went tits up,' snapped Sam. 'That's what I heard.'

'It's a bloody lie, I tell you,' shouted Porter. His finger was twitching on the AK-47, and his head was throbbing with anger. 'A bloody lie . . .'

'But that's what the record says,' said Sam. 'And you can't go back and change the record. Not you. Not any man.'

TEN

Porter could still feel the anger swirling through his veins as he sat down at the desk. He'd taken a quick shower, and changed out of the gym kit he'd been wearing for his training session with Sam, but he still felt charged up. Maybe it was having a gun back in his hands, he reflected. He didn't need to put up with all the crap he had to endure while he was living on the street. From now on, he was taking charge. And if I'm dead in a few days, well, those are the breaks.

A plate of chicken and tuna sandwiches were sitting in front of him, and Porter reached out for a couple. It was amazing how hungry he was all the time. Maybe that was something else that came from living on the streets for too long. Your body became so used to scavenging for food that when it was there you couldn't stop yourself from eating it.

He'd just polished off his third sandwich when Sir Angus Clayton walked swiftly into the room, followed by Layla. She patted Porter on the shoulder, and sat down behind him. Porter didn't recognise the third man. He was in his early fifties, with a greying beard, and hair that straggled down towards his open-necked cream shirt. There was a slight stoop to his walk, and he was carrying a bundle of papers underneath his arm.

'You OK?' said Sir Angus.

From the look on his face, Porter could tell it was a pleasantry, not a question. He doesn't give a toss how I am, or what happens to me. 'Fine, sir,' he replied, pouring himself a coffee from the jug in front of him.

Sir Angus nodded. 'You need that coffee,' he said. 'There are still no leads on where Katie Dartmouth might have got to, and the way the PM is wobbling, our boys might be packing up their bags in Basra by the weekend. So right now, you're still our best shot at sorting out this bloody mess.'

'God help us,' said Porter.

'My thoughts exactly,' said Sir Angus. 'I reckon you're a man who never liked school very much, so we'll try and keep this as short as possible. But we're going to have to cram as much knowledge as we can into your head in a very short space of time.'

He nodded towards the man with the grey beard. 'Professor Gilton here is going to fill you in on as much as we know about Hezbollah. Next up, we've got one of our top hostage guys coming in for a chat. Then we've got the head of Sky News coming down to talk to you about Katie. Over dinner, we'll be giving you your instructions, then packing you off to bed. You'll need all the sleep you can get.' He looked sharply at Porter. 'That agreed?'

Porter nodded.

Professor Gilton leant forward on the desk. He'd already drunk one coffee and was starting on the next. 'How much do you know about Hezbollah?' he asked.

'Bunch of mad fuckers with towels on their heads,' said Porter. He grinned, but quickly noticed that nobody else in the room was smiling and straightened up his lips.

'Yes, well, that's one interpretation, although the towels are more often around their necks, actually,' said Gilton.

Porter shot him a quick glance. 'Hezbollah was formed after the 1982 Israeli invasion of Lebanon,' he said. 'It is a Shiite Islamic organisation, and came together as various extremist organisations joined forces to fight the Israelis. It

103

was largely backed by the Iranians, who sent them large sums of money, and about two hundred armed fighters which formed the backbone of its military strength. But it's important to remember that they aren't just militants. They have plenty of support in the Lebanon as the main resistance to the Israeli occupation of that country, and without that support it is unlikely they would have survived as long as they have. If you go into the Lebanon, you have to remember, you are fighting on their territory. Don't expect any support from the locals.'

The professor took another sip of his coffee. That's shown him not to treat me like an idiot, thought Porter.

'Quite right,' said the Professor. 'Hezbollah virtually invented modern Islamic terrorism. In 1983, it created the suicide bomber when it used them to blow up the American military barracks in Beirut, killing 241 soldiers in one go. And within a few minutes it blew up an apartment block housing French peacekeepers. All the basic elements of Islamic terrorism are there. Suicide bombers. Coordinated strikes. Targets chosen with precision for maximum impact. There is nothing al-Qaeda is doing today that Hezbollah didn't do first, and often more effectively as well.'

'So they're the best,' said Porter. 'I think we already knew that.'

Gilton nodded. 'Afraid so. They started with suicide bombing because they wanted to get the Americans and the French out of the Lebanon, and they just about succeeded. Then they moved on to kidnappings. They're masters at that as well. In 1985, they kidnapped the CIA bureau chief in Beirut, an army officer called William Buckley. They held him captive for fifteen months, tortured him and then they killed him. His body wasn't recovered until 1991, when his remains were found in a plastic bag by a roadside in Beirut. Between 1984 and 1992, they kidnapped and held hostage about thirty Westerners, including the Archbishop of

Canterbury's special envoy Terry Waite, the journalist John McCarthy, and the Ulster writer Brian Keenan. Of course, you know about one of them yourself, Kenneth Bratton. He was one of the very few who was ever successfully broken out. In each and every case, the individual was held for long periods of time, usually in terrible conditions.'

'And what do they want?' asked Porter.

'Power, like all terrorist organisations,' said Gilton. 'You'll get a lot of rhetoric about Islamic revolutions, and fighting the infidel, and all the usual nonsense. That's just to help them recruit. Hezbollah is primarily a political movement intent upon dominating the Lebanon, and particularly southern Lebanon. They are closely allied to the Iranians, and they believe in a Shiite theocracy, but they believe mostly in themselves.'

Porter straightened up in his chair. He knew he was being examined as well as informed: they were looking to see how fast his mind still worked, and how well he could absorb information. He was still feeling hungry, so he grabbed another tuna sandwich. 'Then why do they care about our boys in Iraq?'

'Because the Iranians do,' said Gilton. 'The Iranians are desperate to get the British out of Basra as quickly as possible, because that way they can dominate the area. Southern Iraq is Shiite as well, and it's going to be virtually an Iranian puppet state once we get out of the way.'

'So they're doing the dirty work . . .'

'Precisely,' said the professor. 'The Iranians don't want to start kidnapping British hostages and threatening to behead them. They don't have much of an image in the world, but even for them that is a step too far. They get Hezbollah to do it for them, and since they are the main supplier of money and arms to that organisation, they don't have much choice but to go along. Hezbollah take the girl, demand that British troops get out of Basra, and the Iranians can move into southern Iraq, which is where most of the oil is incidentally, unopposed. Meanwhile their hands are clean.'

'So it's not just some random kidnapping?'

'Not a bit of it,' said Gilton. 'They have a plan, and I have to admit a pretty clever one. It all fits together very well. They know just how vulnerable British public opinion is over Iraq, and they picked Katie Dartmouth because she is young, attractive and popular, and because they knew the story would get round-the-clock coverage. They knew there was a by-election coming up next month as well, and if the government loses that, then the PM is probably toast. Like I said, it's a plan, and a damned clever one.'

Sir Angus leant back in his chair. 'So maybe the only flaw in the plan is you, Porter,' he said. 'They didn't reckon on you.'

'What are their weaknesses?' asked Porter.

'They don't really have any, I'm afraid,' said Gilton. 'Hezbollah is a tight-knit organisation. There are none of the splits between the military and political wings you used to get with the IRA, for example. And there's none of the factionalism you get within al-Qaeda. They have their orders, and they'll execute them ruthlessly.'

'But it's not their war,' said Porter.

'Right, that's our one advantage,' said Gilton. 'They've taken Katie Dartmouth to help the Iranians. They don't themselves care very much whether the British are in Iraq or not. Israel is the enemy for them. If you get into conversation with them, you need to hammer home that point. This isn't really their fight. They're just working for the Iranians. If you can persuade them to believe that, then maybe you can start to weaken their resolve.'

'It's not going to work, is it?' said Porter. 'I mean, they don't care what I think of them.'

The professor remained silent. He probably knows that as well I do, thought Porter, you can't talk these bastards out of anything. There was more coffee, and another plate of sandwiches before Gilton shuffled out of the room and Sir Angus brought in David Provost. A thin, intense man, with reading glasses, and blond hair that was combed across his forehead, he glanced briefly at Porter before taking his seat and reaching for a glass of water. He was described as the Firm's top hostage expert: he'd visited sieges all over the world, and studied the subject for years. There was nothing he didn't know about kidnappers, and how to deal with them.

'There's just one major principle in every hostage negotiation,' he said, looking at Porter. 'Keep the conversation going. It doesn't really matter what you're talking about, or whether the discussion seems to be going anywhere. Every minute you spend talking achieves two things, and they are both important for you. One, it delays the moment of execution. When they're talking, they aren't killing. Next, it draws you closer to the kidnappers. The more of a relationship you build up, the harder it becomes for them to kill the victim.'

'So what do I talk to them about?' asked Porter.

'First, find out what they want,' said Provost. 'One thing you learn about most kidnappers is, they say they want one thing, but they really want something else completely. You need to burrow away at that. Dig and dig, and find out if there is something else that would satisfy them.'

'Like what?' said Porter. 'They've said they want British troops out of Iraq and Afghanistan. How the hell am I meant to negotiate that?'

Provost ran a hand through his stringy hair, and glanced nervously across at Sir Angus. Porter sensed he wasn't being told everything. The Firm had its own ideas and plans, and they weren't about to let him into their secrets. For all I know, he thought, they might even have started negotiating with Hassad without thinking to tell me.

'Again, that's what they say they want,' said Provost

'Don't believe it. They can't really expect a whole British Army to be withdrawn in response to a single kidnapping. So, there's your answer. That's not what they want at all.'

'Then what is it?'

'Publicity,' said Provost firmly. 'Look at how they are operating. Who do they kidnap? A TV journalist. If you want to influence politics, you kidnap a politician. If you want money, you kidnap a businessman. But if it's publicity you want, then you kidnap a journalist, particularly a pretty blonde one.'

'And they've certainly got it.'

'Right,' said Provost. 'But the point is, there is no more perishable commodity. Katie Dartmouth might as well have a sell-by date stamped on her forehead. As soon as they kill her, the story is dead too. So what you need to do is string it out for them. Keep reminding them that when they kill her, they've basically lost. They haven't got the troops out, and in a few days' time they are not going to be in the news any more either.'

'Why the hell should they listen to me?' said Porter.

'That's the first thing to do, engage them in conversation. Make it clear that you sympathise with them, and then they'll start listening. The next thing to do is to get them talking to Katie. From the picture they've put out on the Web, she is bound and gagged. That's no good. Tell them she needs water and food, and she needs to breathe more easily. Do anything to get that gag off her. As soon as you've done that, get her talking. About anything, it doesn't matter what. If needs be, the two of you should sit there chatting. At the moment, she's just a symbol, and they are easy to kill. Turn her into a human being, however, and it gets a lot harder.'

'I need to be able to offer them something,' said Porter.

'We'll get to that later,' said Sir Angus.

Porter nodded. We're not getting anywhere, he told himself. All this talking isn't going to make any difference to anyone.

'When you get out there, Sir Angus will have given you some concessions you can make,' continued Provost. 'Every hostage negotiator always has those. You go in knowing what concessions you'll make, but never make them right away. You need to feed them out slowly. That way the other side feel like they are extracting something from you.'

'Any questions?' said Sir Angus.

Porter rested his arms on the desk. 'So, in your experience, has anyone ever negotiated a hostage out of Hezbollah?'

Provost coughed, and glanced at Sir Angus. 'No,' he said crisply.

'Then I better have a plan B,' growled Porter.

The coffee tasted good. Porter sipped on it slowly as he waited for the next talking head to be wheeled into the room. Layla had disappeared to get a fresh pot by the time Ken Stuart was led into the room. He was wearing cream cargo trousers, a blue jacket and a pink open-necked shirt. His dark hair was worn long, but his face was lined and craggy, making him look a lot older than his forty years.

'Ken is in charge of Sky News,' said Sir Angus. From his expression, Porter judged Sir Angus didn't much care for journalists, and would be relieved when he could get Stuart off the premises. 'We're completely off the record here, and he's agreed that not a word of your mission will be leaked on air. But he knows Katie better than anyone, so he might be able to help us.'

Stuart scrutinised Porter's face like it was an exhibit in a museum: his eyes ran across him, probing and questioning as he scoured his features. 'You're really going out there?' he asked.

'Tomorrow morning,' said Porter.

Stuart nodded. 'She'll be damned pleased to see you.'

'What's she like?'

Stuart paused before replying, giving himself space to think. 'Most TV journalists are pretty tough, particularly the ones that get sent abroad,' he said. 'But even among a hardened breed Katie stood out for her toughness. Forget all that soft-soap stuff we've been putting on air for the last few days about Katie as the nation's darling, the kind-hearted girl from the Hampshire village. It's just for the ratings, twenty-four-hour TV news is a competitive business, and we couldn't afford to let an opportunity like that pass us by. Katie's a great girl. She works hard, and she doesn't mind bruising a few egos if she needs to get a story on the air fast, but her heart's in the right place.'

'What's her background?' said Porter.

'She went to Cambridge, and read English, just like they all do,' Ken answered. 'Then she got a job in local TV news, down in Devon, and did that for a couple of years, before joining Sky. We put her on the regional news beat for a couple of years but she was clearly a star right from the start. The camera loves her.'

'And you think she'll hold up under captivity?'

Stuart sighed. 'We've seen the pictures of her, and there are more you can get off the Web that we haven't even wanted to broadcast. Let's face it, she's bound and gagged, and we don't even know if she's been given anything to eat or drink in the past few days. We can't be certain, but the chances are she knows they are threatening to execute her in a few days' time. I don't know how anyone would hold up in those circumstances. But I'll tell you this much, if anyone can, then Katie can.'

Porter nodded. There was nothing left to ask. The woman was unlucky, that was all. They needed a British TV personality, and she just happened to be in the wrong place at the wrong time. 'One thing you should know,' Stuart added. 'I think she might have had some kind of relationship with Sir Perry Collinson.'

Sir Angus looked bored: that piece of gossip is already on his files, Porter decided.

'You sure?' asked Porter.

Stuart shrugged. 'Just newsroom gossip, which is never the most reliable of sources,' he said. 'But she did a three-part series of specials on him just over a year ago, the same time that his book was on the best-seller charts. Afterwards, they were seen at a couple of drinks parties together. I don't mean to be sexist, but Katie didn't mind sleeping with her contacts, at least from what I hear. It doesn't even have to be that cynical. She's a young single woman, and she likes powerful older men. Nothing strange about that.'

'Thanks, that's all,' interrupted Sir Angus.

Stuart started walking from the room. As he passed Porter, he paused, resting his hand on his shoulder. 'She's not a bad kid, so do your best. We'll all be rooting for you.'

Porter nodded. 'If I can,' he said, 'I will.'

Stuart grinned. 'And don't forget to take some hairspray with you. If by some miracle you get her out of there, we want her right on camera. And if you don't give her something to fix her hair, then you really will be in trouble.'

ELEVEN

The food tasted surprisingly good. A rack of lamb, with a thick herb crust, some minted new potatoes, the plate heaped with other steamed vegetables. All it needed was a nice bottle of Merlot and a shot of vodka and the meal would be perfect. Even the row of brightly coloured vitamin pills laid out on the table couldn't spoil Porter's enjoyment of it.

A condemned man's last meal, he thought to himself, as he chewed on a lamb bone. They know I haven't got much chance of coming back dressed in anything other than a wooden overcoat. At least they're giving me a decent send-off.

Sir Angus stepped into the room. He sat down opposite Porter, picking up a bread roll and chewing on it absent-mindedly. 'Surprised they haven't given you any wine with that,' he said, nodding towards the food.

'If they could –'

'Porter's not drinking right now,' interrupted Layla. 'Doctor's orders.'

'I've drunk enough over the years,' said Porter. 'One more isn't going to hurt me.'

Sir Angus nodded. 'I've seen the medical reports, if they say no juice, then there is no juice,' he snapped. 'Two hundred and fifty grand is a hell of a deal, and for that kind of money, I don't expect you just to be on the payroll, clocking in, keeping your nose clean, and waiting until you can bugger off home.' He leant in so close, Porter could smell the aftershave on his smoothly shaven skin. 'I expect to own you. Whatever I want, you do it. That understood?'

Porter nodded. He spooned some more potatoes onto his plate and carried on eating. They were fattening him for something, he knew that, but like a turkey just before Christmas, it wasn't any reason for not eating the grub. 'If you want someone else to go and get Katie Dartmouth out, feel free, mate,' he said, a slow smile spreading over his lips. 'I won't be offended or anything. In fact, I'm quite happy just sitting here.'

'You're going all right,' said Sir Angus. 'Tomorrow morning.' He spread some papers out on the table. 'OK, this is the plan,' he started. 'Layla, give him the details.'

'When we've finished up here, you get straight to bed,' said Layla. 'We don't really have any idea when you might sleep again, so the more you can get tonight the better. The doctors still want you on antibiotics, so we'll make sure they give you something for some shut-eye as well. The BA flight for Beirut leaves Heathrow at eight, and takes four hours, forty-five minutes. We need to be out of here at six at the latest. I'll be taking you to the airport, and the cars are already booked. There'll be some police vehicles tracking us en route, but nothing high profile. BA have been notified, but we haven't asked for any special favours, except that they put us in the VIP lounge so we don't have to queue up at check-in like everyone else. We've block-booked three rows of seats near the middle of the A320 that BA uses for that route. All of them will be occupied by our people, but they won't be making themselves known to you, and you shouldn't make yourself known to them. It's just a pre-caution so that no one can get close to you on the flight. We aren't expecting any trouble, but in case anything happens, we'll be prepared.'

Danni came into the room, and cleared away the plate of lamb. She put down a bowl of chocolate mousse, and refilled his water glass. Her hand appeared to brush against the side of his jacket, he felt certain of it, and she hovered beside him clearing away the cutlery for a fraction of a second longer than was necessary. Stop kidding yourself, mate, Porter told himself. She's not going to be interested in an old bum like you. There's no harm in looking, never is, but there's no point in fooling yourself you're going to get anywhere.

He dipped his spoon into the pudding. *Chocolate mousse is the closest you're getting to any sensory pleasure this or any other night.*

'Hey, vitamins first,' said Layla sharply. 'Remember what the doctor said.'

'I know, I know,' said Porter, tossing a couple of green pills into the back of his throat and washing them down with some water. 'Deficient in every major vitamin group except B. The amount I've been eating, I must have started fixing that by now.'

'Once you touch down, you say goodbye to Layla here, and walk through customs as normal,' said Sir Angus, interrupting the conversation. 'Ever been to Rafik Hariri airport?'

Porter shook his head. 'Last time I was in Beirut, I was dropped in by a Puma chopper, and I was carrying an M16 rather than a passport.'

'This time we'll try and make it a bit more official,' said Sir Angus. 'Our man in the city will be looking out for you. A chap called Ben Stanton. He's a good man, and he knows the drill so don't bother looking for him. He'll find you and have a car waiting. Once he's got hold of you, just walk casually, and chat to the guy like you're a couple of old drinking mates meeting up for a jolly. Beirut airport is probably teeming with more spies than any other place in the world, and they are all damned good at what they do. The Lebanese may not seem to be up to much apart from running kebab shops on the Edgware Road, but they do know how to spy, so if you do anything suspicious, anything out of the ordinary, you can be damned sure someone will spot it, and then you really could be in trouble.'

'You mean more trouble than turning myself over to a bunch of brutal kidnappers . . .'

A slow smile spread across Sir Angus's lips. 'You volunteered for this gig, remember. I don't want any whinging now.'

'Once you are in the car, Stanton will be in charge,' said Layla. 'We've had some contact with Hassad, and this is the drill. Stanton is going to drive you due south to a place called Sidon, on the coast. He'll drop you at the bus stop. From there you'll get a local bus that will take you the thirty miles or so towards a place called Jezzoine. Next, you'll get on another bus towards Anjar. It's a little place, close to where the borders of Lebanon, Syria and Israel all meet. When you get there, you walk across to the bar directly opposite the bus station. Go in, order yourself a coffee, and then sit down. Don't talk to anyone if you can help it. And don't draw too much attention to yourself. We'll give you some Lebanese money. They use pounds, funnily enough, but there are three of theirs to every one of ours, and we'll make sure you have plenty.'

'I'll get receipts if you want,' said Porter.

'Make sure you do,' snapped Sir Angus. 'This mission is costing us a fortune already.'

For a moment, Porter could see the fear and sweat on the older man's face. It's my life on the line here, he thought. But it's Sir Angus's balls. If this mission goes pear-shaped, and it almost certainly will, then his career is finished. And unlike me, he has a lot to lose. He might act tough, but that's just a show: underneath, I reckon he is a lot more frightened than I am.

'Wait in the bar for as long as you need to,' continued Sir

Angus. 'Don't talk to anyone, but don't avoid people either. Speak if you are spoken to. We'll get you some guidebooks, so you can pretend to be a tourist if anyone asks. At a certain point, one of Hassad's men will come up to you. He'll be looking for a guy with a couple of fingers missing, but it won't be Hassad himself, so make sure you keep your left hand on the table so they can get a good look. They'll use the word "Mahmudiyya", so that's how you know it is them.'

'It's the town in Egypt where Hasan al-Banna, the founder of the Society of Muslim Brothers, was born,' said Layla. 'So I guess that's why they chose it.'

'So long as they use the right password, go with them,' said Sir Angus. 'They'll have transport, and they'll take you to wherever it is they have taken Katie Dartmouth.'

'What about backup?' said Porter.

Sir Angus paused. His fingers were tapping on the table-top. 'There isn't any,' he said. 'Hassad was very clear about that in his messages. The only terms on which he is prepared to receive you is that you come by yourself.'

'Someone could be watching out for me,' said Porter, his tone hardening. 'At a safe distance —'

'Not possible,' snapped Sir Angus. 'Hassad is allowing you to come, but you must be unarmed, and alone. We have virtually no capability in the Lebanon. They're so hostile to us, we can't build a network, and the people who want bribes take the Israeli money because they pay better. The only people with agents on the ground are Mossad, and we can't ask them because they need all their assets for them-selves. If we give you any backup, the chances are that Hezbollah will know about it. This is their home turf after all. Hassad has made it very clear that if you are followed in any way, then he'll execute Katie Dartmouth on the spot, and make sure every TV station in the world has a live feed of the beheading. And when he's holding her freshly severed head in his hand, he'll blame the whole thing on our treachery.' Sir Angus wiped a bead of sweat away from his forehead. 'We can take crap if we need to, it's what we're paid for,' he said sourly. 'But even this organisation doesn't want to have to deal with that.'

'If that's the case, make sure his instructions are obeyed.'

Sir Angus hesitated. 'Of course,' he said.

'So what do I do when I get there?' said Porter.

'Your job is to get Katie Dartmouth out, alive, simple as that,' said Sir Angus. 'That's what we're paying you for, and I expect results.'

His fingers were still tapping nervously on the table. 'This is the plan of action,' he continued. 'First, find out exactly what it is the buggers want. They say they want our boys out of Iraq, but that's probably a front. There'll be something else they will settle for. The PM has authorised us to offer them what he called "a fresh roadmap to peace in the Middle East", whatever the hell that might mean. Frankly I think the only person who believes it is worth anyone pissing away time on peace talks is our beloved leader, but you never know, they might fall for it. Talk to them about that first. But if you aren't getting anywhere, and I suspect you won't, then I'm authorising you to offer them money. We'll do what the French do, which is buy her release. Offer them ten million dollars for starters, but hint that we'd be prepared to go higher if it would help. Tell them they can negotiate directly with me via email. Or, if they prefer, they can talk to Jacques Papiasse. He's a private banker in Luxembourg who the French use to pay ransoms for their hostages, and Hezbollah know him and trust him. He's agreed to act for us, for the usual outrageous fee I might add, and if they want to, they can negotiate with him directly.'

'Like I said earlier, it sounds like I'll need a plan B,' said Porter. 'Because I can't see them going for any of that bollocks. They've had more peace plans than I've bottles of vodka, and if they wanted money, they would have asked for it by now.'

'Then this is where you go next,' said Sir Angus. 'There's a man in Guantànamo Bay, a Hezbollah leader called Fouad Karem. He's been there for a year. We've spoken to Washington, and they've agreed that they'll let us swap him for Katie. Offer them that, and if they bite, then we can sort out the details of the exchange.'

'And what happens when it's Saturday morning?' said Porter. 'Three days' time, and Katie's execution is just hours away. None of these suggestions are working. They won't negotiate, and they won't delay, and they don't give a toss about either of us. What the hell do I do then?'

Sir Angus leant forward, straight into Porter's face. 'I've sent a lot of men into the field since I started working for this outfit, and I've always given them one piece of advice,' he said. 'Don't play the bloody hero. It isn't worth it. You'll probably end up dead, and get us all in the shit. But you know what, Mr Porter. This time round I might just suspend that. If it comes to Saturday morning, and nothing else is working, then play the hero. It's a last resort, remember that, but if everything else fails, use your Regiment training to try and take the buggers out and get the girl out of there.'

'And if I die trying?'

'Then at least you'll have been well paid.'

'Someone tried to kill me,' said Porter, as Sir Angus got up to leave.

'Just wait until you get out to the bloody Lebanon, man,' said Sir Angus. 'Everyone will want to kill you out there.'

'I'm not joking,' snapped Porter. 'A guy tried to run me over.'

'We're investigating,' said Layla.

'And what have you found out?'

Layla hesitated. There was a flicker of indecision in her

expression, and for a moment Porter suspected she was holding something back from him.

'So far, not much,' she said, tossing a lock of hair away from her face.

'There's a mole,' said Porter. 'Someone in this organisation knows what I'm doing and wants to stop it.'

'A Hezbollah spy within the Firm?' said Sir Angus. 'Don't be bloody ridiculous, man.'

Porter got up. 'I'm telling you, it's true,' he growled.

Sir Angus turned and started walking from the room. 'You just concentrate on doing your job,' he said. 'There are no spies in this organisation.'

TWELVE

Porter adjusted the sound on the TV set. Sky News was sticking to its round-the-clock coverage of the Katie Dartmouth story, and so were CNN and BBC News. He flicked through the other channels: there was a celebrity show on ITV, a detective programme on BBC, and a rerun of *Friends* on Channel 4, but it was so long now since Porter had had a TV set he no longer had much idea what was on, or what he liked to watch.

He propped his head back on the pillow, and went back to Sky. There wasn't much new for them to say. It was Wednesday evening now, and Katie had been captured late on Sunday night. There was some fresh footage that had been released of her captivity. All you could see was a woman tied to a stake. Her arms and legs were both bound, and there were three hooded and armed men standing behind her. As the camera zoomed in closer, you could see the cuts and bruises on her cheeks. A gag was stuffed crudely into her mouth, but her eyes were exposed. And as the camera tracked towards them, you could see the despair that had overwhelmed her.

'Shit,' muttered Porter. *In less than twenty-four hours I'm going to be there as well.*

On the news, the Liberal Democrat leader had called today for troops to be brought home from Iraq, and even the Conservatives were calling for a debate. Sky switched to some footage from Prime Minister's Questions at the House of Commons earlier that day. The PM had looked rattled as he repeated his earlier line that everything humanly possible was being done to secure Katie Dartmouth's release, but that they could not negotiate directly on the kidnappers' main demand. 'All I say to people is this,' he repeated, the strain showing in his face. 'There can be no turning back, nor can there be any surrendering to the forces of terror.' The words, however, were met by a stony silence from his own side of the house, and by barracking from the opposition.

On the viewers' poll, Sky was reporting that 72 per cent of people wanted British troops taken out of Iraq if there was a chance that it might save Katie's life. They switched briefly to the launch of a new government initiative to encourage more teenagers to go to the gym. Their political editor came on the screen to dismiss it as an 'eye-catching initiative, designed to deflect attention from the kidnapping story', and within minutes Sky had gone back to the Katie Dartmouth saga. The website showing pictures of Katie's captivity had already received twenty million visitors from around the world. In Trafalgar Square, the 'Vigil for Katie's Release' had grown overnight, and the police now estimated there were five thousand people camping out overnight in the square, and they had pledged to remain there until the PM started negotiating directly for Katie Dartmouth's release. The Sky reporter started interviewing one of them, pointing out that the forecast was for sweeping rains and gales across London tonight. 'We don't care,' said a young woman dressed in a blue overcoat. 'We're staying here until the war is finished, and Katie Dartmouth is brought back from the Lebanon alive.'

Then the coverage switched to some breaking news. Sir Elton John had just announced that he was recording a special version of 'Someone Saved My Life Tonight' with reworked lyrics, designed to appeal for Katie's release. The song was being recorded tomorrow, and would be available as a download on iTunes by Friday morning. Already there were predictions that it would eclipse the massive sales of his reworked version of 'Candle in the Wind' composed for Princess Diana's funeral.

Christ, thought Porter to himself. The whole country is going nuts. And I'm the only man with any chance of bringing it back to its senses.

There was a knock on the door. Porter glanced up. Danni was coming into the room, with her bag of medical kit under her arm. He had already dimmed the lights in his small bedroom, so the room was mainly lit by the glow of the TV screen. He killed the sound, and looked back up towards her, noticing the way the fuzzy light from the tube caught the blonde streaks dyed into her hair, creating a golden glow around her shapely face. 'My medicine,' he said with a smile.

She nodded, kneeling down beside him. 'Roll up your sleeves,' she said.

Porter planted his feet on the floor. He was wearing just a sweatshirt and black jeans, and he pushed up the sleeve on his left arm to expose the bare flesh underneath. Danni had already taken a swab of cotton wool, and was smearing some disinfectant across the skin. Porter closed his eyes as the needle pierced him, wondering if he was about to be put to sleep: he didn't mind injections too much, but didn't like to watch them. 'All done,' she said, within a fraction of a second.

'There's another kind of medicine I need,' said Porter. 'The kind you find in a bottle.'

'You're going tomorrow,' said Danni.

Porter nodded.

'To where Katie Dartmouth is being held?'

'That's why I need a drink.'

Danni flashed a smile. 'Christ, I'd need a drink too if I was going there,' she said. She reached in her bag, pulling out a half-bottle of white wine. 'This do?'

Porter reached for the bottle. It was one of the Australian

whites you buy at Tesco to take home with you when you pick up a ready-meal on the way home from work. It wasn't what he usually liked to drink, but right now he was desperate for anything. This was the first alcohol he'd seen since he'd set foot in the place thirty-six hours ago, and he wasn't about to turn it down. 'Care to join me?'

Danni shrugged. 'OK,' she said.

Porter unscrewed the cap, pouring the wine into two tumblers he'd grabbed from the washbasin. He took a sip, allowing a moment for the alcohol to hit his bloodstream. It was hard for him to remember the last time he'd gone this long without a drink. Living on the streets, he was almost always too short of cash to put a roof over his head, and often too short to get anything to eat either. But he always found money for a drink.

'What happened to you?' asked Danni.

She took a sip of the wine, and sat down just a few feet from him on the end of his bed. As she crossed her legs, Porter noticed the seam of her black tights, running up the side of her shapely legs, and disappearing into the tempting folds of her crisp white skirt. Suddenly, he was aware she was noticing the way he was casting his eyes up her legs, and snapped them away. Stop kidding yourself, he reminded himself. She can't be more than twenty-four or -five. Young enough to be your daughter. And let's face it, mate, even the women your own age aren't interested in you. Don't even think about the young ones.

'I had some bad breaks, that's all,' said Porter.

Danni shook her head, tossing aside her blonde hair as she did so. 'That's rubbish,' she said. 'You were Regiment once. The best of the best —'

'How'd you know that?' said Porter.

Danni laughed, taking another sip of wine. 'This is a very small place,' she said. 'And nobody gossips like an office full of spies. This lot love to know what everybody else is up to.'

Maybe that's why someone tried to kill me, thought Porter. Maybe word leaked out somehow. Maybe it got through to some al-Qaeda or Hezbollah guys in London, and they wanted to take me out before I had a chance to get out to Lebanon.

'You have to be tough to get in, don't you?' said Danni. 'I thought there were special tests?'

Porter could feel his mind flicking back almost two decades. There were special tests all right. He'd spent weeks of his life tabbing through the Brecon Beacons, with a deadweight on his back, and with the Welsh rain lashing into his face. He'd done the rock climbing, and the abseiling, learnt how to fly a plane and drive a tank, and he'd done enough hours running around the killing house to last a man several lifetimes. He'd watched men die as well: two guys had bought it on the selection courses he'd been on, good lads both of them who just wanted to prove they could hack it, but who must have been cold in their graves for almost twenty years now. And for what? A few years taking orders from some jumped-up public schoolboys, before they toss you back on the scrapheap, and walk straight past you on the street when you ask them to help you out with the price of a beer.

'Because you were in a bad way when you came in here,' said Danni. 'I mean, I thought Regiment guys could get good jobs in industry. Or go out to Iraq, and earn two or three grand a week in security.'

Not me, thought Porter. I flunked it. And once you've done that, there is no way back.

'I had . . .' Porter paused, taking a sip of the wine, already wondering if she might have something stronger tucked away in her handbag. What was it I had exactly? he wondered? Why couldn't I get back into the world again? Maybe if I'd been able to figure out an answer to that I wouldn't have been searching around at the bottom of so many beer glasses all my life. 'I was out in the Lebanon. A long time ago. I was going in with my unit to get a hostage out, but I fucked it up.'

'Go on,' she whispered.

He looked up at Danni, his expression solid and strong. He held up his left hand. 'That's how I lost these,' he said, nodding towards the missing fingers. 'But that wasn't the worst of it. I lost three guys from my unit, good men. It was my fault, you see. My own sodding fault. They'd have lived if I hadn't . . .'

Porter stopped talking, leaving the sentence hanging between them. It felt strange to be talking about it. He'd tried to discuss it with Diana, but that was years ago, soon after he came back, but she was so preoccupied with the baby she'd hadn't had any time to listen to him, and pretty soon he found it easier just to have another drink and forget about it. Since then, he'd never spoken about it to anyone. He just brooded on it himself, burying the story deeper and deeper within himself, until it was as much a part of him as the blood running through his veins.

'If you hadn't what . . .?'

He shrugged, emptied the wine glass into the back of his throat, and refilled it from the bottle. 'It doesn't matter.'

'It matters to me.'

'I let a kid live, and then he killed my three mates.'

Danni edged forward on the bed, so that there was only a couple of feet separating them. 'And you think going back there will fix it for you?' she said.

She was looking straight at him, her bright blue eyes alive with curiosity, with a hunger for knowledge that Porter found puzzling. 'I sure as hell hope so,' said Porter with a shrug.

She edged another few inches closer. With her left hand, she was brushing a lock of hair away from her face, and her right hand was resting on the top of the bed. Slowly, she uncrossed and then crossed her legs again, and Porter was struggling to keep his eyes away from her. She was so close to him that Porter couldn't escape the heady smell of the perfume splashed across her body.

'I hope so too,' she said softly, leaving her lips slightly parted, and her eyes half closed as she completed the sentence, 'because it's a bloody brave thing to do.'

Porter's hand edged forwards on the bed, so that it was just inches from hers. Christ, she's coming on to me, he told himself. Unless the signs have changed completely in the years since I last tried it on with a girl, I could be in with a chance here. He could feel his heart thumping. He wanted her, of course. She was blonde, and buxom, and dressed in a white, crisply starched nurse's uniform: what man wouldn't want her in his bed. But when you live out on the streets, he reminded himself, you stop even thinking about women. They aren't on your radar screen. Christ, I'm buggered if I even know what to do any more.

'Not that brave,' said Porter, his tone turning weaker.

'I think you're plenty brave,' she said. 'And strong . . .'

Her hand was almost touching his now. Porter let his right hand stretch out, his fingers creeping across the bedding, until slowly they reached hers. He could feel the warmth of her skin against his, and as he looked up at her face, her eyes were still half closed and her lips still parted a fraction. He moved closer towards her, gripping her hand in his, and suddenly her eyes opened wide, and she looked straight at him and smiled. 'Kiss me,' she said slowly.

Porter leant into the kiss, and in the next instant could feel her tongue lashing into his. The embrace was passionate and urgent, as if they were both painfully aware of how little time there was. He could taste the wine on her lips as he flicked his tongue against hers, and her breath was warm against his skin. He could feel her breasts thrusting into his chest, and even through her lace bra, he could feel her nipples

126

stiffening. Porter ran his hand down towards her legs, making impact just above the knee. Small gasps of pleasure started to moan from her lips as he ran his hand slowly up the side of her thigh, until it was nestling in the warmth of her crotch. Danni's own hands were roaming across Porter's chest, tugging at his sweatshirt. She rolled onto her side, and then suddenly was underneath him, pulling him down into the warmth of her body. 'Fuck me,' she muttered, her voice husky and harsh. 'Fuck me right now.'

Porter pulled away her tunic, and buried his face in her chest. His tongue was lashing against her nipples, enjoying the way her large breasts rose and swelled under his touch. As he did so, her hands were busy unbuckling his trousers. In the next moment, Danni had turned him over, stripping the last of his clothes off him, then making him wait a few tantalising moments as she slowly peeled away her dress and tights, leaving just her lace knickers for him to feast his eyes upon. Jesus, thought Porter, as he lay back on the bed and watched her head disappearing towards his groin, girls have learnt a new trick or two since the last time I did this.

The sex was hot and frantic, over in a matter of minutes, but no less satisfying for that. Porter had worried briefly about someone coming in, but the door was bolted. When they finished, they lay wrapped in each other's arms, and for a second Porter found himself wondering about the security cameras he felt certain they had installed in the room. Sod it, he thought with a wry smile. They can watch if they want to. I might even buy a copy of the tape from them.

Danni lay on the side of the bed, her body still vibrating with pleasure. She looked up into his eyes, then planted another kiss on the side of his cheek. 'They don't think you're coming back, you know,' she said.

'What?'

He could feel her hands tickling his chest, and couldn't help himself from smiling. It was so long since he'd been with a woman – there had been one brief girlfriend when he managed to hold down a job for three whole months quite soon after Diana threw him out of the house but since then nothing – that he'd forgotten how good it felt to have someone's arms around you. It made him feel alive again, pushing away the demons that raged inside his mind: already he was wondering about when he might see her again.

'They were talking about it, I heard them,' said Danni. 'Layla and some of the other case officers.'

'What did they say exactly?'

'They reckon there isn't much you can do,' said Danni. 'This Hassad guy, they reckon he's a ruthless bastard, and whatever you offer him, he won't accept it. He'll kill Katie Dartmouth just like he said he would, and then . . . well, it's not going to leave you in much of a position, is it?'

Her eyes flickered up tenderly towards Porter's.

Porter remained impassive. 'I'll do what I can,' he said firmly. 'Whether I can get her out or not . . .' He shrugged his shoulders. 'Hell, I don't know. It's worth trying, that's all I know.'

'Aren't you scared?'

'Of a few ragheads? Fuck, no. They run around screaming to Allah and all that bollocks, but you put in a bullet into them and they fall over pretty quick.'

'But . . . of dying?' asked Danni.

Porter paused. He'd thought about that sometimes over the last few years. When you lived out on the streets, you got used to the idea you weren't going to reach a ripe old age. 'Dying isn't so bad,' he said. 'There are worse things that can happen to man. Trust me, I've been there.'

Slowly, Danni climbed on top of him, grinding her crotch into his groin. There was a wicked, lustful smile playing across her smudged red lipstick. 'I want to fuck you one more time before you go,' she said.

THIRTEEN

The BMW 520 pulled smoothly away from the kerb, and turned sharp right onto Vauxhall Bridge. Porter sat back, listening to the low hum of the engine. Don't get used to it, he warned himself. They'll take you to the airport in style because it suits them. But once you get off that plane, they'll toss you straight back into hell.

It was only just after six and there wasn't much traffic around at this time of the morning. Living rough, Porter had learnt there was no such thing as a quiet time on the London streets: it was a cliché, he knew, but the place really had forgotten how to sleep. Still, as the BMW turned up through Pimlico and Kensington on its way to meet the M4 heading out towards Heathrow, the school-run mums hadn't yet started wheeling out their Chelsea tractors, and the delivery vans hadn't begun their rounds, so the place was relatively calm. He watched as the silent, darkened streets slipped past, recognising places where he'd kipped down for the night, tried his hand at begging, or grovelled to some puffed-up arsehole for a few hours' work washing up or sweeping steps.

I might never see this place again, he thought. And so what? I won't miss a single street of it.

He'd come down to London after Diana had thrown him out. They had a house they'd bought together soon after Sandy was born on the outskirts of Nottingham: Diana liked it because she'd grown up there, but Porter had come from

Luton, and had never really felt at home that far up into the Midlands. Without Diana, there hadn't been much reason to stay, and, if he was being honest with himself, if you were a heavy drinker, it wasn't a great place to hang around: the pubs all got to know you, and wouldn't serve you any more after your first ten or twelve drinks. He'd come down to London to try his hand on the security circuit, and he'd managed to get a couple of bodyguard jobs, but after they caught him with alcohol on his breath that work had all dried up. Nobody wanted some drunk bastard looking after them. He'd stayed in London, though, even as his life gradually fell apart. You could always get a drink, so long as you had a few pounds in your pocket, and sometimes even when you didn't.

'Sleep OK?' said Layla, sitting by his side in the back of the BMW.

He glanced at her. She was dressed more casually today, in jeans, and a white blouse and blue jacket, and her hair was tied back in a ponytail. She had brought an overnight bag with her, even though she was planning on getting the afternoon flight back to London, because anyone who turned up at airport without any luggage automatically made themselves look suspicious.

'Pretty good,' said Porter gruffly.

That just about described it, he reflected. After making love to Danni for the second time, he'd fallen fast asleep in her arms, and slept probably better and more deeply than he had done for years. By the time he'd been woken up by the ringing of the alarm clock, she was gone, with just the lingering smell of her perfume, and a thin trace of lipstick on the pillow to remind him that she'd ever been there at all. I'll probably never see her again, and might not even want to, he'd thought as he stepped into the shower. She was way too young for their relationship to be anything more than brief or physical, but the few hours they'd stolen together

130

had been memorable all the same. *Something to cheer myself up with when the ragheads are about to put a bullet through my head or a sword through my heart.*

'Medical treatment help you sleep?' said Layla.

Porter looked at her again. There was just a trace of a smile around her lips, and suddenly it was clear to him exactly what had happened.

'How much did you pay her?'

'Pay who?' said Layla lightly.

'The nurse,' said Porter.

'I don't know what you're talking about.'

'I might have had too much to drink over the last few years,' growled Porter. 'But the alcohol hasn't rotted all my brain cells, not yet anyway. I've still got enough going on upstairs to know that young girls don't go to bed with guys old enough to be their father unless somebody is making it worth their while.'

'Maybe she likes you,' said Layla with a shrug.

'I have many faults, but I'm not vain,' said Porter. 'What's the deal?'

Layla paused. The BMW had passed through Hammersmith now, and was roaring along the fast lane of the M4 towards the airport. 'She's not really a nurse at all, although she knows how to give someone an injection, and stick a plaster on them if they're cut. She does the honey traps for us. She beds men, usually middle-aged men, and then we threaten to tell their wives unless they do something we want them to do. It's the oldest trick in the book, of course, but a damned good one all the same, and still works a treat.'

'So why me?'

'One of the psychologists we got to watch a video of you talking suggested it,' said Layla. 'He said he reckoned your self-esteem was low.'

'Well, you just spoilt it by telling me.'

Layla shrugged. 'You'd already guessed.'

131

Porter laughed, 'Well, if by some bloody miracle I get back from this hellhole you're sending me to, tell them I'm still feeling a bit down,' he said. 'I might need a repeat prescription.'

'I'll try . . .'

'And ask her to bring her sister as well.'

The BMW had already pulled up in the short-stay car park at Heathrow. Porter followed Layla towards Terminal 4. They still had an hour and a half to go before the flight, but the check-in rules meant they had to be there in plenty of time. Porter was carrying a single leather holdall the Firm had brought for him, with a spare pair of jeans, a couple of shirts, some shaving kit, and a paperback to read on the plane. He slung it over his back, and walked alongside her in the direction of the check-in. His eye caught a newspaper display. All of them were leading on the Katie Dartmouth story: the *Guardian* had a poll showing support for the government slumping as the crisis worsened, predicting a wipeout in the by-election; the *Mail* had signed up Katie's mum to write a kidnap diary; the *Sun* was carrying a Katie countdown measure – 'D-DAY MINUS 3' screamed its headline.

They whizzed through the VIP lounge, then went on to passport control. Porter naturally hadn't had a passport: it wasn't the kind of thing you needed when you slept rough. The Firm had rustled one up overnight. Amazing what you could do when the fate of the government was on the line, he reflected. Even the picture doesn't look too bad, he decided, as he took the passport back from the immigration officer and tucked it into his jeans. Maybe they didn't have to pay that Danni girl too much for the shag: at the rate my life is improving, he thought with a wry smile to himself, the next one might even be free.

'We'll be staying away from the duty-free, I think,' said

132

Layla sharply, steering him towards the coffee bar in the departures lounge. 'You've got quite enough in your system, without stocking up on the vodka.'

'Maybe I should bring my old mate Hassad a gift from Blighty,' said Porter with a grin. 'A T-shirt with Big Ben on it. Or some nice biscuits from Harrods.'

Layla had already ordered a couple of large lattes and croissants: Porter had grabbed some cereal and toast in his bedroom, but his hunger was still far from satiated, and he wolfed down the croissant in a couple of bites. 'I somehow imagine the Society of Muslim Brothers doesn't break out the Johnnie Walker when they get together for a meeting,' said Layla.

'I could grab a bottle just in case,' said Porter.

'Don't even think about it.'

'Maybe get them all pissed, then sneak out with the girl while they're sleeping it off.'

Layla just rolled her eyes.

'You eating that?' said Porter, pointing towards her croissant.

'There'll be food on the plane, I suppose,' she replied with a shake of her head.

He grabbed the croissant, and ate that in two bites as well. Looking around, Porter couldn't tell where the rest of the flunkies the Firm had ordered to accompany them on the flight might be, but he felt certain they wouldn't be far away. They were flying on an A320, which in economy class had six seats in each row, three on either side of the aisle, making sixteen additional officers once you took out the two seats occupied by Porter and Layla. Quite a party, he thought to himself. They would all be in plain clothes. They would slip quietly into the background. The Firm was good at that: it could tap an endless supply of grey men who shuffled unobtrusively into the shadows, only to appear as if from nowhere when they were needed.

'I need the loo,' said Porter, standing up.

Layla looked at him sharply.

'Don't worry,' growled Porter. 'I'm not doing a runner. I might need my head examining, but I actually *want* to get out there.'

'Just don't be long.'

Porter walked in the direction of the toilets. He glanced towards the duty-free, and couldn't help but notice the vast display of whiskies, vodka and gin stacked high in the shop window. Bloody cheap, he reflected bitterly to himself. Johnnie Walker at twelve quid a bottle. They are practically giving the stuff away. No, he told himself, as he carried on walking. Nothing to drink. Not yet anyway.

The Firm had given him a hundred quid along with his luggage: to head up to Heathrow without any money in your pocket was just one more thing that would make him appear suspicious. He had another five hundred in Lebanese pounds, and Ben Stanton would have plenty more if he needed it. Just beyond the duty-free shop, there was a row of gift and clothes stores. Porter slipped inside one, and told the girl at the desk to give him a pair of jeans, a white shirt, some socks, pants and a pair of trainers, size nine. When she asked what label, he told her he didn't care. And no, he didn't mind what colour the jeans were, whether they were straight or boot cut, nor did he want to try them on. Within a couple of minutes, she had returned with a bulging bag. Porter counted out the money, thanked her and left.

Swiftly, he walked the last few yards to the Gents, then, locking himself into one of the cubicles, Porter quickly undressed. It was a cramped space, but he was soon naked. He ran his hands across his body, making absolutely certain there wasn't any kind of tracking device planted anywhere on him. When he was sure, he took the new clothes from the bag, dressed himself, washed his face, and walked quickly back towards the coffee bar where Layla was waiting for him. Glancing up at the departures board, he could see there were still forty minutes until their flight, but passengers were already being asked to make their way to Gate 26.

'What the hell have you done?' said Layla, looking up at him.

'Changed,' said Porter gruffly.

Layla shook her head, the expression on her face that of a nursery-school teacher faced with a particularly unruly pupil. 'You didn't like the clothes we bought you?' she said. 'Christ, we're taking you to Beirut. We're not going to Milan for a bloody fashion shoot.'

Porter leant over the table. She'd ordered herself as chocolate muffin while he was gone, and he grabbed a piece, putting it in his mouth. 'Like I said in the car, I may have had a bit too much to drink over the past few years, but my brain's not completely gone. Not yet anyway. I have to be absolutely certain you lot haven't planted any tracking devices on me. Because if you've put a tracker on me, then sure as hell Hassad is going to find it. You can slip one into my clothes easily enough, even into the heel of a shoe, or just the button of a shirt. The only way I can be certain I'm clean is to be wearing clothes I just bought in the shop right here. Because if Hassad does find anything, he's going to kill me on the spot. And frankly I wouldn't blame the bastard.'

'Christ, John, don't you trust us?'

Porter shook his head firmly from side to side. 'I trust only myself.'

The flight was only about half full, and that was including the seats the Firm had booked. Not many people flying to Beirut, thought Porter as he walked along the aisles to the toilets at the back of the plane. And who the hell can blame them. No business to be done, half the hotels are shut, and unless you're dressed in a burka or a headscarf, the chances are some nutter will kidnap you and phone home asking for a million quid or he'll chop your head off.

The A320 had been in the air for three hours now, and so far the flight had been pretty smooth. It was the first time Porter had been on a plane in nearly fifteen years, and they'd come on a bit since the charter flight to Spain he had taken with Diana and a three-year-old Sandy on the last family holiday they'd gone on before his drinking meant they no longer had any money for luxuries like that. The wings didn't scream with pain every time the pilot changed direction. The seats were comfier. You could plug forty or more channels of music into your ear. And there was a neat little screen hanging on the ceiling that tracked the progress of the plane over Europe and told you how far you were from your destination. They were just passing over Sicily, Porter noted, and heading out into the Mediterranean. The pilot was banking left to steer them away from Egypt and towards Israel and the Lebanon. Not long now before they started their descent into Beirut.

He looked towards the drinks trolley. The stewardess – a pert little blonde who introduced herself as Chloë while serving Porter his microwaved breakfast – had already been through the cabin offering people a drink but it was still only mid-morning and there weren't many takers. Layla had told her sharply that they didn't need anything, and Porter had had to settle for finishing her breakfast instead. There was a row of tiny, airline bottles: whisky, vodka, gin, rum, several different types of beer, quarter-bottles of red and white wine. Porter could hardly remember the last time he'd seen so much booze in one place. And all of it free as well. He grabbed two vodkas, one gin, and a double-sized serving of Johnnie Walker, and slipped them inside his jacket.

There's only one place they manufacture the kind of courage a man needs to face what I am about to put myself through, he told himself.

A brewery.

He grabbed another vodka bottle, and twisted its cap. It came loose in his hand, and he put it to his lips. He could feel the warm glass against his skin, and then the steady, strong liquid started to trickle down into his throat. Porter had never found a drink he didn't like the taste of. He'd drink paint-stripper if that was all he could find. But vodka was his favourite. A real drinker's drink: maybe that was why the Russians loved it so much. Vodka didn't mess around with flavours or aromas. There was no nonsense about grains or vintages. It was the closest you could get to pure alcohol without visiting a hospital. And it got you fired up with the minimum fuss and the maximum efficiency.

'What the hell are you doing?' snapped Layla.

Porter spun round. She was standing right next to him, her dark eyes alive with anger. Already her right hand had grabbed for the vodka bottle. She was trying to take it from him but had only succeeded in spilling half its contents down his shirt.

'What the fuck do you think I'm doing?' growled Porter. 'Admiring the pretty cloud formations out of the window? I'm having a bloody drink.'

'Put it down,' said Layla, her tone rising sharply.

Porter held on to the bottle. There were only a few drops left in it, but he wasn't about to let them go.

'Put it down,' said Layla again, even more loudly this time.

Porter could hear the roaring of the plane's engines in his ears. It had just hit a patch of turbulence, and the A320 bounced sharply, then plunged downwards. Porter steadied himself against the plane wall with his left hand. Ahead of him he could see that the pilot had switched on the seat-belts sign.

'I know you're practically an alcoholic,' said Layla, trying to keep her grip as the plane rolled and swerved through the sky, 'but you've had a couple of days without a drink, and you're starting to clean up.'

'I needed a drink,' snapped Porter.

'What the hell for?' shouted Layla. 'We're pinning everything on you. We're paying you two hundred and fifty grand. The last thing we need is a fucking wino crawling off the plane too drunk to even remember his own name.'

'One drink, that's all I bloody needed.'

'It's always one drink, then one more,' said Layla. 'You were a sodding tramp. We've taken you in, given you a chance, but we damn well expect to be repaid. That means you deliver what we expect. That's the deal, and if you break it, we'll fucking break you. You hear me, John Porter. We'll break you like a fucking matchstick.'

Porter paused for a moment. He could already feel the vodka he had drunk a few moments ago hitting his bloodstream. The plane was starting to balance out again, but the weather was still rough, and the undercarriage was thumping against pockets of air. The alcohol was already working its lethal magic, calming his nerves and soothing his anxieties. People said the juice stopped you from thinking straight, but they were wrong. He could always see things much more clearly when he had some alcohol inside him, and right now he could see there was some truth to what she was saying. He'd had nothing, not any kind of life to speak of, but now he had a daughter again, and he'd had done something for her, and that was something he could take to his grave and feel proud of. He had the Firm to thank for that. It didn't mean he couldn't handle a drink, though. She was wrong about that.

'What the hell do you know about soldiering?' he said, levelling a stare right into her eyes. 'There are only two rations every commander in history has made sure his men have plenty of before they go into battle. Booze and smokes. In the trenches of the Somme, that was all the blokes lived on. Rum and tobacco. And you know why? Because it is fucking frightening. Most blokes wouldn't be able to fight

138

unless they were too drunk to know any better.' He paused again, waiting for the plane to pass through another patch of rough weather. 'Well, this is a battle, and I reckon it's going to be a bloody nasty one,' he continued, his voice dropping down to no more than a whisper. 'And I'm going to need all the courage I can get. Some men get it from a church, and some from their country. I get mine from a bottle, and that's all there is to it.'

'I don't care about that,' Layla snapped, her face red with anger. 'One more, and we'll turn straight round and go home.'

The stewardess was standing next to them, her eyes switching nervously from Porter to Layla and back again. Trouble, thought Porter. It was what every stewardess feared the most. 'I'll have to ask you to take your seats,' she said. 'The captain –'

'Don't worry, we're sitting down,' said Porter.

He patted the spare bottles tucked into his jacket pocket as he walked back to his seat. Doesn't matter what she says, he told himself bitterly. The woman knows nothing.

'Just stay where you are,' said Layla sourly, making sure his seat belt was fastened. The stewardess was walking quickly away from them, relieved that the trouble had passed. Porter grabbed for some peanuts, pulled open the pack, and threw them into his mouth in a couple of handfuls, chewing on them angrily.

The turbulence had passed, and the clouds had split open, and suddenly Porter was looking out of the window at the clear blue sea leading up to the Lebanese coastline. The last time I was here I was flying in on a Puma to rescue a hostage and my life was about to fall apart. This time, I'm coming in on a commercial flight to rescue a hostage, and my life is almost certainly going to end.

The years roll by, and sod all changes.

FOURTEEN

Layla glanced at Porter's face. She was scowling, and he could tell she was still furious with him for the drink he'd taken on the journey. They had walked off the plane in silence, accompanied by the silent flunkies from the Firm, then followed the signs through to the arrivals hall. Most of their fellow passengers were waiting to collect their bags from the carousel. But Porter didn't have anything to collect. Just the holdall the Firm had given him, and he had that tucked under his arm.

When you've got a life expectancy of about two days, thought Porter, you really don't have to worry about packing. You can even skip baggage reclaim – which just goes to show, there is some upside to every situation.

'You know the drill?' said Layla.

Porter nodded. 'Yes, sir . . .'

'Remember, no heroics,' said Layla. 'Your job is to get Katie Dartmouth out of there, or at least delay her execution, so that we have a chance to organise a rescue mission. We don't need you trying to do this single-handed.'

'We've been through this,' Porter growled, walking towards passport control.

'John,' said Layla.

He turned round.

'Good luck . . .'

Porter smiled. 'Thanks . . .'

She nodded towards him. 'If you get back alive, I might even buy you a drink.'

'Make it a sodding double then,' said Porter.

He turned on his heels and kept on walking towards the desk. Even inside the airport, Porter could feel the heat and humidity surrounding him. He stood in line alongside what appeared to be mostly a group of Arab businessmen passing through security. In total, there were no more than a dozen white faces among the two hundred or so people filling the arrivals hall. Up ahead, there were two armed policemen manning each desk, and they were checking each passport carefully. They were mostly Syrians, Turks and Egyptians, and all of them had visas, but they all needed to be checked. Porter glanced down at his own document. He noted that the Firm had backdated it a couple of years, and it already had Turkish and Lebanese entry and exit visa stamps in it: a passport that had already been used to get into and out of a country a few times was a lot less likely to provoke suspicion than one that was brand new.

'Business?' said the policeman, glancing from the picture on Porter's passport and up into his eyes.

'Social visit,' said Porter.

The policeman nodded but remained suspicious.

'I've made a few friends while doing business here,' Porter continued.

'Hotel?' said the policeman.

His tone, Porter noted, was just on the wrong side of indifference.

'The Marriott,' he replied.

The policemen flicked through the pages, checking the different visas, then lost interest and waved Porter through. He kept on walking, past another row of armed soldiers, then stepped out into the main airport hall. He could feel a sudden shot of adrenalin buzzing through him. This is where the waiting ends, he told himself. Another few hours and I'll be in the thick of it. *God help me.*

People were swarming through the main hall. There were

big families welcoming passengers off the planes. A few taxi drivers were holding up placards with names attached to them, but none of them said John Porter. Up ahead, there was a bank of money changers, car-rental offices, and hotel booking agencies, and just alongside them a group of taxi drivers touting for business. As he paused for a moment to take in the atmosphere, Porter couldn't help but notice the unmistakable smell of the Middle East. It was a mixture of sweat, and dates, mixed with almonds, stewed meat and sweet tea. It clung to the air, and got onto your skin: even one breath was enough to remind Porter that he hated the place, and would be happier turning round and taking the next plane home again.

'Need help with that bag,' said a voice that appeared as if from nowhere at his side.

Porter looked round. Ben Stanton was around forty, with short brown hair, and a deep tan to his face. He was wearing grey chinos and a blue linen jacket, with no tie. His smile was engaging yet distant, as if he could think of places he'd rather be but was too polite to mention them. What does it take to get the Firm's Beirut posting? Porter wondered. You're either the best man they've got, so they give you the toughest posting. Or else you're a loser they don't know what to do with, so they ship you off to some hellhole hoping you'll get yourself shot, and they can save themselves the cost of your pension.

Stanton looked like the latter, but with spies, Porter thought, it was always risky to judge by appearances. The good ones were masters of deception – and the first thing they always lied about was themselves.

'I've got a car waiting,' Stanton continued. 'Follow me.'

Porter glanced from side to side. There were soldiers lining the exits, scanning everyone suspiciously, their machine guns gripped tight to their chests, ready to be fired. Stanton ignored them, walking straight past, as if they were just adverts plastered to the walls. So did everyone else. That's Beirut, thought Porter to himself. Everyone is so used to war, they no longer even notice it.

The car park was five hundred metres from the main terminal. It was a grey, overcast afternoon, with clouds hanging low in the sky. Stanton pressed the locks on a Volvo C70, and slung Porter's bag on the back seat. 'We're heading south, then your bus will take you to the border,' he said, his tone suggesting they were plenty of places he'd rather be going.

'What's it like there?' said Porter.

'Pretty much like the rest of this hellhole,' said Stanton. 'Bloody awful.'

The Volvo pulled out of the car park, and started heading up towards the exit ramps. There was a roadblock with Lebanese soldiers checking vehicles as they left, but Stanton had diplomatic papers and they waved him straight through. He turned onto the roundabout, swearing furiously at a truck that tried to cut him up as they turned towards the highway leading out of the city. A barrage of honking and swearing filled the air, but Stanton tapped his foot on the accelerator, ignoring it.

'Bloody Lebanese,' he muttered, concentrating on the road. 'When they aren't trying to kill each other with guns they're doing it with the sodding cars.'

Porter grinned. Welcome to hell, he thought. I should be right at home.

'What's the situation like up at the border?'

'What is it you army boys say?' said Stanton. 'Snafu − situation normal, all fucked up? That's about it. The war between Israel and Hezbollah is officially supposed to be over, but that doesn't mean they've given each other a big hug and made up. The border region is swarming with armies, some of them private, some of them religious, some of them Lebanese government, some of them Hezbollah.

Basically, you see a bloke with a gun, then he's going to be fighting for someone, but you won't have a clue who until he's put a few rounds of ammunition into you. In short, it's a nasty place, full of very nasty people.'

'That's where I'm going?'

'For starters, anyway.'

'You don't reckon Katie Dartmouth is up by the border anywhere?'

Stanton shrugged. They were out on the main highway now, heading along the coastline that would take you straight into Israel if you kept going for long enough. The traffic was light, apart from some tanks and jeeps hogging the slow lane. There was some sign of damage to the road: places where shelling or Israeli bombers had knocked chunks out of the concrete, but nothing bad enough to stop the flow of vehicles. 'By now, probably not,' he replied. 'They're planning on collecting you up there, so I reckon it's a decoy. Hezbollah might be nutters, but they are as cunning as sewer rats. They wouldn't have survived as long as they have in this hellhole if they weren't. They're picking you up by the Syrian border, so they have to figure we'll think she's somewhere around there. Which means she probably isn't.'

'And you haven't a clue where she is?'

Stanton shook his head. 'We don't have great contacts out here. Iraq has been a bloody disaster for the British in the Middle East. They *all* hate us now, rather than just 90 per cent of the buggers like before. We've been told to spend whatever money is necessary, and we've put the word out on the street that there's some easy cash to be earned by tipping us off about where they've stashed her.'

'No takers?'

'Not a bloody sausage,' said Stanton. 'Usually in these situations there's somebody who wants to move to Geneva with a few hundred grand tucked away in his bank account and will turn snitch. They are Arabs after all. They're not famous for swapping their grandmothers for a new camel for nothing. They tell us where the body is, and we make a discreet payment into a bank account. That's the way it works. This time around, nothing.'

'Why not?'

For a moment Stanton looked genuinely puzzled, as if he had asked himself that question, but had yet to figure out a proper answer. 'You know what, I think they believe they've got us on the run,' he answered eventually. 'This whole show is being run out of Tehran. The Iranians are desperate to get their hands on the oil fields of southern Iraq, and they know the British can't hang in there much longer. The trouble is, everyone else wants a piece of that action as well. The oil is the only thing worth having in Iraq. The Kuwaitis are stirring things up, hoping to install their own strongmen in the south. If they get their way, they'll operate through the locals for a decade or two, then one day you'll wake up and find Basra is a part of Greater Kuwait. They are smart boys, the emirs, and they play the long game – which is, of course, the only game worth playing in this godforsaken part of the world. Then there is the Sunni up in the middle. That's Saddam's old mob, and they need to secure the oil fields as well, since if they don't get their grubby hands on the oil, the only other alternative is date farming, and there isn't much money in that.' Stanton paused, honking furiously at an ancient BMW that was backfiring badly in front of him. 'So you see, the mullahs in Tehran can't hang around. They need the British out now so they can get control of the place. They took Katie Dartmouth as just another piece of the campaign, but they aren't stupid. They read the papers and watch TV, and they can see what an impact it's all made back in Britain. So they are going to play this one hard, and get the maximum leverage out of it if they can. They can see there is a real chance of

145

concessions, and even if there isn't, the British position in Basra will still be weakened, and that's what this is all about.' He glanced over at Porter. 'I don't mean to be negative, and all that. Chin up, et cetera, et cetera.' He chuckled to himself. 'But you've got more chance of shagging the Ayatollah's sister than you have of getting Katie Dartmouth out of that hellhole. Come Saturday night, I reckon the pretty head is going to be rolling off the elegant shoulders and all of it live on TV. And what happens then? Fucked if I know. I reckon our beloved leader will be in even deeper trouble than he is already and the boys out in Basra can start emailing their wives and girlfriends to expect them back for Christmas.'

'Thanks for the encouragement,' growled Porter.

Stanton laughed. 'When you're stationed in Beirut you learn to be a realist.'

The Volvo swung left, down a slip road that took them into Sidon. It wasn't much of a place, Porter noted. It was mid-afternoon now, and the skies were still grey and over-cast, with just a few rays of sunshine breaking through a mile or so out to sea. Although it nestled into a snug cove on the Mediterranean shoreline, there was nothing picturesque or charming about the town. No point trying to get this place into one of the travel supplements in the Sunday papers, thought Porter. Too many armies had marched through it for that. The main bay was dotted with a few fishing boats and a couple of large cargo vessels, but you could also see the damage to the quayside where the shells must have landed. Many of the traditional houses had been destroyed, their place taken by hastily built concrete shacks. Some of the roads had been broken up into rubble by the shelling, and nobody yet had the money or inclination to fix them. Maybe they don't reckon there's any point, thought Porter. The next war will be along in a minute. There's no point in making things easier for the Israeli tanks.

The bus station was just beyond the main square. About five buses, each one painted a pale green, were parked next to it. Stanton pulled up the Volvo next to them, killing the engine. 'The Jezzoine bus leaves in ten minutes,' he said. 'Then again, punctuality isn't rated as very important around here. It'll probably leave when they've got all the chickens they're taking with them to sit down nicely.'

Porter slung his bag over his shoulder as he stepped out of the car. He paused, smelling the stiff breeze blowing in from the nearby shore, its salt flavour mixed with the fried oils, nuts and spices from the row of six food stands lining the edge of the bus station. It was good to smell the Med one more time, he told himself. He wanted to savour as many experiences as possible. When you were almost certainly going to die in the next twenty-four hours, then you saw the world with a fresh eye. It was like being a kid again. Everything seemed funny, interesting, challenging: the desire to embrace the world was all the more intense for the knowledge that you were about to leave it.

'I'm hungry,' said Porter.

He walked over to the food stands, and got Stanton to order a couple of snacks: tiny chicken and lamb meatballs, mixed with chickpeas and a spicy sauce, and served wrapped up in a pitta bread with a bottle of iced tea to wash it all down. Porter ate them in a couple of bites, then asked for another. 'Any advice?' he said.

Stanton hesitated before replying. He was scanning Porter's face, looking, Porter reckoned, for traces of fear. But he wasn't going to find any. He'd been scared before in his life. Going into combat had turned his stomach into jelly the same way it did for all the men. Taking a beating out on the streets had been just as bad. But he wasn't scared now.

'Turn in your resignation,' said Stanton. 'Take a holiday. Phone in sick . . .'

Porter smiled, but remained silent. He walked slowly

147

towards the bus. A couple of women were climbing on board, buying their tickets, talking to each other. Porter handed across a Lebanese ten-pound note, collected his ticket, then nodded towards Stanton. 'Thanks for your help,' he said tersely.

The bus was already running ten minutes late by the time it pulled out of Sidon and started wheezing its way up the hill inland. Porter had positioned himself near the centre of the bus, keeping himself as inconspicuous as possible. The two women in front of him were still chattering away: there were obviously a lot of unfaithful husbands and disloyal daughters in Sidon to catch up on, thought Porter. There were a few old men, a couple of families, and several schoolchildren scattered around the vehicle. Some of them were talking. But mostly, just like Porter, they were looking out of the window and keeping themselves to themselves.

The journey took just over an hour, twisting along the only main road that led up into the mountains that ran along the spine of the coast then down again into the valleys and plains below. There were some farms you could see stretched along the side of the road, growing dates, oranges, lemons and chickpeas, with the occasional herd of goats chewing the grasslands between the orchards and the fields. But the evidence of war was everywhere. Farms that had been abandoned were slowly being taken over by weeds, trees and scrub. Barns and houses that had been broken up by RPGs and mortar fire, roads that had been smashed to rubble, and the occasional burnt-out husk of a tank, or the familiar dugouts used to shelter a machine-gun crew, littered the side of the road.

That's what soldiers leave behind, thought Porter to himself. Lots of shattered communities, and broken lives. Not much of an advertisement for the trade.

Jezzoine wasn't the last stop on the route but it was where

Porter was getting off. He climbed from the bus, and out onto the tarmac of the bus station, glancing quickly around. The clouds were heavier now. It was just after five in the afternoon, and although sunset was still some way ahead, the light was already growing murky. Sidon may not have been much of a place, thought Porter, but compared with Jezzoine, it was Biarritz. There were just three buses waiting at the station, and the tarmac was pitted with holes: some of them might have been left there by shells, but most of them were there because nobody had bothered to fill them up at any time in the last fifty years. The ticket office had shut, and a dog was prowling around it menacingly. Glancing across the street into the town, Porter could see a couple of beaten-up cafés, with a group of surly-looking men outside, sipping cups of thick, black coffee, and one shop selling some food, hardware and car parts.

Not many tourists, thought Porter. I'm going to stand out like Victoria Beckham in the local Primark. I'm probably the first white guy mad enough to come here in years.

He checked the bus schedule. The Sidon bus had rolled into town ten minutes late, but he still had twenty minutes to spare before the next bus headed out to Anjar. Take in the sights, he thought to himself with a grim smile.

Walking across to the shop, he took a bottle of water from the cooler cabinet, chose a couple of bars of chocolate, and handed across a Lebanese twenty-pound note to pay for them. He didn't say anything, and although the woman serving could see he wasn't local, she didn't seem to care. A small boy was emptying out his pockets, seeing if he had enough coins to buy a packet of sweets. He glanced suspiciously at Porter, then looked away. Porter took the coins he'd been given in change, and handed them down to the boy. He started to say something in Arabic, but Porter just shook his head and turned round.

No need for the thanks, mate, thought Porter as he

walked back towards the bus stop. Where I'm going, I won't be needing any loose change.

I'm dealing in a harder currency.

Blood.

Another hour, another bus station.

Porter stepped down from the ten-year-old Mercedes vehicle and glanced around. It was gone six now, and the skies were growing darker: back in England it would be pitch black by this time, but the days were longer out here. The journey had taken longer than expected. His bus had left twenty minutes after the scheduled time, and had taken fifteen minutes longer than it should have done to get to Anjar: the driver had picked one woman up, then turned round and gone back again when it turned out she had forgotten something. The waiting was driving Porter crazy. Just get on with it, he muttered to himself. I want to get stuck into this mission.

There were two food stands at the far end of the bus station, and a couple of guys were hanging around the ticket office. One of them, Porter noted, very obviously had some kind of gun tucked inside his leather jacket. They glanced at Porter, but neither seemed very interested. All through the journey, Porter had been watching, wondering whether the Firm had put some kind of tail on him. It was, he well knew, their most obvious move. After all, he was going to lead them straight to Katie Dartmouth's kidnappers. Follow him, and they'd find her. All they would have to do then was rustle up a crack unit from Hereford to go and get her out. The only risk was, if the tail was spotted, Porter would be killed on the spot. Then they would have nothing. If there was a tail, he had to spot it before Hassad did.

As much as he scanned the bus and the streets for evidence of anyone keeping tabs on him, he felt certain he hadn't seen the same face twice throughout the whole journey. He hadn't seen anyone acting suspiciously. There was nobody lurking in the shadows. And no passing of the watch from one person to another. Not that he could see anyway.

Either they are not here, *or else they are bloody good.*

He started walking towards the bar. It was just a single room, built into a ragged concrete structure on the street directly opposite the bus station. There were a couple of cars parked alongside, and a few plastic tables and chairs. About a dozen guys were sitting around outside, drinking coffee and tea, and there were heaps of dog ends at their feet. Sandwiched close to the Lebanese, Syrian and Israeli borders, it was hardly surprising Anjar didn't exist as anything more than a brutally fought-over dot on a map. Why the hell would anyone want to live here? Porter wondered. There was nothing to tie you to the place except for war, poverty and anger.

Crossing the road, he paused before the entrance to the bar. It had no name, just a dirty brown awning that would provide some shade when the sun was shining. Still, there was no mistaking the place. Anjar only had about four proper streets and two of those appeared to have been abandoned. It had a couple of shops, but this was the only café or bar. Porter started to step inside, yet for a brief moment he could feel himself hesitating. This is the line, he thought to himself. On one side, there's this world. On the other a different one, probably the next world, if that happens to exist.

Cross it and there's no going back.

Sod it, he told himself with a grim smile. There's nothing to go back to. And the next world probably isn't so bad. There's bound to be a place where a bloke can doss down for the night. Who knows, you might even be able to get a drink.

The only trouble is I wouldn't ever see Sandy again.

The guy at the counter looked around thirty, with a black

151

T-shirt, and blue jeans hanging loose over his white trainers. There were a few men inside the bar: where they stashed the women in this place, Porter had no idea, but he hadn't seen any apart from at the shop and on the bus. The men were all drinking tea and pouring over a single copy of a newspaper. There was some kind of discussion going on, but whether it was about sport, or politics, or business, Porter couldn't tell. He nodded towards the barman. There were some beer bottles in the cooler, and Porter felt tempted. A beer was just exactly what he needed right now. Lebanon was a Muslim country, but it wasn't dry like some of them. Still, the locals hardly ever drank, and ordering a beer would only attract attention to himself. And that was the very last thing he wanted.

'A coffee,' he said in English.

He'd learnt a few words of Arabic back in the Regiment, but he didn't want to try them out now. The barman looked at him, his expression puzzled. Not many English guys up here, thought Porter. The only foreigners you ever got around this place were probably Israelis and they didn't usually get out of their fighter jets to say hello.

'You speak English?' said Porter.

The man nodded. 'A little,' he said. 'You want coffee?'

'That's why I asked for it,' said Porter.

The man went to the machine behind the bar. 'Where you from?'

Porter took the small white china cup that had just been placed on the counter, and flicked away two flies that were sitting on the sugar bowl next to it. He pushed a couple of Lebanese one-pound coins across the bar. For a moment, he thought about lying. The British weren't popular in Lebanon: they never had been, and they'd got a lot less so since the Iraq war kicked off. He didn't need to get into any kind of argument with the locals. He could pretend to be Australian or a Kiwi: the trouble was they would probably recognise the accent. And who knows, they probably hate the Aussies as well. 'England,' he said.

A couple of the men from the group around the newspaper looked at him. One of them had narrow eyes and a thick scar that ran down the side of his cheek and into his neck. He spat the half-smoked cigarette from his mouth and ground it beneath the heel of his boot. You don't need a translator to figure out what he's saying, thought Porter. He's tooling up for a fight. And the next thing he wants to put underneath that boot is my face.

'You hear about the English girl,' said the barman. 'The one who got kidnapped?'

Christ, thought Porter. It's even a big story out here.

'Something,' he replied tersely.

'What they think of that back in London?' said the barman, with a smile.

'Maybe they get their soldiers out of our country now?' said the man with the scar, standing up and walking over to the bar.

'We're not in your country,' said Porter.

'The Arab nation is one nation,' said the man. His scar quivered slightly as he spoke, as if it was the wound talking. 'You occupy one land, you occupy all our lands.'

Shit, thought Porter. The last thing I need here is a bar-room brawl.

'I'm sure you're right,' he said firmly. 'I don't really know anything about it. I'm just getting a coffee while I wait for the next bus.'

'What are you doing here?' said the man with the scar. He had edged a foot closer to Porter, and he could smell the cheap cologne and the nicotine clinging to his skin. 'There are no foreigners up here.'

Porter paused for just a fraction of a second. 'Family business,' he said. 'A Lebanese family in London, they need some land sorted out. I've no interest in politics.'

He walked past the man, sitting down at a plastic table at the far end of the bar. Taking two sugars from the bowl, he stirred them into the thick black coffee, then discreetly took out the tiny bottle of Johnnie Walker he had taken from the plane and poured half of it into the cup. He sipped on the small cup, and could instantly feel the rich mixture of caffeine, sugar and alcohol all hitting his bloodstream at the same time. He could feel his head start to spin, and his eyes were getting dizzy, but the whisky worked its magic, the way it always did, and he could feel his head start to clear and his spirits reviving. The guy with the scar had gone back to his group of mates, but he was still looking occasionally across at him, a glint of anger in his eyes.

If only you knew what I was really here for, thought Porter with a grim smile, you'd kill me on the spot.

He glanced at the clock. Six twenty. Hassad hadn't given the Firm any precise time for the pickup. But they expected him to be getting to the bar around five thirty, so they should have scheduled the collection for shortly after that. Maybe it's a set-up, thought Porter. Maybe they are just going to leave me, and then let that bloke with the scar cut my throat open as soon as it gets dark.

A man walked up to the bar. Late forties, Porter noted, with a linen jacket, a bald head and one of those Saddam Hussein moustaches that men wore throughout the Middle East. Is that my contact? wondered Porter. For a moment, he could feel his muscles tensing with anticipation. But the guy just ordered some chilled water and tea, and went to sit outside by himself. Porter emptied the rest of the Johnnie Walker bottle into his coffee cup, and knocked it back in one gulp. Much more of this and I'll be looking for somewhere to spend the night.

Six forty. Porter took out the book the Firm had packed into his bag. Pretty good, he decided, after a few pages, but it was difficult to concentrate on reading anything. One of scarface's friends had left the bar, but the rest of them were still arguing over the contents of that day's paper. The barman had switched on the radio, and as the news came through Porter caught the name of Katie Dartmouth, but the presenter was talking so fast in Arabic he couldn't begin to translate what he was saying. Who knows, thought Porter, maybe the bastards have already killed her.

'Mahmudiyya,' said a voice behind him.

The instant he heard the word, Porter could feel his heart thump against the walls of his chest. This is where it all kicks off, he realised grimly.

Porter looked up. There were two men standing right next to him. The taller of the two was almost six foot, slim with slicked-back hair, around thirty, with the hardened face and the muscles of a man who'd been in plenty of fights. The shorter man was about five eight, with thin dark hair, a face that was running to fat even though he couldn't even have reached his mid-twenties yet. A pair of sunglasses were wrapped around his eyes, and there was a gold chain glinting through the black hairs on his chest that were visible through his open-necked shirt.

This is it, thought Porter. He drained the last few dregs of his whisky-soaked coffee and stood up. Time for the kick-off.

'Let's go,' he said quietly.

The two men remained silent. They turned on their heels, heading towards the door. Scarface and the barman were watching as he left, their jaws dropping slightly, but neither of them moved from their spot. Do they know these goons? wondered Porter. Do I . . .?

A black Toyota 4x4 was parked outside on the tarmac. It looked new to Porter. The smaller man opened the back door, revealing the dark leather seats and blackened-out windows inside. Porter was about to climb in when the taller man touched his arm. 'Wait,' he said.

His tone was low and controlled, with a slight accent, but Porter could tell his English was good. 'Here,' he added.

There was a strip of black cloth in his hand. Porter knew instantly what it was.

A blindfold.

'OK,' he said.

He turned to face the car. The taller man stood behind him, and his height gave him at least three inches over Porter. He was stretching the cloth in his hand, then laid the strip across Porter's face. The skin on his fingers was rough, like a builder's, but his touch was as soft as a little girl's, and Porter could feel himself growing nauseated by the sense of the man's flesh touching his. He wrapped the blindfold around, once, twice, three times, so that the top half of Porter's face was completely covered. The light totally vanished, and Porter could see nothing. A hand pushed him down into the back seat of the Toyota, and as he sunk back into the leather, he could hear the ignition turn, and feel the surge of power as the car started to move out into the street.

The blackness was total. Porter knew this was inevitable. If they were going to the place they had hidden Katie Dartmouth, then they had to be certain he had no idea where they had taken him. If he knew where she was, they would have to kill him, of that there could be no doubt. Even if they were planning to kill him – and he suspected they were – they would still go through the blindfold routine. If they didn't, he'd know he was a dead man, and they'd surely save up that piece of information for later. A condemned man is always a nuisance: he knows he has nothing to lose, and that makes him dangerous. So, whatever the plan, the blindfold was unavoidable.

'Where are we going?' he said.

Silence.

He could hear only the hum of the engine, and the rumble of the tyres against the rough tarmac.

'How long will it take?' said Porter.

Again, silence. He could feel the Toyota turning first left, then right. Whether they were travelling north, south, east or west, he no longer had any idea. No doubt that was the intention.

'I said, how long will it take?'

Silence.

OK, thought Porter. Don't talk if you don't want to. Just take me to Hassad.

FIFTEEN

The Toyota kept ploughing on over harder and harder terrain. Porter had long since lost track of what time it was. Two, maybe three hours they had been driving. It was hard to keep up, as it was to keep tabs on your direction when a blindfold was strapped over your eyes: lose that most basic of the senses, and the others seem to go as well.

How far have we gone? Porter tried to calculate. Sixty, perhaps seventy miles. But in which direction it was impossible to tell.

The roads had been getting rougher as time moved on. He wasn't even sure they were still on a road at all. At a guess, Porter reckoned they had been driving north, but he couldn't be certain. They might well have crossed into Syria by now. Neither of the men up front had uttered a single word the whole time, and Porter had long since given up trying to talk to them. They didn't even talk to each other.

Suddenly, he felt the Toyota judder to a halt. Porter didn't react. It had stopped several times in the past couple of hours as it encountered some obstacle on the road, but each time it quickly restarted. This was different. The engine had been turned off. He could hear doors opening. Somewhere in the distance – outside the car – he could hear voices.

'Get out.'

From the tone of the voice, Porter could tell it was the taller man speaking.

He levered himself out of the back seat, and swung his legs

down onto the ground. Still unable to see anything, he knocked his head against the roof of the car, and he could feel a dull ache where a bruise might be starting to form. He kept on moving, until he was standing, he guessed, just next to the car.

'Where are we?' said Porter.

'Stay quiet,' barked the man.

His tone was harsh and cruel, but there was a hint of amusement in it as well.

Then, a silence.

Porter could sense there were people around him. He couldn't see anyone because of the blindfold. He couldn't hear anyone any more either: if they were there, they were keeping quiet. But he could sense them all the same. There was a body heat in the air all around him. There was a charged, tense atmosphere that you could smell in the air. There are plenty of guys here, he told himself. And probably all of them want to kill me.

'Why won't you answer me?' he said.

'Just move,' hissed the taller man.

'I can't bloody see anything.'

Suddenly a hand was gripping his shoulder. It squeezed tight, and he could feel the muscled fingers digging hard into his flesh. 'Just move.'

'Not until you take my blindfold off.'

Porter dug his heels into the ground. The man was still holding on to his shoulder. Stand my ground, Porter thought. We have to start this right. Once they start treating me like a prisoner rather than a negotiator, then I'm done for.

The grip on his shoulder started to relax.

'You're not allowed to see the outside of the building,' said the taller man. 'It is too dangerous for us. You must understand this. Now, allow me to take you inside. Then we can remove the blindfold.'

'And bring Hassad to see me?'

'You will meet the man you have come to see, yes.'

Porter started walking. The taller man was guiding him. Underneath, he could tell the ground was soft and sandy. Maybe they were out in the Syrian Desert somewhere. He could sense men all around him, and caught a couple of whispers, but no one was talking out loud. Within a few seconds, they had gone inside some kind of doorway. It was warm – he could sense the temperature change instantly – and he was being led along a corridor. He tried counting the paces: without being able to see anything, it was the only way of getting a sense of the size of the place. Thirty, he reckoned, which made the corridor only about twenty metres long. He started to be steered down a staircase. Ten, fifteen, twenty steps, he counted. That meant they were only one floor down, probably in a basement. Another corridor. This time they walked only about five metres. Then they stopped, and the man let go of his shoulder.

'Can we lose the bloody blindfold now?' snapped Porter.

He could hear his voice echoing around the cramped corridor: from the time it took his voice to bounce back from the walls, he reckoned it was just a short corridor, and at most a couple of rooms.

There was no reply.

Porter could hear the sound of a key being turned in a lock. Then a bolt being shifted back. Next, there was a sudden shove against him, and he was bundled into the room.

'Getting your fucking hands off me,' he snarled.

Another shove. This time Porter could feel four pairs of hands pushing him forwards. They were strong: the skin on the hands was gnarled and tough, like the sole of an old boot, and the muscles behind them were toned and fit. The force of the blow took Porter by surprise and he stumbled. His hands were flailing out desperately – the blindfold meant he still couldn't see anything – and that made it even harder for him to regain his balance. His feet were already wobbling beneath him as the next thump hit him in the middle of the spine. A ripple of pain tore through him. A boot was crashing into his ankles. He could feel himself starting to fall. His arms reached out to grab hold of something, but there was nothing there apart from thin air. He was hurtling towards the ground. There was a moment of sheer terror as he realised he had no idea what he was falling towards: it could be hard stone, it might be shards of glass, they could have tossed him into a well to drown him. In a brief instant, he could remember his instructors in the Regiment telling him that one of the ways the Iraqis tortured their prisoners was to blindfold them, then push them downstairs, because the terror of falling without knowing where you were going was more than most men could bear. I can see their point, he thought grimly. He had thrown his arms around his face to protect it. In the next instant, his body was crashing into the ground. There was something soft and damp on the surface of the floor. Straw, maybe. And beneath that stone. He could feel some bruising on his knees and around his ribs where he had taken the worst impact of the fall, but apart from that he was intact. Nothing broken: he'd have felt the pain by now if a bone had snapped. He felt around. Whether the two men were still standing in the doorway, he had no idea.

'Where the fuck is Hassad?' he growled.

Silence.

He could hear one of the men breathing. And he could hear his own voice echoing around the tiny room.

'I'm supposed to be his bloody guest,' shouted Porter. 'Why the fuck are you treating me like this?'

Porter started to lift himself up from the floor. His hands were reaching up to the back of his head to untie the blindfold. But the knots were strong, and it was taking a moment to unpick them. He started to stand up – and as he did so, the door slammed shut. He could hear the turning of the key in the lock. And then he could hear the sound of metal scratching against metal as the bolt was pushed into place.

He pushed himself up against the door, slamming his fists against it. 'Take me to see Hassad,' he shouted.

The words echoed around the room, taunting him like a hundred different mocking voices.

But the only response was the tread of four sets of boots walking away along the corridor. And then a laugh.

'Fuck it,' he muttered.

For a moment, Porter just rested against the side of the door. He was catching his breath. And, more importantly, trying to catch his thoughts as well.

What the hell have they done to me?

Why have they brought me here?

He started to unpick the knots on the blindfold. It was slow and frustrating, but at least it gave him something to do. It stopped the questions raging through his head: Where have they brought me? Why are they treating me like this? Has it all gone wrong already? Slowly the blindfold came free. He unwrapped the black cloth from his face, and threw it to the floor.

'Shit,' he said. *Maybe I was better off not being able to see anything.*

The cell measured ten feet by fifteen. Up by the doorway, there was enough room for Porter to stand up, but the ceiling sloped away fast, so that by the other end it was no more than four feet high. There was a slit window at the far end of the room, measuring no more than a foot across, to a depth of six inches. It looked out onto a wall, and had bars across it. Outside, it was dark already, but the moon was shining, and a few weak glimmers of light were managing to trickle through the tiny window. It took Porter a few

162

seconds to adjust his eyes. For what? he wondered. There was some straw tossed across the rough stone floor, but it must have been here for at least a year, Porter reckoned, because it was damp and sodden with dirt. He knelt down to where he had fallen from the doorway. There was some smeared blood on the floor, but he could tell it wasn't his: it was caked crimson and dry, so it must have been at least a day or two old. Next to it there was a human tooth, with some dried blood caked around its torn root, which looked if it had fallen from a man's mouth during a beating. Porter kicked it away with the toe of his boot, then explored the rest of the cell. There was some writing on the wall but all of it was in Arabic: some of the letters looked like they had been scratched into the walls with a man's fingernails. In one corner was the only object of any sort in the room, a metal bucket with a vile, putrid smell rising out of it. The bucket was half filled with water, and there was a human turd floating on its scummy surface.

So much for the legendary Arab hospitality, thought Porter bitterly.

He leant back against the wall. He felt exhausted. As he looked into the darkness, he tried to take stock of what had just happened. He had thought for the last couple of days about what he would do when he got here, about how he would handle the kidnappers, and how he would handle Hassad. But he'd hadn't expected to be thrown straight into a prison.

Whatever was about to happen next, it wasn't going to be good. There was no point in kidding himself about that.

Maybe I've miscalculated, he thought. Who knows who we killed on that mission all those years ago? A dozen or more Hezbollah guys had been taken out on that job. We weren't even counting. It could have been somebody's father or brother. They might well have been looking for revenge all this time. After all, nobody clings on to a grudge

163

like an Arab. And nobody is ever more determined to take their vengeance in blood.

Maybe Hassad just said I could come out here so that he could kill me.

And who could blame him?

There's unfinished business between us and he probably knows it.

Perhaps this is how it ends. A short, brutal fight in a dark cell. And then a knife to the throat.

Porter sat down on the straw, resting his back against the wall. The clouds had obscured the moon, and the cell was plunged into near total darkness. Up above, Porter could hear a couple of vehicles move around, and then he heard a couple of shouts. One of the commands appeared to be in English, but Porter reckoned he must have misheard. Soon, it fell completely silent. He had no idea what time it was – the Firm hadn't supplied him with a watch and it was years since he'd owned one himself – but he guessed it must be at least midnight. Friday morning already, he told himself. Tomorrow night Katie Dartmouth will have been executed. And they can toss her into whatever grave they have already dug for me.

Peering into the darkness, Porter decided that he didn't mind dying that much, just so long as it was quick and painless. If he was being honest with himself, he'd died a long time ago. The moment that Hassad had come back from unconsciousness and shot my mates, my life was over. There was nothing worth living for after that. I was just punching out the hours at the factory, until the foreman called the whistle on my time.

But now at least I've done something for Sandy, he thought.

And regrets? Christ, where would you even start? But right at the top of the list would be not killing the Hassad bastard.

He could hear the turning of the key in the lock. Porter's muscles tensed as soon as he heard the mechanism start to move. He could hear the rusty, scratchy bolt being thrown back. And then the door started to open.

Porter stood up.

A man was walking into the room. He must have weighed at least three hundred pounds, but like a sumo wrestler, it was strong, meaty flesh, as much muscle as flab. He was wearing black jeans and a black T-shirt. His face was pudgy and mean, dark-coloured, and with tiny eyes and a small nose like a pig's.

And in his hand, he was carrying a strip of thick, black hosepipe.

Porter instinctively stepped backwards.

'Where the hell is Hassad?' he snapped.

The man said nothing.

'We had a deal,' said Porter, the anger evident in every syllable.

The man was cradling the hosepipe in the palm of his fist.

'I spoke to Hassad, and he told me to meet him here,' Porter shouted. 'He gave me his word, soldier to soldier. I saved the bastard's life once. Doesn't that mean a sodding thing to you people?'

The man took another step forward. His eyes were staring straight into Porter, and there was something about his expression that made Porter nervous. He'd seen it dozens of times before on drunks tooled up and high on the prospect of violence.

'Who the fuck are you?' said Porter.

'Your worst nightmare,' replied the man. He spoke in cold, slow English, with a heavy Middle Eastern accent.

He cracked the hosepipe. It lashed through the air, smashing into the side of Porter's chest. The plastic snapped into his shirt and then into his skin with the force of a hailstorm of bullets. Porter screamed out in pain: a howl of agony that started somewhere deep inside his lungs, and erupted through his mouth with the force of a volcano. As he did so, he was staggering backwards, but his head was cracking against the narrow, sloping ceiling. 'Get the fuck away from me,' Porter shouted.

The hosepipe cracked through the air once again. Instinctively, Porter raised his hands to protect himself but it was no good. It smashed past his hands, and laced itself around his chest, neck and throat. The force of the impact rocked him back, crashing his head once more against the low ceiling. He could feel his eyes dancing and his brain spinning. The blows were emptying all the air out of his lungs, and sending a bolt of pain stabbing through him.

Underneath him, Porter could feel his knees buckling. He was reaching out for something to hold on to but there was nothing there.

The whip crashed down once more.

'Who the fuck . . .' mumbled Porter, hardly even able to breathe.

But the words died on his lips.

He had already lost consciousness.

SIXTEEN

Porter opened first one eye, then the other.

He was half awake, half asleep, and in that dreamlike state he could barely remember what had happened to him. His throat was parched dry, and his stomach felt as if it was only slowly recovering from a violent sickness. He could recall the outlines of his mission, arriving in Beirut, travelling halfway across the Lebanon, and then being met by the men who were supposed to take him to meet Hassad.

And then he remembered where it had all gone wrong, and suddenly he woke up completely.

'Shit,' he muttered.

He could hear the fear and dread in his own voice.

Porter was strapped to a chair, and the chair itself appeared to be nailed into the floor. There were ropes around his chest, his arms and his legs, making it impossible for him to do more than twitch a few muscles. They must have come in during the night to strap me up, he told himself grimly. To make sure that I couldn't cause any trouble when I came round from the beating.

But why?

A few pale glimmers of light were sneaking through the tiny window of the cell. It must be morning, Porter told himself, although he had no way of knowing for sure what time it was or even which day.

The door started to creak open. Porter followed it with his eyes, and found it impossible to suppress a glimmer of hope that it might be Hassad. Disappointment, he knew, was inevitable. As the door swung completely open, the same fat bastard who had whipped him into unconsciousness last night stepped slowly into the room. Same black clothes. Same pudgy face. And the same streak of pure violence running through his eyes.

Porter looked straight at him, and he could feel every muscle in his body tensing in anger, but he resolved to remain silent.

The man took two paces forward, so that his imposing bulk was just five feet away from the chair to which Porter was strapped.

'I haven't killed any Zionist, imperialist scum for more than a week,' he said. The words were pronounced in whiny, heavily accented English. 'So I think I'm going to enjoy this.'

It takes character to listen to your own death sentence in silence, thought Porter. But maybe when you don't care any more it doesn't feel so bad.

'It is ten o'clock now,' the man continued. 'The beheading – *your* beheading – is scheduled for one hour.'

Porter flinched. It was an involuntary instinctive twitching of the muscles, one that he couldn't control, and he felt instantly ashamed of himself. Take this like a soldier, he told himself. It is the last shred of dignity left to you.

'Before then, we offer you the chance to make your peace with Allah.'

'I'll make peace with my own God, thank you,' Porter spat contemptuously.

The man smiled. 'You will die in accordance with the teaching of the Koran,' he said. 'That is our way, and if you attempt to resist us, you will only make things worse for yourself. You will be led from here, and taken to a court-yard, where you will be allowed to face Mecca. You will be allowed to kneel, and whether you wear a blindfold or not is up to you.' The man's face creased up in another pudgy smile. 'The blade will be sharp, but of course you are a strong man, with a thick neck, and as I am sure you can imagine, it is hard for even the most skilful swordsman to sever a neck in one blow. I have watched several beheadings and the head nearly always comes away from the neck on the third or fourth strike of the sword.'

Porter could feel the muscles on his arms straining against the ropes that bound him to the chair: if there was even the remotest possibility of release, he would flatten the bastard in a hailstorm of punches. But there was not so much as a millimetre of leeway in his bindings.

The man started to unroll some sheets of paper he was holding in his hand.

'The holy book says, "When a man dies they who survive him ask what property he has left behind. The angel who bends over the dying man asks what good deed he has sent before him."' He paused. 'You should take heed of those words.'

Porter caught his breath inwardly, and remained silent.

The man folded his arms and began to pray, and as he did so, his voice turned from a whine into a slow, respectful chant.

> 'In the Name of God, the Merciful, the Compassionate
> Praise be to God, Lord of the Universe,
> The Compassionate, the Merciful,
> Sovereign of the Day of Judgement!
> You alone we worship, and to You alone we turn for help.
> Guide us to the straight path,
> The path of those whom You have favoured,
> Not of those who have incurred Your wrath,
> Nor of those who have gone astray.'

Porter could feel a bead of cold sweat running down the

back of his spine. I don't mind dying, he thought bitterly. *But I could do without the bloody RE lesson.*

The man had briefly closed his eyes at the end of the prayer, in a moment of religious contemplation, but now he opened them again. 'I will leave these with you,' he said, holding out the few sheets of paper in his hand. 'You are an infidel, and maybe you wish to die an infidel. That is your choice. But we are holy men, and we wish you to have the opportunity to come to know the one and true God before you pass from this world to the next.'

'Maybe I'd rather not die at all,' growled Porter.

'A soldier always wants to die,' said the man.

He placed the sheets of paper down on Porter's lap. It took all the self-control Porter could muster to stop himself from spitting on them. Instead, he merely looked up impassively into the man's eyes. Don't give him the satisfaction of even the smallest victory over you, he told himself. It will just be one more regret to take with you to your grave.

Porter watched as the door clunked shut, and listened as the bolt was slotted into place. Even though he was securely bound to the chair, with no possibility of freeing himself, they weren't taking any chances on his escape. Porter could feel his heart pounding against his ribcage. His blood was beating furiously, and even though the cell was dark and damp it was impossible to stop the sweat dripping down his back.

Now there can be no doubt, he told himself morosely. Within the hour, I shall be dead.

He was afraid, he didn't mind admitting that. When he was a soldier he knew he might die, but that was in a firefight, with a weapon in his hand, when he would at least have had a chance to defend himself. This was different: a cold and premeditated death at the hands of a bunch of religious psychopaths and gangsters. Of all the ways to go, Porter reckoned, being murdered was the worst, for the simple reason that some bastard was getting the better of you.

And it made it worse to die without knowing who was killing you or why they wanted you dead so badly?

He peered into the darkness. His arms were still straining against the ropes binding him to the chair, but he knew it was useless: the wrestling with the bindings was just the instinctive desperate reaction of a condemned man, like a person who has been accidentally buried alive clawing hopelessly at the lid of their own coffin.

Hassad wasn't here, he told himself. Or at least, if he was, he had no intention of showing himself. If it had been a trick all along, just to lure me out here to my death, then I don't suppose he is about to change his mind now. But maybe it isn't a trick? Perhaps someone back at the Firm betrayed me. Maybe someone who wants Katie Dartmouth to die, perhaps so the government will fall? After all, someone already tried to kill me back in London. Who's to say they aren't trying again out here? And this time, they look like making a better job of it.

I can wrestle with the riddle. But unless the bastard chooses to tell me in the last seconds before the sword cuts into the back of my neck, I will never know the answer.

Porter tried to calm himself. He knew he had to keep himself together if he was to walk out of here and face his execution. Avoiding humiliation was the only shred of control he had left over what remained of his life, and he was determined not to squander that now: for all he knew, the beheading might be broadcast on television or the Internet. The minutes were ticking by, although without a watch he had no sure way of knowing how much time was left to him. Half an hour maybe? It could even be less.

What's the bloody point of the last hour? he asked himself bitterly. If they were going to kill me why didn't they just do it in the back of the car last night?

Just then, a noise echoed down through the tiny slit window.

Gunfire.

Porter froze. He felt certain of it.

The noise he had just heard was gunfire.

He tried to turn round but it was impossible. The ropes binding him to the chair lashed him in place. All he could rely upon were his ears. And they were telling him the place was under attack.

Heavy attack.

With RPGs and machine guns.

'Move the fuck up against the wall.'

Porter sat bolt upright, the ropes cutting into his skin as he did so. It was an English voice, he could have sworn it. It was carried on the breeze and drifted down through the slit window at the back of the cell. It was little more than a murmur by the time it reached Porter's ears. He had to strain his ears to catch it above the din of Arabic and the rattle of gunfire. It was enough to give him hope, however.

Maybe the Firm were tracking me? Maybe Katie Dartmouth is holed up in one of these cells and they've sent some boys in to break us both out.

A condemned man will grab hold of just about any straw, he reminded himself. But it could just be true.

He listened harder, aware of the adrenalin surging through him. There was the sound of gunfire, and a couple of mighty explosions as RPG rounds smashed into concrete walls. He could hear shouting above the din, all of it in Arabic, and he started to think he'd just imagined the English voice. The battle had been raging for three or four minutes now, and showed no signs of abating: the flow of noise rocked from side to side, as the two opposing forces unleashed lethal firepower.

Whatever's going on up there, he thought, it's a hell of a firefight.

172

The bolt.

Porter's eyes shot to the door.

He could hear the bolt being slammed back, then the key turning in the lock.

Who is it now? he asked himself.

As the door opened, Porter briefly hoped it might be a Regiment guy, dressed in the olive-grey uniform he'd once been so proud to wear himself: if the Firm was breaking them out, there was only one unit of soldiers who would get the job. But the figure who stepped through the door was dressed in a long black robe, and had dark skin and a thick black beard. He was at least six feet tall, with thick, muscled forearms.

'I hope you have read those verses,' he said, leaving the door open to the corridor behind him. 'Because within a few seconds you will have to explain yourself to Allah.'

In his right hand, he was holding a long, curved, stainless-steel sword. From one end to the other, it must have measured five feet, Porter reckoned, and with its finely chiselled brass handle it couldn't have weighed less than fifty pounds. It might be a medieval piece of technology but that didn't mean it wasn't one of the most deadly weapons ever created. In the right hands, it could do as much damage as a tank. And the thick, stout hands of the man who had just walked into the room looked as if they knew exactly what to do with it.

Porter could feel his neck numbing with fear. 'I thought you were taking me to the courtyard,' he said.

Up above, he could still hear the sound of gunfire. They're under attack, Porter thought. And they want to finish me off while they still can.

'You are facing Mecca,' said the swordsman. 'This is as good a place to die as any.'

He was standing behind Porter now, so close that he could smell the man's warm, stale breath. Porter's hands started shaking slightly as the executioner drew even closer. He put his sword against the chair, and Porter could feel the cold steel of the weapon touching his skin. Drawing a black cloth from his pocket, he placed his warm hand across Porter's face as if to close his eyes, then tied the blindfold into position. As he did so, Porter was plunged into darkness, and a sense of terror started to overcome him. Get ready for it, thought Porter bitterly. It is dark all the time where you're going, mate.

He could hear the executioner picking up the sword. Then he felt a slight stab in the neck, where the swordsman had nicked his skin, drawing a few drops of blood. It was a technique Arab executioners had developed over the centuries to prime their victims for the blow that would kill them: a small nick numbed and stiffened the neck, making it easier for the blade to sever the neck.

And then he could hear the slight movement of the sword through the air.

Porter closed his eyes tight, even though he could see nothing through the blindfold. His knuckles were white and shaking, and he felt as if he was about to vomit.

So this is it, he thought grimly.

'First your tooth,' said the executioner.

Porter was confused. What could he possibly mean?

He felt the man's hand gripping his neck. With his fingers, he prised Porter's jaw apart, and slammed something inside.

Some kind of metal, Porter judged. Maybe a wrench.

He reeled back in pain, and tried to shake his jaw away, but the man was too strong for him.

The wrench was smashing down into his lower left jaw.

Just then, he heard a terrifying crash behind him. It was as if a wall had fallen down.

The noise was so loud that it echoed viciously around the tiny, dank cell. It burst onto Porter's eardrums, exploding within his brain. Then there was a shot, and another. The rattle of gunfire and the smell of smoke filled the room.

He could hear one body falling to the floor. Maybe two. In the confusion, and in the darkness behind the blindfold, it was impossible to tell.

'Who's there?' he shouted.

Nothing. Silence.

'Who the fuck is it?'

Porter could feel a blade against his skin. It was small, but still sharp, and he could feel a hand next to it. There was a sharp sound, then a tug, as the blade cut through the ropes that were binding him to the chair. First the ropes around his hands were severed, then his legs, and finally the bindings around his chest.

For a moment, Porter just sat there, immobilised. Fear and shock had frozen him. Then up above, he could hear the dull rattle of gunfire cranking up again. Whatever kind of danger he was in, it was far from over.

He stood unsteadily to his feet, taking a second to restore his sense of balance.

Reaching behind his neck, he grabbed the blindfold and ripped it free from his face. He blinked once, then twice, taking time to adjust to the dim, fading light of the cell. The wall that led up and out towards the courtyard had been smashed down by a big Mercedes Unimog truck – there was dust and rubble everywhere where the huge front end of the vehicle had punched a hole straight through the bricks.

Porter glanced across to the man standing before him, the man who had just rescued him.

Many years had passed since he had last laid eyes on him. He had grown older, turned from a boy into a man, and the years had hardened as well as aged him.

But there was no mistaking the face. It was burned into Porter's memory, the way a branding iron is burned into the flesh of a bull.

Hassad.

SEVENTEEN

Hassad grabbed hold of Porter by the shoulder. 'We haven't much time,' he hissed. 'Let's get the fuck out of here.'

Porter's eyes were still blinking. Dust and debris were filling the room, and the massive engine on the Unimog was still roaring. Porter's legs were weak and his head was still spinning. He'd kicked back the chair, and glanced only briefly at the executioner: the man was lying flat on the floor, with his sword at his side, his body punctured by three precisely aimed bullets that had smashed through his chest and into his heart.

'Just move,' snapped Hassad, louder this time.

Hassad was already getting into the driver's seat. Porter rushed round the side and climbed into the cabin. He could feel some blood trickling along his gums where the executioner had tried to wrench out one of his teeth, and he had a dozen different cuts and bruises, but otherwise he was in OK shape.

'Let's go,' he muttered.

Hassad hit the reverse gear on the Unimog into position, then tapped his foot on the accelerator. A big piece of machinery built mainly for farmers, the Unimog was like a cross between a pickup truck and a tractor. It had big tyres, four-wheel-drive and an engine powerful enough to kick down a building when it needed to.

It started to edge into reverse. The route it had taken had smashed its way from the courtyard into the room where

176

Porter had been held prisoner, and now it was taking the same route back again. The vehicle shook and shuddered as its tyres crunched backwards over the rubble, but it held steady.

As Hassad flung the steering wheel to the right, turning it swiftly round, Porter looked over to the courtyard. Outside the building, a Honda CR-V had been turned on its side, and was being used as a makeshift wall by four men. By the way they greeted him, Porter guessed they were Hassad's blokes. They were staying close to the underside of the car. All of them were dressed in black, and had neatly trimmed beards and moustaches and close-cropped hair. Two of them had dark glasses pulled down over their eyes. All four had AK-47s gripped tight to their chests, as well as hand pistols and big, lethal hunting knives strapped into their belts. Porter didn't have much idea what they did to the enemy, but they certainly frightened him.

The firefight looked to have subsided.

'Is it safe to leave?' Porter asked.

Hassad barked a few words in Arabic to one of the men behind the Honda, waited for the reply, then looked back at Porter. 'They're all dead,' he said. 'We can move out.'

He gestured to the four men, and one by one they climbed onto the back of the Unimog.

'How many were there?' Porter asked.

'Ten,' said Hassad. 'Tough men as well. We lost men trying to rescue you –'

'Who the fuck *were* they?'

'You don't know?'

Porter shook his head.

Hassad just shrugged. 'If you don't know, then nobody does.'

Porter nodded. 'Thanks for getting me out,' he said tersely.

'I invited you out here,' said Hassad. 'That makes you my guest.'

The Unimog started to roll again. The courtyard was surrounded by a series of farm buildings and barns, as well as the main building where Porter had been kept since last night. Beyond it, at the bottom of the hillside, there was a road leading away from the site. All around him, Porter could see the debris of the battle, and feel the smell of death in the air.

Next to a wall he could see two corpses. And even though both men were covered in dust and blood, Porter could see one of them was white.

'Stop a minute,' snapped Porter.

'We need to leave,' said Hassad. 'There could be more of them.'

'I need to look at these guys.'

He jumped down from the cabin, kneeling down next to the dead body. The guy had taken about two dozen hits, even though the first two or three had probably killed him. The bullets had smashed up his face, turning his skull into paste, and smearing blood over every surface. One eyeball had been blown out, and the other was still bleeding. Even for a corpse he looked in pretty rough shape. From what Porter could see of him, he was almost forty, with dark brown hair, and tanned, grooved skin. He was wearing an olive-green military uniform, the kind you might pick up in an army surplus store. Porter couldn't see any sign of a flag, or insignia. 'Who the hell is he?' said Porter, glancing back up at Hassad.

Hassad just shrugged. Porter didn't get the impression he was very interested in corpses. Maybe he'd seen too many of them.

'What the hell is a white man doing out here, taking British guys hostage?' growled Porter.

He started rifling through his pockets. In one, he found thirty Lebanese pounds, along with some loose change. In another, he found a picture of a woman: dark-haired, with freckled pale skin, pretty but slightly overweight, probably in her late twenties. Other than that, there was nothing that might identify who he was or who he was fighting for. No passport, no credit card, no dog tag. The unknown soldier, thought Porter. And you're welcome to an unmarked grave, mate. *You sodding deserve it.*

'They must have some kit somewhere,' said Porter, looking around.

Hassad grabbed him by the arm. He gestured to the hillside. Now that they were on the other side of the wall, Porter could see the scrubland sloping away to a dusty track. 'We've got to move,' he hissed.

'I need to find out who these bastards were,' snapped Porter.

'We haven't any time,' said Hassad. 'There may be more of them here any minute. There are only a few of us left alive –'

'I need to find out why they bloody took me,' said Porter. 'It might be important.'

Another of Hassad's men was already walking towards them. He was carrying a wounded man who was hobbling, resting on his mate's shoulder.

Hassad flashed him a smile. As he did so, the deformity of his mouth was cruelly apparent: the smile twisted his mouth into a hideous mangled shape that gave no hint of pleasure or humour. 'Welcome back to the Middle East, Mr Porter,' he said. 'Nothing out here is ever what it seems.'

'But –'

'I told you nothing out here is what it seems . . .'

Porter had already noticed the AK-47 slung around Hassad's shoulders was suddenly cocked. His finger was on the trigger, and there was no mistaking the casual way its black metal barrel was pointing straight at Porter's chest. A mistake? Not likely, thought Porter.

'Take your clothes off,' Hassad snapped.

'What –'

'I said, take your clothes off. We need to make sure you are clean.'

As he finished the sentence, he barked something in Arabic to one of his men. The guy came back from the Unimog with a pair of black jeans, a sweatshirt and some trainers, and a can of petrol. Porter realised what they were doing: he'd have done the same in their position.

They wanted to make sure he didn't have any bugs on him before they took him back to their base.

He ripped the clothes off himself, tossing them on the dusty ground. While he was pulling on the fresh jeans, the soldier had already soaked Porter's clothes with petrol, and set fire to them.

'OK,' said Hassad. 'Now we can get out of here.'

EIGHTEEN

The drive took two hours, but it seemed like much longer. The Unimog was at least five or six years old, Porter reckoned, and its suspension had taken a hammering from the rough dirt tracks it had spent its life driving along. There were six of them in total: Hassad, the four men who had survived the firefight, plus Porter. Hassad sat in the front, along with the driver, while Porter was squeezed into the back with the other blokes. The wounded man was brave enough, but every jolt and bump in the road was tearing up the wound in his chest, and he was moaning with pain through most of the trip.

Where they were going, Porter had no idea, and he judged it better not to ask. He reckoned they were travelling somewhere through the Lebanese and Syrian borderlands, but the driver was keeping to the dirt tracks, steering away from anything that looked like a main road, so Porter never got a chance to look at a road sign that might help him establish his bearings. From time to time, he could see the lights of a small village, but even if the track they were on went through it, the driver veered off, and pushed the vehicle cross-country until they could connect with the track on the other side of the village. Whether he was doing it because they didn't want to be seen, or because they didn't want Porter to see where he was going, he couldn't tell. A bit of both maybe, he decided. After driving for an hour, they put a blindfold on him, so after that, Porter had even less idea where they were going.

Porter had tried to talk to Hassad when the Unimog had pulled away from its hiding place, but he told him to be quiet. His men had to rest. He handed around some pitta breads, spread with some kind of chickpea mixture, and they all swigged on the same bottle of water. He was grateful for the food even though it didn't taste of much. Then the other blokes in the back went to sleep. As the vehicle powered forward, Porter couldn't get any rest. He was trying to think, to straighten out in his own mind what had just happened, and what he needed to do next. He had no idea who had captured him, or why they wanted him dead. If it wasn't Hassad, then someone must have leaked where he was, and what mission he was on. And that could only be someone back at the Firm.

By the time the Unimog came to a halt, even Porter was fighting off sleep, struggling to keep himself alert. He judged that it must be nine or ten at night. Only twenty-three hours or so until the deadline set for Katie Dartmouth's execution. And probably my own as well, he reflected.

To Porter, their destination looked like a disused mine. The Mercedes had turned off the track, and down a steep, rough slope that led inside a massive crater. There was a roadblock across the track leading into it, manned by three armed men, and even though they knew Hassad they still checked the vehicle before letting it pass. Taking their security seriously, Porter noted. This place is hard enough to get into. It will be even harder to get out again.

Around him, he could see some tall cranes, and a long conveyor belt led along the length of the crater towards an old, abandoned processing plant. A metal mine, thought Porter. Maybe copper or zinc. The crater must have measured two hundred yards, by a hundred: perhaps they started with an open-cast mine and then went underground, because there were doorways dotted around the crater that looked as if they led down into mineshafts. A perfect place to keep a hostage. Discreet, easy to defend, and virtually impossible to escape from. Even if I did manage to get Katie loose, how would I ever get her out of here?

'Wait here,' said Hassad, as they all climbed out of the Unimog.

Porter stood for a moment next to the vehicle. The wounded man was already being taken towards one of the mineshafts, but the other men stayed behind next to Porter, all of them cradling their AK-47s in their chests. Porter was sure he could smell some wild flowers in the night air, and there was a musty, metallic aroma that came from the piles of broken ore scattered around the crater. Copper, Porter reckoned. He'd had a mate who'd been a plumber once, and whenever you met the bloke for drink, he always had the same smell of burnt copper clinging to his skin after a day's work.

Hassad had returned to the vehicle and was looking straight at Porter. 'Are you here to kill us?'

Porter didn't so much as blink. 'We just want a discussion.'

'Then come,' he said. 'We'll talk inside.'

Porter followed him across the crater. It was a walk of about thirty metres to the mineshaft, and they completed it in silence. As he walked, Porter was trying to make a mental recce of the layout of the place. Alongside the Mercedes, there were two other vehicles: a small Skoda Felicia, and a big Honda CR-V that had a couple of dents in its side. Close by, he saw a small, diesel-powered electricity generator that was obviously powering the place. He'd already seen a few men go in and out of the mineshaft, so he calculated there must be a whole platoon of Hezbollah fighters here. How many? I'm probably about to find out.

Hassad pushed open the doorway. The entrance to the mine opened up into a small, low room, with a single electric lamp at one side. The walls were composed of a sandy, stained rock, cut into deep grooves where the mineshaft had been sunk. Directly in front of them was a metal cage lift. Hassad slung the wire door open, and instructed Porter to step inside before he followed and pulled the lever. The lift started to drop: Porter judged they'd descended at least twenty-five or thirty metres into the ground before the lift came to a juddering halt.

As Porter stepped out, he could see a corridor leading into the interior of the abandoned quarry. Single-bulb electric lights were slung up on the low ceiling every twenty metres, but they did no more than cast a pale, murky light through the space. Hassad unhooked a gas lamp from the wall, turning up its light, and then starting to descend a rickety flight of wooden steps. Porter counted thirty steps down, twisting through a narrow channel carved into the rock. Glimpses of the copper could just about be seen in the walls. At the bottom, the space widened out into a cave, with six different tunnels leading off in different directions. In the centre, there was some broken and rusty machinery that must once have been used to cut out the ore and lift it up to the surface, but from the state of it Porter guessed it must have been years since the mine was worked. Some water was dripping through the roof. Hassad took the first tunnel, a sharp left from the bottom of the staircase.

The passageway was narrow, no more than four feet across, and only six feet high: it had been carved out of the rock to ferry the miners deep into the ground, and there was no room for more than one man to pass at the same time. One bloke with an assault rifle could hold this place against an army of men, Porter reflected grimly. They had chosen it with care. Even if the British did find out where Katie Dartmouth was being held, they could send in a whole battalion and still not have much chance of getting her out.

Not alive anyway.

Hassad led him into a small room. It measured ten feet by six, there was a straw bed in one corner, and some coffee was brewing on a stove made from hot bricks. There was a sweet, sticky smell to the air that Porter found nauseating. In one corner, there was a lamp, but there was a cloth thrown across it, as if Hassad didn't like the light too much. He poured some coffee into two small white cups, and handed one to Porter. 'So now we can talk,' he said flatly.

Porter took a hit of the coffee. It was thick and black, with a sludge of grounds at the bottom. He could feel it hitting his veins, washing aside some the exhaustion that had afflicted him since he'd touched down in this country. He had thought about this moment for the last few days, but now it was here, he realised you couldn't plan a deal like this one. Sometimes a man had to be guided by his wits and his instincts alone. If they weren't good enough to get him through, then it was no use imagining anything else would.

'You know who they were, don't you?'

'Who?' said Hassad.

'The bastards who took me.'

Hassad drained the last of his coffee and grabbed a handful of cashew nuts from a bowl next to the coffee pot. In the semi-darkness of the room, you could hardly see the deformity around his mouth. You could see the tiredness, however. This was a man who spent his life living underground, and only emerged blinking into the daylight for the occasional fierce firefight.

'I went to the café to find you,' said Hassad. 'It was as I had arranged it. When I arrived, you weren't there, but I spoke to the barman, and he said that you had been led away by two men.'

'They had the password.'

'Then you were betrayed,' said Hassad. 'The British can't be trusted. That won't come as news to anyone down here.'

'Who says it wasn't one of your people who betrayed

me?' said Porter. 'There could be plenty of people who didn't want me to come here.'

'Everyone here is loyal to me, and loyal to the cause,' said Hassad. 'There are no traitors within Hezbollah.' A thin smile twisted up his deformed mouth. 'Betrayal is a British speciality.'

'The bastards who took me looked like Arabs to me.'

'They are, but they work for a company called Connaught Security Services,' said Hassad. There was no emotion in his voice. Porter realised he was in the company of a soldier: a man who killed people when he had to, but who always respected his enemy.

'It's a British private security firm, with offices throughout the Middle East. They are in Iraq, in Afghanistan, and out here as well. They work for whoever pays them. Mining companies, oil companies, airlines. And the British government as well when it suits them.'

But why the hell did they take me? Porter asked himself. Who were they working for?

'We have contacts inside their organisation, which was how we found out that they had taken you, and where,' said Hassad. 'Once we knew that, we had no choice but to come and get you. Three of my men died, however.' He looked sternly at Porter. 'Your life doesn't come cheap, Mr Porter. Now it is time to tell me why you are here.'

'To bring Katie Dartmouth home,' said Porter.

Hassad listened to the statement without a flicker of reaction.

'You have details, I suppose, of your government's willingness to bring its troops home from Iraq,' he said flatly. 'We have already said the woman will be released so long as this one simple condition is met.'

Porter took a step forward. 'Is she here?'

Hassad nodded.

'I want to see her.'

There was a flicker of doubt across Hassad's face, but then the twisted mouth turned up into a smile.

'Of course,' he replied.

He started to walk from the room. Porter followed him, out into the corridor, and back along to the main meeting point at the bottom of the staircase. Hassad took another tunnel. It stretched for thirty metres, although Porter quickly realised the lamp wasn't powerful enough to illuminate it to the end. They had walked for ten metres along its length when Hassad suddenly stopped. Right in front of him there was a solid steel door built into the side of the rock. Two men were standing outside, both of them dressed in black, and with AK-47s strapped to their chests. Hassad nodded to them, and they nodded back, but neither of them spoke. Hassad pushed the door open, then stepped inside. 'This way,' he said, glancing back.

Porter started to follow. The pictures of Katie Dartmouth broadcast over the Internet and TV in the days after her captivity had been burned into his memory. But this was different. This was real life.

Hassad extinguished the gas lamp: an electric line had been fed down here from the generator above, and there were two lamps illuminating the room, making it far brighter than anywhere else in the mine. The room was a decent size, significantly larger than Hassad's own room, or any of the other spaces Porter had seen cut into the rock. It was at least fifteen feet deep and twenty wide. The walls were squarer than they were elsewhere, and the room felt dry: there was none of the metallic dampness that filled the rest of the mine. There was a smell of sweat and excrement, like walking past an open sewer. In one corner, there was a webcam fixed to a wooden tripod: Hassad switched it off as soon as they stepped inside. But although the room was probably better than he expected, Katie Dartmouth herself looked far worse. As Porter looked at her, he could feel his heart sinking within his chest. What kind of barbarians could do this to an innocent woman? What kind of political point could possibly be worth this kind of suffering? How low into the pits of cruelty can a man sink that he would make another human being endure this amount of humiliation and pain?

He could feel the anger flowing through his veins. If you didn't deserve to die for what you did to me sixteen years ago, then you've certainly put the ink on your own death warrant with what you are doing right here and right now. No man capable of inflicting that kind of misery can complain about the grisly death that justly awaits him.

Katie was tied to a stake, exactly as she had been depicted on television – though at least the gag had been removed. It was a thick wooden pole, stripped of its bark, and dug deep into the ground. Her hands were strapped behind her back, held in place with thick leather bindings, and her feet and her chest were lashed to the stake as well. It was impossible for her to move a muscle from her neck downwards. She was wearing the clothes she had been captured in, but by now they were stained and filthy. Her blouse was ripped, and there was a gash running down the side of her blue jeans. No one had unstrapped her to allow her to go to the toilet, so it was obvious she had no choice but to soil herself where she was. A vile stench was rising up from her stake, and around her feet it was possible to see small piles of human waste. It was her face that looked the worst, though. Her eyes were bloodshot and wasted, with a dark, hollow look to them, and the skin across her face was already dry, stretched and caked with sweat, dirt and blood. There was a cut across one cheekbone, which had dried into an ugly scar, but with some blood still seeping from the wound. And her hair was matted, thick with sweat, and was starting to form itself into ugly clumps that would soon fall clean away from her head.

The pretty young television star who was filling a

thousand newspaper front pages back in Britain was long gone. Instead, her place was taken by a haggard, beaten person, who was already closer to a corpse than a woman.

How long exactly she had been tied to this stake, it was impossible for Porter to tell. Probably since they took the poor girl late on Sunday night. That made five continuous nights now. It would be virtually impossible for her to get any sleep, nor did it look as if they had been feeding her. There was a jug of water on a table next to her, but there was no way she could reach it with her arms bound behind her back. The closer you looked at her, Porter realised, the more of a miracle it was that she had survived this long. Another day, and the bastards probably wouldn't need to chop her head off. She'd be dead already.

They might not have tortured her – not yet anyway – Porter told himself, but that made no difference. They were treating her worse than any animal.

Her eyes rolled towards his, the eyeballs moving slowly in their sockets. Porter had seen eyes like that before. There were plenty of junkies out on the streets, and they all had dilated pupils and eyeballs they were incapable of moving properly. It was one of the ways of spotting them, and Porter was always quick to steer clear of the crackheads sleeping rough on the streets: they were violent and dangerous, and usually so out of their heads they would attack you for no reason. Her eyes were exactly the same: slow, empty, full of pain, and devoid of any hope. But it wasn't any kind of drug that had made her like that. It was the bastard standing right next to him.

Porter clenched his fists. It would take a man of iron self-discipline not to land a punch on Hassad's face right now. And he had never been a man who had counted self-control among whatever qualities he might possess.

It was clear Katie Dartmouth was finding it hard to focus. Her mouth was immobile, and her face was too caked in

189

blood and sweat for any sort of expression to be read into it. But you could see from her eyes she was confused and terrified. The last few days had taught her to greet every new moment with dread and loathing, and this one was no different. She was looking at Porter, struggling to focus, and yet as she did so, she seemed to flinch. 'Are you . . .?'

She was struggling to speak, but it sounded more like the strangled cry of a dying animal than any noise a human might make. Again, Porter could feel a wave of anger welling up inside him. Her lips were so dry, and her throat so weak that it was clearly painful for her even to finish the sentence. 'Are you . . .?' she started again, this time trying to move her head upwards slightly so that she could see him properly.

'I'm English, yes,' said Porter, looking straight at her.

For the first time it was possible to see something other than despair in her eyes. Not hope exactly, Porter realised. That would be putting it too strongly. But there was some strength there that he hadn't seen when he'd first walked in: a sign that she might be able to struggle through the next few hours at least.

'Who . . .?'

Suddenly she started to cough violently. Her whole body had become badly dehydrated over the last few days and as she started to speak, her throat seized up. Porter could see the shame and humiliation in her eyes as the saliva started to dribble down the front of her mouth. Without being able to lift either of her hands, there was nothing she could do to stop it.

'Who are you?' she said finally when she managed to bring the coughing under control.

'I'm the best news you've had since you got here,' said Porter.

It looked as if she was attempting a smile, but her face was too weak for the muscles to respond. 'I . . . I . . .'

The coughing started up again: a vicious hacking sound

that appeared to throttle her, and caused teardrops to start forming around her strained and tired eyes.

'Give her some bloody water,' snapped Porter.

Hassad remained immobile, neither saying nor doing anything.

'Fuck it, man, she'll be bloody dead by tomorrow morning,' growled Porter.

He walked over to the jug of water, picked it up and poured some into the tin cup next to it. Then he stood next to Katie, holding the back of her head in his hand. The stench was vile, worse than anything he had ever experienced even while he was sleeping rough. Anyone who has ever been homeless has developed a strong stomach, but Porter was struggling to keep himself from vomiting. He pushed the cup up to her lips, holding her head in position to give her any chance of drinking it. Her throat was so dry that at first the water just washed over her lips, the way a heavy rainfall will wash over the land, but eventually she was able to swallow some of the water, gulping it down greedily. When the cup was empty, Porter turned round to refill it from the jug. But Hassad was now holding it. 'Here, let me,' he said contemptuously.

He filled the tin cup, and held it up to Katie's mouth. The first hit of water had started to strengthen her, and she was better able to drink this time: as soon as the cup was at her mouth, she drank down its entire contents in two swift gulps, with hardly a single drop spilling out over her face. 'We need to get you looking alive for the camera,' said Hassad. 'That way it will be all the more shocking when your head is severed from these shoulders for all the viewers watching back at home.'

'You can't execute her,' snapped Porter.

'I can and I will,' said Hassad.

'Who sent you?' said Katie, her eyes darting nervously from Porter to Hassad.

'Nobody sent me,' said Porter. 'I came of my own accord.'

'For . . .' She started to cough again, and it took her nearly a minute to bring it under control. 'For what?'

'I might be able to get you out of here.'

Her head moved slightly from side to side. It was no more than a flick of the neck, and maybe she was just trying to stretch the few muscles she had been left in control of. But Porter could see something else in her expression. She didn't believe him. Even worse, she didn't want to believe him. He'd seen the same looks sometimes in the faces of guys dossing down in the street. They'd given up all hope. They no longer reckoned they could do anything for themselves, nor would anyone else be able to rescue them. They were just waiting to die. And the sooner their lives ended, the better.

'Just wait and see,' muttered Porter, as Hassad took hold of his shoulder, and guided him back towards the door.

But she had already closed her eyes.

Hassad looked back at her. 'One more night of suffering, and then your ordeal will be over,' he said softly.

I'll get you away from these bastards, Porter said to himself. *Or I'll sure as hell die trying.*

NINETEEN

Porter walked alongside Hassad through the narrow, dank corridor. He knew the memory of what he had just seen would remain with him for the rest of his life – all twenty hours of it. The woman tied to that stake was nothing like the young, tough, resourceful woman who was being talked about every night on the television back at home. She had been boiled down to nothing more than a skeleton with some skin and veins wrapped around it.

The bastards had only had her for five days. And they'd already drained every ounce of spirit and resistance out of her.

Porter knew he had to stay calm. Inside he was raging, but he knew he had to conceal that from Hassad. To show even the slightest trace of emotion would be a mistake. He had to make Hassad believe that he was here as a negotiator. He had to convince the man there was something he could do for him, some deal he could offer, that would persuade him to at least postpone the execution for a few days. If nothing else, maybe he could get them to cut her down from that stake, and let her get a few hours' rest.

But what? They had discussed it back at the Firm, and apart from releasing the prisoner in Guantànamo Bay nothing they had suggested sounded very convincing. Sometime in the next few hours, he realised, he would have to make the toughest call of his life so far. Shall I try and negotiate? Or should I just concentrate on breaking Katie out with my bare hands?

But what the hell can I do? Just one man against maybe dozens of them?

It was just a short walk back to the main junction where the staircase down from the lift shaft ended. Hezbollah had obviously chosen this part of the mine as their main base. How far the mine extended, there was no way of telling for sure: from the surface it looked like it had once been a pretty big operation, so it could go on for miles and miles. Even if only a tiny fraction of it was occupied, Hassad and his men would know the entire layout, and would almost certainly have booby-trapped the rest of the place to deal with any potential intruders. Even if by some miracle I knew exactly where we were, and I managed to transmit the location back to London, the Regiment would find this place tough to break into.

Porter was surveying the territory as he walked, making sure he knew every inch of the ground, and committed every face to his memory. The same two guards had still been standing mute outside Katie's door, but he reckoned there must be a shift change, probably three times a day: in any well-organised army, eight hours was the maximum sentry duty you could expect a man to perform before he started getting tired and careless, and Hassad's mob looked pretty professional to Porter. He made a mental note to see if he could figure out the time of the shift change: there might be a few seconds in which there was a chance to sneak into Katie's room unnoticed. As they walked into the main meeting point of the tunnels, Porter took note of another pair of heavily armed men standing guard at the bottom of the staircase. In total, Porter reckoned he had seen between fifteen and twenty different guys since they had arrived here, including the blokes they'd driven with in the Mercedes. As a rough rule of thumb, he calculated there could well be double that: some men would be sleeping, some would just be in different parts of the mine, some would up on guard duty above ground. That meant there could be anything up to forty Hezbollah fighters down here.

Forty to one, thought Porter grimly. That's just suicide.

Hassad steered him towards the third tunnel leading away from the main meeting place. Like the corridor in which Katie was incarcerated, it stretched back about thirty yards, except at the end this one dropped into what looked like a deep crevice the mining company must have cut into the rock. This must be where some of the men kip down, Porter reckoned. There were a few small rooms leading off the corridor, each one with three or four straw beds on the damp ground. Electric lamps illuminated part of the way, but some of them had been turned off, probably to save power. He saw a few men sitting around in each room. Some of them were cleaning their guns, or repacking the ammunition in their belts. One or two were reading or writing letters. The rest were just staring into space. Same as soldiers anywhere, thought Porter. They were trying to get as much rest as they could before the next firestorm kicked off.

'This will be your room,' said Hassad. 'So long as you are our guest, then you can stay here.'

How long are they expecting me to stay here? Porter wondered. Their plan is to kill Katie tomorrow evening. Maybe I'm the next hostage after they've finished with her.

He pushed open the door. It was no more than a cave: a space where the miners had blasted into the rock years ago. It was four metres deep and about three metres wide. Hassad knelt down to switch on an electric lamp, which filled the space with a pale, golden light. There was a straw bed and a bucket in the corner with some water in it. From the smell of the place, some men had been kipping down here pretty recently, but they seemed to have cleared out. 'Wash,' said Hassad. 'We will eat in twenty minutes, and then we will get some rest.' He smiled to himself. 'Tomorrow, after all, is a pretty big day for us.'

Porter turned to face him. The last time they had been this close was seventeen years ago when he had been about to plunge a knife into the man's neck. 'Let me take her place,' he said.

Hassad shook his head.

'You need blood, then take mine,' growled Porter. 'If you let her go, then I'll happily replace her.'

Again, Hassad shook his head. There was no trace of emotion in his eyes. Not even a trace of interest.

'We need headlines,' he said flatly. 'It's the only weapon your leaders understand. Certainly the only weapon with which we can match them blow for blow. And I'm afraid your face isn't pretty enough to make the same kind of impact on the television screens.'

'Then think of the headlines if you release her,' snapped Porter. 'You'll get massive sympathy right throughout the country. And you still have a hostage you can behead if the government doesn't give in to your demands.'

Hassad paused. In his eyes, Porter reckoned he could see a flicker of interest. His twisted mouth was set in a look of concentration, and Porter knew he had to press home what-ever advantage he might briefly have. 'Just think about it,' he said. 'You'd have released Katie, and that would get you a lot of support. I'd be a hero for getting her out of this hellhole. And now it would be my life on the line. The pressure to save me from execution would be intense. You'd be closer to your goal than you can ever imagine.'

Porter was watching Hassad's eyes, and he could see the proposal dying even as he spoke. The man was losing interest, turning away. 'Interesting,' he said finally. 'But not possible.'

'Why the hell not?' said Porter.

He grabbed hold of the fabric of Hassad's T-shirt, but immediately regretted doing so. Don't show too much emotion, he told himself. Don't let the bastards get to you.

Just get closer and closer to them until you can start to win them over. Hassad touched the side of hand that was holding on to his T-shirt disdainfully, and Porter instantly withdrew it. 'Because it would show weakness,' he said. 'You've been a soldier yourself, so you surely know that to show the slightest flexibility, to admit even the possibility of doubt, would be mistake. We are the underdog, remember, and we have to be harder and if necessary crueller than our enemy if we are to get anywhere.'

Porter was about to reply, but Hassad was already leaving. 'One of our men will collect you shortly,' he said.

The door shut behind him, and Porter was confined and alone. He noticed at once that the door wasn't locked. It was just a relatively flimsy piece of wood, wedged into a frame that had been built into the rock. It didn't have a lock, not even a bolt. Even if it did, one strong heave from the shoulders would probably take the whole thing down. Porter tapped against it twice. Chipboard, he decided. Cheap, and weak. If I wanted to, I could walk straight down this corridor, and find my way out of this place.

Except I'm not going to.

They haven't locked me up because they know I'm not going anywhere. Not without Katie Dartmouth anyway.

He walked across to the metal bucket in the corner. The smell of the room wasn't too bad: you could tell blokes had been kipping down on the straw, and certainly nobody had been in to change it, but when you'd been sleeping rough for a few years, you got used to far worse. The air was bad, however: there wasn't any proper ventilation down here, and what oxygen managed to filter its way into the mine was already stale and old. You could taste the bodies it had already passed through with every breath you took, and it made Porter feel more unclean than he had at any point in his life. Dipping his hands into the water, he scooped up the cold water, and splashed it across his face and his hair. It was the same way he'd washed when he was living on the street. At least I'm used to it, he reflected bitterly.

There was no mirror in the room, and no shaving kit either. Porter hadn't shaved since he'd left his room in the Firm, and that was getting on for forty-eight hours ago now. A beard was growing on his face: he'd always been a man who could put on a beard in a few days if he stopped shaving, and, living rough, he'd often had one when he hadn't been able to get to a proper bathroom. Out here it might even be an advantage, he decided. If by some miracle I escape, then it will help me blend in among the local Arabs.

Porter paced around the room once then twice. Even though he didn't know exactly what time it was, he thought it was late on Friday night. The execution was scheduled for eight tomorrow night: that meant if he didn't make any progress with Hassad and the rest of the raghead bastards tonight, he wasn't likely to get a second chance. Tomorrow, they'd all be sharpening their swords, ready for their big moment on TV.

He reckoned that for all their talk – and for all Peregrine Collinson's talk in particular – the Firm hadn't made any more progress in the last forty-eight hours. Katie was right here, and it was as clear as hell that the boys back in London didn't have the faintest clue where 'here' was. If they had, they'd be raiding the place. Tonight. They wouldn't leave it until the last minute. Too risky.

Porter paused for a second. He splashed some more water on his face, trying to clean the dirt that had clung to him from the cell and the firefight. There were a couple of small scabs from the cuts he'd picked up, but they flaked away easily enough. It was nothing too serious. If they do know where she is, then they might come tonight. If the Regiment have discovered this mine, they'll send in a unit, probably around three or four in the morning. Even with regular shift changes, the guards were always a lot sleepier around then, and that pushed the odds up in your favour. They'd probably sneak in a few men first, and try and cut a few throats quietly before they set off the big fireworks. I need to be watching out for that in the next few hours. I might be in the middle of making my own move when suddenly a couple of dozen Regiment guys start rampaging through the place. Dressed the way I am, the bastards will probably shoot me on sight. I'll be just one more incident of 'friendly fire'.

There was a knock on the door. Porter spun round. There was a boy standing in the corridor. He couldn't have been more than thirteen or fourteen, Porter reckoned. His short hair was jet black, and his brown eyes shallow and dark, but there was nothing nervous or immature about the way he held himself. He stood up straight and tall, and carried himself with confidence. You remind me of someone, thought Porter. Someone from years ago. Of course, he told himself. The kid looked just like Hassad did the night I should have killed him all those years ago. A nephew, maybe. Or even a son. Christ, it looks like kidnapping, terrorism and torture is a sodding family business down here.

'Come,' he said. 'We eat now.'

Porter followed him down the corridor. The men had emptied out of the rooms, but he noticed there were still three guys with guns strapped to their chests standing where the corridor hit the main meeting point. They don't trust me that much, thought Porter. If I'd tried to walk out of here, those men would have stopped me.

The boy pointed left. In his head, Porter was starting to get a rough layout of the mine. The staircase brought you down to the meeting point. In one direction, they had the cells, where Katie and maybe a few other unfortunate souls were locked up. In another, there were the few rooms he'd seen earlier where the men kipped down. Next to that, there were a couple of cells with open bars. Inside one, he could see a pair of young Israeli soldiers chained to the wall: from the looks of them, they were slowly starving to death. And now there was this corridor, the one the boy was leading him along. This must be where they do the cooking, and keep all the kit.

As he glanced inside a couple of the small rooms cut into the rock, Porter could see a vast array of munitions. There were stacks of assault rifles: AK-47s mostly, but also a few of the American-made M16s he used to fight with when he was in the Regiment, and some IMI Galils they must have captured from the Israeli Army. There were at least a dozen machine guns, with thirty or forty neatly stacked boxes of ammo. A dozen RPGs. At least ten boxes of hand grenades. And a wall full of handguns: Berettas, Brownings, Colts. A whole bloody alphabet of the things.

Enough to kit out a small army, thought Porter with a grim smile.

Then he corrected himself.

This is a small army.

And the bastards back at Vauxhall expect you to deal with them single-handedly.

The boy led him to the largest room he had yet seen in the mine. It was at least twenty metres deep, and twenty wide, cut to a height of about two and a half metres. The floor was mostly covered with straw, but there were a couple of rugs at its centre. There were no chairs – the blokes were all squatting or kneeling on the rugs – but at the far end there were a couple of long wooden tables with plates of food on them. Along one side, there was a wall of electric lights: about six in total, filling the room with a busy glow. And next to that, there was a bank of computer kit. Porter counted five PCs, each one on its own work table, and two flat-screens TVs that were picking up satellite broadcast signals. Beside them, there was a mess of wires and routers that were feeding data into and out of the cave.

Hunched over them, there was one boy who didn't look more than twenty. Thin, with a straggly beard, and a T-shirt that was at least one size too small for him, he was busily programming one of the computers. The IT department, Porter reflected. That's how they are communicating with the rest of the world. And that's why we can never track them. That kid is smart enough to route any message they send through so many hijacked PCs around the world, the source always remains untraceable.

All the men in the room turned to look at him as soon as he stepped inside. In total, Porter calculated there were around twenty guys in the room. They ranged in ages, from the boy who had led him here, up to a couple of guys who looked like they were past sixty. The bulk of them, however, were in their twenties or thirties. Old enough to know how to fight, thought Porter. But also young enough to be fast on their feet. Just the kind of men you'd want in any army.

Three were clean-shaven, but the rest of them all had black beards. There was no formal uniform. Most of the men were dressed in jeans, trainers and a shirt. All of them were armed. There were curved, brutally sharp knives tucked into the waists of their trousers, and pistols tucked neatly into their pockets. A few still had their assault rifles strapped to their chests, others had checked them in at the door. Christ, thought Porter, a man feels underdressed in this place if he doesn't have at least a couple of hundred rounds on him.

'You must be hungry,' said Hassad.

His tone was formal, polite, yet distant as well, Porter noted. He must remember that he killed my mates, and he must know that I'm not likely to forgive that. I'd be distant as well if I thought a bloke had travelled a couple of thousand miles just to cut my throat.

'Starving,' said Porter.

It was true as well. Porter hadn't had anything proper to eat since he'd picked up some grub at the bus stop. He hadn't thought about it, but now he could feel the hunger chewing away at his stomach. The men were eating out of tin containers, very similar to the ones Porter had used out in the field when he was in the army. There were plates of food spread across the wooden table: piles of flat, warm pitta bread, some salads made of olives, cucumbers and chickpeas, and piles of cold lamb and chicken, all of them covered in spicy sauces. Porter chucked come chicken and lamb into the pitta, and put some of the salad on the side. Then he took a knife and fork, and followed Hassad towards the centre of the room. 'Why not give Katie something to eat?' he said.

Hassad shook his head. 'I know you think we are cruel men, but really it isn't true,' he replied. 'A woman dies better on an empty stomach.'

'Bollocks,' snapped Porter. 'Even on death row they give a man a decent last meal.'

'That is not our way,' said Hassad, his voice barely more than a whisper. 'Believe me, when a person is beheaded, then their bowels automatically empty. It is better if there is nothing there. We do not wish to humiliate her. Insofar as it is possible, we would like her to have a dignified death, one she can be proud of.'

'There's no pride in dying.'

'That is where you are wrong, my friend,' said Hassad. 'Osama bin Laden himself has spoken eloquently on this subject. The difference between our two civilisations is that while you celebrate life, we celebrate death. For us, there is no shame in dying, no fear either.'

'You didn't see it that way when you were a kid,' said Porter. 'I was about to kill you then, and I decided not to. Maybe that's because, as you say, we celebrate life.'

Hassad paused, and for a moment Porter thought he

might have got through to the man, but then he started to pick at the food he had piled onto his plate. They were sitting down now, on a rug to the left of the tables full of food. There were three men next to them, and they introduced themselves briefly: Nasri, Jabr and Asad. Nasri looked to be around sixty, but the other two seemed to be in their early thirties, the same age as Hassad. From the way they acted, Porter reckoned the four of them were in charge of the place: they looked more senior than any of the other guys, although what the hierarchy was between the four of them, Porter couldn't figure out.

'That's different,' said Hassad, when Porter had sat down. 'I was just a boy then. I didn't ask you to spare my life, although I am grateful that you did, and I recognise the debt that I owe you. But I was fighting as a warrior for my people and my God that day, and if I had died I would not have objected.'

Porter started to eat. He took a chunk of the pitta filled with chicken, and swallowed it quickly. There were jugs of water on the rug: he poured some into a cup, and gulped it down, drawing strength from the food and water. 'We can negotiate,' he said, looking back at Hassad. 'That's what I'm here for.'

Hassad raised his hand. 'We'll listen to what you have to tell us,' he said. 'But you should know my colleagues didn't want you to come here.'

Nasri leant forward. 'It is Hassad's debt,' he said softly. 'He owes you his life, we know that, but his debts are not our debts. So you see, your coming here can only create problems for us. Indeed, three of our men have already died, and one has been wounded, because you were captured on the way.'

'All I'm asking is that you listen to what I have to say,' said Porter. 'A woman's life is at stake.'

He was still trying to figure out which of the men was the most senior: Hassad spoke with the most authority, and seemed to make more decisions, but Nasri was the oldest, and the Arabs respected years. If I can get through to Nasri then maybe he can bring the rest of them round.

'Then talk,' said Nasri. 'But we don't have much time, so talk quickly.'

Porter looked at the man. His hair and his beard were greying, and his face was lined and weather-beaten, but he had a rock-like strength to him which reminded Porter of the sergeants who'd trained him. His muscles were like lumps of stone, and his eyes were as fierce and unyielding as storm clouds. At a guess, Porter would say he was the guy in charge of the fighting. He trained the men, and gave them their orders. And if I have to fight my way out of here, it's you I'm going to be up against.

'I've offered to take her place, and that offer still stands,' Porter started.

'And I've already told you, we're not interested,' Hassad interrupted.

He turned to the others, smiled and muttered something in Arabic. They laughed briefly yet harshly, then all looked back at Porter again.

Christ, how did I ever get myself into this job? Porter wondered. The only thing I've ever been able to negotiate is a couple of quid to buy myself a drink. And I wasn't even much good at that.

'I've been told I can bring you a message from the British Prime Minister,' said Porter, recalling the lines he had been fed back in Vauxhall. 'He has a "Roadmap to Peace" which he is prepared to kick-start so long as you let Katie Dartmouth go. He can talk to the Israelis and to the other regional players, and start . . .'

At his side, Porter could see Jabr slamming his fist down into the rug. 'The Jews don't care what any British Prime Minister thinks,' he growled. 'There will never be peace. Not until the Jews are driven back into the sea.'

'He says he'll talk to the White House,' said Porter. 'If the American President gets behind the roadmap —'

'Nice try, but it's not going to work here,' said Hassad. He was chuckling as he spoke. 'Everybody knows that the Americans couldn't care less what the British think. You are just the poodles.'

Nasri jabbed a finger in Porter's direction. 'America is controlled by the Zionists. They do what the Israelis want them to do. The British are America's poodles, so it follows that you are the tools of the Zionists as well.'

Porter knew he was struggling. He hadn't imagined they would be interested for a moment in the offer of peace talks. But he was being paid to speak to them. I'll do my job the best I can. And then I'll take matters into my own hands.

He took a helping of salad on his fork, then some more meat, and when he had finished he held the knife in the palm of his hand. 'How about money, then?' he said. 'If a man isn't interested in peace then he should at least be interested in cash.'

Again Hassad paused before he answered. You could get a better measure of the deformity around his mouth when you were sitting close to him. It stopped him from speaking properly, and when he chewed, his lips contorted upwards, making it impossible for him to conceal the food he was swallowing. 'How much money is on the table?'

For a brief moment, Porter could feel his pulse racing. Maybe it was just money they were after all along. They didn't look like gangsters. There were plenty of guys here, and they were living in pretty rough conditions. Men put up with that because they believed in a cause, not because they wanted to make themselves rich. Gangsters would be hanging out by a pool somewhere down in Beirut, with a harem of Russian hookers, a fridge full of cold beer and a big satellite dish beaming down Sky Sports. They wouldn't be down here reading the Koran to one another.

'A million at least,' said Porter looking Hassad straight in the eye.

Hassad turned away to speak to his colleagues, talking quickly. While he was doing so, Porter slipped the knife inside the belt of his trousers. Then he took another chunk of food in his hands, and ate it quickly. 'If a million, why not more?' said Hassad looking back at him. 'Why not two million or three million?'

'Name your price,' snapped Porter. 'Then we can negotiate.'

'But the money doesn't matter, does it?' interrupted Nasri. 'One million, five million, ten million, what difference does it make? The British government just takes the money out of the bank, hands it over and carries murdering our people. The money doesn't change anything.'

'You take money from the French,' said Porter.

'That's different,' said Asad. 'The French aren't occupying our lands.'

It was the first time he had spoken, and his voice was by far the weakest of the four men. He was paler than the others, and his beard was struggling to cover his face. Maybe the brains of the outfit, thought Porter. In any terrorist cell, there would be a planner, a frontman and a fighter, and Porter's was guessing that Asad was the planner. Maybe he was the man to convince?

'So you see, money won't work for us,' said Hassad. 'If we wanted money, we'd just steal it.'

'Then what?' said Porter. 'Arms?'

'We can get all the weapons we need from Iran,' said Hassad.

'We've told you,' Nasri butted in. His tone was amused, but with an underlying layer of contempt. 'British troops must be taken out of Iraq and Afghanistan. Then the girl may live.'

'Then why are you rejecting the PM's roadmap?' said

Porter. 'If there was peace, then the troops could come home. Believe me, I don't think any of the poor bastards want to be there.'

'Your PM's promises mean nothing, no British promises do,' said Asad. 'It is the British who have brought war to this region. The British let the Jews into Palestine, and drove our people out. And now the British are in Iraq, keeping our people oppressed.'

'They've liberated the country,' Porter growled.

'Some liberation,' Asad spat. 'Men are tortured in jails. Women are raped by your soldiers. Families are blown up daily. You call that liberation?'

'You think it would be better if they left?' said Porter. 'It would be a sodding bloodbath.'

There was a silence. Porter scooped up the last of the food from his plate, and stuffed it into his mouth. He could feel the blood raging through his veins, and food was about the only way he could think of to keep his mouth shut. Talk any more, and he was only getting himself into worse trouble.

Keep the conversation rolling, that's what they'd told him to do at the Firm. Engage their sympathy. Get them on your side. Well, they chose the wrong man for the job. I've never been able to persuade anyone of anything. If I had been, I wouldn't have found myself sleeping in the gutters.

I've got one more card, Porter decided. And there isn't going to be a better time to play it than now. 'Fouad Karem,' he said. 'Heard of him?'

'Karem?' said Hassad. 'He's one of our leaders, of course we've heard of him.'

'The imperialists have him,' said Asad. 'In Guantànamo.'

'We could arrange for him to be released,' said Porter. 'An exchange. You give us Katie Dartmouth, and we'll give you Fouad Karem.'

Not so much as a second passed before Asad replied, Porter noticed. They weren't even going to consider it.

'Hezbollah doesn't do prisoner exchanges, not with the Israelis, not with the Americans, not with anyone,' he said. 'Every person who joins us is willing to lay down their life for the cause. That is the deal, and they accept it.'

'He's your own man,' said Porter. 'You could get him out of there.'

'And make your life easy?' said Hassad. 'If we did that, every time you wanted something, you'd take one of our people and then offer to release them in exchange. We've told you. We don't negotiate with the infidel. That's our policy, and it is final.'

Turning away from Porter, he shouted across to the boy fiddling with the computers. 'Get us the British news,' he said, with a broad grin on his face. 'Let us see how they are preparing for the country's biggest execution since they cut the head off King Charles.'

TWENTY

Even though the signal was being dragged down from a distant satellite, the reception was crystal clear. Porter folded his legs under him, and looked up at the screen as the Sky News logo flashed across it. This was the ten o'clock news, which, since Beirut time was two hours later than London time, meant that it was midnight here.

Saturday morning, Porter reflected. The day set for Katie Dartmouth's execution.

And probably my own. It's forty blokes against one. How can any man survive odds like that?

Porter could feel an icy shiver down his spine. He'd thought about the death plenty of times – any soldier had – but he had never felt it so close as he had over the past forty-eight hours. It was so near, he could almost reach out and touch it. Embrace it, he told himself. Show no fear. That's the only way to handle it.

'KATIE DARTMOUTH, MINUS TWENTY-TWO HOURS' beamed the headline on Sky News.

Porter glanced around the room. Most of the men had stopped eating and were looking up at the screen. Some of them were talking feverishly, but Porter couldn't make out a word they were saying: obviously they didn't talk in English, but they seemed to understand it well enough on the television. He could smell their mood, however: the unmistakable, triumphal aroma of soldiers who believe they are winning the battle.

'With twenty-two hours left before the scheduled time for the beheading of the Sky News reporter Katie Dartmouth, we'll bring you the latest on the story,' said the newsreader. 'The PM makes a last-minute appeal for calm. Sir Perry Collinson is already in Beirut to mastermind the hunt for Katie. Thousands gather in Trafalgar Square for an all-night vigil for peace. Stop the War protestors plan a mass rally tomorrow through London calling for British troops to be brought home. And we'll be live in Katie Dartmouth's home village getting the latest reactions from friends and family.'

On the screen, Porter could see the familiar figure of the PM standing on the steps outside Downing Street. 'I just want to say this,' he began. 'I know people have many different views on the war in Iraq, and I respect that, but in the end we're there to do a job, and we have to stay there until the job is done. So I say to the kidnappers of Katie Dartmouth, we have offered you talks, I have said I am willing to fly to the Middle East, to bring all the sides together, so that we can find a way of stopping the bloodshed. I am willing to meet the leaders of Hezbollah to discuss a way forward. But we can't start moving soldiers out of a country just because one group or faction wants us to. We are willing to talk, but we are not willing to surrender. So delay this terrible act by at least a few days, so that we can start discussions.'

'You see,' Hassad muttered towards Porter. 'He's not interested in peace.'

'He's just interested in war,' Asad spat. 'That's all the British ever want.'

Porter remained silent. He looked back at the screen. 'We're now crossing live to Beirut, where Sir Peregrine Collinson landed tonight. Our reporter Sam Davenport spoke to him outside the British Embassy in the city. Sam . . .'

In the next instant, Collinson's face appeared on the

screen. He was wearing a casual shirt, and his face had the worried, concerned, slightly disappointed look he could recall seeing on the face of every Rupert whenever they were about to dump you right in the crap. 'I can assure everyone back at home we're doing everything we can to locate Katie Dartmouth and bring her back out alive before tomorrow,' he said, his tone serious yet also calm. 'We're getting help from our allies, from the local authorities, and also from the ordinary Lebanese people who are shocked and horrified at what is being done in their name.'

There was a jeer from the men in the room. They were talking in Arabic, but Porter didn't need a translation. Whatever the raghead word was for 'tosser', that's what they were saying. If the local Lebanese are shocked and horrified, thought Porter, then somebody forgot to tell these blokes. In fact, they forgot to tell the whole sodding country, judging by the people I met when I was travelling through it.

'But have you got any leads?' asked Sam, putting his microphone up close to Collinson. 'Does anyone have any real idea where Katie is being held captive?'

Collinson nodded. The same look, Porter noted. The one the Ruperts adopted when they were about to lie to you. 'I can't give away any confidential information that might help our enemies,' he said. 'But I can assure people that the net is closing all the time. As Winston Churchill once said, "If you are going through hell, keep going." Well, that's just what we are going to do. Keep going, until we are victorious.'

'No one will have spoken to that fool,' said Hassad. 'This hiding place is totally secure. Even most of the leadership of Hezbollah don't know where we are.'

'Tomorrow, I shall be travelling to Israel,' continued Collinson. 'The Israeli government has promised us every support and assistance.'

'I told you,' snapped Nasri, slamming his fist on the ground, and looking in Porter's direction. 'The British and the Zionists are working hand in hand, just as they always have done. That's why we can never negotiate.'

The rest of the news bulletin scrolled by. Porter watched it, with dread mounting inside his heart. There was a report from the all-night vigil in Trafalgar Square. A couple of women were weeping hysterically as they held up 'Stop the War' posters: at least ten thousand people were now planning to spend the night out in the Square, according to the police. The peace march scheduled for tomorrow morning was expected to be hundreds of thousands strong, snaking its way through Parliament Square, and up to Downing Street. Sky's political editor popped up, explaining that the PM was planning to travel down to Chequers tomorrow morning, and so wouldn't see the demo, but would be monitoring the situation from there. According to government sources, he explained, the PM was now relying on Sir Perry to find Katie Dartmouth, and had given up on a diplomatic solution. The by-election on Thursday was now looking like a disaster, if the execution went ahead, and there were rumours of a leadership challenge. The news bulletin switched to a live report from Katie's home village in Hampshire. Her family were no longer talking to the press, explained the reporter. Katie's mother had been taken to hospital after suffering a stress-related collapse. A couple of people from the village said how shocked they were, and how they all hoped for a miracle tomorrow. A special prayer service was being held on Saturday morning, said the reporter as he closed the bulletin. Better pray for a miracle, thought Porter grimly. The big guy upstairs might be the only person who can help us now. Finally, the thumping, insistent piano chords of 'Someone Saved My Life Tonight' rolled out across the room as the break for the adverts began. A soft-focus picture of Katie stared out at them from the TV screen: a pretty, vibrant young woman, a million miles away from the beaten husk tied to a stake less than a hundred metres from where they were sitting.

'I don't understand why they play this song all the time,' said Nasri. 'This Elton man, with the funny glasses, is he some sort of religious figure?'

Porter tried to smile, but his heart wasn't in it. 'He's just a singer,' he said.

'You think the British will break?' said Asad, looking closely at Porter.

He sighed. He felt revolted sitting among these men. Whatever their cause, this was no way to fight. Skulking away in a bunker, torturing a woman, manipulating the media. If you wanted a war, it should be honest combat, man to man. But, much as he hated it, he could see that it was having an impact. The country was going crazy. The bastards down in this mine might be evil, but they were effective: what they were doing to Katie was hitting home a lot harder than lobbing a few bombs at the British Army down in Basra. 'Never,' snapped Porter. 'We stood up to the Nazis and we'll stand up to you.'

Christ, he thought to himself. I sound just like that tosser Collinson. But what else am I meant to say?

'Then we just have to put more pressure on them,' said Hassad. He stood up. 'Follow me.'

They started to move. Hassad was leading the way, and Nasri, Jabr and Asad were following on behind Porter. He walked down the corridor, through the meeting point of the tunnels, then straight towards the room where Katie Dartmouth was incarcerated. The door swung on its hinges, and Hassad stepped inside. Porter glanced into the room. Katie was still tied to the stake. She seemed close to losing consciousness. Her head had drooped to one side, and her eyes were so swollen it was as if they were bulging out of their sockets. There was a rotting stench of decay all around her, as if she had already died and her body had started to decompose. Maybe she already has died inside, thought Porter. Maybe she's just waiting for the rest of her body to catch up.

Not many people would have the strength to survive five days in this hell.

Hassad muttered something in Arabic. In response, Asad walked across to the camcorder. He trained it straight on Katie, and then switched on a powerful light that illuminated her face. You could see her much more clearly now: every cut, bruise and scab on her skin was bathed in white light. Her eyes flinched from the lamp, and she tried to look away, but there wasn't even enough strength in her eyeballs to turn away. A tear rolled down the side of her cheek. Then a gasp of pain escaped from her lips.

Christ, I can hardly bear to look, thought Porter. What the hell are the bastards doing now?

'I need you to make a statement,' said Hassad firmly, standing two feet in front of Katie, looking straight into her face.

'Wha . . . wha . . .'

She was trying to speak, but the words died on her lips.

Hassad took half a step forwards. Porter could see Katie flinching. Like an abused child, she now expected to be hit whenever anyone approached her.

'We will hold up some words on a card in front of you,' he said. 'We want you to look at the camera and read them out. We will send them through to the TV station you work for, and post them onto the Internet. When they wake up in the morning, the British people will be able to hear you making one last desperate appeal for your life.'

'For Christ's sake, man,' growled Porter. 'The woman is in no fit state to talk.'

'Shut up,' shouted Hassad.

'You're killing her tomorrow, isn't that enough?' said Porter.

'I've already told you to keep out of this,' said Hassad. There was a flash of anger across his face as he turned to Porter. 'She will do exactly what she's told to do.' He turned back to face Katie again. 'Now read,' he snapped coldly.

Asad was standing behind the camera. Above his head, he was holding a strip of white card with letters neatly stencilled in black ink. Porter glanced at it. 'My name is Katie Dartmouth,' it said. 'I am scared. Very scared. I don't want to die. These are not bad men, and their cause is a just one. They just want British soldiers off their land. So I appeal to the British people, go out of your homes, demand that your government brings your soldiers home. Please. Because if you don't, I will die, and my blood will be on all of your hands.'

Christ, thought Porter. They can't make her read that. *Can they?*

'Read it,' repeated Hassad.

Katie rolled her eyes towards the card. She was struggling to focus. Porter watched as her bruised and swollen eyeballs screwed up, trying to get a fix on the words. Slowly, from the expression on her face, he guessed that she was starting to make sense of the rows of black stencilling.

'Fu . . .' she stuttered.

The words still wouldn't come.

Hassad took a step sideways. He grabbed the jug in the corner, filled a tin cup, and took two steps towards Katie. She flinched. Grabbing hold of her chin with his left hand, he pushed the water to her lips with his right. She drank quickly, drawing down the liquid in two fierce gulps. 'Now speak,' said Hassad.

'Fuck you,' spat Katie.

Although his face remained as impassive as lump of rock, Porter was smiling inside. That's the spirit, girl, he told himself. Show the bastards what you're made of.

Hassad took a moment to compose himself.

'Fuck you,' spat Katie again. 'You can kill me if you want to, but I'm not reading that shit for you.'

Hassad looked at Nasri. 'Deal with her,' he said curtly.

Nasri vanished from the room, but within an instant he'd returned. In his right hand he was holding a long stretch of hosepipe. 'You want to read?' said Hassad, turning menacingly back towards Katie.

'Fuck you.'

Nasri took two steps forward then paused. He raised his right hand high in the air, and flicked the hose so that it was hanging over the side of his back. For a moment he just held the pose, giving Katie a moment to look straight at him. The dread was already evident in her eyes: she knew the pain that was about to be inflicted on her, and she was scared witless. Her lips were shaking, and it looked as if a trickle of urine was dribbling down her leg. Nasri tensed his muscles. He was a thin but strong man, and his biceps were like cannonballs: round and as hard as steel. An unimaginable strength was about to be transferred into the lash. 'No,' muttered Katie, the words so weak they were barely audible. 'Please no . . .'

Nasri started to raise his arm. In the still, dank silence of the room, you could hear the plastic start to cut through the fetid air. Porter lunged forwards. He moved with an agility that surprised even him. Crashing through the five metres of space that separated them, he collided hard into Nasri's ribs, knocking him off balance. The hose was already travelling through the air, but its flight had changed. It cracked viciously, but was hitting only thin air. Porter pummelled one fist, then another, into Nasri's ribcage. The man had the strength of an armoured vehicle: putting your fist into his muscles was like slamming your hand into the skin of a tank. He rolled with the first punch, but the second hit a nerve, sending him crashing to the floor, a cry of pain escaping from his lips. Porter fell on top of him, bringing his knee up sharply as he did so, so that it crashed hard into Nasri's chin, sending his neck snapping back. Porter could feel a surge of adrenalin running through his bloodstream as the blows hit home: I've built up so much anger towards these bastards since I've been here, he reflected, that it is good to finally get some of it out of my system.

There's plenty more where it came from as well.

He could feel a set of hands on his shoulders. They were tugging at his sweatshirt, pulling him back. He roared with anger, and tried to shake them away, but it was too late. Another set of hands was grabbing him around the chest. Both Hassad and Jabr had caught hold of him and were tugging him away. He lashed out a fist, aiming for Nasri's face, but missed, hitting only air. Jabr had a lock on his chest, and with one swift movement, heaved Porter upwards, and threw him up against the wall. Porter could feel his back slamming into the stone, bruising the skin.

Hassad slammed a fist straight into the centre of his stomach. The blow landed hard, knocking the wind out of his lungs. Porter started coughing violently. As he looked sideways, he could see Nasri getting to his feet. He had taken a couple of bruises where Porter's kneecap has smashed into his chin, but otherwise he wasn't badly hurt. Leaning over, he picked the hose up from the floor, reeled it back into the air like a fishing road, then lashed it through the air. The tip of the hose slashed across Porter's chest. Its impact was softened slightly by his sweatshirt, but it still stung viciously. Porter cried out as the pain ripped through him. In front of him, he could see a cruel smile cross Hassad's face. 'Next time, we kill you,' he said.

Nasri had already turned round. The hose was high in the air. It flicked back, then lashed into Katie's side. The sound of plastic ripping into skin filled the small room, then there was a brief moment of silence. Porter already knew what was happening from painful experience. It took a moment for the brain to figure out what the body had just experienced. The pain didn't register instantly. But when it did, it was like having a hundred sharp blades cutting into your skin in the same moment.

'No,' screamed Katie. 'No, no, no . . .'

Nasri had already drawn the hose back again. His muscles were tense and bulging. In that moment, Porter realised he had only made things worse. The man's blood was up now. There was real anger in each blow. The hose was moving through the air with the venom of a snake. It curled through the air, then kicked into Katie's skin, cutting through the cloth that was covering her, and drawing a line of blood that ran across her belly and up into her breast. 'Please no, please no, please no,' she whimpered.

Don't lose it again, Porter commanded himself. It doesn't matter how much they provoke you. It only makes things worse.

Hassad raised a hand. Nasri had already drawn the hose behind his back, but he paused. 'You'll read now?' said Hassad.

'I'll . . .'

'You'll read, or you'll keep tasting the whip,' snarled Hassad.

There were tears streaming down Katie's cheeks, but they were tears of pain, not regret. Specks of blood had splattered across her chest, and her face was so pale and beaten, it was as if she had already taken another step into the grave. They planned this, Porter realised. He felt another stab of fury drilling into his heart. They knew she'd refuse, and they'd decided to whip her, just so she would look even more pitiful for the camera. Every move, every step, was planned with a brutal, unfeeling callousness that disgusted him.

What was it that bastard Hassad said? We celebrate death. He wriggled his leg to make sure the knife he'd hidden inside his trouser pocket was still there. I'll give that fuckhead something to celebrate, all right. Just as soon as I find the moment to strike.

'My name is Katie Dartmouth,' she started.

Her voice was fractured and rough, but you could see the sincerity in her eyes, and you could hear the pleading in her voice. Porter could see Hassad smiling to himself. He knew what he was doing when he kidnapped a TV reporter. He needed someone who could play for the cameras, and Katie was just perfect. Even in death, she could deliver.

'I am scared,' she continued. 'Very scared. I don't want to die. These are not bad men, and their cause is a just one. They just want British soldiers off their land. So I appeal to the British people, go out of your homes, demand that your government brings your soldiers home. Please. Because if you don't, I will die, and my blood will be on all of your hands.'

Asad snapped the camera shut, and switched off the light. The small room was suddenly dark and silent: only the sound of Katie sobbing gently broke the stillness.

'Thank you,' said Hassad. 'Your words have served a noble purpose.'

Katie snivelled. The tears had blocked up her nose and her throat. The lash of the whip would still be stinging, Porter reckoned: the pain from where the hose had cut into his own skin was still burning through him, and he knew it would be hours before it started to subside.

'I don't care about that,' Katie stuttered. 'I just want to die.'

'Soon enough,' said Hassad. 'There are less than twenty hours for you to wait now.'

'I want to die now,' Katie screamed. There was a sudden energy and violence in her voice, as if she had suddenly found some strength from somewhere.

'I've told you to wait.'

'Now,' said Katie, gasping for breath. 'I've had enough. If you're going to do it, just fucking get it over with.'

'The deadline has been set,' snapped Hassad.

'Film it now, do whatever you want, I just can't take this any more.'

There were tears streaming down her face and Porter could see in her eyes that the will to live had abandoned her. It happened sometimes to men on the battlefield: once their spirits were broken, they'd just march straight into the line of fire. When they knew they were going to die anyway, they just wanted to get it over with. It was the waiting they couldn't stand.

His eyes met hers, and suddenly he saw a spark of anger flicker within her. She wants to know why I haven't saved her yet. And it's a bloody good question.

'Tonight at eight, precisely,' said Hassad. 'We're expecting a huge global audience. We don't want to disappoint them.'

Katie fell silent. The moment of hysteria had passed. Now she just looked sad and bitter, as if she was reflecting on the life that was about to be snatched away from her. 'Leave me alone with the Englishman,' she said quietly.

'What?' asked Hassad.

'I want to be alone with one of my own people.'

Porter listened closely. Has she got a plan? he wondered.

Katie was looking up now. 'You said you weren't cruel men,' she said. 'Well then, you'll grant a woman one simple request before you kill her.'

Hassad looked at her, then at Porter. 'No tricks,' he said.

Porter nodded.

'A man will be posted at the door,' said Hassad. 'Five minutes, that's all. Then we're taking you out of here.'

He walked from the room, the others following behind him. The door slammed shut. For a couple of seconds, Porter remained silent. He reckoned he knew something of what she was going through. Only a day earlier, the bastards who captured him told him he was about to be beheaded, and he'd believed them. He'd sensed the fear, the dread, the expectation of the pain, and the challenge of dying alone and miserable in a strange and hostile place.

'Do you think they'll really do it?' asked Katie.

Porter nodded. There was no point in trying to kid her. That wasn't going to do any good now.

'They're bastards,' he muttered. 'They'll do anything.'

Katie started to speak, but she choked on the first word. Maybe some small part of her had hoped through the past week that it was just a bluff, that when the moment came, they'd call it off. Lock her up instead. He'd heard that men on death row often thought that. It was the only way they could handle the pressure. If so, he'd punctured that now. The flat certainty with which he delivered the answer had extinguished what hope remained as surely as a closed fist will extinguish the flame on a candle.

'It won't be so bad,' he said. 'It'll be quick. And . . .'

He paused, trying to complete the sentence, but it was hopeless. It wasn't going to be quick, and she knew it. That was why she was so afraid.

'Kill me now,' she said.

Porter could hear the desperation in her voice.

'At least it will be over,' she continued.

'There's still hope,' he persisted. 'That's one thing you learn in the army. While you're still alive, there's still a chance. Something may turn up.'

'Have you negotiated?' asked Katie, her voice pale and frightened.

Porter shrugged. 'They're not interested.'

'Did they . . . did they give you anything to offer?'

'Just the bollocks you'd expect,' said Porter. He sighed. 'Some half-arsed peace talks. Some money. That's not what they want though, is it? They want our boys out of Iraq. And we're not going to give them that.'

A tear was falling down the side of Katie's cheek. 'Did . . . did Perry get involved?'

'Collinson?' said Porter.

Then he remembered. She'd been tied to this miserable stake for the past week. She had no idea what was going on at home.

'We were . . .'

'I know,' growled Porter.

There's no need for her to know the history between us. It will only make things worse. If that was possible. 'He's meant to be heading up the effort to rescue you,' said Porter. 'I saw the latest broadcast. He's been in Beirut today, and he might be in Israel by tomorrow.

'If there's a way, he'll find me,' sniffed Katie.

Dream on, girl, Porter reflected bitterly. If he can find a TV camera, he'll pose for it. The bastard would have trouble finding his own arse and elbow. And if he did, he wouldn't know how to get them in the right order.

'You have to hold on in there,' he said grimly. 'If they have any idea where we are, they'll come tonight.'

'But you don't think there's any hope?'

Porter shrugged. He'd thought about it ever since he'd been here. He'd done hostage raids himself, he'd been trained for it, and there was no more difficult military operation, particularly if you wanted to get the hostage out alive. Even when it was on open ground, you had to get in quickly enough and take out enough of the opposition to secure control of the area before they killed the hostage. To stand much of a chance, you needed detailed maps, and you needed an access point where you could get a lot of men in fast. They didn't have either. If they did get the location, they might try pumping some kind of nerve gas down into the mine to paralyse everyone down below: officially, those kinds of chemical weapons didn't exist, but he'd heard rumours in the Regiment they were stockpiled somewhere for an emergency. They were meant to be sodding dangerous – unstable, rarely tested, and with potentially carcinogenic side effects – but that was all just hearsay. It was something they needed to be prepared for, though. If they had them, they'd surely use them tonight.

'This place is bloody hard to find, and even if you get the location, it is going to be a bastard to break into, even for the Regiment.'

'Stand closer to me,' said Katie. 'I'm scared.'

No point in telling Katie about the possibility of a chemical attack, Porter thought. It will only make her even more frightened. And I'm not sure there is much more terror she can handle.

'Are you religious?'

Christ, no. The last thing I need right now is a lot of mumbo-jumbo. Porter shook his head. 'Not really.'

'I'm a Catholic.' She stifled another tear. 'At least, at school. I'm not really a churchgoer or anything.' She steadied herself, trying to stop her lips from trembling. 'But I would like you to read me the last rites.'

'I . . .' Porter hesitated, unsure what to say. 'I don't think I know them.'

She leant her head forward, and whispered two short sentences.

'I'm not a priest,' said Porter, and immediately felt stupid for such a weak and pointless remark.

Katie attempted a smile. His lips were too battered, however, to turn up more than a couple of millimetres. 'I'll call one then, maybe.'

She looked at Porter. 'You're the only person here.'

Porter took a step closer. He was standing just inches away from her. The stench was unbearable: a suffocating mixture of rotting excrement, sweat and blood. Like a cross between an abattoir and a boghouse, he decided bitterly. With his right hand, he crossed himself, then closed his eyes so they were half shut. 'Through this holy anointing, may the Lord in His love and mercy help you with the grace of the Holy Spirit,' he said softly.

'The rest,' said Katie weakly. 'Please.'

'May the Lord who frees you from sin save you and raise you up.'

'Hold me,' said Katie.

Porter leant into her, and wrapped his arms around her body. She was thin, wasting away, and he could feel the cuts and fractures and bruises that covered her skin. She was dry, like an piece of old fruit, and her limbs seemed to be rotting away. 'I'm so scared,' she whimpered.

Hassad stepped into the room. He glanced first at Katie, then at Porter. 'It's time for you to leave,' he said, a soft smile twisting up his deformed lip. 'Next time you see her, she will be dead.'

TWENTY-ONE

The two men walked in silence down the length of the corridor. The path was dark, and even though they were deep underground, Porter could sense the night all around them. Two guards were already in position outside the door where Katie was being held captive, and two more where the corridor hit the meeting point. They looked strong and alert, and they were well armed. Nobody's going to try to catch a few minutes' kip on their watch tonight, Porter decided. They know just exactly how much is at stake.

If the Regiment does try and come in tonight, it's going to be a slaughterhouse.

Hassad turned into the next corridor, and led Porter towards his room. As he passed through the sleeping quarters, Porter could see that most of the men were resting. The lights were out and there were bodies stretched out on the floor. He could hear a couple of guys snoring. Hassad pushed the door open. There was a dim light shining from a candle in one corner of the room he had been shown into earlier. As Porter glanced around, he suddenly felt something hard stabbing into the small of his back. He knew instinctively what it was.

A gun.

He spun round. Hassad was pointing a Beretta handgun right at him.

'What the fuck?' spat Porter.

'Don't worry,' said Hassad. 'I'm not going to hurt you. Just as long as you do what I say.'

Porter looked at the gun, then up into the man's eyes. There could be no doubt that he would kill him if he resisted. He nodded towards a stake driven into the ground in the far corner of the room. Porter could see precisely what was about to happen. The bastard was going to tie him up.

'My apologies,' said Hassad politely. 'But you are a British soldier, and we can't leave you roaming around here all night. And you have already attacked one of my men.'

Porter kept his eyes on the Beretta as he walked towards the stake. Inwardly, he was shuddering: maybe they're planning to behead me as well. There was no point in arguing right now: any trouble and they would probably just whack him on the head, then tie him up anyway while he was out cold. His vengeance would come later, he felt certain. The stake was a thick piece of wood, driven deep down into the floor, with about a metre protruding from the surface. Hassad nodded to him to lie down on the straw next to it, then took a rope and started to tie his foot to the stake. Next, he took Porter's right arm, and bound that behind his back. The ropes were rough, and cut into his skin, but he had space to move and breathe, and if he curled up, he could lie flat on his side on the straw and get some sleep.

'I'm sorry that your journey has been a wasted one,' said Hassad, as he slipped the last of the knots into place. 'I might have talked . . . but Nasri, and the others, wouldn't allow it.'

'I make one last appeal to you,' said Porter, his eyes rolling upwards so that he could look directly into Hassad's face. 'Put me in her place. Leave the girl alone.'

Hassad shook his head. 'We've already discussed it,' he said. 'Nothing can change the plan. Unless your government gives us what we want, the execution will go ahead as planned.'

'I spared your life,' snapped Porter.

'And now *I'm* sparing yours.'

'She's sodding bricking herself. She can't deal with this. I can.'

Hassad shrugged. 'Everyone can deal with death,' he said, speaking with a weary sigh. 'There's really nothing to it.'

Porter was about to speak, but Hassad had already stood up. He was walking towards the door. He looked exhausted, Porter thought, and he probably wasn't going to get much kip either. Nobody would, he reflected bitterly. Not in this hellhole, with a young woman's blood waiting to be spilt.

'Now, get some sleep, if you want to,' said Hassad. 'Tomorrow, after the execution, we will blindfold you so that you won't know where you've been, and we'll drive you to a safe spot, and we'll make sure you have directions and enough money to get back to Beirut. You can report to the British Embassy, they'll take care of you.'

Porter grunted. We'll both be dead long before then, mate, he decided.

'I owed you a debt for sparing my life all those years ago,' Hassad continued. 'That's why I agreed that you should come out here. But after tomorrow, that debt is paid in full. We are men on different sides of a war that may last for generations, and there should be no more dealings between us.'

Before Porter could reply, Hassad had already left the room. The door had been slammed tight shut, and he could hear a bolt being slid into place.

Porter lay back. The room was not completely dark: there was the single, small candle burning in a pool of molten wax in the corner. The straw felt damp, and he could feel the dirt within it. There was a drip somewhere in the room where some water was coming through the stone out of which it was carved.

'Shit,' he muttered.

He tried to make a mental calculation of the time. It had been midnight locally when they'd watched the news bulletin from London, and at least an hour had passed since then. So it could be one, possibly pushing two in the morning. The dead of night. If there was a rescue attempt coming, his best guess was that the Regiment would strike between three and four in the morning. There was no way of knowing for sure, but he reckoned nobody was coming. All that posturing on TV from Collinson: it suggested to Porter the bastard didn't have a clue where Katie had been hidden. Hassad's men were loyal, professional and dedicated, and they were operating in their own country.

He turned onto his side. The ropes were tight, but it was only his right leg and right hand that were immobilised, and that gave him space to move. He slipped his left hand into his jeans, and took out the knife he'd hidden there during the meal. It only measured five inches, with a black plastic handle, but it had a good sharp steel blade on it. It would do, Porter reckoned. Hassad must have decided that one arm and one leg was enough. A man couldn't untie a knot with one hand: certainly not when the hand in question was short of a couple of fingers. *But he could cut one.*

Porter glanced towards the door. It was shut tight, and he reckoned they were leaving him alone for the rest of the night. It would be five, he judged, before the place came back to life. That gave him a couple of hours to play with. What was it Clayton had said to him? Play the bloody hero if you have to.

Gripping the knife in his left hand, he moved his body around until he was level with a piece of clean rock. Turning the blade flat, he started to slowly sharpen the blade by grinding it into the stone. The ropes binding him were thick, made from a plastic cord: the blade right now was nowhere near strong enough to cut through it, but with enough work he might be able to get it into shape for the job.

It was slow, painful work. A couple of times the blade sprung from his grasp, spinning across the rock, and once he was afraid it might be out of reach. The rock was certainly no grinding stone – just ragged, blunt ore – but if you drove it hard, the blade gradually sharpened. The work was dull and repetitive, but Porter was grateful for it. It took his mind off what was likely to happened next.

Within half an hour, the blade was sharpened. It wasn't a razor, but the steel was thin, and pointed, and it would do the job. Twisting himself around, he positioned the blade in his left hand. Porter had never been naturally dexterous with that hand, and after he lost his fingers he'd found it wasn't good for much more than holding the second bottle of vodka if he was ever lucky enough to get his hands on two at the same time. Still, he got a good enough grip between his thumb and his palm and, leaning forward, slashed it into the rope binding his right foot. The knot was strong, and so was the artificial fibre the rope was made from, but the knife was now sharp enough to saw its way through. In just a few seconds, it had been severed. With a kick of the knee, Porter shook his leg free of the stake. Still squatting on the ground, Porter kept the blade wedged tight into the palm of his left hand. A rope was still tied tight around his chest, strapping his right hand to him, but he quickly cut it open. Free, he told himself with satisfaction.

Porter looked up at the bolted door.

OK, he thought, feeling the resolve stiffen inside him. Let's see if we can't make some trouble for these bastards.

He collected the tiny candle, holding it up close to the door. There was enough of a crack that he could see out into the corridor. From here, it looked empty, but that didn't mean there wasn't a guard just a few metres away. The bolt was made from metal, and slotted into position in a socket about four feet off the ground. Porter positioned himself close to the door, and held up the candle so that he had as much light to work with as possible. He slotted the knife into the gap in the door, and slowly worked it against the bolt: he dug the tip into the metal, twisted it to get as much grip as possible, then used all the strength in his wrist to flick it backwards a couple of millimetres. It didn't move much, but it did shift a fraction, and to Porter that was all that mattered. He would get there eventually.

It took ten minutes, maybe fifteen, but eventually the lock was freed. He reckoned it was three fifteen in the morning now, although he couldn't be certain. The door swung open: Porter had to grab hold of it to stop the thing from crashing back and raising the alarm. He blew out the candle, and held his breath tight in his chest. Very slowly, and with the knife gripped in his right hand, he squeezed the door ajar. He glanced into the corridor. The light was murky – there were some lamps in the meeting point but nothing in the corridor – and although he had got used to the semi-darkness it still took a second for Porter to adjust his eyes. So far as he could see the corridor was empty. He inched out, keeping one foot inside the door, so that he could snap back inside if necessary.

Porter already had a plan mapped out. He'd have liked to go straight to Katie, but that route was too well guarded. There was no way he could get through equipped just with an eating knife. Instead, he'd slip through to Hassad's room. It was a distance of about twenty metres through the tunnels, and he calculated there would only be one guard along the way. The odds of success weren't great, he thought. But at least they weren't suicidal.

He moved quietly forward. The guard was standing just where the tunnel met the meeting point. He had his back to it, and he was leaning against the wall. Whether he was drowsing or alert, it was impossible to say from here. Porter inched out further, his back flat against the wall. The knife was nestling in the palm of his hand. He was gradually adjusting his eyes to the soupy light. He could see the barrel of the man's gun. An AK-47: the lamp in the meeting point was catching on the gleaming wood of its polished stock.

Porter kept moving. He was about ten metres from the man now. He was holding his breath: he knew from his time in the Regiment that it was the sound of your breathing that usually gave you away. The floor was just dust and grit so at least it wasn't scratching against his trainers. Five metres. His back was tight against the wall, slipping into the shadows, making sure he was virtually invisible against the rock. Three metres. He could see the man's shoulders twitch. He was a big man, Porter noted: six foot, with hefty shoulders, taking his weight up to two hundred pounds. He could hear him grunt. Or maybe a snore. His hand rose upwards. For a moment, Porter was certain he was going for the gun. All he had to do was look round, and he could spray the space with bullets: Porter would be shredded to pieces within seconds. He tried to melt into the rock. The man picked at his nose, grunted again, then slumped back against the side of the rock. Porter took a step closer, then another. He raised his right hand, and steadied himself. With a sudden, swift movement, he darted forward. He cupped his left hand around the man's mouth, dragged back hard with all the muscles in his shoulders. He could hear the man starting to cry, but the hand was effectively stifling the noise. He was starting to shudder, and as his muscles absorbed the sudden shock of the attack, he heaved backwards. Porter struggled to contain him. You've only got a fraction of a second, he reminded himself. Once you get into a fair fight with this bastard, then you're a dead man.

In an instant, Porter's right hand was thrusting towards the man's neck. The knife pierced the skin, making a neat incision, in the space between the jawbone and the collar bones where a blade could cut straight through to the wind-pipe. Porter had barely a moment, and he knew he had to slice the man open as skilfully as any surgeon: except his purpose was to end the creature's life, not preserve it.

There was a hiss of air: the unmistakable sound of oxygen

wheezing out of a collapsing windpipe, like an old tyre with a puncture. Porter twisted the knife around, letting it complete its deadly work, while at the same time keeping his hand gripped tight on the man's mouth. He stifled a bolt of pain as his victim summoned up enough strength to bite into the palm of his hand, but that was the man's last moment of resistance as the life drained out of him. Giving the blade a final twist, Porter made sure the windpipe was completely cut open, making it impossible for any air to get through to the brain. He removed his hand from the man's mouth, and checked his pulse. Dead. He yanked his body back, lying him down flat on the ground.

No time to hide the body, he decided. The shifts could change at any moment, and as soon as someone came along, they would know the base was under attack and raise the alarm. They might even think they were under a full-scale assault from British special forces. If that was the case, so much the better. In the chaos, some kind of opportunity to escape might open up.

Porter pulled the knife free from the man's throat, and wiped the blood away on the back of his jeans. You'll taste more before this night is out, he told himself grimly.

He picked up the man's handgun and tucked that into his jeans. A compact Browning M1900, Porter was familiar enough with how it worked. He walked swiftly across the meeting point. He knew where Hassad's quarters were.

Porter turned into the corridor. The moment of truth has arrived, he told himself.

The light leading up to Hassad's room was dim, but Porter's eyes had already adjusted to the murky conditions, and he didn't have any trouble identifying the right door. He laid his palm flat against it, and exerted the slenderest amount of pressure. It gave. Hassad slept with his door unlocked, the way Porter had figured he would. Soldiers didn't bolt themselves in, especially when there was possibility of any enemy assault. They needed to be ready to move the moment an attack started: in the time it took them to unlock their doors, they might already be dead.

Porter held the knife in his hand, savouring the cold sharpness of its blade against his skin. If he could, he'd use that rather than the gun: a shot would alert the whole base, and there would be a dozen soldiers on top of him within seconds. He paused for a brief moment, controlling his breathing. He suddenly recalled Steve, Mike and Keith. He could see them laughing as they went into the battle. He could hear the jokes and the banter, and then the desperate commands as the action kicked off. And then he could recall the moment when he'd seen the three stretchers with white cloths covering them being carried out of the chopper. He remembered the funerals, and the moving tributes from their mates as the bodies were buried in the ground. And he could remember the looks of all the other guys in the base back at Hereford. The looks that said, 'Here's the bloke who let three of his mates die because he didn't have the bollocks to finish off some raghead kid who was intent on killing the lot of them.'

OK, boys, Porter thought bitterly. It's a bit late, I know. This is a cheque that should have been cashed years ago. But you're about to get your payback on the bastard that killed you.

He pushed the door open. Hassad was lying on a simple straw mattress by one wall of the small room. In the corner there was a small candle floating in a pool of wax that filled the room with a pale light. He was still wearing the jeans and sweatshirt he wore during the day, although he'd kicked off his trainers and put them at the bottom of the mattress. Next to it, there was a paperback book in Arabic left half open and a tin cup of water. There was also an open packet of some kind of medicine although Porter couldn't read at this distance what it was. His AK-47 was laid down flat on the straw right next to him. There was a knife as well. Under attack, he could reach for both within seconds. What was under the cushion he was using as a pillow Porter couldn't tell. But it was more likely to be a pistol than a spare pair of pyjamas, he thought with a half-smile.

Porter had a fraction of a second. That was all the time available to determine success or failure. He kicked against the stone floor, and threw himself across the few metres that separated the doorway from the straw mattress.

He landed hard on top of Hassad. Immediately, the Arab woke up, looking straight at Porter, his eyes ablaze with anger. But it was too late. Porter was lying right across him. He was a big man, with at least a fifty-pound weight advantage on Hassad, and the sheer bulk of his body was pinning him down to the floor. Porter could feel a heady sense of elation surging through him. Almost as good as double vodka, he told himself. Right now, I've got this bastard exactly where I want him. And now he's going to help me get Katie out of here.

Porter drew back his right hand just a few inches, hovering close to Hassad's neck. His blade was sharp, it would only need the minimum of force to break open the man's skin. His hand held steady and his eyes darted across the man's body, scanning it the same way a butcher glances across a carcass, looking for the best places to cut up the meat. He could feel a surge of anger running through his veins. I've waited too long for this, he told himself grimly. Far too bloody long.

He jabbed the knife forwards, using the strength in his elbow. It collided with the skin, nicking open a cut, and suddenly the blade was crimson with blood. In the same moment, however, Hassad had rolled his head to one side, stretching enough of his neck muscles to deflect the worst of the attack. Porter was still lying flat on top of the man, crushing him into the straw bedding, and making it impossible for him to move. 'Stay still, you murdering raghead scum,' Porter spat viciously.

He could see the fear in the man's eyes, and smell the sweat pouring off him. It was the same look he'd seen seventeen years ago, the one that had persuaded him to spare the life of a small frightened boy. But this time it was the expression of a man, not a kid, and rather than sympathy it aroused only contempt. This time you're going to do exactly what I tell you, Porter thought. And no mistake.

'You killed my mates after I spared your life. Now I'm going to kill you, you bastard. Now take it like a bloody man . . .'

Hassad bucked forward. He was desperately trying to loosen Porter's vice-like grip on him, but the dead weight lying across his chest made it impossible for him to get up enough strength to free himself.

'I didn't kill anyone, I swear it,' Hassad pleaded.

'Don't give me that bollocks, you Arab scum,' Porter hissed. 'I spared your life once before, and you took out three of my mates.'

'I didn't kill anyone,' Hassad squealed.

'You lying bastard.'

Porter drew his hand back the few inches necessary to skewer the knife into the man's neck. He'd already scanned the flesh, and knew exactly where the windpipe was. With little more than a flick of the wrist he could sever the bastard's life.

And this is the moment . . .

'It was that man on television,' said Hassad. 'Collinson.'

Porter paused. 'Who?'

'The man on TV.' Hassad's body was wheezing with fear, and there was a foul stench of sweat all over him. 'I recognised him. It was the same man on the raid, I swear it, and it was because of him the British soldiers died.'

'You're just a lying raghead scum,' Porter growled.

'You're just trying to save your miserable skin. I bloody know it. Well, it's not going to work, I tell you. I was going to kill you nice and quick, but now it's going to be slow and bloody painful, just so you know not to start telling lies.'

'It was Collinson, I tell you,' said Hassad. 'The man was a fucking coward.'

Porter's hand paused again.

What if he's right? he wondered suddenly. Christ, maybe, just maybe, the bastard isn't lying to me.

Hassad's hand snapped sideways so it was resting on the barrel of the AK-47. Porter immediately slammed his fist down on the hand so that he couldn't pick up the gun. 'Take it,' said Hassad. 'Take the fucking gun, and hold it on me. I've got no chance of escaping. I'll tell you the real story of that day, and if I don't convince you, then you can shoot me all the same.'

'It's a trick,' snarled Porter.

'No trick,' snapped Hassad.

'You've got ten seconds,' said Porter. 'No more.'

He dropped the knife from his hand, and grabbed the AK-47. He climbed off Hassad's chest, and knelt beside him, jabbing the muzzle of the gun straight into the man. 'OK, mate,' he said roughly. 'Tell me what really happened that night.'

Hassad pulled himself up. He was sitting now, with his back to the wall. He had sweat dripping off his face: the cold, angry perspiration that Porter had smelt before on men who were convinced they were about to die. There was a deep cut on his neck where the knife had caught his skin, and some blood was still oozing out of the wound, although a scab would soon start to form around it. The side of his neck and the top of his sweatshirt were both stained crimson. But in his eyes there was a brightness again: the hope of saving his life had begun to return.

'You knocked me out cold,' he said, some calm in his

voice now. 'I remember that as clearly as if it was yesterday. But you didn't make a great job of it. A couple of blows to the head, enough to make me dizzy, but not enough to put me out for long. Perhaps it was because I was so young. Boys can take a terrible beating and come back pretty quickly.'

'Go faster,' growled Porter. 'Don't play for bloody time.'

'I think it was only a few minutes later that I came round. I was scared out of my life, and so I just lay there on the ground, with my eyes mostly shut. Playing dead, or at least unconsciousness, seemed like the best strategy. But I could see enough of what was going on, and hear it as well. That man Collinson was insisting on taking command, and the others were arguing with him. There was a lot of shouting between him and the other guys. You'd already been evacuated, and they were clearing a space for another chopper to come in to take them out. Just then, a unit of Hezbollah reinforcements arrived. About a dozen men in all. It started to turn nasty. There was a lot of shooting, and a few grenades. The British managed to subdue the attack, but it was impossible for the chopper to come down to the roof. There was too much incoming fire. I didn't reckon there was any serious danger, though. Patience and a little perseverance, that was all that was required. But Collinson panicked. I could see and hear it. He was shouting a series of stupid and contradictory orders. He wanted a couple of them to march out of the building straight into the line of fire so that he could get up onto the roof. They were screaming at him not to be an idiot.'

Keeping his eyes on Porter, his expression turned deadly serious. 'Then he shot one of them in the back, and told the other two they were bloody cowards, and if they didn't go forward he'd make sure they were going to be court-martialled on charges of desertion. They started to run towards the man who had been shot in the back, but he was right by the window and the poor guys had no chance. They were both mowed down by raking machine-gun fire. While that was happening, Collinson used the cover to sneak up to the roof, and guide the chopper home. There was no point in fighting any more, and the Hezbollah guys fell back. The chopper took off. I just stayed there, must have been a couple of hours at least, waiting until I was sure the fighting had all died down.'

Hassad's expression was now calm and composed. 'So whatever the official report said, the reason three of your guys died was because that Collinson man lost his nerve.'

Porter could feel a hardening of his skin. It was the same feeling you got when the doctor gave you a local anaesthetic. Your body gradually turned numb. The nerves stiffened up, and all your senses withered away. The last seventeen years, he told himself, had all been a lie.

I've wasted an entire lifetime regretting something that never even bloody happened.

'That fucker,' he muttered aloud.

'What . . . ?'

'He said you came round and shot Steve, Mike and Keith. That made it my fault for not finishing you off when I had the chance. But it was his fault all along . . . the cowardly fuckhead didn't know how to fight, and he didn't know how to take the rap when he screwed things up either.'

He let three men die because of his cowardice, thought Porter bitterly.

He let another man die inside because he didn't want to take the blame.

And offered the choice between believing Hassad's version of what happened and Collinson's, then Hassad's seem the more credible.

I always knew Collinson was a coward.

I saw it the moment he started puking up when he stepped off that Puma and into the fighting.

TWENTY-TWO

Porter was still holding the AK-47. His finger was still twitching nervously on the trigger. And the gun was still pointed straight at Hassad's chest.

'I owe you my life, nothing else,' said Hassad.

'Take me to her,' said Porter.

Hassad remained silent. His eyes were fixed on the barrel of the gun. 'And you expect me to help you?'

'I'll kill you if you don't.'

'You are my enemy,' said Hassad softly. 'I allowed you to come here because I owed you, but now that you have discovered the truth, all the debts between us are ended. And the woman dies at eight tonight.'

Porter caressed the trigger of the AK-47. 'This gun says differently.'

'Kill me if you want to,' Hassad snapped. 'If that's what you came for, just do it, then . . . the woman stays right where she is.'

For a moment Porter was about to fire. Why the hell not? he asked himself. Whatever the truth of what happened seventeen years ago, Hassad was still a brutal terrorist who had tortured an innocent woman until the will to live had been drained out of her. Even if he didn't deserve to die for killing Steve, Mike and Keith, then he certainly deserved to die for that.

His finger stopped.

I don't have it in me to pull the trigger, he thought.

As he gripped the barrel of the AK-47, everything was slotting into place for Porter. Someone had tried to kill him back in London – someone who knew the details of the mission he was about to go on. When he arrived, he was captured by a British-led private military corporation – by someone who knew precisely where he was going, and what passwords needed to be used.

That person could only be Sir Peregrine Collinson.

Why? Because he was desperate to prevent me from seeing Hassad again, for the simple reason that I might learn the truth of what happened on that bungled mission to Beirut all those years ago.

The bastard is going to pay for that.

'Take me to her,' Porter growled.

'I can't.'

Porter stood up, and jabbed the barrel of the AK-47 into Hassad's chest. He could feel the hard, solid muscle as he prodded it with the cold steel of the gun. 'You bloody well can, and you bloody well will,' Porter snapped. 'I just want to talk to her, that's all. I won't cause any more trouble, not for you anyway.'

Hassad got slowly to his feet. Maybe he's just playing me along, Porter thought. Perhaps he's just going to walk me straight into a trap. I have to take that chance: it's the only hope I have of breaking Katie out of here.

They strode briskly through the meeting point. Hassad glanced at the one corpse Porter had left behind, then glanced at Porter. He could tell from the expression on his face that he knew exactly what had happened. Porter jabbed him forward with the AK-47. They kept walking towards the room where Katie had been tied to a stake. Porter was struggling to keep track of time: he reckoned it was three thirty in the morning, but it could be as late as four. The two soldiers stood rigidly to attention as they saw them approach. Their own assault rifles were snapped into position.

240

'It's OK,' said Hassad softly. 'We're just going inside for a moment.'

Smart, thought Porter. He knows they could shoot me, but it would be a bloodbath, and probably all four of us would die. Once you started letting off AK-47s in a confined space, the bullets would shred everyone. Better to let me inside: there's still a chance he might be able to talk me into dropping the gun.

Pale light had spread across the room. Porter glanced at Katie. It was only a couple of hours or so since he had last seen her, but her condition was even worse. So far as he could see, she had lost consciousness: she could be sleeping, but with the pain she had endured Porter reckoned she'd gone under.

He kept his gun trained on Hassad.

'Untie her,' he snapped.

He knew his drill. Get her off the stake, then try and fight his way out of here, room by room. It was probably the worst plan he'd ever heard. Against so many men, there was practically no chance of success. But at least this way they'd take a few of the bastards with her. And it wouldn't be on worldwide TV.

'No,' said Hassad, with quiet determination.

As he spoke, Porter could see Katie's eyes slowly open. He could see the pain each movement caused her, but there was a glimmer of defiance in her expression. Her boss was right, thought Porter. The woman has nerves of steel. She glanced first at Hassad, then at Porter. 'I . . .' she croaked, coughing as she struggled to form the words on her lips.

Porter raised a hand to stop her from speaking. He pushed the AK-47 closer to Hassad's chest. 'Then she'll at least have the satisfaction of watching you die first,' he said. 'And then I'll untie her myself.'

'I hope she enjoys the show.'

'Please just do . . .' started Katie, her voice turning into a cough.

While Porter's attention was distracted, Hassad leapt forwards, smashing the AK–47 from Porter's grip as he did so. He jammed as hard as he could on the trigger, loosening off a few rounds of bullets, but the barrel of the gun had already been deflected, and the shots smashed harmlessly into the solid stone walls of the cell. Christ, thought Porter. The noise of that gunfire is certain to alert the rest of the guards.

Hassad was forcing him onto the ground, crushing him with his weight. Using his right hand, Porter curled his fist, and smashed it into the man's jaw. He could tell at once the blow was a good one: he could feel his knuckles crunching into the bone underneath the skin. Hassad reeled back, the pain shooting through him. A smear of blood was trickling away from his lips.

Hassad was preparing to strike back, and even though he'd been unbalanced by the blow, his boot was drawing back, and Porter could see at once he was about to take a kicking. He started to try and scramble to his feet, moving as fast as he could to deflect the impact of the first inevitable blow.

A huge explosion rocked through the mine.

For a second, Porter was too stunned to react. His mind went numb. He could hear the sound of explosives detonating, and the crumbling of rock. How far away? he wondered. The explosion was muffled at first, but the noise was rumbling through the tunnels and rock like a train rumbling through the night.

Christ, he thought. Maybe it's the Regiment. *Maybe they've come for us.*

Let's hope to God that's what it is.

Hassad was looking around desperately, then running for the door. Outside, Porter could hear men screaming, and the din of a rolling series of aftershocks from the first explosion, rattling though the mine like a persistent, steady cough. 'What the fuck is it?' he shouted.

'A bunker-busting missile, I reckon,' Hassad snarled, his expression grim.

Porter could hear more shouts, and more screams. An ugly smell was drifting under the closed door. It took Porter a moment to recognise it – he had smelt it once before on the battlefield: a mixture of scorched foam and stewed meat, it was the distinctive smell of men burning to death. Christ, he told himself. The place is going up in flames.

If we don't get out of here, we're all going to die.

'Cut her down,' yelled Porter, gesturing towards Katie.

Hassad was reaching for the door, throwing it open. Outside, the corridor was filled with a thick, noxious smoke, and he instantly slammed it shut again. He looked back at Porter.

'We need to get her out of here,' Porter shouted, his voice hoarse. 'She's no bloody good to you dead, is she?'

There was no reply. Hassad looked to have been stunned into muteness.

'If it's a British attack, and she dies, then we've fucking won, haven't we?' screamed Porter, handing him a knife.

Snapping back to attention, Hassad took two steps forward. With a swift movement of his hand, he slashed at the ropes that bound Katie to the stake. The knots were strong, and expertly bound, and it took several attempts to free her completely. But then she fell forwards. Porter caught her in his arms. She was so groggy, she was close to losing consciousness, but if they could just get out of here, there was still a chance of saving her.

'What's happening?' she muttered.

Porter no longer had any idea. When he first heard the explosions he reckoned it must be the Regiment coming in to rescue them, but now he wasn't so sure. They might have used some stun grenades to prepare the way for an assault. Maybe some gas. But this looked like some kind of cruise missile making a direct hit on the mine. Why the hell would you do that? It would risk killing the very people you were meant to be capturing.

Her voice was cracked and weak, but as Porter cradled her in his arms, he could feel some of the strength coming back to her. For the first time in days she believed she might live, and it was amazing what resilience that knowledge could give a person.

'Reckon we can get out of here?' said Porter, glancing at Hassad.

He didn't reply, but the brutal expression on his face suggested he didn't think so. Porter pointed his gun straight at the man, nudging him forward, while holding on to Katie as well. He pulled the door ajar, reeling back as a cloud of thick black smoke hit him straight in the face. He coughed violently, his whole body shaking as his lungs tried to get rid of the air he'd just breathed. 'Corpses,' he whispered, his face drained of all colour.

Porter put Katie onto the ground, and held his breath as he slipped his face around the door, glancing out into the corridor beyond that ran down to the meeting point. It took a moment for his eyes to adjust to the clouds of smoke, and the fumes that were stinging his pupils, but as he focused it was clear that the mine had been turned into a scene of total devastation. The two fighters who normally stood guard against the door had been reduced to a couple of charred skeletons, and there were more corpses as you looked towards the meeting point. A huge fireball, Porter reckoned, must have swept down the corridor, burning everything it met, then, as it sucked all the oxygen out of the space, it would have extinguished itself, leaving behind the heavy clouds of smoke. Only the thick door to Katie's cell had saved them. Even so, to get out they would have to fight their way through the smoke, and the secondary fires and explosions still rippling through the rest of the mine.

Porter tore the shirt from his back. 'Tear this into three strips, then dunk them in water and put one over your mouth,' he barked. 'It's the only chance we've got.'

'You were pointing a gun at my chest five minutes ago,' Hassad growled.

'And you bloody deserved it,' Porter snapped. 'But unless we work together, none of us has a chance of getting out of here alive, so let's just get free of this place, and then carry on our fight later if we have to.'

Throwing the AK–47 he had taken from Hassad across his back, Porter knelt down, and tied the strip of wet cloth across Katie's face. It would help the keep the fumes out of her face. Then he slipped a strip around his own mouth, knotting it tightly around the back of his head. He hoisted Katie into his arms, and headed for the corridor. She was a good-sized woman, at least five eight, and when she was fit would probably have weighed considerably more than she did now. He could feel at once how frail and weak her body had become. Even a fit person would have trouble walking through these fumes, he thought bitterly.

For a weak one, it could be fatal.

'Try not to breathe too deeply,' he muttered.

Porter stepped out into the corridor, pressing Katie's face into his chest to try and keep her mouth away from the smoke. The fumes were so heavy, and the light so poor, it was impossible to see more than a few metres ahead. From somewhere, Porter heard a shout, telling him that not every-one was dead. Not yet anyway. Hassad was already striding towards the meeting point. Porter plunged forward, ignoring the carnage all around him. As he stood alongside Hassad at the centre of the mine, there were at least five bodies strewn across the ground, all of them burnt beyond recognition.

'How the hell do we get out of here?' Porter shouted, though his voice was muffled by the wet cloth strapped across his mouth.

'All the exits are blocked,' said Hassad.

Porter glanced around. The timbers the miners had wedged into place to hold up the roof years ago had been incinerated in the blast. Some were still burning and the roof was starting to sag badly: Porter reckoned it might not be long before the whole thing came down, bringing a couple of hundred tons of rock collapsing onto their heads. The staircase that led down from the lift into the meeting point had been totally destroyed. Flames were still licking upwards where the timber frame of the stairs had once been. It was totally impassable.

'We'll take the back way,' said Hassad.

Along one of the tunnels, Porter could hear an explosion. There was suddenly a blinding flash of light that cut through the fumes and illuminated the meeting point. Porter shielded his face as he felt a blast of heat wash over him. He gripped tighter onto Katie, and tried to follow Hassad. He'd already started marching towards a tunnel, motioning to Porter to follow him. Porter stepped forwards. The fire was gathering pace behind him, and he could hear a scream as it collided with one of the men trying to escape, frying him in an instant. Keeping hold of Katie, he followed Hassad into a narrow channel cut into the rock. There were a couple of bodies at its entrance, but Porter just stepped over them and pressed on. Behind him he could hear the sound of another roof collapsing somewhere, and more screams.

Hassad was twisting his way through a tunnel that was narrowing all the time. The light from the flames licking up around the meeting point had illuminated the first few metres, but it was fading fast, and within a few seconds Porter was struggling to keep track of Hassad through the darkness. A wall loomed up ahead of them, but to the right-hand side, there was a crack that appeared to lead upwards. It was part of an old ventilation shaft that must have been built years ago. 'Here,' said Hassad. 'This will take us to the next level. Where the lift is.'

'The lift won't have survived this carnage,' said Porter.

'There's another exit from there. If we can get through . . .'

Hassad started to lever himself up into the hole in the rock. There was enough room for a man to crawl through it – just – but not enough to carry Katie.

'You push her, I'll pull,' shouted Hassad as he disappeared into the tunnel.

With a heave of his forearms, Porter hoisted Katie up to the mouth of the tunnel. He pushed her into position, ignoring the cry of pain as she smashed her elbow into the rock. 'Just grab his hand,' he shouted, struggling to make his voice heard over the crashing of collapsing timbers behind them.

Porter pushed her again, then pulled himself up into the vertical tunnel. It measured just three feet in diameter: enough space for a person to crawl through, but only just. The surface of the tunnel was pitted and rough, but there were plenty of places to get a grip on the rock. Using the muscles in his legs to propel himself forwards, his arms pushed Katie up. Hassad was dragging her along with his arms. It was hard going but they were making steady progress. Porter could hear a couple more explosions behind him but he reckoned most of the blokes down there must be dead by now. They were lucky just to have made it this far.

They were getting closer. Another ten metres, Porter thought. He could see Katie was using her fingers to try and claw her way to the surface, but she was so desperately weak it was hard for her to summon the strength to propel herself upwards. Hassad was reaching the surface now. He paused, then pulled himself free of the narrow tunnel. Turning round, he held out a strong hand, pulling Katie up, while Porter pushed her from behind, following swiftly in her wake.

They had emerged into a dark cavern that must have once formed a part of the main mine. It was so dark, Porter had no idea how big it was or where it led: the only light was the soft glow sneaking up the tunnel from the fires raging one level below them. 'Where the hell are we?' said Porter.

'One level below the surface,' said Hassad. 'It's a big mine, and we were using only a tiny part of it. These tunnels go on for miles.' He nodded in front of him. 'But to get out we have to go that way.'

Porter picked Katie up again and looked ahead. He could see nothing through the darkness. 'How far?'

'About seven hundred metres along this tunnel, there should be an old emergency exit that will take us up to the surface.'

'You think it's on fire?'

'How the hell should I know?' snapped Hassad.

Porter hoisted Katie onto his back. He was still wondering if Hassad was tricking him, maybe leading him straight into a troop of Hezbollah fighters on the surface. I'll fight that battle when I get to it, he told himself. 'Then we better get moving.'

From down below, another explosion echoed towards them. There were tons of munitions down there, Porter realised, and one by one, the flames were reaching the stock-piles of weaponry, igniting vicious fireballs. The ground beneath them shook, and a pile of dusty debris scattered loose from the ceiling, showering them with fragments of rock and ore. Porter started to pick up the pace, jogging alongside Hassad. As they moved away from the shaft they had climbed up, they lost all contact with the light. Within seconds, they were shrouded in darkness. It was too dangerous to run: they could see nothing, and the path was littered with rocks and pits they could easily trip over. Hassad was hugging the wall, feeling his way forwards with his hands, and Porter was following on behind. The metres were covered painfully slowly. A couple of times Porter could feel himself starting to fall as his feet collided with a rock – and a fall might easily finish Katie off in her weakened condition – but he just about managed to recapture his balance in time.

Eventually they reached a doorway. A light was shining underneath it: the glow of burning flames. Even standing ten feet from it, Porter could feel an intense heat from the other side. 'It's on fire,' he said, looking towards Hassad. 'There must be another way.'

Hassad shook his head. 'Back there, the mine just goes deeper and deeper underground.'

'It's burning up over there.'

'It's the only way,' Hassad snapped. 'Otherwise, we die down here.'

He took a couple of paces forwards. The exit was made from an old metal fame, with a wooden door inside it. There was a padlock, but it didn't look very strong. Hassad pushed his shoulder against it, then stepped back a couple of metres and charged the door. It snapped free on impact. The padlock broke away, and the rusty hinges collapsed, sending the door crashing to the ground. Porter followed Hassad through. Katie was still clinging to his back, wheezing heavily as a fresh blast of smoke hit them in the face. He was looking into a long thin room, maybe thirty metres deep by five across. A burst of heat hit him in the face. At the far end, he could see the lift that led down to the level below, but it was smashed to pieces and twisted beyond recognition. Flames were licking up from that level, creating the waves of heat that had hit him in the face. Behind the lift shaft, there was a thick, broad channel, reaching down into the mine, and above up to the night sky. Porter reckoned that must have been where the bunker-busting missile came in: its hardened, titanium nose would have pierced the ground, and then bored its way easily through the levels of the mine, before exploding viciously deep underground. Bunker-busters were designed to take out the reinforced concrete layers that protected nuclear or biological weapons: it was no surprise that it had shredded the mine like a carving knife through a sandwich.

Not many countries have access to bunker-busting technology, thought Porter.

But the British do. And the Israelis.

'This way, quick,' yelled Hassad. 'We haven't much time.'

Porter now saw he was pointing towards a corridor that led away from the main room.

Porter glanced around. The area near the lift where they had come in last night was clearly impassable. The missile had left a pile of burning debris. Even the rock looked red-hot: touch it and it would set fire to you instantly. The timbers along the room had ignited and burnt, and the floor was now a smouldering mess of ash and embers. There was no way they could cross it. But the corridor Hassad was pointing to looked OK. If I can trust him, thought Porter.

Checking that Katie was secure on his back, Porter started to run across the open space towards the corridor. He could feel great waves of raw heat from the lift, and a couple more explosions rocked through the mine in quick succession. The ash and embers on the floor were burning into his feet: running as fast as he could, he could feel it singeing the soles of his trainers. The ground was vibrating all around him, and the walls were shaking. Another explosion, and then a vicious fountain of sparks shot upwards from the lift shaft like a display of fireworks. This mine can't take much more punishment, Porter reflected grimly. Any moment now, the whole place is going to blow.

Hassad had already turned into the corridor. Porter ran after him. The tunnel was long and thin, twisting up and down through the rock. It was held in place by a series of wooden timbers, many of which were already burning. The heat was searing, like stepping straight into a microwave. Porter could feel the sweat dripping off his skin, and on his back, Katie was coughing viciously, the flannel across her face doing little to control the heavy fumes from the fires all around them.

They covered ten, twenty, then thirty metres. Porter wasn't sure how much more he could take. The temperature was rising all the time. His head was throbbing and his vision was starting to blur: beyond a certain point, he knew that men just dropped from heat exhaustion.

'We can't make it much further,' he shouted to Hassad.

'Just another ten metres.'

Porter pressed on. He could see the tunnel opening up ahead. There was a wooden structure up in front of them, with flames already licking around it, and beyond that a rickety wooden staircase that had not yet caught fire. Behind him, the heat was growing more intense by the second, and he'd already heard the sound of rocks crashing to the ground. As they burnt, the timbers could no longer support the weight of the roof. It was groaning, threatening to collapse at any moment. Ignoring Katie's cough, he pushed on harder, picking up the pace. There might only be seconds left before the whole place collapses, he told himself. Each step could well be the last one.

The wooden entrance was now covered in flames, and for a moment Porter paused. There was no way through, not without risking setting fire to yourself. Already, Hassad had ripped the shirt from his back. He was using it to beat back the flames, creating a space large enough for a single man. 'Take her through,' he shouted. 'I'll follow on behind.'

Porter threw himself past Hassad, and towards the staircase. It stretched up for ten steps or so.

Suddenly he heard a scream.

Hassad.

He was shouting something in Arabic.

Porter looked round.

Part of the wall had come away. Hassad was lying flat on the ground, a heavy timber pinning down his leg and his groin. Flames were licking along the wood, getting closer all the time. He tried to lever himself up so that he could push the timber away, but it was no use. He was trapped, and from the look on his face he knew it. Any moment now, he was going to die.

'Help me,' he shouted.

Porter rested Katie on the staircase. The flames hadn't reached this far yet, but sparks were spitting all over the place, and the heat was intense so it might not be long before the steps went up as well. 'You going to be OK?'

She nodded. 'I . . .'

The words ended in another fit of coughing.

'Just stay right there,' said Porter. 'Don't try to move.'

He turned and ran back towards where Hassad was lying on the ground. The timber wasn't that heavy – no more than a hundred pounds – but it was hot. More than half of it was alight now, and the sparks were spitting into Hassad's leg. Porter grabbed it with both hands, and started to heave it away.

Then he paused. He looked straight at Hassad.

'This is the second time I've saved your life,' he said.

Hassad glanced towards him.

'This time I want something in return,' said Porter. 'You have to help me get Katie out of here, and across the border.'

'Just release me,' shouted Hassad.

The flames were getting closer all the time. A couple of sparks spat on his clothes, singeing his skin. Porter could feel his own face burning up, and his cheeks reddening.

He lowered the burning timber just a fraction, so that it was still pinning Hassad down. 'Give me your word.'

'I'll get her to the border, I swear it,' screamed Hassad.

With a heave of his shoulders, Porter hoisted the timber up into the air, and tossed it clean away from Hassad's legs. He reached down a hand, and grabbed hold of the man, pulling him up to his feet. 'Then let's get the fuck out of here,' he said. 'Before the whole bloody place collapses on top of us.'

TWENTY-THREE

Their way was blocked by what looked to Porter like no more than an old and rusty manhole cover. Unhooking the AK–47 still strapped to his back, and flipping the gun around, Porter smashed its butt into the disc, pushing it open. His hands grabbed the sides of the hole and he pulled himself up with one swift movement. He glanced anxiously around to see if anyone could see him, but the way was clear. Instantly, he plunged his hands back into the mine. 'Grab hold of these,' he shouted.

Katie was just below him, and had enough of her wits about her to grip on to Porter's wrists. He pulled her sharply upwards, dragging her out onto the land. Hassad followed on swiftly behind them. 'What do we do now?' said Porter, his voice breathless.

'Run like hell,' said Hassad. 'It's not safe here.'

Porter hardly had time to take in the scene around them. It was still night-time, and visibility was limited. They had emerged about eighty metres from the main entrance to the mine. There was a huge crater in the ground where the missile had smashed into the site, throwing up a ton of hot, molten rock as it cleaved its way through the ground. A few corpses were scattered around the entrance: men who must have been killed when the missile first struck. However, up to a dozen more were still standing, grouped twenty metres behind that, too far away for them to be able to see Porter. Guys who were out on patrol or too far from the missile strike to be killed on the first impact, he reckoned. Probably trying to figure out what the hell has just happened to them.

And whether there is anything they can do for the poor bastards trapped down below.

Porter grabbed hold of Katie, and slung her onto his back. With some food and water and medicine she might be up to walking soon. But not yet. Never mind, Porter decided, as he started to walk steadily forwards. I'll carry her all the way back to London if I have to. It would be worth it just to see the look on that bastard Collinson's face.

'This way,' hissed Hassad.

He was tabbing across the open ground. The mine was at the centre of a big, open-cast pit, like a moon crater but filled with old and rusting machinery. The banks rose up steeply, taking you back to level ground, but there were pathways and tracks where the trucks must have carried the finished metals they dug here out towards the railways and ports. It was about thirty metres, heavy going with Katie clinging to your back, but they made it. A couple of times, Porter could feel the ground shake beneath him, like the tremors from an earthquake. Some of the soldiers near the entrance a hundred metres behind them were running around, shouting as holes appeared in the ground where the mine was collapsing. One or two men appeared to have made their way out to the surface, but not many. More explosions, Porter reflected grimly, as he listened to the ground cracking beneath his feet. Finishing off whatever poor sods are still down there.

Sweat was pouring off his skin as he marched on. He'd ripped the wet mask off his face: the air up here was clear and fresh, and just getting some oxygen into his lungs was doing him good, but he was half naked, and his body had taken a terrible beating in the past few hours. There were cuts and bruises all over him, and his skin felt charred from the intense heat of the mine. His lungs felt as if he'd just smoked about two million cigarettes, and his head was spinning.

Even as he walked, the questions were starting to loop through Porter's mind.

Who the hell fired that missile? The British? The Israelis? But why?

If they knew where we were, why not just send in a Regiment unit to try and break us out?

Whoever fired that monster must have been reckoning to kill everyone in the mine.

Including us.

As they reached the top of the pathway, Porter laid Katie on the ground. Up over the ridge, the first glimmers of dawn were starting to break through the night sky. It must be five thirty, maybe six in the morning, Porter thought.

Saturday.

The day scheduled for the execution.

But the danger was far from over. Indeed, it might be just beginning.

I've no idea where the border is. Or how far we are from safety . . .

He knelt down and wiped some of the soot away from Katie's forehead with the palm of his hand. Christ, we better keep this girl away from a mirror for the next couple of days, he thought. Her eyes were like a couple of squashed tomatoes, and her complexion had turned the mucky grey of school-dinner stew. There were scabs across her cheek where she had been cut. And her body was wasting into little more than a skeleton with some ill-fitting skin stretched over it.

'We're getting you home,' he said.

'Thanks,' she croaked.

'Just hang in there, that's all.'

They had paused just where the mine met an old road, made from broken and chipped concrete. Porter was already looking at Hassad suspiciously, wondering if he could be trusted to keep his word or if he was about to call out to his mate. 'Over there,' hissed Hassad, pointing towards a tin shack with half its roof blown away. 'There's a car we can use. We stashed a few around the edge of this mine in case we needed a quick escape. The keys are left in them, and there's fuel in the tank.'

Only another twenty metres, Porter thought. They were even further from the Hezbollah guards now, and unlikely to be spotted. But he wasn't sure Katie should be carried any longer. 'Bring it here,' he muttered.

Hassad jogged across the road. Again, Porter wondered if he'd escape. Maybe go and get his mates and come and capture Katie again. Or just escape in the car. He checked the AK-47 on his back, making sure there was still some ammo left in its magazine. If he had to, he'd take the bastard down, and escape on foot himself. But Hassad had given his word when he saved his life back there in the mine. Just so long as he kept it . . .

The car was an old, grey VW Polo, with what looked to Porter like a hundred thousand miles on the clock. It reeked of diesel and cigarette fumes. Its engine roared and stuttered, but seemed to be spinning fine. Hassad twisted the wheel around, pulling it up next to Porter, and flung the door open. Porter grabbed Katie, pulled back the passenger seat, and laid her flat down on the back. She was in no state to sit up, he judged. He pulled the seat belt down to fasten it around her so that she wouldn't get knocked around too much. There was no telling what kind of roads they might meet. Nor what kind of opposition.

'Drive carefully,' he muttered towards Hassad. 'She can't take much more.'

'We still have to get past the soldiers.'

'Do what –'

'You think they're going to be happy to see you drive off with their hostage?'

'You bloody promised you'd get us to the border.'

'But my promise doesn't extend to the rest of Hezbollah.'

Porter looked around. They were on a ridge on the top of the open-cast mine. The road twisted around its edge, before linking up with the main highway about a mile away. Porter didn't know how many soldiers had remained on the surface and survived the missile strike, but enough to put up a stout resistance should they catch wind of what was afoot. Behind them was a tall, rocky set of mountains. The dawn was starting to break through now, spreading a fresh orange light across the landscape, and yet as Porter surveyed the rocks, he could see there was no way through. Not by car anyway. They might be able to make their way on foot, but the condition they were in, and without any water or supplies, they might easily die within a few miles.

'Is there a side road?' said Porter.

Hassad shook his head, gunning up the engine at the same time.

'Do we look like idiots?' he said. 'We chose this old mine because it's simple to monitor anything coming in or out. You take the main road, which always has some guards on it, or else you have to walk through the mountains and desert, but that's a hard and difficult journey.'

Hassad tapped his foot on the accelerator. The Polo roared and started to rev, then spun along the track, kicking up a cloud of dust as it did so. 'They think we're still down in that mine, and that means they think we're dead,' said Hassad. 'They won't be looking for us.'

Porter glanced round. Katie was lying motionless on the seat. Her eyes were half closed and she was breathing slowly. They had to get her some food and water soon. She wasn't going to last much longer.

How far is it to the border? Porter asked himself again.

The Polo was powering steadily. Around the perimeter of the open-cast mine was about half a mile, and for its age, the

VW had plenty of acceleration left in it. Hassad was just keeping the engine ticking over, not trying to push it too fast. The road was rough and pitted with stones, and even if you did try to push it above fifty miles an hour, you would probably just crack the suspension. 'Put your head down while I drive past the soldiers,' muttered Hassad. 'And then we just need to get through the roadblock.'

Porter ducked. He buried his head in his knees: in that position, if they drove past anyone at speed, they probably wouldn't notice him. He glanced back at Katie. No need to hide her. She was already lying flat on her back.

As he dipped his head below the windscreen, Porter could see they were approaching the main road on the far side of the mine. A makeshift roadblock had been set up across the track: it consisted of two mounds of old tyres, with a wooden bar slung between them. Normally, Porter reckoned, there would be two or three soldiers there monitoring who came into and out of the mine, but there was so much chaos down below where the missile had struck there was just one guy, sitting by the side of the road, an AK-47 cradled in his arms.

At his side, Porter could see Hassad tapping his foot hard on the accelerator.

'There may be an impact when we go through the bar,' said Hassad. 'Steady yourself.'

'Won't they let you through?'

'This is Hezbollah,' said Hassad proudly. 'Nobody comes in or out of this mine without their vehicle being checked.'

Porter put his hands around his head. The Polo was accelerating now, touching sixty. Suddenly, there was a crunching noise, as the nose of their car collided with the wooden pole. Porter was thrown forward, his head bashing against the cheap plastic of the glove compartment. In the back, Katie jerked upwards and groaned in pain. The Polo served to the right as the impact deflected it off its path.

Hassad was gripping the steering wheel, pulling it back onto the track. Behind them, Porter could hear shouting. And then a rapid burst of gunfire exploded behind them.

Porter heard the sickening crunch of a bullet colliding with the back the car. It pierced the steel skin of the vehicle, but lodged itself harmlessly in the boot. Porter glanced again at Katie. There was no chance of moving her now, Porter realised. Too dangerous. But lying on the back seat, she was the most vulnerable of any of them: any bullets that pierced the back window were heading straight for her.

'Can't you move any bloody faster?' he shouted.

'I'm trying,' yelled Hassad.

His foot was jamming hard on the accelerator, but instead of gaining power, the Polo was losing it. The speedometer had touched sixty-five as they burst through the wooden barrier, and started heading down the slope that led towards the main road. But now it was slowly dropping down to sixty, then fifty-five.

Porter glanced in the wing-mirror.

The soldier had climbed on board a motorbike. His assault rifle was slung over his back, but there was a pistol clearly visible in the belt of his trousers. The bike was roaring fast, gaining on them with every metre they covered.

Hassad's grip tightened on the steering wheel as he tried to move them back onto the centre of the road.

'He's on a bike,' Porter growled.

'The car won't move, the tyre is punctured.'

'Fuck it.'

The Polo was still slowing, dropping down to forty-five now. It must be the back wheel, Porter thought grimly. There was no way the car was going to build up any speed with a back tyre blown out. He could see exactly what was about to happen. The bike was going to overtake them within not much more than a minute. The soldier would spin past them, stop the bike in the middle of the road, then turn his AK-47 on them.

Hassad might be one of the leaders of this gang, Porter told himself, but he'd seen these boys in action. Everything was sacrificed to the cause.

And everybody.

If they thought he was pissing off with their hostage, they wouldn't hesitate to shoot him.

And the hostage.

'I'm bailing out,' snapped Porter. 'Keep driving.'

Before Hassad had a chance to reply, Porter had flung open the door on the Polo. As it ripped through the air, Porter curled himself into a ball and kicked back with his legs. Hitting the ground with a heavy thump, a hundred bolts of pain started shooting up through his spine as his back absorbed the impact of the fall. It was only a couple of feet from the Polo's passenger seat to the dirt track they were driving down, but it felt like at least a hundred. He rolled, keeping his body as curved as possible to smooth the landing, but he was still moving fast over the ground, his naked back taking a dozen different cuts and bruises from the pebbles littering the path.

He could hear a horrible crunching sound where his ankle hit a stone, and prayed to God it wasn't broken.

No time to worry about it now, he told himself.

I could be dead before the next five seconds are up.

The AK-47 was still in his right hand. Porter rolled to his feet, steadied himself by the side of the road, then whipped the gun into his fists. The Polo was still moving away down the side of the hill, and in its wake, the motorbike was accelerating fast: a Honda, Porter noted, with at least a one-litre engine, the machine should be able to reach eighty or ninety on a track like this, and it was probably hitting those speeds now. He gripped the AK-47 tight in his hands, his fingers closing down on the trigger. The bike was close now, but amid the dust kicked up in the Polo's trail it was unlikely its driver would have noticed Porter bailing out. The bike sped past. In the same instant, Porter slammed his finger into the trigger of the AK–47, unleashing a hailstorm of bullets. The munitions ripped through the bike. The sound of metal colliding with metal cracked through the still morning air. Porter took a step forward. He kept his finger glued to the trigger, the bullets still rattling out of the barrel of his gun, tracking the target as it moved across the rough surface of the ground. The bike was wobbling. Some petrol had started to leak from its tank, and the driver had taken a couple of bullets to the back, and at least one to the leg. He was hanging on desperately to the machine beneath him: enough of his brain was still working to know that the bike was now his best chance of escaping the attack. But the machine was spinning violently out of control now. The bullets had severed the brake lines, and even though it was losing power fast, the driver had no way of slowing it down as he tried to straighten up and get down the hill. It twisted brutally, and the man no longer had the strength to hold onto its jerking handlebars. He was spun out across the dirt track, while the bike crashed into a rock close to the edge of the road. The front wheel broke off on impact, rolling down the hill, while the rest of the bike fell to the ground, the engine still coughing and spluttering.

Porter took another step forward.

The man was fifteen metres in front of him on the road.

He was reaching down for the pistol tucked into the belt of his trousers. There was blood pouring out of the wounds in his back, but he still had enough life left in him to hold a gun. Porter raised the sights of the AK–47 to his eyes, and squeezed the trigger. One bullet, then two, then three, smashed into his chest. Porter moved the AK–47 just a fraction of a millimetre, keeping his finger squeezed on the trigger. The next three bullets smashed into his neck and chin, blowing his face wide open.

The gun dropped from his hand.

The man fell dead into the dust all around him.

Porter started to jog down the road, looking anxiously for the Polo: if Hassad wanted to escape this was his moment. The light was rising all around the mine now. He could see the car had pulled up about two hundred metres down the road. Glancing behind him, Porter didn't think any more soldiers were giving chase. He ran faster, flinging back the door of the car and jumping inside.

'Let's get the hell out of here,' he muttered. 'Before any more of the bastards come after us.'

'Those bastards are my people,' said Hassad.

Porter paused.

The AK-47 was still gripped in his hand. It would take just a fraction of a second to kill Hassad, and if he had to, he would. From the look on his face, he guessed that Hassad understood that.

'We made a deal,' he snapped. 'Just get us to the border, and this is all over.'

TWENTY-FOUR

They had been gone for around an hour, Porter calculated, and twenty minutes of that was spent by the roadside, with the two men changing the burst tyre on the Polo as quickly as they could. Porter kept his eyes on the road around them, trying to get a fix on where they were: according to Hassad they were still in northern Lebanon, but up close to the Syrian border. The road was decent enough, Porter noted. Half a mile from the mine they'd hit some fresh tarmac, and even though the Polo had taken a couple of bullets to its rear, it seemed to be driving OK.

They'd get there. Just so long as nobody else started shooting at them on the way.

It was a day's drive to the Israeli border, Hassad had said: a total of a hundred and ten miles, but the territory was rough as you got closer to Israel, and progress would be slow. Porter wanted to drive straight there, but Hassad insisted they stop first. He'd take them to a safe house he knew first. They would get themselves cleaned up, then complete the journey. No, just get us there, said Porter. Hassad was adamant. Katie needed some fluids in her: without them, she was probably going to die. And the Lebanese–Israeli border was the heaviest, most heavily militarised on the planet: without any proper weapons they didn't stand a chance of getting through.

Porter glanced a few times at Katie, but she seemed to have fallen asleep. Porter reached back to check her pulse. It was weak, fading all the time. 'Hang in there,' Porter muttered under his breath. I didn't go to all this trouble just to bring a corpse across the border.

His own condition wasn't too bad. The shirt had long since been ripped off his back, and he'd taken a battering to his back when he jumped out of the car. His jeans had been torn in a couple of places, and the soles of his trainers had been burnt when they were escaping from the burning mine. There was a hole in the left shoe and the right one wasn't in much better shape. His chest was a mess of cuts and bruises, and there wasn't even any water in the car to start washing them.

Hassad's right, I need to get myself cleaned up, he told himself. There's still a long way to go before we get out of this hellhole.

'Here,' said Hassad.

He pulled the Polo up outside a modest one-storey house, set five hundred metres back from the main road. There was a petrol station about a mile up the road, and eight or nine hundred metres back there was a warehouse. Otherwise the place was completely isolated. A set of hills rose up behind the house, and there was flat plain in front of it, but the ground was too dusty, dry and hard for anything other than a few rough-looking bushes to grow. Safe enough, Porter decided. They could rest for a couple of hours, get themselves back in shape, and get the hell out of here.

Hassad had fished out some keys from a compartment hidden inside the spare wheel. There were at least a dozen on the ring. Hezbollah kept a string of safe houses within a short drive of the mine, he explained. They permanently expected Israeli tanks to come rolling across the border towards them, and were always prepared to evacuate in a hurry. All the keys to safe houses were kept in the cars hidden around the perimeter of the mine. Anyone could grab one at any time and make a clean getaway if the mine came under attack.

Preparation, thought Porter. They plan every move meticulously. That's what makes them such a dangerous enemy.

He picked Katie up from the back seat of the car, cradling her in his arms. She was half asleep, but also half unconscious. Hassad had already pushed the door open. It was just after eight in the morning, and there was a slightly chill breeze in the air, but the house was warm enough. He followed Hassad through from the hallway into the main room. There wasn't much furniture: the walls were painted plain white, and there was a sofa, and a couple of cheap wicker chairs, but at least it was clean, and it was the most luxurious place Porter had seen since he left Beirut airport. He laid Katie down on the sofa. She moaned softly as his arm caught one of her many bruises. Porter looked over to Hassad. 'We need food and medicine,' he said. 'She's in a bad way.'

They walked through to the kitchen area. Even without the full tour, it didn't take Porter long to get the layout of the place. It had everything you'd expect of a safe house: a few places to kip down, a kitchen well stocked with dried and tinned foods, and plenty of water; a cabinet bursting with every kind of medicine you could think of; and a stash of weapons. There was a TV and a radio, and the house even had a small oil-fired generator to keep the power supply secure. But there was no sign of a phone. If there had been, Porter might have checked in with the Firm, and organised a chopper to come and lift them out. But it would be quicker to try and get to the border themselves, and he still didn't trust Hassad enough to rely on him to organise a safe line back to London.

Porter grabbed a bottle of water, some cereals and dried crackers, and some medicine. He knelt down beside Katie. Putting his hand to her forehead, he could tell that she was running a slight temperature. There was a film of sweat over her body, and her eyes were still very swollen. Porter had had some basic medical training back in the Regiment, but it was years since he'd tried to use it. He stripped her down to just her knickers. He grabbed some cotton wool and some disinfectant, and started to fix the cuts across her skin: she winced as he treated the worst tears with raw alcohol, washing them carefully, then spreading thick strips of plaster across them. Within moments, she looked more like an Egyptian mummy than a woman. He rifled through the medicines he'd collected from the chest. Among them was some penicillin. He quickly unwrapped a syringe and jabbed it into her arm. She winced, but she was still too weak to register much of what was happening. Next, he took some blood plasma, and pumped that into the vein as well. Along with the fluids, that should help her pull through the next twelve hours or so they needed to get to the border, then they could get her to a hospital.

Right now, some sleep will probably do her more good than anything else.

He patched up some of his own wounds, then grabbed a fresh pair of jeans, a T-shirt and a pair of trainers. The shoes were a size ten, a size bigger than his own feet, but at least they didn't have a hole in them. He mixed up a bowl of cereal with some dried milk and wolfed it down. It tasted like stale cardboard, but it was the first thing he'd had to eat in ages and at least there was some strength in it. All I need now is a vodka, he thought.

Porter glanced around. Hassad was standing behind him with an AK-47 he'd just taken from the stockroom clutched to his hand.

'Shit,' Porter muttered.

'Don't worry,' said Hassad. 'I've had enough chances to kill you already, and maybe I should have taken them. I've said I'll get you to the border, and I will. I'm just equipping myself with some kit in case we get attacked again.'

'I thought you said this was a safe house?'

'This is the Lebanon,' said Hassad with a shrug. 'Nowhere is safe.'

Porter had already checked out the munitions room. It was a big store cupboard just off the small kitchen. From a distance, it looked like a larder. Inside, there was enough weaponry to have a crack at taking Tel Aviv single-handed. Porter counted twelve assault rifles, each with a couple of hundred rounds of ammunition. There were six boxes of hand grenades neatly stacked in boxes. Two RPG launchers. One machine gun, plus a couple of belts of rounds. And a selection of handguns, hunting knives, ropes, handcuffs and chains.

Porter finished eating his cereal, then suddenly stopped. He could hear something.

Out in the scrubland.

He was sure of it.

He moved swiftly towards the window.

Scanning the land outside, he couldn't see anything. A couple of trucks rolled by in the distance, but none of them seemed to be stopping. There were no cars parked anywhere in view apart from the Polo outside. But still he felt certain he'd heard something.

A voice.

An English voice.

'Got any binoculars?' he said to Hassad.

After rooting around in the munitions store, Hassad returned with a cheap pair of field glasses.

'You think there's someone out there?'

'I'm sure of it.'

He scanned the landscape once more. At first glance, all he could see was scrubland. Acres and acres of dust stretched into the distance. No, he told himself. There is something there. I am sure of it.

A man.

He flicked the field glasses a fraction of a millimetre to the left, twisting the lens to increase the magnification.

A man was lying flat on his belly. He was covered head to toe in dusty-coloured uniform, effectively camouflaging him. To the naked eye, he was just a ridge of dirt in the ground. Porter locked the binoculars tight onto him. The man was fifty metres away, between the road and the house. Although he was flat on the ground, he was advancing steadily towards them. He passed the glasses across to Hassad. 'We're under attack,' he said.

'How many?'

'I can only see one guy,' said Porter. 'But there will be more of them. We can be sure of it.'

Somewhere behind him he heard a crash. He ran to the back of the house. A fragmentation grenade had been lobbed through the window. Glass was shattered across the floor. The grenade was lying in the hallway: there was no time to get rid of it before it blew. Porter clamped his mouth shut, and ran towards Katie. He hauled her over his back, ran towards the front door and flung it open. Looking around desperately, his eyes were searching for some cover. Without it, they were about to get cut down like dogs. There was a small wall close to where they had parked the Polo, only four feet high but just tall enough to provide some shelter. 'Get the fuck out of there,' he shouted at Hassad.

He dived towards the wall, flinging himself and Katie to the ground. Behind him, he could hear the grenade blowing inside the building, throwing a cloud of dust and smoke into the air. In the same moment, Hassad emerged coughing and spluttering from the house. He must have taken a lungful of fumes when the grenade blew, Porter guessed. Let's just hope it's not enough to put him out of action.

There could be a dozen of the bastards out there.

Are they Hezbollah? Porter asked himself. Maybe Hassad only brought me here so he could finish us both off.

Katie was muttering something, but there was no time to listen to her now. He unhooked the AK-47 from his back, and checked there was still some ammo left in the clip.

Hassad was running towards them, covering the ten metres from the house to the wall. He hurled himself down next to the others, and promptly threw up on the dusty ground. 'Puke it up, man,' Porter snapped. 'It's the only way to get the bloody smoke out of your lungs.'

Another explosion rocked through the house. Porter turned round. They must have put at least two, maybe three grenades into the place, igniting the munitions dump. A huge fireball rocked up into the sky, followed by a heavy cloud of thick black smoke. Porter tried to ignore it. A diversion, he told himself. The bastards are trying to move us out of here. Then they can gun us down.

Porter found a gap in the wall. Carefully, he slipped the AK-47 through it, so that only his hand was exposed, and even that was mostly protected by the muzzle of the assault rifle. He squeezed hard on the trigger, unleashing a barrage of fire into the space directly in front of them.

He heard a man scream, then another one.

The bastards were charging me, he noted with grim satisfaction.

But who the hell are they? And how did they know we were here?

'Lay down some fucking fire,' he shouted at Hassad.

He pulled the AK-47 back from the wall, discarding the empty clip. Glass and plaster had blown out of the house, covering the area with debris. He could feel the dirt clinging to his face. A hole had been blown in the roof, and waves of intense heat were billowing out of the burning building.

'Fucking fire,' he screamed.

Hassad spat the last of the vomit heaving out of his chest onto the ground. He lifted his head to the edge of the wall, his finger poised on the trigger of his gun.

'Keep your fucking head down,' shouted Porter, jamming a fresh clip into his own rifle. 'They're coming straight at us.'

Both guns were lodged over the wall, and Porter and Hassad fired in unison, unleashing a lethal barrage of bullets. Porter heard another scream, and the sound of a man roaring with pain. Suddenly there was a thump as something collided with the wall. He felt his heart skip a beat. In the next instant, a man had landed on the ground, just five feet from where Porter was positioned. He was about six foot tall, with a stocky build, and jet-black hair. His skin was tanned and lined, but he didn't look more than thirty. He didn't look like an Arab either, Porter noted. He crashed straight into Hassad, knocking him to the ground. Blood was pouring from his shoulder where he must have taken a bullet while charging the wall. His gun had fallen to the ground, but a hunting knife was gripped in the palm of his right hand, and was pointing straight at Hassad's throat. Porter aimed the AK-47 at him, and tried to line up a shot. It was too difficult. As the two men struggled, they turned into a blur. Shoot and the chances were he'd kill Hassad as well. Glancing at the wall, he could see that there were no more men jumping over. He threw the gun aside, and jumped across to where the two men were wrestling. Hassad was lying on the ground. His right hand was sticking up, gripping his assailant's arm, trying to stop him plunging the knife straight into him. Porter rammed a fist straight into the man's ribcage. It was as hard as rock. The man barely flinched. He spat down into Hassad's face. 'Die, you bastard,' he said.

Porter punched again. This time the blow connected, and he could feel a rib cracking under the force of the blow. The man groaned. He spat a mouthful of his blood down onto Hassad's chest. Porter clenched his fist, drew his arm back, and smashed it into exactly the same spot. He could feel the man's ribcage splintering: one, maybe even two bones cracked open as the blow hit home. He screamed in pain, rolling off Hassad onto the dusty ground. In the same moment, the knife in his hand lashed out. Porter leapt backwards, narrowly avoiding the blade slicing open his stomach. He stamped hard, bringing his new trainer down on the man's hand. The knife fell away. Porter ground his foot down, making sure the fingers were driven down into the dirt. With the other foot, he kicked hard into the man's stomach. The wind emptied out of him, and more blood dribbled out of his lips.

Hassad had already picked himself up from the ground. He had grabbed hold of the knife and was holding it tight into the man's throat. 'Who the fuck are you?' Porter growled.

The man remained mutely silent.

Porter paused. Glancing again over the short wall, he could see three bodies. All of them looked dead, killed as they tried to run into the wall. At his side, the safe house was still burning, throwing off an intense heat. It looked like there had been a total of four men making the assault, and they had now dealt with all of them. He looked back at the man. 'I said, who the fuck are you?'

The man looked back at him. His eyes were bloodshot and swollen, but although there was fear in his expression, there was defiance as well.

'Piss off,' he spat.

Even through a couple of broken teeth, and a mouthful of blood, Porter recognised the accent. A Scouser.

'What the fuck are you doing out here?' he said. 'There's nothing to nick. Now tell me who sent you –'

'Fuck off.'

Porter glanced towards Hassad. 'Cut him,' he snapped. 'Work on the gunshot wound.'

Hassad leant into the man's chest. He ripped open his shirt, and sliced open a wide, deep cut in his shoulder. Blood bubbled up out of the open wound, spilling down into the ground.

Porter knelt down, leaning into the man's ear. He picked up a handful of dust and dirt and chucked it into the open wound. 'The Arabs are fucking savages, and so am I,' he said. 'Now just tell us, and then you can go out and sleep in the scrub with your mates.'

There were tears of pain streaming down the man's cheeks.

Porter punched him hard in the stomach. He coughed violently, and a fresh river of blood tipped out of the gaping wound in his stomach.

'Just tell me,' Porter growled, 'and I'll let you fuck off to the great Scouser-nicking shop in the sky.'

'We work for Connaught Security,' he shouted. 'Perry Collinson is ultimately in charge of it. He sent us out here to kill you.'

Porter slammed another foot into the man's stomach. 'Fucking mercenaries,' he spat. 'There's a lot of competition for who's the lowest scum in this hellhole. But I reckon you blokes are right at the bottom.'

I'm bloody through with bastards trying to kill me, he told himself. I'm going to take it out on someone.

'Why?'

Another half-pint of blood spilt onto the dusty ground.

'Why?' shouted Porter, louder this time.

But the man's eyes had already closed.

I already know why, Porter thought. *And the only man I have left to speak to is Collinson himself.*

TWENTY-FIVE

Katie felt heavy in Porter's arms. He lifted her clean from the ground, and ran quickly towards the car. The safe house might be isolated, and there wasn't much in the way of law and order in this part of Lebanon, but the explosions in the house would attract attention. We don't want to be around when the police or the Hezbollah militia show up, Porter thought.

'Want me to finish him?' said Hassad, pointing towards the wounded man on the ground.

'Let him die slowly,' said Porter. 'A quick death is too good for that bastard.'

With Katie still in his arms, Porter ran across to the Polo. She needed rest, and the firefight had only made her worse: if he didn't treat her gently she wasn't going to make it through the next few hours. Waves of heat were rolling out of the house as the flames licked up inside it. Across the scrubland that separated it from the road, there were three dead bodies, all of them lying face down in the dirt, their bodies shot to pieces. It hadn't been much of an attack, Porter reflected grimly. Whoever that bastard Collinson was using to do his dirty work for him, it wasn't Regiment guys. These blokes had no proper training. First they'd tried to kill them with fragmentation grenades inside the house, and when that hadn't worked, they'd created a diversion with some more grenades and had reckoned that would be enough to allow them to charge the wall. Idiots, thought

Porter. The Regiment would have taught them that a well-dug-in target, with plenty of ammunition, had to be taken by surprise or ground down slowly and relentlessly. Otherwise you were just committing suicide.

He flung open the door of the Polo, but it came away clean in his hand. The car had been caught in the crossfire as Porter and Hassad had opened fire with their AK-47s and been shot to pieces. The windscreen had been shattered and the petrol tank pierced, spilling its fuel out over the ground. It was a miracle the thing hadn't gone up in flames.

'Sod it,' he muttered. 'Now we've no transport.'

'We can't walk,' snapped Hassad. 'It's still a hundred miles to the Israeli border.'

Porter nodded to the petrol station a mile up the road. He waved his AK-47, then slipped it over his shoulder, making sure he slipped a fresh mag of ammo into place as he did so. 'Then we'll just have to borrow one,' he said. 'And I reckon one of these could be pretty persuasive.'

He still didn't have a watch on, but by now he reckoned it must be at least eleven on Saturday morning. The sun had risen in the sky, but it wasn't especially hot: no more than a mild twenty degrees centigrade. He was still carrying Katie on his back, though. He was cut, bruised and exhausted. And he had no idea when, if ever, they were going to get home.

They paused a hundred metres short of the filling station. It was a small place. Four pumps on a dusty forecourt, with a back office and a repair shop. Porter reckoned the best plan was to wait for a driver to pull up, then hit him just after he'd paid for his petrol. If you're going to nick a car, you might as well take one with a full tank, he told himself with a half-smile.

The mechanic glanced up at them suspiciously as he walked across the forecourt to the car he was working on. Maybe he's seen the guns on our backs, thought Porter. Or maybe this is the kind of road where you don't talk to strangers. He scanned the highway. A couple of trucks rolled by, then a van, but nobody was stopping for petrol. It was Saturday morning, and business was probably slow anyway.

Porter put Katie down at the side of the road. Hassad was sitting next to her, gripping the side of his shoulder with his hand. 'I need a doctor,' he said. 'I'm hurt.'

Glancing towards him, Porter couldn't see what the fuss was about. There was blood where the knife had cut into him, but it was only a field injury. 'You'll be OK,' he snapped. 'Once we get to the border, you can get yourself sorted.'

'I need a doctor now,' he said. 'There a place nearby we can go. It's safe.'

Porter shrugged. What we really need is a drink. But I suppose it isn't going to do us any harm to get ourselves fixed up before we try to travel much further. God knows how many more people are going to attack us before we manage to get across into Israel.

He still wasn't sure whether he trusted Hassad. But it wasn't Hezbollah who had just attacked them. It was Collinson's men. *I can trust Hassad more than my own side.*

'I'll take the mechanic,' said Hassad.

He started walking towards the garage. Porter watched from a distance, noting a couple of shouts as Hassad knocked the man out, then tied him up. A Fiat van came up the road, turning into the garage. One driver, Porter noted. The van had pulled up next to a diesel pump, and the driver was filling his tank. After he finished, he walked towards the office to pay. Porter could see that Hassad was waiting for him, his AK-47 still strapped to his back. Within seconds, Hassad had pointed the gun at the man, taken his keys off him, then bound and gagged him. He ran back out onto the forecourt towards the van. The engine was still warm, and started with the first turn of the key. He gripped the wheel, slammed his foot on the accelerator, and turned the Fiat round, steering back towards the side of the road. 'Get the hell in,' he said, pulling up alongside Porter and Katie. 'We haven't got much time.'

There were some chickens in the back of the van: live ones, trussed up three to a crate. Hassad put Katie alongside them, then climbed into the passenger seat. 'Ten kilometres, straight ahead,' he snapped. 'Then we'll see the doctor.'

'Why not go straight to the bloody border?' Porter growled.

'I told you, I need the doctor,' said Hassad.

'And I need to get out of this craphole.'

'Then you can do it by yourself.'

Porter paused. It was a possibility. He had the van, and Katie was probably well enough to survive the journey. The plasma and fluids pumped into her at the safe house had perked her up already. But it was a hundred miles to the border, and it was heavily fortified. He had a hostage he'd snatched from Hezbollah with him. They controlled this territory, and they'd be looking for both of them. I need help. And in this hellhole, Hassad is likely to be the only person I can even begin to rely on.

'We only stop for an hour maximum,' said Porter.

'One hour,' said Hassad nodding. 'Then we hit the border.'

He put on the radio. There was some terrible local pop music, then the news bulletin. It was eleven in the morning. Outside, the sun was up now, but some clouds were starting to drift across the sky. The road was long and straight, a stretch of tarmac rolled out like a carpet across an arid and dry piece of scrubland. A few miles up ahead, Porter could see a turning off to the left, and a dusty, grey smudge on the landscape that looked like a village. In the back of the van, some of the chickens were starting to squawk as Porter slammed his foot hard on the accelerator, pushing the van up close to its top speed of ninety miles an hour. On the radio, the newsreader was talking in Arabic. The sound washed past Porter: he was too busy concentrating on the road.

Then he heard the words 'Katie Dartmouth'.

Porter turned the volume up.

'What's he saying?' he asked, glancing across at Hassad.

Hassad raised a hand. He was listening intently to the broadcast. In the back of the van, Katie had woken up. Porter could see her lifting herself up. Her eyes looked clearer, and some of the vigour had returned to her skin. She still looks pretty terrible. But she's a tough young woman. With the right treatment, she's going to be OK again.

'They're talking about –' she started.

'Quiet,' Porter hissed.

They waited a few more seconds until the broadcast finished. When the terrible Arabic singing started up again, Porter leant across to switch off the sound. 'What was he saying –'

'Here,' said Hassad, pointing to the turning. 'The doctor is down this road.'

Porter flicked the indicator, and started to pull the van across the corner. 'What were they saying about Katie?'

'They don't know anything,' said Hassad.

'Nothing about the explosion?'

Porter looked across at Hassad. His face was tight and taunt, as if the muscles in his skin were being stretched out on a rack.

'They are just saying the execution is scheduled for eight o'clock this evening.'

The road was rough, just a dirt track, and there were a few goats grazing alongside it. The village up ahead looked to be no more than a single street nestling into the side of a hill, with a dozen houses, a shop and a couple of workshops. Up in the hills behind there were some cultivated fields, making a break from the scrubland all around them. 'Why are Hezbollah saying nothing about an attack?' he asked, looking back at Hassad.

'Because they don't want to admit it,' said Hassad.

'But Katie's with us,' said Porter. 'They must know that.'

'Then it looks like they're planning on getting her back by eight tonight. This is their country, remember. So long as they find her, then the execution can still go ahead.'

Porter pulled the van up on the side of the road. A farmer was heading up towards the hills with a tractor and donkey. He turned round, looking at the van suspiciously, then when he saw Hassad climb out, quickly turned back and started driving faster. Porter killed the engine, and got down from the driver's seat. As he did so, he unhooked the AK-47 from his back and tucked it under his arm. He could feel the smooth wood of the weapon next to his skin, and checked the mag. Plenty of ammo, he noted, feeling reassured by that. It doesn't matter what the PR department at Hezbollah is telling or not telling people, he reminded himself. There's no execution tonight. We'll fight our way out of here by ourselves if we have to.

A cat was snarling at them as Porter helped Katie down onto the track. 'You OK?' he asked.

She nodded. Her legs were wobbling, and she clung on to Porter for support, but there was enough strength in her knees for her to stand. 'I think so.'

'Good girl.'

The street smelt of dried olives and raisins. It was around midday now, and there were no people on the street of the tiny village. There were some fruit and vegetables on sale at the single shop, but Hassad had already walked through an open doorway ahead of them. Porter took Katie's arm, guiding her forward. She was walking unsteadily, like a toddler. 'Ever broken a leg?' Porter asked.

Katie shook her head.

'You've been strapped to a stake for a week by these bastards,' said Porter. 'The nerves in your legs have packed up, same as when you have a plaster cast on. It takes a week or two to learn how to walk properly again. You'll need some physio. You can get used to anything.'

'Like your fingers?' she said, looking down at the hand that she was holding on to.

'Yeah, that took a lot of getting used to.'

'How did it happen?'

'That bastard's lot right up there,' said Porter, nodding towards Hassad.

'How . . .'

'It's a long story,' interrupted Porter. 'I'll tell you about it over a long cool beer when we're tucked up on a couple of first-class seats on the British Airways flight home.'

'That would be nice,' she said, attempting a smile.

As her lips creased up, Porter could see that the cuts and bruises covering her were making her wince with pain. They were following Hassad into a small building two doors down from the shop. It was basically one room, measuring twenty feet by fifteen. There was a kitchen at one end, and a curtain sealing off a bedroom area at the other. The only light was coming through a couple of skylights built into the roof. Close to the door, there was desk and a chair, and a collection of elderly pieces of medical equipment: some scales, a blood-pressure pump, a stethoscope and a few reusable syringes.

Out of the shadows, there emerged a woman. She was dressed entirely in black, with a face like a pickled walnut. Her eyes were piercing, but her skin was dried up as if she had been left out in the sun for too long, and she walked with a slight stoop. From the way she looked up at Hassad, it was clear that she knew him, but there was no smile, nor any kind of a greeting. She merely pointed at the chair, and waited for him to sit down.

Hassad took off his sweatshirt. The woman examined the shoulder silently. The knife had dug into the skin, then been twisted, creating a nasty corkscrew wound. Porter had seen those kinds of injuries before, indeed he'd taken a few himself over the years, and although they hurt like hell, he knew they weren't serious. Taking a swab of cotton wool, the woman drenched it with raw alcohol and pushed it hard into the raw skin. Porter winced. He knew how painful that was: he admired the way Hassad sat there impassively, taking the pain, with nothing more than the clenching of a fist to suggest what he was going through.

When she'd finished, she bound up the wound with gauze. Next, the woman looked at Katie. She worked quickly and swiftly, checking where Porter had patched up her cuts and wounds, redressing them, and then giving her another dose of antibiotics. She muttered a few words to Hassad in Arabic.

'She's going to be fine,' Hassad said to Porter. 'She needs a few days in hospital, with maybe a drip to get some fluids and calories back into her, but apart from that she'll be OK.'

Porter could see the look of relief on Katie's face. She was getting stronger by the minute, and you could see it in her face and eyes. Just knowing she had a chance of escaping had brought her back to life again.

'Now you,' said Hassad, pointing Porter towards the chair.

'I'm fine,' Porter growled.

'She needs to check you out.'

'I said I'm fine,' snapped Porter. 'A few cuts and bruises, that's all. Nothing I can't handle. Now let's get the hell out of here before the rest of your mates show up and start trying to chop people's bloody heads off again.'

The small room was dark and gloomy, but even in the dismal light it was possible to see that Hassad's face was reddening with anger.

'She needs to look at your teeth.'

Porter laughed. 'I'll get a check-up when I get home, thanks,' he said with a rough grin. 'I'll even make sure I floss regularly.'

'Your teeth, now,' Hassad snapped.

He was standing just two feet from Porter, with the old woman another three feet behind him. Porter was looking hard into his eyes, still questioning whether he could trust the man. 'Let's just get on –'

'If you won't let me do this, there's no point in trying to get to the border.'

'This is ridiculous.'

Hassad moved closer, so that he was standing just a foot in front of Porter. 'They sent a missile straight into the mine,' he said, his voice calm and controlled but with a thread of anger running through it. 'We were tracked to the safe house. They know exactly where we are.'

'You mean . . .' said Katie.

She hobbled towards John and Hassad, using the desk for support. She was looking from one man to another, her face confused.

'You mean the missile was a British one?'

Hassad nodded curtly. 'British or Israeli. A bunker-busting missile is a sophisticated piece of kit.'

Porter paused. He already knew that was true. If it was a bunker-busting bomb that attacked the mine, then it was almost certainly a GBU-28, a piece of kit manufactured by Lockheed in America, but sold to both the British and Israeli air forces. It was made up of 80 per cent TNT, and 20 per cent aluminium powder which powered up the conventional explosive. On tests, the GBU-28 had blasted its way through twenty feet of concrete, and cut through as many as fifteen different layers of bunker. It had probably been delivered by two fighter jets: one to mark the target, and a second to deliver two bombs. It was the only weapon

282

capable of causing the kind of damage seen in the mine. And not many people had them.

'And the soldiers who attacked us just now, they were British as well?'

Hassad glanced at Porter. 'You tell her.'

'They worked for a firm called Connaught Security,' said Porter. 'It's a private military corporation operating throughout the Middle East. It's run by Perry Collinson.'

Katie slumped back. Suddenly, Porter noticed, the blood seemed to have drained from her face. 'If they knew where we are, why didn't they come in and rescue us?'

'Because they want us dead,' says Hassad, jabbing a finger at her. 'So long as you die in an explosion, that suits them fine. They just don't want to be seen to be giving in to any of our demands.'

Katie shook her head. 'They'd get me out if they could.'

'Collinson wants me dead,' said Porter.

'But he's . . .'

'Your boyfriend?' said Porter. 'I know. The trouble is, he's also a coward and a fraud. He's terrified that I'll find out from Hassad here the truth about what happened on a mission seventeen years ago, and unfortunately for him I already have. He'd rather we both died than let us come back alive.'

'He told me . . .' The words trailed off on Katie's lips. But the shock on her face was evident.

'He loved you?' said Porter. 'Maybe the bastard did, but he was lying about that along with everything else. Take it up with the agony aunt when you get home.' Porter grinned. ' "My boyfriend fired a bunker-busting missile at me. Do you think that means he isn't committed to a long-term relationship?" '

Porter looked back at Hassad. 'I reckon you're right,' he said. 'Collinson's got control of the whole op, and he fired that missile into the mine to try and kill us. It's a result for them if we get killed that way and the execution doesn't get shown on live TV. They can just say it was an accident. Then he realised we'd escaped, so he sent his boys from Connaught in to quietly finish us off.'

'This issue is,' said Hassad, 'how do they always know where you are?'

'What do you mean?'

'They knew you were in the mine, and they knew you were in the safe house. How did they know that? How did they even know you'd escaped from the mine?'

Porter shrugged. He wondered that himself. The trouble was, he had no idea of the answer.

'They must have a tracking device,' said Hassad.

'I'm not a bloody idiot,' Porter snapped. 'I checked myself, and you checked. There's nothing. Maybe there's something planted on you?'

Hassad shook his head. 'It's you they're following.'

'Then maybe a satellite?'

'There's no satellite that can look into a mine,' said Hassad. 'Before they sent you out here, did they do any dental work on you?'

Porter paused. 'They fixed up my teeth,' he admitted.

'A crown? Implants?'

Porter nodded.

'Then get in the chair.'

Porter sat down.

Hassad muttered something to the woman in Arabic. She leant forward, switching on a torch so she could have a better look at Porter's mouth.

'Open wide,' said Hassad, tapping his shoulder.

Porter felt certain he could detect a hint of pleasure in the man's voice.

'Is she a dentist?' he asked, glancing back at Hassad.

'In a tiny village like this, you have to be a bit of everything,' Hassad replied. 'Don't worry, yours aren't the first teeth she's examined.'

He could feel a spatula pressing down his tongue, the cold steel pressing into his flesh, and then winced slightly as she started tapping on his teeth. Her breath was warm on his skin as she worked: a mixture of goat's milk and stewed fruits filled the air around him. Next, she started prodding them with a scalpel, nicking his gums in the process.

She paused, looking up at Hassad, talking quickly in Arabic.

'Two of the crowns feel odd to her,' said Hassad quietly.

'Meaning?'

'There may be some kind of tracking device inside them.'

'In a tooth?'

Hassad nodded. 'I've heard of it before, but I've never seen it done.' He shook his head, in sorrow as much as anger. 'Usually you can't put a tracker inside a tooth because the tooth blocks out the signal, but if you use a mostly hollow crown then it's possible, although the signal is never great.'

'What can we do?'

'Pull it out and take a look, of course.'

Porter looked at the old woman suspiciously. 'Can she do that?'

'If there's a tracker, the guys from Connaught are going to find us anytime soon, and they'll almost certainly finish us off before we get to the border.'

He said something to the old woman, then looked back at Porter. 'You're not scared, are you?'

His deformed lips twisted up into a mocking smile.

'I don't suppose there's any chance of an anaesthetic is there?'

Hassad rolled his eyes.

'How about a shot of vodka then?'

'Just do it,' said Hassad to the old woman. 'Open your mouth and shut up. Every minute we waste you may be transmitting signals back that tell Collinson exactly where we are. For all we know, they are preparing their assault right now.'

'Then get on with it.'

Porter gripped the sides of the chair. He closed his eyes, and opened his mouth. He could smell the stewed fruit washing over him as the old woman leant into his face. She said something to Hassad, and he replied, but Porter couldn't make out a single word. She tapped one tooth then another with a scalpel: two of the teeth that had been replaced for him back at the Firm's headquarters. Porter could feel a clamp being placed inside his mouth to hold it open, then a wrench being screwed on to one of his teeth. Hassad knelt down, pressing a strip of leather into Porter's hand. 'Here, pull on this,' he said quietly.

Don't yell, he told himself grimly.

The woman yanked at the wrench. Porter could feel a bolt of pain jabbing right through him as the nerves attaching the tooth to the jaw screamed out in agony. It was like having a needle threaded straight into your veins. There was a crunching sound, then the scratching of metal against bone. Porter gripped hold of the strip of leather, twisting it into his hand, trying to keep the pain under control.

Another yank. A fresh wave of pain swept through every nerve in Porter's body. Christ, he muttered, making sure he kept his mouth open and the word to himself. He could feel the sweat dripping off his brow. The woman said something to Hassad. Porter opened his eyes. He could tell the wrench was still clamped to his tooth. Hassad was leaning into the wrench, a grimace on his face. Porter steeled himself, shut his eyes tight and gripped hard on the sides of the chair. He could feel the force of the wrench smashing into his gums. Then a snapping sound. A searing pain ran up through his mouth, colliding inside his head.

He opened his eyes. He could feel some blood hitting the

back of his throat, and washing across his tongue. The side of his mouth was numb from the impact. In front of him, Hassad was holding the tooth inside the wrench, showing it to the old woman. There was still some blood dripping from the stem. 'It's clean,' said Hassad with a shrug. 'Maybe it's the other one.'

'Christ!'

As he spoke, some blood and fragments of broken tooth spat clean from his mouth.

Hassad nodded towards the old woman. 'I wouldn't take the name of any of the prophets in vain in here,' he said casually. 'She's very devout, and Muslims revere Jesus as well as Muhammad. Make her angry, and she might not be so gentle with you.'

Porter closed his eyes. The pain was stinging through his jaw, but he knew there was no choice. *There has to be some explanation for how they found out where I was, and I can't think of a better one. If we don't pull the tooth, Collinson's going to have his men onto us any moment, and then I'll never get a chance to kill the bastard.* 'Then do it.'

He could feel the tapping of the scalpel, then the cold hard steel of the wrench clamping on to his tooth. This time it was on the right side of his mouth. The woman moved away, and as he briefly opened his eyes, Porter could see Hassad gripping hold of the wrench with his muscular fists. Even with the wound in his shoulder, he was a strong guy. Porter gripped on to the strip of leather. He twisted hard on it, pulling it between both hands. Closing his eyes again, he could feel a stuttering series of jabbing pains as Hassad started to put pressure on the tooth. There was nasty crunching sound inside, and he could feel more blood trickling into the back of his throat where the wrench was nicking against the side of his gums.

'One more heave,' Hassad muttered.

He slammed his fist down hard. Porter's head snapped

sideways. The force of the blow was ripping into his neck muscles, making it impossible for him to hold himself steady. The pain was searing through him now, making his eyes water and his head spin. It was like having a jackhammer drill into the side of your jaw. 'Hold his head,' Hassad growled to the old woman.

Her medical training had equipped her with enough English to follow the command. Porter felt her hands clamping around the side of his head, gripping him tight, while her frail body pushed into him, providing a countervailing force to the wrench. Hassad immediately leant into a fresh blow. The tooth creaked. Porter summoned up one more ounce of resistance, trying to bring the pain under control. If this doesn't work, maybe they should just toss me aside. Let Katie get to the border by herself. Collinson's men can catch up with me and I'll just have to deal with them as best I can.

Suddenly there was a sound like a floorboard cracking open. Porter's eyes shot open. He could see Hassad rocking backwards, the wrench still in his hand, blood dripping from the small lump of white tooth at its tip.

The old woman was handing Porter a glass of water. He took it from her, but his hands were shaking so badly he was hardly able to hold the thing, and spilt much of it down the front of his shirt. A terrible pain was throbbing through his jaw. He swilled the water back, rinsing out his mouth, and spitting out the blood and tooth debris into the bin at the side of the chair. Next, she handed him six white pills. Porter took them in his shaking hand, and swallowed them methodically. Painkillers, or cyanide? he wondered to himself as the tablets sunk down the back of his throat. Let's hope it's the latter. That's the only thing that's going to make this pain go away.

'They put that one in with concrete,' said Hassad, holding the tooth in front of Porter. 'I guess they didn't want to take any chances of it falling out if you got into a fight.'

'You found something?'

Tears were still streaming down Porter's face, and he was finding it difficult to speak.

Hassad nodded, pointing to the underside of the tooth. Porter's vision was still fuzzy, and the pain ripping through his head was making it hard for him to concentrate. The painkillers were still a long way from kicking in. But he could see a sliver of dark matter on the underside of the tooth.

'Silicon,' said Hassad. 'A micro tracking device, sending out a signal that can be picked up by a satellite.'

'Bastards,' Porter muttered. 'They promised me I was going in clean.'

He could feel the anger burning inside him. He'd walked into the Firm voluntarily. He'd put himself into the line of fire for them, because he wanted to get Katie out. And this was how they repaid him. By putting a tracking device into his tooth, and then trying to kill both of them. And just so they could save face.

Hassad chuckled. 'Never trust the British government,' he said. 'That's a lesson we learnt out in this part of the world a long time ago.'

TWENTY-SIX

The truck had Jordanian number plates, and it looked empty. That means it is on the way home, Porter decided. Completely the opposite direction to us. He checked that the driver was still in the café next to the shop, then knelt down, pulling out a piece of chewing gum he'd found in the Fiat, and carefully sticking the tooth to the underside of the lorry. 'That'll take care of them,' he said, glancing back at Hassad. 'Collinson's boys will spend half the day searching for this vehicle, and when they catch up with it, they'll just have a Jordanian truckie and bunch of empty crates.'

They climbed back into the Fiat. Hassad had taken the wheel, explaining that he knew the roads better, and was less likely to attract attention from other drivers. As they'd left the old woman's house, they had borrowed a burka for Katie. It covered up her face effectively, and it made sure no one would recognise her as they drove towards the border.

It was close to mid-afternoon. After an hour's drive, Hassad had suggested they stop for some food, and wait for darkness. They were fifty miles from the Israeli border by now, and Hassad was convinced they needed to plan their breakout. The strip of land between Lebanon and Israel was used by Hezbollah to launch its rocket attacks on its neighbour. The territory was swarming with fighters, making it one of the most heavily militarised places on earth.

'Where's the best place to get through?' asked Porter.

While they were still in the van, Hassad pointed to the

map the driver kept on the front seat. 'Here,' he said.

Porter glanced down. Beit Yahoun. It meant nothing to him.

'Never heard of the place,' he said.

'It's a border village, and one of the main crossing points between Lebanon and Israel,' said Hassad. 'There used to be about ten thousand people living there, but the place has been shelled to bits over the years. There are about a thousand people there now, and most of them are soldiers.'

'Can't we sneak through somewhere a bit quieter?'

Hassad laughed, but his expression quickly turned serious again. 'Quiet? On the Israel–Lebanon border?' He shook head. 'There is no such place. Every inch is heavily fortified, and if the soldiers see you, they shoot you on sight. That goes for the Israelis as well. They see us coming through the wire, they'll open up their machine guns, and worry about who the hell we are later on.'

'And you think this Beit Yahoun place is safer?'

'There's a demilitarised zone of about a mile, a bit like the no-man's-land that used to exist between the Berlin Wall and the West. There isn't much trade or traffic that goes between Israel and Lebanon, but what there is, mostly goes through there. Get into the no-man's-land, and we should be able to walk through to Israel without being shot.'

Porter glanced around. 'Then let's go,' he said.

'Not yet,' said Hassad.

Porter checked the time. It was just after four in the afternoon. The execution was scheduled for eight, and he'd have wanted to get Katie out of this hellhole long before then. 'When?' he snapped.

'We have another fifty miles to travel, and the roads aren't great,' said Hassad. 'Plus there are roadblocks to get through. It will take us about six hours. We stay here about two more hours, and travel when it's starting to get dark. It's safer that way.'

The time passed slowly. They stayed in the van. Porter managed to buy some more painkillers, and swallowed most of the packet. They would make him feel drowsy, and slow his reaction times if they came under attack, but it was better than the terrible pains that were still throbbing through his jaw and up into his head. Porter tried to nap. Sleep was impossible, however. He was too wired up. Another few hours, he told himself. Then I can get Katie out of here, deal with that fucker Collinson, and start getting on with the rest of my life.

As soon as we get back to Britain, I'll reveal that man's treachery to everyone.

And maybe even see Sandy again.

By six, it was getting dark outside. Hassad judged it was safe for them to start moving again. After buying some bottles of water and some food from the café, they loaded themselves back into the Fiat van. Hassad took the wheel, while Katie sat between then, her face completely covered by the burka. Porter had tucked the AK-47 underneath his feet, but he made sure the mag was full again, and that he could reach it within a couple of seconds. They could have used the ammo that had been destroyed back at the safe house, Porter thought bitterly, and another couple of guns. If it hadn't all been blown up by Collinson's men.

The first hour passed without incident. The road was long and straight, and there wasn't much traffic around. The weather was clear enough. It was turning cold, and there was some cloud spitting across the night sky but the half-moon would occasionally break through. It is always the same, thought Porter. The closer you get to the end of a mission, the more you long for home.

It was close on seven in the evening by the time they turned due south. The road they were on snaked along the border, and would eventually take them all the way down to the coast. The road was terrible. The surface of the tarmac was regularly broken up into rubble. For the past couple of years, the Israelis and Hezbollah had been shelling each other across this narrow strip of land, and the Israeli tanks had rolled through it, decimating everything they encountered. There were a couple of villages along the way, but they had long since been abandoned: just collections of empty, crushed buildings, without even any wild dogs still living in them. After ten miles, there was a single petrol station, but it only had two pumps, the price was double what it was in the rest of the country, and the owner had put up a steel bunker to hide the payment kiosk. Territory doesn't get much more hostile than this, thought Porter. And we're driving straight into it.

'If anyone stops us, just leave the talking to me,' said Hassad.

They managed another ten miles without any trouble. The roads were practically empty. The Fiat slowed down to a crawl. There were so many potholes in the road it was impossible to take the van much above ten or fifteen miles an hour. A couple of times, Porter had to climb out and push when a back wheel dropped into a shell hole. The chickens squawked furiously as he pushed, and Porter suggested ditching them, but Hassad said it would look better if they had some kind of cargo. As they progressed steadily on, Porter could sense that Katie was becoming more and more afraid. She'd been living with death for a week now, but she still hadn't learnt how to handle the fear. On the rare occasions a truck or a car passed them in the other direction, he could feel her shaking. She's right on the edge, Porter realised. Much more, and she's going to fall completely to pieces.

'Roadblock,' said Hassad. His voice was tense and strained.

Porter peered into the darkness up ahead of them. He could see a couple of cars pulled across the road. Next to it there was a brazier with some hot coals in it, where some men were keeping themselves warm. In total, there looked to be about three men, all with AK-47s hung over their shoulders. But there could be many more lurking in the background.

Hassad slowed the Fiat to a crawl. Between the two cars, a long wooden plank had been placed, and beneath that there was a net studded with nails. You could try to ram your way through, but the nails would blow out your tyres. You'd be easy meat for the gunmen standing right behind you.

'Leave this to me,' whispered Hassad.

A man was leaning into the side of the car. Hassad wound down the window, and they exchanged a few terse words in Arabic. Katie was sitting still, her face covered by the burka, while Porter had wrapped a scarf he found on the floor of the van up high around his neck. In the dark, with the weather-beaten appearance his skin had had ever since he started sleeping rough, it wasn't hard for him to pass for an Arab. Even so, his hand was under the seat, holding the AK-47.

The door opened. The soldier's gun was raised, and he was snapping something at Hassad, but Porter couldn't follow the conversation. Another soldier walked over. An older man, Porter judged. Thirty maybe, with a close-cropped black beard, and eyes as hard as steel. He tapped the younger man on the shoulder, and leant forwards. Porter glanced across. It was clear that he recognised Hassad. They exchanged greetings but there was no warmth there, Porter noted. More words. Then suddenly the door slammed shut, and Hassad had fired up the engine. The plank and the net that were slung across the road were removed, and the Fiat was moving on again.

Porter remained silent, but inwardly he was breathing a sigh of relief. He took a quick look back, making sure they were a safe distance from the roadblock and that no one was following them.

'Do they know Katie's escaped?' he asked.

Hassad shook his head. 'Not yet, but they might soon. Apparently a lot of communications are down because of the missile strike, and it's going to take a few days to get them back up again. Until then, they won't know that she's out.'

'That should make things easier for us.'

'Maybe,' said Hassad with a shrug. 'Or maybe nobody has spoken to the guys at this roadblock. We don't know about the next one.'

'Just so long as we get out here,' said Katie, speaking through her burka.

'We will,' Hassad snapped. 'Trust me.'

They picked up some speed. The road flattened out as they put the roadblock behind them. There were fewer potholes in the tarmac, and the landscape looked less damaged. On the left-hand side of the road, they were snaking close to Israel: at some points it was perhaps only twenty miles to the west of them. Another hour or so to the border point, Hassad told them. It was nearly nine now. They should hit it at around ten.

The Fiat pushed on into the darkness. Nobody was speaking. Porter was scanning the road ahead, keeping a watch out for more Hezbollah patrols. There were miles of empty countryside, broken only by the occasional small village. He saw some vans go by, and a couple of private cars. At one point he saw a truck full of Hezbollah fighters, their arms bristling with weapons, but they paid no attention to the van. As the countryside rolled by, Porter was thinking, planning. The pain in his mouth was terrible, the jawbone aching in a dozen different places, but he knew he had to concentrate on what happened next. With any luck, in the next couple of hours they would get across the border into Israel. But could they get in touch with the British

Embassy in Tel Aviv, or would that just alert Collinson?

'Does Sky have a correspondent in Tel Aviv?' he said to Katie.

'Of course,' she said. 'Jamie Breakton. You'll get him at the Tel Aviv bureau. If he's not answering, I can call the Fox News bureau, or *The Times*'s guy.'

'Then we'll ring him just as soon as we get over the border.'

Katie pushed her burka aside, and Porter saw her face for the first time in hours. There was still a starved, vacant appearance to her eyes, but her strength and confidence were steadily recovering.

'The sooner we get this story on the air the better. The reason is, we can't trust the British government, not with that fucker Collinson on the loose,' said Porter, shaking his head. 'Get Sky News to pick us up rather than the embassy, and we'll be OK. If Collinson wants to shoot us, then he'll have to do it live on TV.'

'He wouldn't —'

'He bloody would,' Porter snapped. 'He's already tried to kill us twice. Me, three times.'

The town of Beit Yahoun loomed up in the distance. A few lights, and some smoke rising in the air were all there was to mark it out from the rest of the desolate landscape. Porter saw the road sign, and then the outskirts of the place itself. The road worsened as they pulled into the first street leading down towards the demilitarised zone. The tarmac was cracked in so many places it might have been better to get out and complete the trip on foot, Porter thought. Along the way, there were the remains of houses, but they had been shelled virtually to oblivion. All that was left were the foundations, and the heaps of rubble that had collapsed into them. There were no street lights working, but about a mile away there were some streaks of neon shooting up into the night sky.

296

'The demilitarised zone runs for about a mile to the west of here,' said Hassad. 'Get into there, and we'll be OK.'

'Any checkpoints?' asked Porter.

Hassad nodded. The strain was evident in the man's eyes, Porter noted. He was delivering them to the border, just the way he promised. But now he was up against his own people, and you could tell that troubled him. 'One, and it's heavily guarded,' he replied. 'But we got through the last one, so we have to hope for the same again.'

The suspension on the Fiat was creaking as it ploughed through the potholes in the road. Porter reckoned the machine wouldn't hold out much longer. You needed an off-roader and preferably a jeep for this kind of territory. As they drew closer to the checkpoint, he could see a few men on the streets, but they were all soldiers or militia. Either the civilians had fled or they were cowering in their houses.

'Just keep your faces covered, and don't say anything,' said Hassad. 'I'll take you to the border, then drop you there and make my own way home.'

Porter nodded.

Even if I wanted to say something, my mouth hurts too much, he thought.

At his side, he could feel Katie shaking. He gripped the side of her arm to provide some reassurance: the fear was getting to her, the same way he had seen it get to Collinson seventeen years ago. 'Just try and hold yourself together,' he whispered. 'We'll be out of here soon.'

The checkpoint was brightly lit. There were two big wooden watchtowers, reaching thirty feet into the sky, each one with a searchlight flashing onto the ground. Porter glanced up. A machine gun was placed in the centre of each tower, on a pivot so that it could fire in any direction. The road led to a gate. There were two sentry posts on either side of it, and beyond that the empty desolate scrubland of the demilitarised zone. Cross that, Porter told himself, and we're safe.

'What's your story?' said Porter, glancing across at Hassad.

'My story?'

'You've got to give them some reason why you're driving a van into Israel. What is it?'

Hassad paused. 'Medical supplies,' he answered. 'I'll tell them we're delivering some blood.'

'With a couple of dozen chickens in the back?'

Hassad laughed. 'This is the Lebanon. Everyone trades in chickens on the side.'

Porter looked back ahead. There were two soldiers manning the sentry posts, and three more checking the vehicles moving through. It was just before ten at night, Porter noted. Not a time when many people were likely to be attempting to get across any border, never mind the boundary between Lebanon and Israel. There was no more dangerous crossing anywhere in the world, he thought. No one would try to get through it unless they had to.

Back in Britain, people would be anxiously waiting for news about Katie. They might be starting to suspect something had happened. So far, however, they would have no idea what.

Two vehicles were parked at the side of the road: one van and one car. The car looked to be empty, and the van's driver was standing outside it, smoking a cigarette. No traffic was coming through from the Israeli side. Hassad had pulled the Fiat up, but left the engine idling. One of the soldiers was walking towards them. Porter pulled the scarf up high around his neck, and made sure that Katie's burka was drawn completely across her face. His hand was dropped beneath the seat, cradling the tip of his AK-47.

The soldier's eyes flashed through the cabin of the Fiat. He was no more than twenty-five, with a clean-shaven face, and close-cropped black hair. But from the neat creases to

298

his uniform, Porter reckoned he was some kind of Rupert, or Mustafa, or whatever the hell they called them out in this place. He was looking closely at Katie, his eyes running over her head, and down the length of her body. She was sitting rock still. How do they feel about lifting a burka round here? Porter wondered. In Britain, the border police are too politically correct, but I reckon around here they don't give a toss. If they want to take a look they will.

The soldier snapped a couple of brief commands at Hassad.

Hassad tried to smile, then shrugged and muttered a few words in reply.

The soldier barked another command. One of his colleagues walked over from the gate, and stood right behind. His finger, Porter noticed, was twitching on the finger of his AK-47. No more than a teenager. Trigger-happy didn't even begin to capture the look on his face. Trigger-bloody-ecstatic, Porter told himself grimly.

He gripped harder on the tip of his own assault weapon. Every muscle in his body was poised for action.

Another series of barked commands. Hassad was arguing, his face turning red. Then he suddenly smiled. He turned to look at Porter. 'They're letting us through,' he said. 'You're out of here.'

TWENTY-SEVEN

Hassad slammed the door of the van shut behind him. Porter watched as the man walked slowly back into the Lebanon. He wasn't so bad, Porter thought. He did what he said he was going to do, and you couldn't ask for more from a guy than that.

Shifting across to the driver's seat, he grabbed hold of the wheel and tapped his foot on the accelerator. Up ahead, the gates were starting to swing open. The road stretched into the demilitarised zone, and there was one more set of Hezbollah guards on the other side, but they had already been cleared, and Porter wasn't expecting any trouble from them.

'We've made it,' he said, looking at Katie. 'We're back.'

He could see the relief flooding through her. 'Thank Christ for that.'

Porter drove slowly. It was a mile across the demilitarised zone, and then they would have to get through the Israeli border controls as well. Driving too quickly would only make the guards suspicious, Porter warned himself. Better to take it gradually.

The Fiat slid through the gates, which shut quickly behind them. Just ahead, about two hundred metres in the distance, Porter could see a guard flagging them down. The man was six feet tall, wearing a Hezbollah uniform, with some kind of scarf covering his face. He was holding an AK-47 in his arms, and motioning for the van to pull over.

'Shit,' Porter muttered.

'What does he want?' Katie asked anxiously.

'How the hell should I know?'

Looking ahead, Porter wondered whether he should jam his foot on the accelerator, and make a dash for the Israeli border. He could see the one guard flagging them down, and two more men standing behind him. To the side, there was a small hut that seemed to be serving as a sentry post, but could be hiding more men. The Fiat wasn't in bad shape, but it was still only a van, and there wasn't much acceleration in the engine. The chances of getting away were minimal.

'Maybe they only want some paperwork,' said Porter.

He slowed down, pulling the Fiat to a stop at the side of the road. The tall soldier was walking towards him, his pace deliberately slow. Act casual, thought Porter. Don't try and pretend to be an Arab, you'll never fool them. Just tell them you need to get to the other side. Fast.

The man was standing right next to the van now. The two other soldiers were standing astride the road, their faces also masked, but with their guns gripped to their chests. In the blink of an eye, they could shatter the van with bullets, Porter realised. There's no escape.

He wound down the window. 'Good to see you again, Mr Porter,' said Perry Collinson. 'For a while there, we thought we'd never bloody find you.'

Porter froze.

The words had sliced straight through him, like a dagger cutting through his skin.

'Now I suggest you and your lady friend step out of the vehicle, and walk across to the hut with me,' he said.

Porter remained silent. He could feel the blood pumping through his veins, red with fury.

The AK-47 was still positioned next to his feet. Its mag was full: there were more than enough bullets in there to finish Collinson and his two men. Tempting, he told himself. But there was not enough time to get the gun out, and slam the trigger. They'd have shot him to pieces before he'd even got it in his hands.

It was just suicide.

'C'mon, man,' Collinson growled. 'We haven't got all night.'

'John, I –' Katie started.

'Do as he says,' Porter snapped.

He pushed open the door of the van, stepping down onto the tarmac. It was completely dark now, and there was a bite the air. As he looked back, he could see they were firmly on the neutral side of the border. The gates had been shut behind them, and the Hezbollah soldiers had already gone back to their positions. Collinson must have come down to this position, and overwhelmed the Hezbollah guards in this hut, so that he could catch us after we came through the Lebanese border, but before we reached Israel, he thought.

He means to kill me. There can't be any doubt about that.

Katie was now standing next to Porter. She was looking at Collinson, but there was no warmth in her expression. Her hands were shaking, and her skin was pale. 'This way,' said Collinson, pointing his AK-47 towards the hut.

Porter started to walk. It was ten metres across the empty ground from where he'd pulled up the van to the hut. It was a small, one-room structure, made out of concrete and corrugated iron. There was one glass window, looking out onto the road that led through the demilitarised zone. It was the kind of hut that was familiar to border guards right around the world. Porter could see the two soldiers from the road take up position behind him, walking five paces to his rear, their guns pointing straight at his back. More men from Connaught Security, he reckoned. And they won't hesitate to fill my back with lead if they need to.

Collinson had already opened the door, and was pointing

them inside. Porter stepped through. There was a coal brazier in one corner filling the small room with cosy warmth. A kettle and some cups were stacked up on a table next to the fire, and there was a bucket with some water in it. Otherwise, the room was empty.

With a slow movement of his hand, Collinson shut the door.

Porter and Katie were standing next to the wall. Collinson was standing next to the door, and the two soldiers were standing by the window.

'You come with me, young lady,' said Collinson, gesturing towards Katie. 'We'll make sure you get safely home.'

His voice was smug and self-satisfied: a mocking tone, with a note of vindictiveness threaded through it.

Only a single word was rattling through Porter's mind. *Bastard.*

Collinson's eyes rested for a second on Porter's face. 'And this bugger can die right here.'

'Just so you can take the credit like you did last time, you bloody coward,' said Porter.

Collinson took a pace forward. His two soldiers were standing rigidly to attention, both their guns pointing straight at Porter. 'You know about that, do you?' he said.

'I know exactly what happened,' Porter snarled. 'Steve, Mike and Keith died because of you. And you let me take the fall for it.'

He could see the edge of Collinson's lip twitching. 'I might be a coward, but at least I'm not a bloody loser,' he said, his voice sombre. 'And I'm not scared of killing a man in cold blood either.'

Slowly and deliberately, Collinson took from his belt a Beretta 9000S compact handgun, the first lightweight polymer gun the company had ever made, with twelve rounds stored in its clip. He motioned to Katie to come towards him.

'How the hell did you know we were here?' Porter snapped.

Collinson smiled. 'It was a nice trick sending your tooth to Jordan,' he said. 'But once we reached it, we knew you'd found that tracking device. That meant you were coming here. It's the only place to get across the border. The Israelis let us come through, and we took out the men on this side of the gate. So long as we checked every vehicle coming through, and there aren't many of them at this time of night, we knew we'd find you eventually.'

'Just like you got the Israelis to drop a bunker-busting missile into the mine,' said Porter. 'To kill us both.'

'Quite so,' said Collinson curtly. 'You've figured everything out. Just a shame it's a bit late in the day for you.'

He looked back at Katie. 'Now come here, and we'll get you home. There's a camera crew that can be got ready to record the moment when *I* rescued you.'

She was still standing next to Porter. She glanced into his eyes, but Porter already knew there was nothing she could read there. They had been emptied of all emotion. Slowly and painfully, she started to move away from him, hobbling across the ten feet that separated the two men.

With his left hand, Collinson reached out to grab hold of her arm, pulling her towards him. He looked back to Porter, a twisted smile on his lips and a smirk in his eye. Then he raised his Beretta.

'To quote Sir Winston, "The armies must cast away the idea of resisting behind concrete lines or natural obstacles, and must realise that mastery can only be regained by furious and unrelenting assault,"' he said. '"And this spirit must not only animate the High Command, but must inspire every fighting man."'

He looked straight into Porter's eyes, and chuckled. 'And indeed, that spirit animates me today.'

I don't mind dying if I have to, thought Porter. But I don't think I can listen to this tosser much more.

He could see Collinson's finger hovering on the trigger. And he could see into the man's eyes, and tell that he meant to kill him.

There was a movement. Somewhere behind the window.

Suddenly, the rattle of a machine gun filled the air. The window had shattered, and a lethal storm of bullets had ripped through the hut, slicing into the backs of the two men standing guard. They had both tried to respond, their fingers reaching for the triggers of their guns, but the ordnance had already smashed up their spinal cords so badly they were no longer able to control their muscles. They had collapsed on their faces, their weapons sprawling out on the floor in front of them.

Porter threw himself to the ground, narrowly missing the bullets that were starting to slam into the wall behind him: he could feel the used rounds falling onto his body as they pinged off the wall. As he dropped to the ground, he caught sight of the man standing behind the window.

Hassad.

His AK-47 gripped to his fists, he was spraying round after round of bullets through the window and into the bodies of the men who had taken them captive.

Porter reached forward, grabbing hold of one of the guns that had spilt out onto the floor. He rolled away, so that his back was against the wall, then flashed the gun up and lashed his finger onto the trigger. It was pointing straight at Collinson.

Outside the firing had stopped. Hassad must have realised he'd already killed the two men, Porter guessed. To get any more he'd have to come inside.

He doesn't need to bother, Porter told himself grimly. That's my job.

As he looked up, he could see that Collinson had shaken

Katie free. She was standing next to him, tears of terror and exhaustion streaming down her face. In his right hand, Collinson was still holding the Beretta. Porter gripped the AK-47 tighter in his hands, and although he hadn't had time to line up a shot, that probably didn't matter. Press the trigger, and he should be able to pump out enough bullets to bring the man down.

'Drop it,' Collinson spat, 'and I'll let you go back to the ragheads.'

Porter stood up. 'I'm not going anywhere,' he said.

Katie's eyes were darting from one man to the other. She was standing six inches to Collinson's left: close enough to be a threat, Porter judged, but not close enough to stop the bastard from shooting me.

'Go back to ragheads, man,' Collinson sneered. 'They can fix you up with a bottle of vodka and a nice archway to kip down in.'

Outside, Porter could hear Hassad moving towards the door, but it was still too dangerous for him to come inside. There was no sign the guards back on the Lebanese side of the border were going to intervene. Maybe they hadn't heard the gunfire, or else they didn't want to move into the demilitarised zone.

There were only two men who were going to sort out this fight, Porter told himself. And they are both in this hut.

'I'll give you one more warning,' said Collinson.

Porter held the gun steady. He was pointing it straight at Collinson's stomach and groin. When he fired, he didn't much care any more if Collinson shot him back. He just wanted to rip out the man's guts and his balls before he went down.

'Take your shot,' Porter snapped.

He could see beads of sweat starting to pour from the man's brow. His hand was trembling, the same way he'd started trembling back in Beirut seventeen years ago.

'We'll see who the coward is now,' said Porter. 'Take the fucking shot.'

Collinson remained motionless.

'You're fucking afraid, aren't you, just like you were all those years ago,' Porter snarled. 'Except this time, you're not going to have me to blame.'

The hand was shaking perceptibly now.

Porter held steady, the sights of the AK-47 lined up straight.

A shot.

Porter could see the recoil on the Beretta as the gun kicked back.

He could feel a bullet winging his shoulder, taking out a chunk of flesh, and biting off a piece of bone.

His feet remained rooted to the ground. He swallowed hard, ignoring the pain raging through him.

He could see Katie jumping out of the way.

He squeezed the trigger on the AK-47.

The bullets flew out of the barrel of the assault rifle. One smashed into Collinson's guts, spilling blood and intestines onto the ground. Another clipped his groin, taking at least one ball with it as it chewed its way through his body.

Collinson fell back onto the floor. He was clutching his stomach, trying to hold his intestines in place, but his hands were drenched with his own blood. He was screaming for his mother.

Porter kept the AK-47 tight in his hand, and walked the few paces of empty ground that separated him from the dying man.

He looked down. Collinson was writhing in agony. Porter put his boot down on his chest to hold him still. Then he looked into his eyes. They were pale and watery as the life slowly drained out of him, but the man was still conscious. Porter smiled. 'I've got a quote from Winston bloody Churchill you might enjoy,' he said. ' "When you have to kill a man, it costs nothing to be polite." '

He pressed the barrel of the rifle into the soft flesh at the side of Collinson's neck. 'So, goodnight, sir, and sweet fucking dreams.'

Porter squeezed the trigger once, then twice, then three times.

He tossed the gun aside. The mag was empty, and it was no more use to him now. The bullets had smashed through the man's neck, effectively decapitating him. His head was lying to one side, the last of his blood draining away into the cracks in the wooden floorboards of the hut.

It's over, he thought to himself. *At last.*

Porter grasped hold of Katie. She was shaking with fear, but she was still standing. There was nasty flesh wound to his shoulder where Collinson's bullet had hit him, but he strapped that up with a strip of his sweatshirt to staunch the bleeding, and he knew that a decent bandage was all he needed to sort himself out.

'Let's get the hell out of here,' he said.

Hassad had already pushed his way through the door. He looked at the three corpses, then across at Porter. 'You OK?'

Porter nodded, permitting himself a brief, tense smile. 'How'd you know we were in trouble?'

'I could see the van had been stopped,' said Hassad. 'That shouldn't have happened. This is just an observation post, strictly neutral. The guards here shouldn't stop anyone . . . so when I saw you'd been pulled up I knew something was wrong.'

They were outside now, helping a weak and frightened Katie to walk towards the van. Porter opened the door, and helped her into the passenger seat. Looking around, he clasped Hassad on the shoulder. 'We're quits,' he said.

Hassad nodded. 'Good luck . . .' he said.

'I'll need it.'

'And don't come back to the Lebanon,' he said crisply. 'The amount of trouble you cause . . .'

Porter laughed. He'd climbed into the driver's seat, and fired up the engine, not even looking back as Hassad turned and started walking back to the border.

He kicked on the accelerator, and pulled the Fiat back onto the road. It was less than a mile now to the Israeli border, and they could cover that in minutes. He increased his speed, anxious not to waste any time. The sooner we're out of here the better.

'We made it,' he said, glancing towards Katie. 'We'll be eating hot buttered toast at the Tel Aviv Hilton tomorrow morning.'

'And you know what,' said Katie, wiping the tears out of her eyes. 'It's not even midnight local time. If we could just make to it a newsroom, we could definitely make the second edition of the Sunday papers.'

EPILOGUE

Vauxhall, London: Wednesday, 20 December 2006
As he walked back from the Gents, Porter glanced only briefly at the sparkling lights from the Christmas tree in the foyer of the Vauxhall Travel Inn. Some seasonal music was playing in the background, and outside he could see the beginnings of a hard frost starting to bite on the open ground. Doesn't matter, Porter told himself with a smile of satisfaction. I'm not sleeping out there. Not tonight. Not any night.

He looked up at the bar. A friendly looking blonde was polishing some glasses, and a couple of business guys were settling into the second or third pint of the evening. In the fold of his pocket, Porter could feel a crisp roll of twenty-pound notes. Bar, he thought to himself. Plus money. For most of the last two decades there had been no doubt about what those two equalled.

A bender.

Nah, he told himself. Just leave it. You know where that road goes.

Sandy was waiting for him at the table. She looked like a million dollars, he thought proudly. It's good to have the chance to get to know her properly.

He sat back down, poured some more non-alcoholic grape juice, and tucked into the pudding they'd ordered. Porter wasn't quite sure why he'd chosen the Travel Inn for a pre-Christmas dinner. Christ, it's hardly the best food in London, he thought. And he knew better than most people that the guys in the kitchen all hated the bloke running the place. Still, there was something satisfying about spending an evening on this side of the rope rather than the other. It was another way of closing the books on his past life. And another way of reminding himself that he had started again.

'How's work?' said Sandy.

Porter shrugged. 'It's good. I'm lucky to have it.'

For the last week, he'd been working as a driver for Sky TV, ferrying their studio guests to the west London headquarters. After coming out of the Lebanon with Katie he'd told her that he didn't want any publicity. Just tell them an SAS guy came in and got you out, and that he didn't want his name or face to be revealed since it might jeopardise future operations. She stuck to that end of the bargain, as he knew she would: it sounded more exciting when she told and retold the story on air anyway. The Firm had ferried them both back to London, and they'd spent a couple of days in debriefing. They said they hadn't known about Collinson slipping the tracking device into his tooth. Porter wasn't sure if he believed them, but there was no point in arguing about it now. The official line was that Collinson had been killed in a separate Hezbollah attack while looking for Katie. Sir Angus had been effusively grateful for bringing Katie back, and offered to find Porter a job in the organisation, but he'd turned him down. There was no way he wanted to go through that again, he told them. He just wanted to do something simple, earn a few quid, and stay sober. He mentioned it to Katie during one of their debriefs, and she fixed him up with the driving job at Sky. It suited him just fine. He'd found a small flat in Stockwell, he had the Sky Mercedes to get around in, and that was all he needed.

'You get all sorts of people in the back of the car,' he said.

'Celebrities?' asked Sandy.

Porter shrugged. 'I probably wouldn't recognise them even if they were.'

'Let me buy you something, Dad,' she said. 'For Christmas.'

Porter laughed. He'd made sure the £250,000 was paid into their joint account, and then he'd taken his own name off it. He didn't want the money, and he wasn't sure he'd trust himself even if he had it. There was a lot of vodka you could buy with that kind of wedge. Sandy had her place at UCL, starting next September, and was planning a trip to Africa with one of her girlfriends during the summer holiday. She could use some of the money for that, use some to pay her tuition fees, then maybe use the rest to buy herself somewhere to live while she was at college. He'd started looking at some places for her. Maybe something that needed restoration. He could work on it when he wasn't driving the car for Sky.

'Just seeing you is enough,' he said. 'And knowing that you're doing well.'

'I'll make it a surprise then,' said Sandy.

Porter laughed. 'I've had enough of those for a while, thanks.'

Porter glanced up at the waitress delivering the bill. Another Czech girl. He didn't recognise her, but then they turned over very fast in this place. Most of them didn't stick it for more than a couple of weeks, and this one would probably be gone after Christmas as well. 'Who's washing up tonight?' Porter asked.

'Excuse me,' she said. 'I don't . . . understand.'

Porter put down the money for the bill, then peeled off another couple of twenties from the roll in his pocket. 'Tell the guy he's doing a great job, and give him this.'

The girl nodded, looked at him as if he was mad, then walked away.

Porter collected his coat, helped Sandy with hers, and together they stepped outside into the cold night. They walked for a while along the Thames, towards where Porter had parked the Mercedes. A wind was whipping across the river, blowing hard into their faces, and Porter pulled the collar up around his coat, protecting his skin. His shoulder had mostly healed now, and he'd had a couple of new teeth fitted where he'd lost them, but he knew he still had to take things easy. It would be several months before he was completely better.

Taking another twenty from his pocket, Porter paused to give it to a man lying on the ground close to Vauxhall Bridge. He had a rough, beaten-looking face, and he smelt of beer and blood. Give the money now, thought Porter. Because in a few months' time you'll probably have forgotten all about them. You'll walk straight past them, as if they weren't even there, just like everyone else.

'Thanks, mate . . . Merry Christmas.'

'And you too,' said Porter.

He clicked the car keys, and the doors on the Mercedes lit up as the locks sprang open. He opened the door for Sandy to climb inside. He'd run her up to St Pancras and get her on the last train to Nottingham before going home to get some kip.

'Next time we have dinner, maybe I can get Mum to come along,' said Sandy. 'Or perhaps you could come up on Boxing Day or something.'

Porter laughed, climbing into the driver's seat and snapping the seat belt into its lock. 'I don't mind taking on the bloody Hezbollah,' he said. 'But I don't know if I'm brave enough to face your mother again.'

Porter glanced across the station forecourt. Last time he'd stepped across it, someone had tried to run him down. Now he knew it must have been one of Collinson's men: the bastard had known exactly where he was going, and wanted to stop him ever getting out to the Lebanon and finding out about what happened all those years ago. He checked the cars. There were no drivers sitting anxiously at their wheels. Collinson is dead, Porter reminded himself. That's all finished with now.

He opened the door on the Mercedes, fired up the engine and pulled the car gently out into the road. It was just after nine, and he was done in for the day. All he wanted to do was catch some sleep.

'Did she buy that story about you just being a driver for Sky?' said Layla.

Porter looked round. She was sitting in the back seat, dressed in a crisp black suit, and with a pair of dark glasses dropped over her eyes.

'It's not a story,' Porter snapped.

She leant forward, and he could smell a trace of perfume on her neck. 'You work for us, Mr Porter,' she said. 'The driving job is useful cover. It will make people think you're living a normal life.'

'I'm finished with soldiering, I told you that.'

'We don't pay two hundred and fifty thousand pounds for one week's work,' she said. 'What do you think this is? Goldman Sachs —'

'We had a deal,' said Porter.

'And we want to get our money's worth,' said Layla. 'Or would you rather we took it all back, and Sandy found out that her daddy wasn't such a big shot after all?'

Porter paused. The traffic lights had switched to green, but he didn't feel like putting the gear back into drive. Behind him, someone was starting to hoot. 'What is it you want?' he said finally.

'There's someone else we want you to get in touch with for us,' said Layla. 'Another man you came across during your time in the Regiment.'

'Who?'

'An Irishman . . . from the bad old days.'